PENGUIN CLASSICS

DEAD SOULS

NIKOLAI VASILEVICH GOGOL was born in 1809; his family were small gentry of Ukrainian cossack extraction, and his father was the author of a number of plays based on Ukrainian popular tales. He attended school in Nezhin and gained a reputation for his theatrical abilities. He went to St Petersburg in 1829 and with the help of a friend gained a post in one of the government ministries. Gogol was introduced to Zhukovsky, the romantic poet, and to Pushkin, and with the publication of *Evening on a Farm near Dikanka* (1831) he had an entrée to all the leading literary salons. He even managed for a short period to be Professor of History at the University of St Petersburg (1834–5). *Diary of a Madman* and *The Story of the Quarrel between Ivan Ivanovich and Ivan Nikiforovich* appeared in 1834, *The Nose* in 1836, and *The Overcoat* in 1842. Gogol also wrote the play *The Inspector* (1836), *Dead Souls* (1842), and several moralizing essays defending the Tsarist régime, to the horror of his liberal and radical friends. He lived a great deal abroad, mostly in Rome, and in his last years became increasingly prey to religious mania and despair. He made a pilgrimage to Jerusalem in 1848, but was bitterly disappointed in the lack of feeling that the journey kindled. He returned to Russia and fell under the influence of a spiritual director who told him to destroy his writings as they were sinful. He burned the second part of *Dead Souls*, and died in 1852 after subjecting himself to a severe régime of fasting.

DAVID MAGARSHACK was born in Riga, Russia, and educated at a Russian secondary school. He came to England in 1920 and was naturalized in 1931. After graduating in English literature and language at University College, London, he worked in Fleet Street and published a number of novels. For the Penguin Classics he translated Dostoyevsky's *Crime and Punishment*, *The Idiot*, *The Devils*, and *The Brothers Karamazov*; *Oblomov* by Goncharov; and *Lady with Lapdog and Other Tales* by Chekhov. He has also written biographies of Chekhov, Dostoyevsky, Gogol, Pushkin, Turgenev and Stanislavsky; and he is the author of *Chekhov the Dramatist*, a critical study of Chekhov's plays, and a study of Stanislavsky's system of acting. His last books to be published before his death were *The Real Chekhov* and a translation of Chekhov's *Four Plays*.

NIKOLAI GOGOL

DEAD SOULS

TRANSLATED WITH AN INTRODUCTION BY

DAVID MAGARSHACK

PENGUIN BOOKS

PENGUIN BOOKS

Published by the Penguin Group
Penguin Books Ltd, 27 Wrights Lane, London W8 5TZ, England
Penguin Putnam Inc., 375 Hudson Street, New York, New York 10014, USA
Penguin Books Australia Ltd, Ringwood, Victoria, Australia
Penguin Books Canada Ltd, 10 Alcorn Avenue, Toronto, Ontario, Canada M4V 3B2
Penguin Books (NZ) Ltd, 182–190 Wairau Road, Auckland 10, New Zealand

Penguin Books Ltd, Registered Offices: Harmondsworth, Middlesex, England

First published 1961
25 27 29 30 28 26 24

Copyright © David Magarshack, 1961
All rights reserved

Printed in England by Clays Ltd, St Ives plc
Set in Monotype Bembo

CONTENTS

INTRODUCTION

THE origin of *Dead Souls*, Nikolai Gogol's greatest masterpiece, presents no difficulties to the literary historian. It is the final catastrophe that overtook it and its author that provides perhaps the most puzzling problem of literary history, for it raises the fundamental question of an author's personal involvement in his work, of how far, that is, a creative artist's outlook on life can impinge on the lives of his heroes without leading, as in Gogol's case, to insanity and suicide.

Gogol spent about eight years, from 1834 to 1842, on the writing of the first part of *Dead Souls*, and about ten years, from 1842 to 1852, on the writing of the ill-fated second part. The third part which, according to Gogol, should have crowned his magnificent literary edifice of vice turned into virtue, was never even begun. The subject of the novel was suggested to Gogol by Alexander Pushkin. 'He [Pushkin] presented me with his own subject,' Gogol wrote in his *Author's Confession*, 'which he wished to make into some sort of a poem and which, according to his own words, he would not have given to anyone else. This was the subject of *Dead Souls*.' Gogol must have begun writing the novel some time towards the end of 1834, for long before his departure from Russia in June 1836, he had read, as he declared later in one of his 'Letters apropos of *Dead Souls*', the first chapters of the novel to Pushkin, who 'grew gloomier and gloomier and at last cried, Good Lord, how sad is our Russia!' It is doubtful whether anything of those chapters has been retained in the final version of the novel. For Gogol revised everything thoroughly when he sat down to his work on the novel in Switzerland in the autumn of 1836 and later on in Paris between November 1836 and February 1837. Most of his work on *Dead Souls*, though, was done in Rome in the autumn and winter of 1837 and the first half of 1838. The following account, given by Gogol himself to some friends in Moscow, shows how he wrote at least parts of the novel:

This is the sort of thing that happened to me. I was travelling one July day between the little towns of Genzano and Albano. Half way between

7

those towns is a miserable little inn, standing on a small hill, with a billiard table in the main saloon, where people are constantly talking in different languages and the billiard balls never cease clicking. I was writing the first volume of *Dead Souls* at the time and never parted from my manuscript. I don't know why, but I felt like writing as soon as I entered the inn. I ordered a small table to be brought and sat down in the corner of the saloon. I took out my manuscript and, in spite of the noise made by the rolling balls, the rushing about of the potboys, the indescribable din, the smoke, the close atmosphere, I became completely lost to the world and wrote a whole chapter without stirring from my place. I consider this chapter the most inspired in the whole novel. In fact, I have seldom written with such inspiration.

It is a pity Gogol never revealed what chapter it was, but it might well have been the sixth chapter describing Chichikov's visit to the miser Plyushkin. Indeed, according to an account left by Pavel Annenkov, the literary historian and memoirist who acted as Gogol's amanuensis in Rome when he was revising the novel in 1841, it was that chapter that Gogol dictated 'with a feeling of particular elation', accompanying his dictation with 'proud and imperious' gestures. Annenkov writes:

At the end of this remarkable chapter, I was so excited that, putting the pen down on the table, I said frankly, 'I think, Nikolai Vassilyevich, this chapter is a real work of genius!' Gogol gripped the manuscript in his hand and said in a thin, hardly audible voice: 'Believe me, the others are not worse.' But raising his voice at the same moment, he went on: 'Do you realize we've still lots of time before dinner. Come, let's have a look at the Gardens of Sallust, which you haven't seen yet, and we may as well knock at the door of Villa Ludovisi!' From the beaming look on his face and his proposal, one could see that the impression made on me by his dictation gave him great pleasure. This showed itself even more when we went out into the street. Gogol had taken an umbrella in case of rain and as soon as we turned to the left of the Barberini palace into a deserted lane, he burst into a gay Ukrainian song and then broke into a dance and began twirling the umbrella over his head with such abandon that in two minutes it flew off, leaving only the handle in his hand. He picked it up quickly and went on with the dance. It was in this way that he expressed the gratified feelings of an artist.

Gogol was never in doubt about the sensation *Dead Souls* would produce on its publication in Russia. As his work on the novel proceeded, its theme took on more and more grandiose proportions in his mind. At first he began writing it, as he admits in his *Author's Confession*,

without forming any definite plan in my head. I simply thought that the droll project which Chichikov attempts to carry out [that is, the purchase of dead serfs or 'souls' whose names still appeared on the census and who could therefore still be mortgaged] would naturally lead me to the invention of all sorts of characters; that my bent for laughter would of itself create a large number of comic episodes, which I intended to intersperse with moving ones. But at every step I stopped myself with the questions: Why? What is it all for? What should such a scene and character express? You will ask what is one to do when such questions occur to one. Get rid of them? I tried to, but I found it impossible to get rid of them. ... I saw plainly that I could no longer write without a clearly defined plan, that I must first of all explain to myself the purpose of my work, its absolute usefulness and necessity, as a result of which the author himself would be filled with a genuine and powerful love for it. ...

It seems pretty clear, therefore, that while his creative imagination held him under its spell, Gogol was not worried about the ultimate purpose of his novel, but that when his inspiration left him, which happened quite often, especially during the latter part of his work on the novel, these questions returned to haunt him with nightmarish insistence. He tried to get rid of them by travelling all over Europe. He came to regard 'the open road' as a cure-all for all his mental ills, but the thought of the final aim of his work never deserted him for a moment. Three weeks after leaving Russia in 1836 he wrote to the poet Zhukovsky: 'I swear that I shall do something no ordinary man could do. I feel a lion's strength in my soul....' Again, writing to the same correspondent from Switzerland, he declared in a reference to *Dead Souls*: 'If I do this work as it ought to be done – oh, what an enormous, what an original subject! What a heterogeneous crowd! The whole of Russia will appear in it. It will be the first decent thing I have written. It will make my name famous.' But quite soon the fact that the whole of Russia would appear in his novel was no longer enough to satisfy him. He was getting more and more convinced of his messianic mission to save Russia and he began to regard *Dead Souls* as the means Providence had given him for accomplishing this task. 'I see quite clearly,' he wrote to a close friend in Moscow from

Rome in March 1841, 'God's holy will: such ideas are not humanly inspired. A man would never think of such a subject!'

The first part of *Dead Souls* already contains hints of how Gogol hoped to fulfil his mission of saving Russia. Indeed, he felt that Russia herself was looking up to him (as he declares towards the end of the first part) 'with eyes full of expectation', and that there was some mysterious connexion between her and him. Brooding over the fate of mankind in general and of his countrymen in particular, he was puzzled by man's perverse habit of straying from the road which lay wide open before him and which, if he followed it, would lead him to 'a magnificent palace fit for an emperor to live in', and of preferring instead to follow all sorts of will-o'-the-wisps to the abyss and then asking himself in horror, Which is the right road? Which is the way out? Still more puzzling was the amazing way in which every new generation laughed at the mistakes of its forebears and in the end followed a path that led to the same abyss. Gogol hoped, therefore, that by revealing the mysterious substance that he believed lay buried deep in the Slav soul and by introducing 'colossal figures' in his novel and letting it follow 'a grandiose lyrical course', he would 'widen the horizon' and, by stopping the bolting *troika* from rushing no one knew whither, save Russia from the predicament in which she found herself. This hope was itself a will-o'-the-wisp which brought Gogol to the abyss into which he finally precipitated himself. At the time of the publication of the first part of *Dead Souls*, however, and indeed up to the last moment he believed in it, though, fortunately, it was too late to reshape the first part of the novel in accordance with his fantastic dream.

If anything was capable of bringing Gogol down to earth from the clouds in which he seemed to have lost himself in the search for the key of what he considered to be 'the riddle of his existence', it was his encounter with the censors from whom he had to obtain permission for the publication of the first part of his novel. He was, as usual, in dire financial straits and any delay in the publication of *Dead Souls* spelt disaster to him. Immediately on his arrival in Moscow from Italy in January 1842, he sent the novel to the censors, who flatly refused to pass it, chiefly, it seems, on the ground that its title *Dead Souls* showed, as one learned censor expressed it, 'that Gogol was taking up arms against immortality'. Gogol, therefore, sent the manuscript of his novel to the Petersburg censors, who at once took objection to

Gogol's blisteringly satirical *Tale of Captain Kopeikin*. Gogol was therefore obliged to revise the Tale thoroughly so as to put the blame for his misfortunes on Kopeikin and not on the authorities. (In this translation Gogol's original version of the Tale is given.) The Petersburg censors also insisted that the title of the novel should be altered to *Chichikov's Adventures or Dead Souls*, to which Gogol agreed. The novel, or 'poem' as Gogol preferred to call it, using the word 'poem' in the sense of an epic narrative, was published on 2 June 1842. Although its reception was as enthusiastic as Gogol expected, he was not particularly impressed by its success himself. He regarded it, as he wrote to a friend, merely 'as a pale introduction to the great epic poem which is taking shape in my mind and which will finally solve the riddle of my existence'. To the poet Zhukovsky he wrote three weeks after the publication of his masterpiece: 'I have revised it thoroughly since the time I read the first chapters to you, but for all that I cannot help feeling that it is quite insignificant when compared to the other parts which are to follow. It reminds me of the front steps of a palace of colossal dimensions hastily constructed by some provincial architect.' In the second part, as he hints at the end of the first part,

people will catch the sound of other hitherto untouched chords and get a glimpse of the untold riches of the Russian soul, of a man endowed with divine valour or of a wonderful Russian girl ... possessing all the wondrous beauty of a woman's soul, full of generous instincts and self-sacrifice. And all the virtuous men of other races will seem as dead beside them as a book is dead beside the living word. And Russian emotions will rise up ... and everyone will see how deeply what merely skims over the surface of the nature of other nations has sunk into the Slav nature. ...

The difficulties of building this 'palace of colossal dimensions', in which 'the untold riches of the Russian soul' should be housed, became apparent to Gogol as soon as he sat down to write the second part of *Dead Souls* after he had again left Russia for Italy on 4 June 1842. 'Several times', he later wrote in his *Author's Confession*, 'I sat down to write and could produce nothing. My efforts almost always resulted in illness and suffering and, finally, in such attacks that made me give up my work for a long time.' He decided that before he could carry on with his work on the novel and bring about the spiritual regeneration of a crook like Chichikov, he had to undergo a spiritual regeneration himself. But the austere regime of prayer and fasting he imposed on himself sapped his health and, of course, hindered rather than helped the work on his novel. In reply to inquiries from his friends, he declared that 'the subject of *Dead Souls* has nothing to do with the description of Russian provincial life or of a few revolting landowners. It is', he went on in the prophetic vein which he was beginning to use more and more in his correspondence, 'for the time being a secret which must suddenly and to the amazement of everyone (for as yet none of my readers has guessed it) be revealed in the following volumes. ...' His inability to reveal this secret, however, drove him into a state of nervous collapse by the beginning of January 1845, and at the end of June he burnt all he had written of the second volume of *Dead Souls*. For the next seven years his resumed work on the second part of the novel was laborious and painful. He had to drag out each word as though by a pair of pincers, he complained to a friend. But at last the second volume was finished and he read different chapters of it to his friends. Unfortunately, he had fallen under the influence of a religious fanatic, a priest of most obscurantist views, who regarded his literary work as an abomination in the eyes of the Lord. The priest, Father Matthew Konstantinovsky, apparently demanded that his disciple should destroy the second volume of *Dead Souls* and atone for his sin of writing the first volume by entering a monastery. After a tremendous inner conflict, Gogol decided to carry out Father Matthew's wish and burnt the complete second part of his novel on the night of 24 February 1852. He then took to his bed, refused all food, and died in great pain nine days later, on 5 March 1852.

All that remains, therefore, of the second volume of *Dead Souls* is a number of various fragments of four chapters and one fragment of what appears to be the last chapter. These were found after Gogol's death and seem to belong to an early draft of the novel. Some idea of what the first chapters of the completed second part were like can be gathered from an account left by Leo Arnoldi, a brother of Alexandra Smirnov, a former lady-in-waiting and the wife of a high Russian official and one of Gogol's closest friends. Arnoldi was present at one of Gogol's readings at his sister's country house. The first chapter of the second part of *Dead Souls*, he writes in his reminiscences, ended with General Betrishchev's loud laughter. The second chapter contained a description of a day at the general's country house. Chichikov stayed to dinner at which, besides Ulinka, there were two more persons: a taciturn Englishwoman, Ulinka's governess, and a Portuguese gentleman. Nothing particular happened at dinner. The general kept cracking jokes and Chichikov ate with great relish. Ulinka looked sad and pensive, her face growing animated only at the mention of Tentetnikov's name. After dinner the general played chess with the Portuguese gentleman and then with Chichikov, who showed his usual shrewdness by first making it very hard for the general and then allowing himself to be mated by him. Pleased with having defeated so strong an opponent, the general invited Chichikov to call on him again together with Tentetnikov. On his return to Tentetnikov's estate, Chichikov told the young man that Ulinka seemed to be pining for him and that the general was very sorry to have insulted him and intended to pay a call on him and apologize for his rudeness. Tentetnikov, however, was so glad of the opportunity of seeing his Ulinka again, that he insisted on visiting the general himself and making it up with him. Chichikov of course approved his decision and confessed to Tentetnikov that in his attempt to bring about a reconciliation between him and the general he had told the general that he, Tentetnikov, was writing a history of the generals who had taken part in the campaign of 1812. Chichikov implored Tentetnikov not to deny the story he had made up on the spur of the moment and in good faith. Next followed a description of Tentetnikov's arrival with Chichikov at the general's country house and Tentetnikov's meeting with the general and Ulinka. According to Arnoldi, the description of the dinner that followed was one of the best parts of the second volume. In the course of it, the general referred to the book Tentetnikov was supposed to be writing and, to avoid humiliating Chichikov, Tentetnikov pronounced a panegyric on Russia in which he emphasized the need of all classes of the population to unite in their feeling of love for their country, a feeling which they had displayed in so remarkable a fashion during the war of 1812. Betrishchev, of course, was so deeply moved by Tentetnikov's speech that he forgot the ill-feeling he bore towards him, and as for Ulinka, she was so filled with adoration for the young man that she at once decided to marry him. After visiting her mother's grave, she went to see her father and asked him to give his consent to her marriage to Tentetnikov. After demurring for some time, the general at last gave his consent and as soon as he heard of it, Tentetnikov, Arnoldi writes, 'beside himself with happiness, leaves Ulinka for a moment and runs into the garden. He wants to be left alone with himself: his happiness is choking him! Here,' Arnoldi goes on, 'Gogol had two wonderful lyrical pages. A hot summer day, at midday, Tentetnikov alone in the dense, shady garden, and all around him profound stillness. The garden was painted with the brush of a great master, every branch of the trees, the broiling heat, the grasshoppers in the long grass and all the insects, and at last what Tentetnikov himself was feeling, happy, in love, and his love reciprocated. I remember vividly,' Arnoldi writes, 'that this description was so powerful, so full of colour and poetry that it took my breath away.' Tentetnikov burst out crying from sheer happiness and at that very moment Chichikov appeared in the garden and, taking advantage of Tentetnikov's overwrought condition and his declared desire to do anything for the man who had been instrumental in bringing about his engagement to Ulinka, proceeded to tell him the story of his fictitious uncle to whom he had to prove that he owned three hundred serfs before he could become his heir. 'What do you want dead souls for?' replied Tentetnikov. 'I'm quite willing to let you have three hundred living ones. You can show the deed of purchase to your uncle and we shall then destroy it.' Chichikov stared at him in amazement. 'Aren't you afraid,' he asked, 'that I might deceive you and ...' But Tentetnikov did not let him finish. 'Doubt you?' he exclaimed. 'I who owe you more than my life?' Thereupon they embraced and Chichikov accepted Tentetnikov's offer with alacrity. Next day General Betrishchev, who was not sure how his aristocratic relatives would react to the news of Ulinka's engagement to a comparatively poor landowner, consulted Chichikov who offered to go and visit his relatives in order to convey the news to them in his best diplomatic manner.

This is all that Arnoldi could remember of Gogol's reading, but his sister, to whom Gogol had read nine chapters of the second part, told him of another character in the novel, an 'emancipated' society woman of over thirty-five who had spent her youth at court in Petersburg as well as abroad. Like Platonov in the extant fragments of the second part, she is bored with life. The two of them meet in the provinces and their meeting seems a great stroke of luck to them. They become attached to one another and mistake this feeling for love. But their happiness is only of short duration, for they soon realize that there can be no question of genuine love between them, that, in fact, they are no longer capable of love, and so they become even more bored with life than ever.

These few incidents perhaps help to bridge the gap between the four chapters of the second part, but as recounted by Arnoldi they do not amount to much. In fact, no final judgement of the completed second volume of *Dead Souls* can be based on what has come down to us of it. The idealized landowner Kostanjoglo and the even more idealized government contractor Murazov are not living men at all but simply pegs on which Gogol hangs his naïve ideas on the complex social and political problems of his time. No less nebulous a figure is the governor-general who apparently is quite ready to forgive both Chichikov, who forged a rich woman's will, and the officials, who aided and abetted him, on the ground that injustice could not be rooted out by punishment and that the only way of restoring the reign of justice in Russia was to appeal to the inbred sense of honour which, according to Gogol, resided only in a Russian's heart. The only living characters of the second part are Chichikov and the gormandizer Petukh, but even they are merely pale reflections of the remarkable characters in the first part.

Nothing perhaps shows up the utter unreality of Gogol's attempt to effect a lasting reconciliation of the hostile social and economic forces in Russia so much as the fact that the regime of serfdom, of which he himself was in favour, was finally abolished only eight years after his death. The 'secret' which was to be revealed by the two subsequent volumes of *Dead Souls* and the conversion of Chichikov and even Sobakevich into shining examples of virtue, everything, in fact, that Gogol the moralist had set his heart on and that Gogol the creative artist had found so difficult to achieve, has proved to be an idle dream, while the things Gogol had so little use for at the end of his life, the creations of his genius, have made his name famous far beyond the borders of Russia. The 'souls', the serfs on which the whole of the Russian economy in Gogol's time was based, are today truly 'dead', while the superb gallery of characters he created in his novel have achieved immortality as universal human types.

D. M.

PART ONE

Chapter 1

A SMALL, rather smart, well-sprung four-wheeled carriage with a folding top drove through the gates of an inn of the provincial town of N.; it was the sort of carriage bachelors usually drive in: retired lieutenant-colonels, majors, and landowners with about a hundred serfs – in short, all those who are described as gentlemen of the 'middling' station of life. The gentleman in the carriage was not handsome, but neither was he particularly bad-looking; he was neither too fat, nor too thin; he could not be said to be old, but he was not too young, either. His arrival in the town did not create any great stir, nor was it marked by anything out of the ordinary; only two Russian peasants standing at the door of a public house opposite the inn made certain remarks, referring, however, more to the carriage than to the gentleman in it. 'Lord,' said one of them to the other, 'what a wheel! What do you say? Would a wheel like that, if put to it, ever get to Moscow or wouldn't it?' 'It would all right,' replied the other. 'But it wouldn't get to Kazan, would it?' 'No, it wouldn't get to Kazan,' replied the other. That was the end of the conversation. Also, as the carriage was driving up to the inn, a young man happened to walk past wearing very narrow and very short white canvas trousers, a swallow-tail coat with some pretensions to fashion, disclosing a shirt-front fastened with a pin of Tula manufacture in the shape of a bronze pistol. The young man turned round, took a look at the carriage, held on to his cap which a gust of wind nearly blew off his head, and went on his way.

When the carriage had driven into the courtyard, the gentleman was met by a servant of the inn, or a floorman as waiters are called in Russian inns, who was so lively and restless that it was quite impossible to make out what sort of a face he had. He came running out promptly with a napkin in his hand, a long figure in a long cotton frock-coat, the waist of which nearly reached the nape of his neck, tossed back his hair, and briskly conducted the traveller upstairs and along the whole length of a wooden gallery to show him the room Providence had provided for him. The room was of the familiar sort, for the inn too was of the familiar sort, that is to say, the sort of inn that is to be found in all provincial towns where for a couple of roubles a day travellers are given a quiet room with cockroaches peering out from every corner like prunes, and with a doorway always blocked up by a chest of drawers leading into the next room occupied by a quiet, taciturn, but extremely inquisitive man, who is interested in finding out all the facts about a new arrival. The façade of the inn corresponded entirely with its interior: it was very long and had two stories; the lower one was not faced with stucco but had been left in small dark red bricks, dirty looking, to begin with, but which had become even grimier from the boisterous changes of weather; the upper story was painted in the everlasting shade of yellow; and the basement was occupied by small shops selling horse collars, ropes, and ring-shaped rolls. In the corner shop, or, to put it more exactly, in the window of it, sat a man who sold hot spiced honey drinks next to a red copper *samovar*, so that from a distance one might think that there were two *samovars* in the window, were it not that one of the *samovars* had a beard as black as pitch.

While the new arrival was inspecting his room, his things were brought in: first and foremost a white leather trunk, a little the worse for wear and showing signs that it was not the first time it had been on the road. This trunk was carried in by the driver Selifan, a shortish man in a sheepskin coat, and the gentleman's valet Petrushka, a fellow of about thirty in a large well-worn coat that had obviously belonged to his master, a fellow with a somewhat surly expression, very thick lips, and a big nose. After the trunk a small mahogany box inlaid with slivers of Karelian birch was carried in, as well as boot-trees and a roast chicken wrapped in blue paper. When all these things had been brought in, the driver Selifan went off to the stables to see to the horses, while the valet Petrushka began settling down in a small anteroom, a very dark cubby-hole into which he had already managed to take his overcoat and with it a peculiar smell of his own, a smell which was also imparted to the sack in which he kept his various personal belongings and which he took in after the coat. Against the wall of this cubby-hole he fixed up a narrow three-legged bedstead, covering it with something that looked like a mattress, squashed and flat like a pancake and perhaps also as greasy as a pancake, which he had succeeded in wheedling out of the innkeeper.

While the servants were busying themselves and putting everything in order, their master made his way into the public room. Every traveller has a very good idea of what these public rooms are like: the walls are always the same and they are covered over with oil paint, grimy near the top from tobacco smoke and shiny at the bottom from the backs of innumerable travellers and, more especially, from the backs of the merchants of the district, for the merchants repaired there regularly on market days with six or seven companions to drink their customary two cups of tea; there was the same grimy ceiling, the same grimy chandelier with a multitude of pendant glass drops, vibrating and tinkling every time the waiter ran across the worn oilcloth, smartly brandishing a tray with as large a number of teacups as there are birds on the seashore; the same oil paintings covered the whole of the wall, in short, everything was the same as everywhere else, the only difference being that a nymph in one of the pictures had such enormous breasts that the reader cannot possibly have seen anything like it before. Such freaks of nature, however, are to be found in some historical paintings brought to Russia no one knows when, whence, or by whom, sometimes even by some of our rich noblemen, lovers of the arts, who bought them in Italy on the advice of the couriers who accompanied them on their travels. The gentleman took off his cap and unwrapped from his neck a woollen rainbow-coloured scarf, such as wives are in the habit of knitting with their own hands for their husbands, furnishing them with suitable instructions on how they should wrap themselves up; who provides them for bachelors I'm afraid I cannot tell – goodness only knows – I have never worn such scarves myself. Having unwound his scarf, the gentleman ordered dinner. While they were serving him with the various dishes one usually finds in all inns, such as cabbage soup with puff pasties, specially kept for travellers for weeks, brains with peas, sausages with cabbage, roast chicken, salted cucumbers, and the invariable sweet pastries which are always there ready to be had; while all these things were being served, either warmed up or simply cold, he kept asking the waiter all sorts of stupid questions, such as who used to keep the inn before and who kept it now, whether it was profitable and whether the proprietor was a great scoundrel, to which the waiter, as was customary, replied: 'Oh, yes, sir, he is a great rogue.' As in enlightened Europe, so also in enlightened Russia, there are nowadays many worthy men who cannot have a meal at an inn without having a chat with the waiter and sometimes even having a good laugh at his expense. The visitor, however, did not always ask stupid questions: he was extremely meticulous in finding out who was the governor, who was the president of the court, who was the public prosecutor, in short, he did not pass over a single official of any importance; with even greater exactitude, if indeed not with sympathy, he inquired about all the leading landowners: how many souls or serfs each of them owned, how far their estates were from town, what sort of characters they had, and how often they came to town; he made very careful inquiries about the state of the district, whether there had been any illnesses in their province, any epidemics, any sorts of deadly fevers, small-pox and the like, and he did it all in great detail and with a preciseness that betrayed more than mere curiosity. There was something solid in the gentleman's manners, and he blew his nose extremely loudly. It was a mystery how he did it, but his nose sounded like a trumpet. This apparently quite innocent accomplishment, however, inspired so great a respect in the waiter that every time he heard the sound, he shook back his hair, drew himself up more respectfully, and, bending his tall frame, asked whether the gentleman required anything. After dinner the gentleman had a cup of coffee and sat down on the sofa, propping his back against a cushion which in Russian inns is stuffed not with soft wool but with something extremely like bricks or cobblestones. At this point he began to yawn and asked to be shown to his room, where he lay down and slept for a couple of hours. After his rest, he wrote at the request of the waiter his rank, his Christian name, and his surname on a piece of paper, so that it might be communicated to the proper quarters, namely the police. As he went downstairs, the waiter read laboriously the following words on the piece of paper: 'Collegiate Councillor, Pavel Ivanovich Chichikov, landowner, travelling on private business.' While the waiter was still reading the note syllable by syllable, Pavel Ivanovich Chichikov himself set off on a sightseeing tour of the town with which he apparently was satisfied, for he found that it was in no way inferior to other provincial towns: the yellow paint on the brick houses hit you in the eye, while the wooden houses were of a more modest dark grey. The houses were of one, two, and one-and-a-half stories, with the everlasting mezzanine which provincial architects consider to be very beautiful. In some places these houses seemed lost in the midst of a street as wide as a field and with interminable wooden fences; in others they were huddled together and it was there that a more lively and bustling traffic of people could be observed. One came across shop signboards with ring-shaped rolls or boots on them, almost washed away by the rain, and others with painted blue trousers and the name of some Warsaw tailor; in one place there was a shop with ordinary and service caps and a signboard inscribed: 'Vassily Fyodorov, Foreigner'; in another a signboard showing a billiard table with two players in frock-coats, such as are worn on the stage by extras who make their appearance in the last act. The billiard players were depicted taking aim with their cues, their arms slightly twisted and drawn back and their legs askew, as if they had just been executing an *entrechat* in the air. Beneath all this was written: 'To the saloon'. Here and there stalls were set out simply in the street with nuts, soap, and treacle cakes that looked like soap, and somewhere else an eating-place with a signboard on which was painted a big fish with a fork stuck in it. More often, though, one caught sight of the grimy two-headed imperial eagles which have since been replaced by the laconic inscription: 'Public House'. The roadway was everywhere in bad repair. He also looked into the town park, which consisted of some spindly trees which had not taken root properly and which were propped up from below by triangular supports very beautifully painted with green oil paint. However, though these trees were no higher than reeds, the local newspapers, reporting some public fête, declared that: 'Thanks to the solicitude of our Mayor, our town has been adorned with a park of spreading, shady trees providing coolness on a hot sunny day', and that 'it was very touching to observe how the hearts of the citizens were throbbing in an excess of gratitude and pouring out floods of tears in recognition of the great services rendered them by our town governor'. Having questioned a policeman in great detail which was the shortest way to the cathedral, to the government offices, and to the house of the governor of the province, Chichikov went to have a look at the river which flowed through the centre of the town. On the way he tore off a playbill nailed to a post, intending to read it more carefully on returning home, looked intently at a lady of attractive appearance who was walking along the wooden pavement followed by a boy in army uniform with a bundle in his hand, and once more casting a glance over it all, as though wishing to make sure that he would remember where everything was situated, he went back to the inn and straight to his room, slightly assisted up the staircase by the waiter. Having had his tea, he sat down at the table, ordered a candle, took the playbill out of his pocket, moved it nearer to the lighted candle, and began to read it, screwing up his right eye a little as he did so. There was very little of any interest in the bill, however: it announced the performance of a drama by Herr Kotzebue in which the part of Rolla was to be played by Mr Poplyovin, and that of Cora by Miss Zyablov, the rest of the cast being even less distinguished; however, he read through all their names, getting even to the prices of the stalls and discovering that the playbill had been printed at the printing works of the provincial administration; he then turned the playbill over to find out if there was anything on the back of it, but finding nothing, rubbed his eyes, folded it neatly, and put it in the mahogany box in which he was accustomed to stow away everything he happened to pick up. The day was apparently concluded by a portion of cold veal, a pint of sour cabbage soup, and a sound sleep in which he snored away like a suction pump in full blast, as is the saying in some parts of our spacious Russian empire.

The whole of the following day was devoted to visits; the newcomer went to pay his respects to all the high officials of the town. He paid a call on the governor, who was, as it turned out, like Chichikov, neither fat nor thin. He wore the order of St Anne round his neck and it was even rumoured that he had been recommended for the order of St Stanislav; he was, however, a good fellow and sometimes even did embroidery on tulle. Chichikov next called on the vice-governor, then paid a visit to the public prosecutor, the president of the court, the chief of police, the Liquor Tax contractor, and the superintendent of the government factories. I am sorry to say it is a little difficult to remember the mighty ones of this world; suffice it to say that Chichikov displayed quite an extraordinary activity in paying visits: he even paid his respects to the inspector of the health department and the town architect. Then he sat a long time in his carriage trying to remember whom else he might visit, but there were no more civil servants left in the town. In his talks with these potentates, he showed great skill in flattering each of them in turn. To the governor he hinted somewhat casually that to enter his province was like entering paradise, that the roads were everywhere as smooth as velvet, and that governments which appointed such wise dignitaries were worthy of the highest praise. To the chief of police, he said something very flattering about the policemen in the town; and in his talks with the vice-governor and the president of the court, who were still only State Councillors, he twice said by mistake 'your Excellency', which was greatly to their liking. As a consequence of this, the governor invited him that same evening to a party and the other civil servants, for their part, also invited him, one to dinner, another to a game of boston, and a third to tea.

The newcomer apparently avoided saying a great deal about himself; when he did say something, he spoke in general terms and with marked modesty, and on these occasions his speech assumed a somewhat bookish turn, to wit, that he was but an insignificant worm in this world and was unworthy of people paying any great attention to him, that he had undergone many trials in his time, had suffered in the cause of justice while in the service, had many enemies, some of whom had even attempted his life, and that wishing at last to settle down to a quiet life, he was looking for a place of permanent residence and that, having arrived in this town, he considered it his bounden duty to pay his respects to its leading dignitaries. That was all that the people of the town ever learnt about this new personage, who very soon did not fail to put in a prompt appearance at the governor's evening party. The preparations for this party took him over two hours and here the new arrival showed such an extraordinary attention to his toilette as is rarely to be found anywhere. After a brief after-dinner nap he said he would like to wash and he spent an extremely long time soaping his cheeks, pushing them out with his tongue from inside; then, taking a towel from the waiter's shoulder, he wiped his chubby face all over, beginning behind his ears, first snorting twice right in the waiter's face. Then he put on his shirt-front before the looking-glass, plucked two hairs sticking out of his nose, and immediately after that appeared in a gleaming cranberry-coloured swallow-tail coat. Dressed in this fashion, he drove in his own carriage along the interminable wide streets, lit up by the feeble illumination that came flickering here and there from windows. The governor's house, however, was illuminated as though for a ball; there were carriages with lanterns, two gendarmes standing in front of the entrance, postilions shouting in the distance – in short, everything as it should be. As he entered the ballroom, Chichikov had for a moment to screw up his eyes, dazzled by the blaze of the candles, the lamps, and the ladies' gowns. Everything was flooded in light. Black frock-coats glided and flitted about singly or in swarms here and there like so many flies on a sparkling white sugar-loaf on a hot July day when the old housekeeper chops and breaks it up into glittering lumps in front of an open window, the children gather round and look on, watching with interest the movements of her rough hands raising and lowering the hammer, while the aerial squadrons of flies, borne on the light breeze, fly in boldly, just as if they owned the place and, taking advantage of the old woman's feeble eyesight and the sunshine that dazzles her eyes, cover the dainty lumps in small groups or in swarms. Already satiated by the abundant summer, which sets up dainty dishes for them on every step, they fly in not so much to eat as to display themselves, to stroll up and down the pile of sugar, to rub their hind legs or their front feet together, or to scratch themselves under their wings, or, stretching out both their front legs, to rub their heads with them, then turn round and fly out again, and again fly in with new tiresome squadrons.

Chichikov had barely time to look round when the governor grasped him by the arm and at once introduced him to his wife. The new arrival did not discredit himself here, either: he paid her some compliment which was most becoming in a man of middle-age whose rank was neither too high nor too low. When the couples of dancers had taken up their positions and pressed everyone back against the wall, he put his hands behind his back and looked at them very attentively for a minute or two. Many ladies were very fashionably dressed; others were dressed in what the good Lord had thought fit to send to a provincial town. The men here as everywhere were of two kinds: the thin ones kept dancing attendance on the ladies; some of them indeed were difficult to distinguish from Petersburg dandies: they had the same kind of carefully and tastefully combed whiskers or the same good-looking and very smoothly shaven oval faces; they sat down beside the ladies in the same casual way, spoke French, and made the ladies laugh just like the gentlemen in Petersburg. And the other kind of men were either fat or, like Chichikov, neither too fat nor too thin. These, unlike the others, looked askance at the ladies and stepped out of their way, merely looking round to see whether the governor's servants were getting the green card tables ready for whist. Their faces were full and round, some of them had warts, and some were even pock-marked; they did not wear their hair either in quiffs or in curls or in 'the devil take it' manner, as the French say; their hair was either closely cropped or plastered down, and their features were rather rounded and rugged. These were the more distinguished government officials of the town. Alas, fat men know better how to manage their affairs in this world than thin men. The thin are mostly employed as civil servants on special missions or merely have their names on the Civil Service list and just rush about back and forth; their existence is somehow too light and airy and completely insecure. The fat, on the other hand, never occupy secondary posts but always first-class ones, and if they do sit down anywhere, they sit firmly and securely, so that their seat is more likely to creak and give way under them than they are to be dislodged from it. They do not like outward show; their coats are not as elegantly cut as the thin men's, but their money-boxes are full of the Lord's blessings. In three years the thin man will not have a single serf left unmortgaged in the State Bank; the fat one, on the other hand, has no worries whatever and before you know where you are he has a house somewhere at the end of the town purchased in his wife's name, and at the other end of the town another house, then a small estate near the town, then, later, a big estate with acre upon acre of forest and arable land. In the end, after having served God and the Emperor and won general respect, the fat man resigns the service, goes to live on his estate, becomes a landowner, a fine Russian gentleman, a hospitable host, and lives on and lives well. After him, as is the Russian custom, his thin heirs make short work of their father's fortune. Chichikov, as a matter of fact, was occupied with almost the same kind of reflections as he scrutinized the company and, in consequence, he at last joined the fat ones among whom he found almost all the familiar faces – the public prosecutor with his very black, thick eyebrows and with his left eye that kept winking slightly, as if to say: 'Come along, old man, let's go into the next room where I shall tell you a thing or two', a serious and taciturn man withal; the postmaster, a short man, but a wit and a philosopher; the president of the court, a most reasonable and amiable gentleman – all of whom greeted Chichikov as an old acquaintance, to which he responded by bowing a little to one side, though no less amiably for that. It was here that he made the acquaintance of Manilov, a most obliging and courteous landowner, and Sobakevich, a somewhat clumsy-looking landowner, who as soon as he was introduced to him trod on his foot saying, 'I beg your pardon!' It was at this point that they thrust a card for whist into his hand, which he accepted with the same polite bow. They sat down at the card table and did not rise till supper was served. All talk came completely to an end, as always happens when people become engrossed in some sensible occupation. Although the postmaster was an extremely talkative person, he too assumed a thoughtful expression as soon as he picked up his cards and, covering his lower lip with his upper one, he remained like that all through the game. When he played a court card he struck the table violently with his hand, saying, if it were a queen, 'Be off with you, you old priest's wife!' and if it were a king, 'Be off with you, Tambov peasant!' The president of the court kept saying: 'And I've got him by the moustache! And I've got her by the moustache!' Sometimes as the cards were flung down on the table the players would give utterance to such expressions as: 'Oh, hang it all, I've nothing else, diamonds it is!' Or simply to exclamations such as: Hearts! Heartache! Spades! or Spadefulls! Spade-a-little-lady! or simply, Speedy! – names with which they had christened the different suits among themselves. At the end of the game they argued, as is usual, rather noisily. Our newly-arrived visitor joined in the arguments, but, somehow, extremely skilfully, so that everyone realized that, though arguing, he was arguing agreeably. He never said: 'You led', but 'You were so good as to lead', or 'I had the honour to beat your two', and more in a similar vein. To propitiate his opponents even more on some point or other, he would hold out to them his silver enamelled snuff-box at the bottom of which they could see two violets placed there for the sake of the scent. Chichikov's attention was particularly drawn to Manilov and Sobakevich, the two landowners mentioned earlier. He at once made inquiries about them, drawing the president of the court and the postmaster aside to question them. Some of the questions he put to them showed not only his love of knowledge, but also his good sense, for he first of all inquired how many peasants each of them possessed, and what was the condition of their estates, and only afterwards asked what were their Christian names and patronymics. Within a very short time he succeeded in making them find him completely fascinating. Manilov, not by any means a middle-aged man, with eyes as sweet as sugar, which he screwed up every time he laughed, was absolutely enchanted by him. He kept pressing his hand

and he begged him most earnestly to do him the honour of visiting his estate which, according to him, was only about ten miles from the town gates. To which Chichikov replied with an extremely polite inclination of the head and a warm pressure of the hand, adding that he was not only anxious to do so, but would consider it his most sacred duty. Sobakevich said a little laconically: 'Come to see me, too', scraping his foot shod in a boot of such a gigantic size that it would be hardly possible to find a foot to fit it, particularly in these days when even in Russia men of heroic build are beginning to grow scarce.

Next day Chichikov went to dinner and a party at the house of the chief of police, where after dinner at three o'clock in the afternoon they sat down to whist and played till two o'clock in the morning. It was there, incidentally, that he made the acquaintance of Nozdryov, a landowner of some thirty years of age, a sprightly, happy-go-lucky fellow, who proceeded to address him familiarly after the first few words. Nozdryov was on most familiar terms also with the chief of police and the public prosecutor; but when they sat down to play for high stakes, both the chief of police and the public prosecutor watched his tricks most closely and scrutinized almost every card he played. Chichikov spent the following evening with the president of the court who received all his guests, including two ladies, in his rather soiled dressing gown. Then he spent an evening at the vice-governor's, attended a big dinner at the liquor tax contractor's, and a small dinner at the public prosecutor's which was, however, just as good as, if not better than, the large one; he was also present at a buffet lunch given by the mayor after morning mass which, too, was the equal of a dinner. In short, he had not to spend a single hour at his room at the inn and he went there only to sleep. The newcomer somehow or other was never at a loss and he showed himself to be an experienced man of the world. Whatever the conversation was about, he was always able to keep up with it; if they were discussing stud farms, he talked about stud farms; if they were talking about pedigree dogs, he was able to make very sensible observations on that subject too; if they discussed some investigation conducted by the provincial treasury department he showed that he was not uninformed about legal jiggery-pokery, either; if there was some argument about billiards, he knew all there was to know about a game of billiards, too; if virtue was discussed, he spoke very eloquently about virtue too, and even with tears in his eyes; if the question of the distillation of vodka was raised, he knew all there was to know about the art of distilling spirits; if the conversation turned on Customs and Excise officers, he delivered himself of so authoritative an opinion as though he had himself been a Customs and Excise officer. But the remarkable thing was that he could invest all this with a certain air of gravity, that he knew how to conduct himself with the utmost decorum. He spoke neither too loudly nor too softly, but just as one should. In short, whichever way you looked at it, he was a man of the utmost respectability and honesty. All the civil servants were pleased at the arrival of the new-comer. The governor gave it as his opinion that he was a right-think-ing person; the public prosecutor said that he was a sensible fellow; the colonel of gendarmes said that he was a man of learning; the presi-dent of the court that he was a well-informed and honourable man; the chief of police that he was an honourable and amiable man; the wife of the chief of police that he was a most courteous and most well-mannered person. Even Sobakevich, who very rarely said any-thing good of anyone, said on his return rather late from town to his scraggy wife, after undressing and getting into bed beside her: 'I spent the evening at the governor's, dear, and dined with the chief of police and made the acquaintance of Pavel Ivanovich Chichikov, a Col-legiate Councillor – a most agreeable man!' To which his wife re-plied: 'Mmmmmm!' and gave him a shove with her foot.

Such was the opinion, extremely flattering to the new arrival, that was formed of Chichikov in the town, and it persisted till the moment when an odd peculiarity of his and an undertaking, or as they say in the provinces, a proper how-d'you-do, of which the reader will soon learn more, threw almost the whole town into a state of utter per-plexity.

Chapter 2

THE newly arrived gentleman had been in the town for over a week, driving about to evening parties and dinners and having, as they say, a very pleasant time. At last he decided to extend his visits out of town and, as he had promised, pay a call on the landowners Manilov and Sobakevich. He had perhaps another more important reason for this, a much more serious matter, something that was nearer to his heart ... But the reader will learn about all this gradually and in good time, if only he has the patience to read through this very long story, which will assume greater and much vaster dimensions as it nears its end, which crowns all.

Selifan, the driver, had been given orders to harness the horses to the familiar carriage early in the morning; Petrushka was told to stay at the inn and keep an eye on the room and the trunk. This is perhaps the best place to acquaint the reader with these two house-serfs of our hero's. Although, of course, they are far from prominent characters and are what might be called secondary or even tertiary characters, although the plot and the mainspring of the poem have little to do with them and perhaps only here and there touch upon them and concern them but slightly, the author nevertheless likes to be extremely circumstantial in everything and even in this particular matter and, though a Russian, he wishes to be as precise as a German. This will not take up too much time or space, however, for there is little more to add to what the reader knows already, that is to say, that Petrushka used to walk about in a rather roomy brown coat which used to belong to his master, and, as is usual with people of his calling, had a big nose and thick lips. He was more taciturn than talkative by nature; he even had a noble urge for enlightenment, that is to say, for reading books, without bothering too much about their contents: it made no difference to him whether it was a tale about the adventures of a love-lorn swain or simply a primer or a prayer book – he read everything with equal attention; if someone had slipped a book of chemistry to him he would not have refused it. He liked not so much what he read as the reading itself, or, to put it more precisely, the process of reading, the fact that the letters were always forming a word which sometimes meant the devil only knew what. His reading was mostly done in a recumbent position in the anteroom, on the bed and on the mattress which, as a result, became as flat and as thin as a wafer. Apart from his passion for reading he had two more peculiarities which formed two other of his characteristic traits: he slept without undressing, just as he was, in the same coat, and he always carried about with him a peculiar atmosphere, a smell of his own, which recalled the stale air of a stuffy room, so that it was quite enough for him to fix up his bed some-where, even in a room which had not been lived in before, and to bring his overcoat and belongings there, for it to appear as if people had been living there for a dozen years. Chichikov, being an ex-tremely particular and in some respects even fastidious person, could not help making a wry face as he inhaled the air in the morning while his nose was still unaccustomed to it, and, shaking his head, used to say: 'Goodness only knows what's the matter with you, my dear fel-low. You're sweating, aren't you? I wish you'd go to the baths once in a while.' To which Petrushka made no answer, but tried to busy himself at once with one thing or another; he either went to brush his master's coat which was hanging on a nail, or simply tried to tidy up something in the room. What was he thinking while he was silent? Perhaps he was saying to himself: 'You're a fine one too! Aren't you tired of repeating one and the same thing a hundred times?' God knows, it is hard to tell what a house-serf is thinking when his master is telling him off. This is all that can be said of Petrushka for a start. The driver Selifan was quite a different sort of man. ... But knowing from experience how loath his readers are to strike up an acquaintance with persons of the lower orders, the author feels rather ashamed to take up so much of their time with them. A Russian, I am afraid, is like that: he has a passionate desire to bolster up his own importance by striking up an acquaintance with anyone who is at least one rank above him, and a nodding acquaintance with a count or a prince is much more important to him than the most intimate relationship with people of his own class. The author, in fact, is a little apprehen-sive for his hero who is only a Collegiate Councillor, that is to say, a civil servant of the sixth grade. Court Councillors, or civil servants of the seventh grade, may perhaps strike up an acquaintance with him, but those who have already attained the fourth or third grade, that is to say, the rank of general, those may, if he is lucky, cast upon him one of those contemptuous glances a man proudly casts at everything that grovels at his feet, or, if he is not so lucky, pass by with an indifference that cannot but have a devastating effect upon the author. But however regrettable that may be, we have to return to our hero.

And so, having given all the necessary orders the night before, he woke up very early in the morning. He washed, rubbed himself down from head to foot with a wet sponge, which he did only on Sundays (and that day happened to be a Sunday), and shaved himself so that his cheeks were as smooth and shiny as satin. He then put on his gleaming cranberry-coloured swallow-tail coat and his overcoat lined with bearskin, descended the staircase, supported now on one side and then on the other by the waiter, and got into his carriage. The carriage thundered out of the gates of the inn and into the street. A passing priest took off his hat, while several street urchins in dirty shirts held out their hands crying, 'Spare a copper for an orphan sir!' Noticing that one of them was trying hard to sneak a ride on the foot-board, the driver took a crack at him with his whip, and away went the carriage, bumping over the cobblestones. It was not without relief that the black-and-white striped toll-gate barrier was seen looming in the distance, for it was a sign that, like any other instrument of torture, the cobbled roadway was coming to an end; and after striking his head rather violently several times against the box of the carriage, Chichikov at last was rolling along on soft ground. No sooner did the town disappear in the distance than all sorts of stuff and rubbish began to pass quickly before our hero's eyes on both sides of the road, as is only to be expected in our country: hillocks, young fir-trees, low, scanty bushes of young pine, charred trunks of old pine-trees, wild heather, and such like trash. They drove past villages consisting of one long straight street, their buildings resembling old stacks of timber covered over with grey roofs, the carved wood ornaments under them looking like embroidered towels. As usual a few peasants in their sheepskin coats sat gaping on benches in front of the gates. Peasant women with fat faces and tightly bound bosoms were looking out of the upper windows; out of the lower ones a calf stared or a pig thrust out its blind snout. In short, the scenes were familiar enough. Having driven past the tenth milestone, Chichikov remembered that according to Manilov his village should be somewhere near. But the eleventh milestone flew past and still there was no sign of the village, and if two peasants had not happened to pass by on the road they would scarcely have got on the right track. Asked how far the village Zamanilovka was, the peasants took off their caps and one of them with a wedge-shaped beard, who was more intelligent, replied:

'You mean Manilovka, and not Zamanilovka, don't you, sir?'

'Very well, Manilovka.'

'Manilovka! Well, sir, you drives on for another mile and you comes to it. I mean, sir, it's there on the right.'

'The right?' Selifan repeated.

'The right,' said the peasant. 'That will be the road to Manilovka, sir. There's no such place as Zamanilovka. That's what it's called, sir. I mean its name is Manilovka. There's no Zamanilovka to be found hereabouts. You'll see a house up there, sir, on top of a hill. A brick house it is. A two-storied house. That's the manor house, sir. I mean the house where the gentleman himself lives. Well, sir, that's Manilovka. But there's no Zamanilovka here at all. There's never been such a place here, sir.'

They drove off in search of Manilovka. After driving for about a mile and a half, they came to a country road on the right, but even after driving for another two or three miles there was no sign of a two-storied brick house. Then Chichikov remembered that if a friend invites you to visit him in the country ten miles away, it turns out to be a good twenty miles at least. The village of Manilovka could not boast of being a beauty spot. The landowner's house was situated in an exposed position, that is to say, on a height exposed to all the winds that might chance to blow. The slope of the hill on which it stood was covered with a lawn. On the lawn were scattered, English fashion, two or three flower beds with lilac bushes and yellow acacia; five or six birch-trees in small clumps raised here and there their scanty fine-leaved tops. Under two of them a summer house could be seen with a flat green cupola, pale-blue wooden pillars, and an inscription: 'The Temple of Solitary Meditation'; a little lower down was a pond overgrown with weeds which, however, is nothing unusual in the English gardens of Russian landowners. At the foot of this eminence and partly along the slope itself, dark patches of nondescript wooden peasant cottages were visible, and for some mysterious reason our hero began at once to count them, and he counted more than two hundred of them; nowhere among them was there any growing tree or vegetation of any kind; there was nothing but timber to be seen anywhere. The scene was enlivened by two peasant women who, hitching up their skirts picturesquely and tucking them up on all sides, were wading up to the knees in the pond, dragging by two wooden poles a torn net in which could be seen two entangled crayfish and a glistening roach; the peasant women were apparently quarrelling and having words about something or other. A pinewood of a depressingly bluish colour showed up darkly on one side in the distance. Even the weather itself seemed to be perfectly in keeping with the scene: the day was neither bright nor overcast, but of a light-grey hue, such as one sees only on the old uniforms of garrison soldiers, an army pacific enough, though not altogether sober on Sundays. To complete the picture, a cock, the harbinger of changeable weather, crowed very lustily, though his head was picked almost to the very brain by the beaks of other cocks because of his well-known philandering habits, and even flapped his wings, which were as ragged as old bast mats. As he drove up to the courtyard, Chichikov caught sight of the master of the house himself standing on the front step, wearing a green shalloon coat and holding his hand to his forehead like a shield over his eyes to get a better view of the approaching carriage. The nearer the carriage drew to the front steps the merrier his eyes grew and the broader his smile.

'Pavel Ivanovich!' he cried at last when Chichikov got out of the carriage. 'So you have remembered us at last!'

The two friends kissed each other warmly and Manilov conducted his visitor into the house. Though the time during which they will be passing through the hall, the anteroom and the dining-room is somewhat brief, we shall do our best to make use of it to say a few words about the master of the house. But at this point the author must confess that such an undertaking is very difficult. It is far easier to depict characters on a grander scale: there all you have to do is to fling handfuls of paint at the canvas – black, burning eyes, beetling brows, a furrowed forehead, a black or fiery scarlet cloak thrown over a shoulder, and the portrait is finished; but these are all gentlemen of whom there are a great many in the world and who are very much like one another in appearance, and yet when you look at them more closely, you discover that they possess a great number of the most elusive peculiarities – such gentlemen are terribly hard to portray. In cases like these, you must concentrate all your attention before you can force all these subtle and almost invisible traits to disclose themselves to you, and, generally, you have to train your eye, already expert in the science of uncovering the secret places of the heart, to penetrate more deeply.

God alone could say what Manilov's character was like. There is a type of man who is described as 'so-so', neither one thing nor the other, neither fish, flesh, nor good red herring, as the saying is. Perhaps Manilov should be included in that company. In appearance he was an impressive-looking man; his features were rather pleasant, but this pleasantness, one could not help feeling, had much too much sugar in it; in his manners and turns of speech there was something that seemed to be asking ingratiatingly for favours and friendship. He smiled seductively. He had fair hair and his eyes were light blue. During the first minute of conversation with him, you could not help saying, 'What a kind and pleasant person!' During the following minute you would say nothing, and during the third you would say, 'Damned if I can make him out!' and you would get away from him as far as you could, for if not, you would be bored to death. You would never hear a single stimulating or even arrogant word from him, such as you might hear from almost anyone if you touched on a subject that concerned him deeply. Everyone has his own craze: one is crazy about Borzoi dogs; another believes that he is a great lover of music and is marvellously sensitive to its most profound passages; a third is a past master at dining and wining; a fourth is all for playing a part in the world which is at least one degree higher than the one he has been cut out for; a fifth, whose desires are more limited, dreams about going walking on the promenade with an aide-de-camp of the Emperor to show off to his friends, acquaintances, and strangers, too; a sixth has been blessed with a hand that feels an irresistible desire to turn down the corner of an ace of diamonds or a two and so double his stake, while the hand of the seventh simply itches to put things right somewhere and to get within striking distance of a station-master or a coachman – in short, every man has his own idiosyncrasies, but Manilov had nothing. At home he spoke very little, and was mostly pondering and thinking, but what he was thinking about, the Lord only knows. It could not be said that he was busy with the management of his estate. Indeed, he never drove out into the fields, and the estate seemed to carry on by itself, somehow. When his agent said, 'It would be a good thing, sir, to do this or that,' he would usually answer, 'Yes, that's not a bad idea,' smoking his pipe, which had become a habit with him while he was still serving in the army in which he was considered a most modest, tactful, and cultured officer. 'Yes, it's not a bad idea at all,' he would repeat. When a peasant came to him and, scratching the back of his head, said: 'I've been offered some work, sir, and I'd like to go away for a while to earn enough to pay off my taxes,' 'Go by all means,' he would reply, puffing at his pipe, and it never even occurred to him that the peasant was merely going off to get drunk. Sometimes as he stood on the front steps gazing at the yard and the pond, he used to say what a good idea it would be if a subterranean passage could be tunnelled from the house, or a stone bridge built over the pond with shops on each side of it and shopkeepers sitting in them selling all sorts of small articles required by the peasants. As he said this, a look of the utmost sweetness would appear in his eyes and his face would assume a most contented expression; all these projects, however, never went beyond words. In his study there was always some book lying about with a marker on the fourteenth page, a book he had been reading continuously for the last two years. In his house there was always something lacking. The furniture in his drawing-room was very good and it was covered in magnificent silk material which must have cost him a great deal of money, but there was not enough of it for two of the armchairs and these stood covered simply in bast matting. The master of the house, however, had for several years been warning his guests every time they entered the drawing-room, saying, 'Please don't sit on those armchairs, they aren't ready yet.' In some of the rooms there was no furniture at all, although he had said to his wife shortly after their marriage, 'Darling, tomorrow we must see to it that some furniture is put into this room, at least for the time being.' In the evening a very magnificent candlestick of dark bronze with the three Graces and a magnificent mother-of-pearl shield was put on the table, and next to it was set a plain brass cripple of a candlestick, lame, lop-sided, and covered all over in tallow, but neither the master nor the mistress nor the servants seemed to notice it. His wife ... Still, they were perfectly happy with one another. In spite of the fact that they had been married for over eight years, they would still offer each other either a piece of apple or a sweet or a nut and say in a touchingly tender voice, expressing the deepest affection: 'Open your little mouth, darling, and let me pop this in.' It goes without saying that the little mouth was opened very gracefully on such an occasion. They always used to plan surprises for each other's birthdays, such as a bead case or a toothbrush. And very often as they sat on a sofa, for no apparent reason at all, he would suddenly put down his pipe and she her needle-work, if, that is, she happened to have it in her hands at the time, and they would imprint such a long and languishing kiss upon each other's lips that one might easily have smoked a small cigar while it lasted. In short, they were what is called 'happy'. Of course, it might have been pointed out that there were many other things to be done in the house besides exchanging prolonged kisses and planning surprises, and a great number of questions could well be asked. Why, for instance, were the meals in the kitchen prepared so foolishly and haphazardly? Why was the pantry practically empty? Why was the housekeeper a thief? Why were the servants so drunken and dirty? Why did all the household serfs spend most of their time sleeping and larking about? But all these things were too trivial and Mrs Manilov was well brought-up. And, as we all know, a good education is to be obtained in young ladies' boarding schools, and, as we also know, in young ladies' boarding schools three principal subjects constitute the founda-tion of all human virtues: the French language, indispensable for the happiness of family life, the pianoforte to provide agreeable moments for husbands, and, finally, domestic science proper, such as the knit-ting of purses and other surprises. However, there have been all sorts of improvements and changes in methods, especially in modern times; all this depends largely on the good sense and the abilities of the principals of the ladies' boarding schools. In some boarding schools, therefore, they begin with the piano and follow it up with the French language and then domestic science. In others they start with domestic science, that is, the knitting of surprises, and follow it up with the French language and, finally, with the piano. There are all sorts of methods. One might perhaps make the further observation that Mrs Manilov ... But, I must confess I'm very much afraid of talk-ing about ladies and, besides, it is time I returned to our heroes, who have been standing for several minutes before the drawing-room door, each entreating the other to pass through first.

'Don't worry about me,' Chichikov kept saying. 'After you, sir.'

'No, no, after you, sir,' Manilov kept saying, pointing to the door. 'You are our guest, sir.'

'Why, no,' Chichikov kept saying, 'after you, sir. Please, please, don't put yourself out on my account.'

'I'm very sorry, sir, but I cannot possibly permit such a charming and cultured guest to follow me.'

'Why cultured? Please, sir, after you.'

'No, after you, sir.'

'But why, sir?'

'Well, just because, sir!' Manilov said with an agreeable smile.

At last the two friends went through the door sideways, squeezing each other a little.

'Allow me to introduce my wife,' Manilov said. 'Darling, this is Mr Chichikov.'

Chichikov, indeed, caught sight of a lady whom he had completely failed to notice while exchanging bows with Manilov in the doorway. She was quite good-looking and was becomingly dressed. She wore a well-fitting silk morning dress of a pale colour; her delicate little hand threw something hurriedly on the table and clutched a cambric handkerchief with embroidered corners. She got up from the sofa on which she was sitting. It was not without pleasure that Chichikov bent to kiss her hand. Mrs Manilov, pronouncing her r's a little in the Parisian fashion, said that he delighted them by his visit and that not a day passed without her husband's mentioning him.

'Yes,' said Manilov, 'you know she kept asking me, "And why doesn't your friend come?" "Wait, darling, he'll come." And now at last you have honoured us with your visit. Oh, sir, you have given us such pleasure. ... A name-day. ... A name-day of hearts. ...'

On hearing that things had gone as far as a name-day of hearts, Chichikov felt a little embarrassed and replied modestly that he owned no illustrious name nor, indeed, an outstanding rank.

'You have everything,' Manilov interrupted with the same engaging smile. 'You've got everything and even more.'

'And how did you like our town?' Mrs Manilov said. 'Have you passed your time agreeably there?'

'It's a very excellent town, ma'am,' Chichikov replied. 'A magnificent town. And I've spent a most agreeable time: the society there is most affable.'

'And how did you find our governor?' said Mrs Manilov.

'Don't you think he is a most estimable and most obliging person?' added Mr Manilov.

'Perfectly true,' said Chichikov. 'A most estimable person. And how admirably he performs his duties! How well he understands them! I wish we had more people like him.'

'How well he receives people, you know, and how considerate he is in everything he does,' Manilov added with a smile, almost closing his eyes with delight, like a tom-cat who is being gently stroked behind the ears.

'A most courteous and agreeable person,' Chichikov went on. 'And how clever he is with his hands! I could never have imagined it. How excellently he embroiders all sorts of patterns! He showed me a purse he made: not every lady could have embroidered it so beautifully.'

'And the vice-governor,' said Manilov, again screwing up his eyes a little, 'don't you think he is a most charming person?'

'A most, most worthy man,' replied Chichikov.

'And pray, what did you think of our chief of police?'

'A very agreeable person, isn't he?'

'A most agreeable person, and what an intelligent, well-read man! We played whist at his house with the public prosecutor and the president of the court till the small hours. A most, most worthy man!'

'Well,' Mrs Manilov added, 'and what's your opinion of the wife of the chief of police? A most charming woman, isn't she?'

'Oh, she is one of the worthiest women I've ever known,' replied Chichikov.

After that they did not omit to mention the president of the court and the postmaster, and in this way ran through the names of almost all the civil servants in the town, who all turned out to be most worthy persons.

'Do you spend all your time in the country?' Chichikov at last put a question to them in his turn.

'Mostly in the country,' replied Manilov. 'Sometimes, however, we go to town, chiefly in order to be in the company of cultured people. One gets out of touch with things, you know, if one lives shut up all the time.'

'That's true, quite true,' said Chichikov.

'Of course,' went on Manilov, 'it would be quite a different matter if one had nice neighbours. I mean, if there was someone with whom one could, as it were, have a chat about the importance of being polite to people, the importance of good manners, or follow the development of – well – some science so as to stir up the mind a little, something to make you aspire to some high ideal ...' At this point he was about to give expression to something else, but noticing that he had let his tongue run away with him, he just waved his hand vaguely in the air and went on: 'Then, of course, the country and solitude would have many charms. But, I'm sorry to say, there's absolutely no one ... All we can do is read the *Son of the Fatherland* occasionally.'

Chichikov agreed with this entirely, adding that there was nothing more agreeable than to live in solitude, enjoy the spectacle of nature, and to read some book occasionally ...

'But, you know,' Manilov added, 'all the same, if you have no friend with whom you can share ...'

'Oh, that's true, that's perfectly true,' Chichikov interrupted. 'What are all the treasures in the world then! "Not money, but good company!" a wise man has said.'

'And you know, sir,' said Manilov with an expression that was not merely sweet, but cloyingly sweet, like the medicine a clever society doctor has sweetened unmercifully in the hope of pleasing his patient, 'then you feel a sort of, as it were, spiritual enjoyment ... I mean, just as now when chance has given me the happiness, if I may say so, sir, the supreme happiness of chatting with you and enjoying your agreeable conversation ...'

'Good Lord, sir, what agreeable conversation do you mean? I'm an insignificant person and nothing more,' replied Chichikov.

'Oh, sir, do let me be frank with you. I'd gladly give half of all I possess for a few only of your excellent qualities!'

'On the contrary, sir, for my part I should consider it the greatest ...'

It is hard to say what point this mutual effusion of feelings between these two friends might have reached, had not a servant entered to announce that dinner was served.

'Please, sir,' said Manilov. 'You must excuse us if our dinner is not the sort of dinner that is served in great houses and in capital cities. We've just ordinary Russian cabbage soup, but we offer it in all sincerity. Please ...'

Here they again argued for some time as to who should go in first and at last Chichikov went sideways into the dining-room.

Two boys, Manilov's sons, were already in the dining-room. They were of an age when children are allowed to sit at table, but still on high chairs. Their tutor, who bowed constantly and with a smile, was standing beside them. The mistress of the house sat down behind the soup tureen, the guest was placed between his host and hostess, and the servant tied napkins round the children's necks.

'What charming children,' said Chichikov, glancing at them. 'How old are they?'

'The elder is eight and the younger was six only yesterday,' said Mrs Manilov.

'Themistoclus!' said Manilov, turning to the elder boy who was trying to free his chin from the napkin which the servant had fastened round it.

Chichikov raised a brow slightly when he heard this partly Greek name to which for some unknown reason Manilov had attached the suffix 'us', but at once tried to regain his normal expression.

'Themistoclus, tell me which is the finest city in France?'

At this point the teacher concentrated all his attention on Themistoclus and looked as if he would jump straight into his eyes, but at last was completely reassured and nodded his head when Themistoclus said: 'Paris.'

'And which is our finest city?' Manilov asked again.

The tutor again concentrated all his attention on his pupil.

'Petersburg,' replied Themistoclus.

'And what other?'

'Moscow,' replied Themistoclus.

'What a clever little boy!' Chichikov commented aloud. 'Really,' he went on, turning to Manilov and his wife with a certain air of astonishment, 'such knowledge at such a tender age! Let me tell you this child shows great abilities.'

'Oh, you don't know him yet,' replied Manilov. 'You can't imagine what a bright little fellow he is. Now the younger one, Alcides, is not so quick, but this one, if he comes across anything, a small insect or a beetle, his little eyes light up at once. He runs after it and starts observing it immediately. I intend him for the diplomatic service. Themistoclus,' he continued, turning to the boy again, 'would you like to be an ambassador?'

'I would,' answered Themistoclus, chewing a piece of bread, and shaking his head from side to side.

At that moment the footman standing behind his chair wiped the ambassador's nose and it was just as well he did so, for otherwise a largish, superfluous drop would have dropped into the soup. The conversation at table turned on the pleasures of a quiet life, interrupted by their hostess's observations about the town theatre and its actors. The tutor gazed attentively at the speakers and the moment he noticed that they were about to laugh, he opened his mouth and laughed with the utmost zeal. He was probably a person of a grateful nature and was anxious to repay his employer in this way for the good treatment he received. On one occasion, however, his face assumed a stern expression and he rapped on the table severely, glaring at the children sitting opposite him. He was not a moment too late, for Themistoclus had just bitten Alcides' ear and Alcides, screwing up his eyes and opening his mouth, was about to burst out sobbing piteously, but realizing that he might well be left without a sweet, he restored his mouth to its normal position and began tearfully to gnaw at a mutton bone, which made his cheeks shine with grease. The lady of the house very frequently turned to Chichikov with the words: 'But you're not eating anything, you've not taken enough.' To which Chichikov each time replied: 'Thank you very very much, ma'am, I've had enough. Agreeable conversation is better than any dish.'

They rose from the table. Manilov was exceedingly pleased and, supporting his visitor's back with his arm, was about to conduct him to the drawing-room, when suddenly Chichikov declared with a very significant look that he would like to have a talk with him about a very important matter.

'In that case,' said Manilov, 'allow me to take you to my study,' and he led him into a small room, the window of which looked out on some woods, showing blue in the distance. 'This is my den,' said Manilov.

'What a pleasant little room!' said Chichikov, looking round.

The room, indeed, was far from unpleasant: its walls were painted a bluish-grey colour; there were four chairs, one armchair, a table on which lay the book with the marker which we have already had occasion to mention, several sheets of scribbled paper, but most of all tobacco of every shape and form: in paper packets, in a bowl, and simply piled up in a heap on the table. There were also little heaps of pipe-ash on both window-sills, arranged not without care in very neat rows. It was obvious that this provided the master of the house with a very agreeable pastime.

'Do sit down in this armchair,' said Manilov. 'You'll find it more restful.'

'If you don't mind I'd rather sit on an ordinary chair.'

'I'm afraid I do mind,' said Manilov with a smile. 'This chair is for our visitors: whether you like it or not, you will have to sit in it.'

Chichikov sat down.

'Do let me offer you a pipe, sir.'

'Thank you, but I don't smoke,' replied Chichikov amiably and as though with an air of regret.

'Why not?' said Manilov, also amiably and with an air of regret.

'I'm afraid I haven't formed the habit. I'm told a pipe dries you up.'

'If you don't mind my saying so that is a prejudice. Indeed, in my opinion, smoking a pipe is much healthier than taking snuff. There was a first lieutenant in our regiment, a most excellent and cultured man, who never let his pipe out of his mouth, not only at table but, if you don't mind my saying so, in every other place. He's now in his forties, and, thank God, as strong as a horse.'

Chichikov observed that this did indeed happen and there were hundreds of things in nature that could not be explained even by the greatest intellects.

'But allow me first to make a request,' he said in a voice in which there was a strange, or almost strange, note, and for some reason he looked round him immediately. Manilov, too, for some reason looked round. 'How long is it since you sent off the census list of your peasants?'

'Oh, that must have been some time ago. As a matter of fact, I can't remember.'

'And have many of your peasants died since then?'

'I'm afraid I don't know. I expect I'd have to ask my agent about it. You there! Please, call the agent. He should be here today.'

The agent appeared. He was a man of about forty who shaved his beard, wore a frock-coat, and apparently led a well-contented life, for he had a plump and well-fed face, and his yellowish complexion and half-shut eyes showed that he was all too familiar with feather beds and bolsters. One could see at once that he had followed his calling as all landowners' agents do: to begin with, he was simply an errand boy in the house who could read and write, then he had married some Agashka, a housekeeper and a favourite of the mistress, had himself become a house steward and, later on, an agent. Having become an agent, he quite naturally did as all agents do: kept company and made friends with the better-off villagers, levied higher taxes on the poorer families, got up at nine o'clock in the morning, waited for the *samovar*, and drank tea.

'Look here, my dear fellow, how many of our peasants have died since the last census?'

'How many? Why, lots of them have died since then,' said the agent and hiccoughed, covering his mouth slightly with his hand as with a shield.

'Well, I must say, I thought so myself,' Manilov interposed. 'Yes, yes, lots have died.' Then he turned to Chichikov and added: 'Yes, indeed, lots, lots have died.'

'You don't know the exact figure by any chance?' asked Chichikov.

'Yes, what is the figure?' Manilov put in.

'Well, sir, I'm afraid I can't tell the figure. You see, sir, it's not known how many have died. No one has counted them.'

'Yes, that's it,' said Manilov turning to Chichikov. 'I too thought there had been a high mortality. It's quite impossible to say how many have died.'

'You'd better count them,' said Chichikov to the agent. 'And, please, make a detailed list of all of them by name.'

'Yes,' said Manilov, 'all of them by name.'

The agent said: 'Yes, sir,' and went out.

'And what do you require it for?' asked Manilov, after the agent had gone.

This question seemed to have put the visitor into a quandary. His face assumed a sort of strained expression, which even made him go red in the face as a result, no doubt, of an effort to express something that he could not put into words. And, indeed, Manilov was at last to hear strange and extraordinary things no human ear had ever heard before.

'You ask me for my reason. Well, my reason is this. I'd like to buy peasants who ...' said Chichikov, hesitating, and not finishing his sentence.

'But if you don't mind my asking you, how do you wish to buy these peasants? With land, or simply to take away, that is, without land?'

'Well, no, sir,' said Chichikov. 'I don't want real peasants. I want to have dead ones.'

'I beg your pardon? I'm sorry, I'm a little hard of hearing. I thought I heard you say something rather odd ...'

'You see, I'd like to acquire dead souls, who are still registered as living on the census,' said Chichikov.

Manilov dropped his pipe with the long mouthpiece on the floor and remained standing with a gaping mouth for several minutes. The two friends, who had been discussing the delights of a life of friendship, remained motionless, staring fixedly at each other like those portraits which in the old days used to be hung facing each other on each side of a looking-glass. At last Manilov picked up his pipe and glanced at Chichikov's face from below to see if there were not some ironic smile on his lips, to make sure he had not been pulling his leg; but he could see nothing of the sort – on the contrary, if anything, Chichikov's face looked graver than usual; then he wondered whether his visitor had by any chance taken leave of his senses, and looked at him intently in some alarm; but the visitor's eyes were perfectly clear; there was no sign of any wild, restless fire in them, such as flashes in the eyes of a madman; everything about him was respectable and in perfect order. However hard Manilov tried to think what to do and how to behave, he could think of nothing better than to blow out in a thin spiral the smoke still left in his mouth.

'And so, I should like to know whether you could transfer such peasants to me, peasants who are not alive in reality, but who are still alive legally. Could you cede them to me or transfer them to me in any way that seems best to you?'

But Manilov was so confused and embarrassed that he just stared at him.

'Am I right in thinking,' observed Chichikov, 'that you find my proposal a little difficult?'

'Me? No, it isn't that,' said Manilov. 'But I can't quite grasp it. I'm sorry. I haven't, of course, had such a brilliant education as you, which, if I might say so, er – can be observed in your every gesture. I – I – haven't – er – the high art of expressing myself. ... Perhaps, in what you've just said, there's some hidden meaning. ... Perhaps you've just put it like that for the sake of saying something original.'

'No,' Chichikov put in, 'of course not. I meant exactly what I said, that is to say, the peasants who are really dead.'

Manilov was completely dumbfounded. He felt he had to do something, to ask some question, but what question goodness only knows.

He ended finally by blowing out some more smoke, but this time not from his mouth, but through his nostrils.

'Well,' said Chichikov, 'if there aren't any obstacles, we might, with God's help, set about drawing up a deed of purchase.'

'A deed of purchase for dead souls?'

'Oh, no,' said Chichikov, 'we shall put down that they are living, as indeed it is stated in the census list. You see, it's my practice never to depart from the letter of the law. Though I've had to suffer for it in the service, duty is sacred in my eyes. The law, sir – I'm speechless when confronted with the law.'

These last words appealed to Manilov, but he could still not make head or tail of what it was all about, and, instead of an answer, he began sucking at his pipe so violently that at last it started wheezing like a bassoon. It seemed as if he wished to extract from it an opinion about such an incredible business. But the pipe only wheezed and – nothing more.

'You're not having any doubts about it, are you?'

'Good heavens, no. I'm not saying that I have anything against you, that I'm blaming you for anything. But don't you think there's something in this undertaking, or, to put it more precisely, in this business deal – don't you think there's something in this business deal that does not quite conform to the code of civic law and the future prosperity of Russia?'

Here Manilov, having made a slight movement with his head, looked very significantly into Chichikov's face, displaying in all the features of his own face and in his tightly pursed lips an expression so profound as had never, perhaps, been seen before on a human face, except perhaps on the face of some extremely clever minister and that, too, only when confronted by some brain-racking problem.

But Chichikov said simply that such an undertaking or business deal would in no way be inconsistent with the civic code and the future prosperity of Russia, adding a minute later that the treasury would even profit by it, for it would receive the legal fees ...

'So you think ...?'

'I think that it's all right.'

'Oh well, if it's all right, then it's a different matter. I've nothing against it,' said Manilov, and he was completely reassured.

'Now it only remains to agree on the price. ...'

'How do you mean, on the price?' Manilov said again, and he

paused. 'You don't think I'll accept money for souls who, in a certain sense, have ended their earthly existence? If, I mean, such a fantastic wish has entered your head, I'm quite willing, for my part, to let you have them without a penny and I'll pay the costs of the deed of purchase myself.'

The chronicler of these events would feel greatly deserving of reproof if he failed to state that the visitor was overcome with delight at the words uttered by Manilov. Sober and sensible as he was, he had to force himself not to skip about like a goat which, as we all know, happens only in moments of violent outbursts of joy. He turned round so rapidly in his armchair that the woollen material covering the cushion split open; Manilov himself stared at him in some perplexity. Overcome with gratitude, he gave utterance to so many expressions of thanks that Manilov felt embarrassed, blushed all over, shook his head deprecatingly, and at last declared that it was absolutely nothing, that he merely wished to give him some proof of his heart-felt sympathy, of the magnetism of souls, while the souls of the dead peasants were, in a way, absolutely worthless.

'Worthless? Not at all!' said Chichikov pressing his hand. At this point, a very deep sigh escaped him. It looked as if he were just in the right mood for heartfelt effusions, and it was not without emotion and expression that he finally uttered the following words: 'If only you knew the great service you have rendered by these seemingly worthless souls to a man without kith and kin! Yes, indeed, what have I not suffered? Like some barque tossed by tempestuous seas. ... What oppressions, what persecutions have I not experienced, what sorrow have I not endured and for what? Why, for doing what was right, for having a clear conscience, for stretching out a helping hand to the helpless widow and the poor orphan!'

At this point he even wiped away a tear with his handkerchief.

Manilov was deeply touched. The two friends pressed each other's hands for a long time and gazed in silence into each other's eyes in which tears were starting. Manilov would not let go of our hero's hand, but continued to press it so warmly that Chichikov was at a loss how to extricate it. At last, having quietly freed it, he said that it would not be a bad idea to draw up the deed of purchase as soon as possible and that it would be as well if Manilov paid a visit to the town himself. Then he picked up his hat and began to take his leave.

'Good heavens, you're not going already?' said Manilov, coming to himself suddenly and almost frightened.

At that moment Mrs Manilov walked into the study.

'Please, darling,' said Manilov with a somewhat pitiful air, 'Mr Chichikov is leaving us!'

'I suppose it's because Mr Chichikov got bored with us,' replied Mrs Manilov.

'Madam,' said Chichikov, 'here, here,' he laid his hand on his heart, 'yes, it's here that the delightful time I've spent with you will be preserved for ever. And, believe me, I can't think of any greater happiness than to live with you, if not in the same house, at least in the closest vicinity.'

'But, you know, my dear sir,' said Manilov to whom this idea appealed very much, 'it would indeed be a most excellent idea if we could live like this together under one roof, or in the shade of some elm-tree where we could air our views on any subject under the sun and delve deep into the mysteries of life!'

'Oh, that would be paradise itself!' said Chichikov with a sigh. 'Good-bye, madam,' he went on, going up to Mrs Manilov and kissing her hand. 'Good-bye, my most estimable friend. Do not forget my request!'

'Oh, you can be sure of that!' replied Manilov. 'I'm parting from you for no more than two days.'

They all went into the dining-room.

'Good-bye, my dear little ones,' said Chichikov, catching sight of Alcides and Themistoclus, who were playing with a wooden hussar, who had already lost an arm and a nose. 'Good-bye, my little darlings, I am sorry not to have brought you any presents, but, you see, I did not even know of your existence. But I shall most certainly bring you some when I come again. I'll bring you a sword, would you like a sword?'

'Yes, sir,' replied Themistoclus.

'And you a drum,' he went on, bending over Alcides 'You would like a drum, wouldn't you?'

'Dlum,' Alcides replied in a whisper, hanging his head.

'Very good, I shall bring you a drum, such a lovely drum. It'll go all the time rat-tat-tat-tat-tat – Good-bye, my little darling, good-bye.' Then he kissed him on the head and turned to Manilov and his wife with the sort of little laugh with which one usually turns on parents when one wishes to make them realize the innocence of their children's desires.

'But please do stay, Mr Chichikov,' said Manilov when they had all gone out on the front steps. 'Just look at those clouds!'

'Those are only little clouds,' replied Chichikov.

'But do you know the way to Sobakevich's?'

'I wanted to ask you about that.'

'If you don't mind I'll tell your driver at once.'

And with the same politeness Manilov gave the directions to Chichikov's driver, going so far as to address him once as 'sir'.

Hearing that he would have to pass two turnings and take the third, Selifan said: 'Don't worry, sir, we shall manage it,' and so Chichikov drove away, accompanied for a long time by the bowing and waving of handkerchiefs of his host and hostess, who stood on tiptoe for the purpose.

Manilov stood for a long time on the steps, following the receding carriage with his eyes, and when it could no longer be seen he was still standing there puffing at his pipe. At last he went inside, sat down on a chair, and gave himself up to meditation, genuinely glad to have been able to give his visitor some slight pleasure. Then his thoughts concentrated imperceptibly upon other subjects and at last soared away goodness only knows where. He was thinking of the happiness of a life spent among friends, about how delightful it would be to live with a friend on the bank of some river, then he began constructing a bridge over the river, then a huge house with a belvedere so high that one could see Moscow from it, and where one would drink tea in the evenings in the open air and discuss some very agreeable subjects. Then he fancied that he and Chichikov arrived in a splendid carriage at some social gathering where they enchanted everyone by their exquisite manners and that the Czar himself, learning of their great friendship, made them generals, and he went on giving full play to his fancy so that in the end he did not know himself what was happening. Chichikov's strange request suddenly interrupted his day-dreaming. His mind somehow refused to take in the idea; however much he turned it over in his head, he could not make any sense of it and he sat there puffing away at his pipe until it was time for supper.

Chapter 3

MEANWHILE Chichikov was sitting contentedly in his carriage, which had been rolling along the highway for some time. From the foregoing chapter it is already clear what was the chief subject of his predilections and inclinations and it is therefore no wonder that he was very soon immersed in it body and soul. The plans, calculations, and reasons which were reflected on his face were apparently most agreeable, for they left traces of a satisfied smile every moment. Pre-occupied with them, he paid no attention to his driver who, satisfied with the reception given him by Manilov's household serfs, was making extremely sensible observations to the dappled-grey side-horse harnessed on the right side. This dappled-grey horse was a very cunning animal and merely pretended to be pulling, while the bay shaft-horse and the light chestnut on the left-hand side, called 'Assessor', because he had been acquired from some assessor, laboured with all their might so that the pleasure they derived from their work could be perceived in their eyes. 'Cunning, aren't you? Well, I'll be more cunning than you!' said Selifan, standing up and flicking his whip at the slacker. 'Do your work, you German Pantaloon! The bay is an honest horse, he does his duty; I'd be glad to give him an extra measure of oats, because he's an honest horse, and the Assessor, too, he's a good horse. Now, then, what are you shaking your ears for? Listen when you're spoken to, you fool! I shan't teach you nothing wrong, you lout. Look where he's crawling now!' Here he again flicked him with his whip, saying: 'Oh, you barbarian, you damned Bonaparte, you!' Then he shouted at all of them: 'Away with you, my hearties!' and flicked his whip at all three of them not by way of punishment but to show that he was pleased with them. Having given them that pleasure, he again addressed the dappled-grey side-horse: 'You think I don't know what you're up to? No, sir, you must deal fairly if you want to be treated with respect. Now the servants of the gentleman we visited were good people. I'm glad to talk to a good man. With a good man I'm always friends, the best of pals: any time I'd be glad to have a cup of tea or a bite with a good man. Why, if he's a good man everyone respects him. Take our master, for instance. Everyone respects him because, you see, he was in government service, a collegiary councillor he is ...'

Reasoning in this way, Selifan at last got himself involved in most far-fetched abstractions. If Chichikov had been listening, he would have learnt many details relating to himself personally; but his thoughts were so preoccupied with his own plan that it was only a loud clap of thunder that made him come down to earth and look round him: the whole sky was completely covered with clouds and the dusty highway was sprinkled with drops of rain. Then another clap of thunder resounded more loudly and this time nearer and the rain suddenly poured down in bucketfuls. At first coming down in an oblique direction, it beat on one side of the carriage and then on the other; next, changing its tactics and coming down absolutely vertically, it began drumming on the top of the carriage; and, finally, drops of rain began to splash against his face. This forced him to draw the leather curtains with two small round windows, whose purpose it was to afford a view of the landscape, and he ordered Selifan to drive faster. Selifan, interrupted in the middle of his speech, realized that this was not a time for dawdling; he pulled out some grey cloth rags from under the box, put them over his sleeves, caught hold of the reins and shouted at his team of three horses who were scarcely moving their legs, for they felt pleasantly relaxed as a result of his edifying speeches. But for the life of him Selifan could not remember whether he had driven past two or three turnings. Thinking it over and trying to remember something of the road, he realized that he must have passed a great number of turnings. But as a Russian is never at a loss what to do at a critical moment, he turned without wasting any time on any further reflections to the right at the first crossroads and, shouting at the horses: 'Away with you, honest friends!', he set off at a gallop, without thinking where the road he had taken would lead him.

The rain, however, seemed likely to go on for a long time. The dust on the road was very soon churned into mud and every minute the horses found it harder to pull. Failing to catch sight of Sobakevich's village for a long time, Chichikov began to be seriously worried. According to his calculations, they should have arrived there long ago. He kept peering out of the carriage on either side, but it was so dark that one could see nothing.

'Selifan,' he said at last, poking his head out of the carriage.

'What is it, sir?' asked Selifan.

'Have a look, can you see a village anywhere?'

'No, sir, can't see none nowhere.' After which Selifan, waving his whip about, struck up not what you might call a song, but something long-drawn-out that seemed to go on for ever. Everything went into it: all the encouraging and inciting cries with which horses are regaled from one end of Russia to the other, all sorts of adjectives without discrimination just as they happened to come first to his tongue. It went so far, indeed, that he began at last to call them 'secretaries'.

Meanwhile, Chichikov began to notice that the carriage was rocking from side to side and jolting him violently; that made him realize that they had turned off the road and were probably bumping along a recently furrowed field. Selifan himself probably realized it too, but he never said a word.

'Where are you driving, you rogue?' cried Chichikov. 'What sort of road is this?'

'Can't do a thing about it, sir. Look at the weather. Can't see my whip, I can't, it's so dark!'

Having said this, he wheeled the carriage round at such an angle that Chichikov was forced to hold on with both hands. It was only then that he noticed that Selifan had had a drop too many.

'Stop, stop!' he shouted at him. 'You'll overturn us!'

'No, sir, I won't overturn you,' said Selifan. 'It's bad to overturn people, I know that. No, sir, I won't overturn you at all!'

He then began to turn the carriage round gently; he kept turning it round and round till he finally tipped it over completely on its side. Chichikov tumbled out into the mud on his hands and knees. Selifan, however, did stop the horses; they would have stopped anyhow, because they were utterly exhausted. He was struck dumb at such an unforeseen accident. Getting off his box, he stopped dead in front of the carriage with his arms akimbo, while his master floundered in the mud and tried to scramble out of it. 'Well, I never!' said Selifan after a moment's reflection. 'So it has overturned after all!'

'You're as drunk as a cobbler,' said Chichikov.

'No, sir, how could I be drunk? I know it's bad to be drunk. I just had a chat with a friend, seeing as how it's a good thing to have a chat with a good man. There's nothing wrong about it, is there? And we

51

had a bite together. There's nothing wrong in having a bite, is there? One can have a bite with a good man.'

'And what did I tell you last time when you got drunk?' said Chichikov. 'Forgotten, have you?'

'No, sir, how could I have forgotten? I know what's good for me, sir. I know it's no good to be drunk. I just had a chat with a good man, because ...'

'I'll give you a thrashing and it'll teach you to have a chat with a good man!'

'That's as you wish, sir,' replied Selifan who was quite willing to agree to anything. 'If it's to be a thrashing, then a thrashing let it be. I don't mind, I'm sure. Why not give a fellow a thrashing if he's deserved it? That's what a master is for. Aye, a thrashing's all right, because a peasant, sir, likes to take liberties, and order, sir, must be preserved. Why, sir, if he's deserved it, then thrash him. Why not thrash him?'

The master was completely at a loss how to reply to this kind of reasoning, but at that moment fate itself seemed to have decided to take pity on him. The barking of dogs could be heard in the distance. Overcome with joy, Chichikov ordered Selifan to whip up the horses. The Russian driver has an excellent scent that serves him better than his eyes; that is how it sometimes happens that, speeding along with his eyes shut, he always gets somewhere in the end. Selifan, though he could not see a thing, directed the horses straight to the village and stopped only when, the shafts of the carriage striking against a fence, it was absolutely impossible to drive any farther. All Chichikov could see through the thick curtain of the pouring rain was something that looked like a roof. He sent Selifan off to look for the gate which, without a doubt, would have taken him a very long time to find were it not that in Russia savage dogs do the work of porters, and these announced his arrival with such loud barking that he had to stop up his ears with his fingers. There was a glimmer of light in one of the windows and its misty gleam, reaching the fence, showed our travellers the gates. Selifan started knocking and soon the wicket gate opened and a figure appeared covered in a peasant coat, and master and servant heard a hoarse peasant woman's voice saying: 'Who's knocking? What's all this row?'

'We're travellers, my good woman,' replied Chichikov. 'Put us up for the night, will you?'

'A smart one, aren't you?' said the old woman. 'What a time to come! This isn't an inn: it's the house of a lady.'

'I'm very sorry, my good woman, but you see we've lost our way. We can't spend the night in the steppe in such weather, can we?'

'Yes, ma'am,' added Selifan. 'It's a dark night and the weather's foul.'

'Shut up, you fool,' said Chichikov.

'And who are you?' asked the old woman.

'A nobleman, my good woman.'

The word 'nobleman' seemed to make the woman think it over for a while.

'Wait, sir, I'll tell the mistress,' she said, and in a couple of minutes she was back with a lantern in her hand.

The gates were opened. A light appeared in another window. Driving into the courtyard, the carriage stopped before a small house which it was difficult to make out in the darkness. Only half of it was lit up by the light from the windows; a large puddle could be seen in front of the house, on which the light from the same windows fell directly. The rain was pattering loudly on the wooden roof and flowed in rippling streams into a tub specially placed to catch it. In the meantime the dogs were barking in all sorts of voices: one of them, his head tossed upwards, was howling in such a drawn-out voice and so painstakingly as though he were getting goodness only knows what wages for it; another one was snapping it out rapidly like a sacristan; between them, like a postman's bell, the voice of what sounded like a puppy rang out in a restless treble; all this was capped by a bass voice, probably of an elderly hound endowed with a sturdy canine nature, for he was as hoarse as a *basso profundo* when a concert is in full blast and the tenors, in their anxiety to take a high note, are standing on tiptoe and every man in the choir is straining upwards, tossing back his head, while the bass alone, his unshaven chin tucked into his necktie, squatting on his haunches and almost sinking to the floor, lets out from there a note which sets the window-panes shaking and rattling. From the very barking of the dogs composed of such musicians, it could be concluded that the village was of a decent size; but, chilled to the bone and soaked to the skin, our hero could think of nothing but his bed. The moment the carriage came to a stop, he leaped out on to the steps, stumbled, and nearly fell. Another woman, a little younger than the first, but very like her, came out on to the steps. She conducted him to a room. Chichikov cast a couple of cursory glances round him: the room was hung with rather old striped wallpaper; pictures of some kind of birds; between the windows were small old-fashioned looking-glasses in dark frames in the shape of curled leaves; behind each looking-glass was stuffed either a letter or an old pack of cards or a stocking; there was a clock on the wall with flowers painted on its face – Chichikov was too tired to notice anything else. He felt that his eyes were sticking together, as though someone had smeared them with honey. A minute later the mistress of the house came in. She was an elderly woman wearing a kind of night-cap hurriedly put on and a piece of flannel round her neck, one of those dear old ladies, owners of small estates, who complain of bad harvests, losses, hold their heads slightly on one side, and yet little by little fill variegated canvas bags with money and stow them away in different drawers. Silver roubles will be put in one little bag, fifty copeck pieces in another, and twenty-five copeck pieces in a third, though at first sight it seems as though there were nothing in the chest of drawers but linen, nightgowns, and reels of cotton, not to mention an unpicked old-fashioned woman's coat put away for a time to be turned into a dress later on, if the old one should get scorched while baking cakes and meat and onion pasties for the holidays, or should simply wear out. But the dress will not get scorched or worn out, for the old lady is thrifty, and the coat is destined to lie unpicked for a long time and will then be left in her will to a niece together with a heap of other rubbish.

Chichikov apologized for disturbing her by his unexpected arrival.

'Not at all, not at all,' said the mistress of the house. 'In what terrible weather the good Lord has brought you! Such a dreadful storm! What a turmoil! You ought to have something to eat after your journey, but it's so late we can't get anything ready for you.'

The old lady's words were interrupted by such a strange hissing sound that the visitor was almost alarmed; the noise was not unlike the noise made by a roomful of snakes; but looking up he was reassured, for he realized that the clock on the wall had taken it into its head to strike. The hissing sound was followed immediately by a wheezing and, finally, straining with all its might, the clock struck two with a sound as though someone were hitting a cracked earthenware pot with a stick, after which it went on again ticking quietly to right and left.

Chichikov thanked the old lady and told her that he did not want anything, that she was not to trouble and that all he asked for was a bed, all he wanted to know was into what parts he had strayed and whether it was far from here to the estate of Sobakevich. The old lady replied that she had never heard that name and that there was no such landowner.

'But you know Manilov, don't you?' said Chichikov.

'And who is Manilov?'

'A landowner, ma'am.'

'No, I've never heard of him. There is no such landowner here.'

'Who are the landowners here?'

'Bobrov, Svinyin, Kanapatyev, Kharpakin, Trepakin, Pleshakov!'

'Are they well-to-do or not?'

'No, sir. I'm afraid there aren't any very rich people here. Some own twenty serfs, others thirty, but as for owning a hundred, there are none such here.'

Chichikov perceived that he had got into the real wilds.

'Can you tell me at least if it's far to the town?'

'About fifty miles, I suppose. I'm very sorry, sir, I have nothing for you to eat. Would you like some tea perhaps?'

'No, thank you, ma'am. I don't want anything except a bed.'

'I suppose after such a journey you would be wanting a rest badly. You can lie down here, sir, on this sofa. I say, Fetinya, fetch a featherbed, pillows, and a sheet. What awful weather God has sent us, sir! What thunder! I've had a candle burning before the icon all night. Good heavens, sir, all your back and side is covered in mud like a hog's!'

'Thank God I'm only muddy. I must be grateful I have no ribs broken.'

'Dear me, how awful! But shouldn't your back be rubbed with something?'

'No, thank you, ma'am. Don't trouble, just tell your maid to dry and clean my clothes.'

'Do you hear, Fetinya?' said the mistress, addressing the woman who had come out on to the steps with a candle and who had managed to drag in a featherbed, and after beating it up with her hands on both sides, let loose a whole shower of feathers all over the room.

'Take the gentleman's coat and underwear and dry them first in front of the fire as you used to do for your late master, and afterwards have them well brushed and beaten.'

'Yes, ma'am,' said Fetinya, spreading a sheet over the featherbed and laying down the pillows.

'Well, here's your bed all ready for you, sir,' said the old lady. 'Good night, sir, sleep well. Are you sure you don't want anything else? Perhaps you're used to having your heels tickled for the night. My late husband could not get to sleep without it.'

But the visitor refused to have his heels tickled as well. As soon as the mistress of the house had gone out of the room, he hastened to undress at once, giving Fetinya all his stripped off trappings, upper and lower, and Fetinya wishing him good night, too, carried off all these wet accoutrements. Left alone, he glanced not without satisfaction at his bed, which almost reached the ceiling. Fetinya was obviously a past master at the art of beating up featherbeds. When, putting a chair beside it, he climbed on to the bed, it sank almost to the floor under his weight and the feathers, forced out of the seams, flew all over the room. Putting out the candle, he pulled the cotton quilt over him and, curling up under it, he fell asleep at once. He woke rather late next morning. The sun was shining straight into his eyes and the flies which had been quietly asleep on the walls and the ceiling the night before had now turned their attention to him: one of them sat down on his lip, another on his ear, a third was trying to settle on his eye, while the one who had had the temerity to settle close to his nostrils he had, in his sleep, drawn up into his nose which made him sneeze violently, and that was really why he had woken up. Glancing round the room, he now perceived that the pictures were not all of birds; among them hung a portrait of Field-Marshal Kutuzov and an oil painting of an old gentleman with red cuffs on his uniform as worn in the reign of Paul I. The clock began hissing again and struck ten. A woman's face peered through the door and immediately disappeared, for in his eagerness to have a more peaceful sleep Chichikov had thrown off absolutely everything. The face that peered in seemed to him somehow familiar. He tried to remember who it could be and at last realized that it was the mistress of the house. He put on his shirt; his clothes, dried and brushed, were lying beside him. Having dressed, he went up to the looking-glass and sneezed again so loudly that a turkey-cock who had come up to the window at that moment – the window was very near the ground – suddenly began gobbling something very quickly to him in his strange language, probably saying, 'Bless you, sir,' to which Chichikov replied by calling him a damn fool. Going up to the window, he began to contemplate the scenes before him: the window almost looked on to the hen-run; at least the narrow little yard was filled with all sorts of domestic birds and every kind of domestic animal. There were hundreds of turkeys and hens; among them a cock was strutting about with measured steps, shaking his comb and turning his head on one side as though listening to something; a sow was there too with her family; rooting about in a heap of rubbish, she devoured a chick in passing and, without even noticing it, went on gobbling the rinds of water-melons as before. This small yard or hen-run was surrounded by a wooden fence beyond which stretched an extensive kitchen garden with cabbages, onions, beetroot, and other household vegetables. Here and there about the kitchen garden apple-trees and other fruit-trees were scattered, covered with nets to protect them from the magpies and sparrows; the sparrows were flying in huge oblique clouds from one place to another. With the same end in view, several scarecrows had been set up on long poles with outstretched arms; one of them was wearing a bonnet belonging to the mistress of the house herself. Beyond the kitchen garden were the peasants' cottages which, though scattered in all directions and not arranged in regular streets, showed, from what Chichikov could observe, that the inhabitants were quite well-off, for they were well kept: where the planks on the roofs had decayed, they had been replaced everywhere by new ones; the gates were nowhere lop-sided, and in the peasants' covered barns facing him he noticed an almost new spare cart in one and as many as two in another. 'Why, her village is not at all so small,' he said to himself and at once made up his mind to have a good talk to the lady of the house and to get to know her better. He glanced through the crack in the door out of which her head had appeared and, seeing her sitting at the tea table, went in to her with a cheerful and friendly expression on his face.

'Good morning, sir, have you slept well?' said the old lady, rising from her chair. She was better dressed than on the night before – in a dark dress and no longer in a night-cap, but she still had something wrapped round her neck.

'Thank you, very well indeed,' said Chichikov sitting down in an armchair. 'And you, ma'am?'

'Very badly, my dear sir.'

'Why's that?'

'Insomnia, sir. I've an awful pain in my back and my leg, too, keeps aching above the ankle.'

'That will pass, ma'am, that will pass. You mustn't take any notice of it.'

'God grant it may. I've been rubbing it with lard and bathing it with turpentine. And what will you have with your tea, sir? There's some fruit brandy in that decanter.'

'That's not a bad idea at all, my dear lady. Let's have some fruit brandy by all means.'

The reader, I suppose, has already noticed that in spite of his friendly manner, Chichikov was talking to her much more freely than to Manilov and did not stand on ceremony at all. It must be said that if we in Russia have not caught up with foreigners in some things, we have far outstripped them in the art of behaviour. It is quite impossible to enumerate all the shades and subtleties of our manners. No Frenchman or German will ever grasp or even suspect all their peculiarities and distinctions; he will speak in almost the same tone of voice and almost the same language to a millionaire or a small tobacconist, though, of course, at heart he will do his utmost to grovel before the former. But with us it is quite different. We have clever fellows who talk in quite a different way to a landowner with two hundred serfs and to one with three hundred serfs; and to one with three hundred they will talk differently again from the way they will talk to one with five hundred, and in a different way again from one with eight hundred – in short, even if the number were to grow to a million they would still find different shades for it. Let us, for instance, imagine some government office – not here but in some Ruritanian kingdom – and let us also suppose that this office has a chief. Please, have a look at him as he sits among his subordinates – why, you would be so awe-stricken that you would not be able to utter a word! Pride and nobility and what else does not his face express? All you have to do is to pick up a brush and paint him – a Prometheus, a veritable Prometheus! Looks like an eagle, walks with measured, smooth steps. But that very eagle, when he has left his office and is approaching the office of his own chief, scurries along like a partridge with papers under his arm, as fast as his legs will carry him. In society and at an evening party, if everyone is of a lower rank, our Prometheus remains a Prometheus, but if they are ever so little above him, our Prometheus undergoes a metamorphosis such as even Ovid never thought of: a fly, less than a fly, he has reduced himself to a grain of sand! 'But,' you say to yourself, looking at him, 'this can't be Ivan Petrovich! Ivan Petrovich is much taller, while this man is short and thin; Ivan Petrovich talks in a loud deep voice and never laughs, while this one talks in goodness only knows what sort of a voice: pipes like a bird and keeps laughing all the time.' You go nearer, you look – it is Ivan Petrovich after all! 'Aha,' you think to yourself. ... However, let us return to the characters of our story. Chichikov, as we have seen, had decided not to stand on ceremony at all, and so, taking the cup of tea in his hand and pouring some of the brandy into it, he began to speak in this manner:

'You have a nice little village, my dear lady. How many souls are there in it?'

'Souls, sir? Why, I should think about eighty all told,' said the old lady. 'But the trouble is the times are bad. Last year too, you see, there was such a terribly bad harvest!'

'The peasants, however, look sturdy enough and their cottages are well-built. But, I'm sorry, I forgot to ask your name, ma'am. I was in such a state – arriving in the middle of the night ...'

'Korobochka, a collegiate secretary's widow, sir.'

'Thank you very much, ma'am. And your Christian name and patronymic?'

'Nastasya Petrovna.'

'Nastasya Petrovna? A lovely name – Nastasya Petrovna. An aunt of mine, my mother's sister, is called Nastasya Petrovna.'

'And what's your name, sir?' asked the lady landowner. 'You are not a tax assessor, are you?'

'Why, no, ma'am,' answered Chichikov with a smile. 'I'm certainly not a tax assessor. I'm just travelling on a little business of my own.'

'Oh, so you're a dealer! What a pity I sold all my honey to the merchants so cheaply. I expect you would have bought it all from me, sir.'

'Not your honey, I'm sorry to say.'

'What else then? Hemp? I'm afraid I haven't got much hemp left, either. Not more than twenty-five pounds or so.'

'No, ma'am, I'm after a different kind of merchandise. Tell me, have any of your peasants died?'

'Dear me, sir, eighteen of them!' said the old lady, sighing. 'And all such excellent fellows, too. Hard workers all of them. It's true that some have been born since, but they aren't much use, are they? They're all such small fry. But the tax assessor came – "Must pay tax on every soul," he says. The peasants are dead, but you have to pay for them just as if they were alive. Last week my blacksmith was burnt, such a clever blacksmith! Could do a locksmith's work, too.'

'Did you have a fire, ma'am?'

'The good Lord preserved us from such a calamity, sir. A fire would have been worse. No, no, sir, he caught fire himself. Something inside him caught fire. Must have had too much to drink. Only a blue flame came out of him and he smouldered, smouldered, and turned as black as coal. And he was such a clever blacksmith, too! And now I can't drive out at all. There's no one to shoe the horses!'

'It's all God's will, ma'am,' said Chichikov with a sigh. 'It's no use murmuring against God's wisdom. … Why not let me have them, ma'am?'

'Have whom, sir?'

'Why, all these dead peasants.'

'But how can I let you have them?'

'Oh, quite simply, or if you like you can sell them to me. I'll give you money for them.'

'But how is it to be done? I'm sorry, but I just can't make any sense of it. You don't want to dig them out of the ground, do you?'

Chichikov realized that the old lady had gone a bit too far and that it would be absolutely necessary to explain to her what it was all about. In a few words he made it clear to her that the transfer or the purchase would take place only on paper and that the dead peasants would be registered as though they were living.

'But what do you want them for?' asked the old lady, staring goggle-eyed at him.

'That's my affair.'

'But they are dead!'

'Why, who said they were living? It's because they're dead that they're such a loss to you: you have to pay the tax on them, but now I will relieve you of all worry and expense. Do you understand? And I'll not only do that, I'll give you fifteen roubles besides. Well, is it clear now?'

'I really don't know,' said the old lady, hesitatingly. 'You see, I've never sold dead peasants before.'

'I should think not! It would be a miracle if you could have sold them to anyone, or do you think that there really is any profit to be made out of them?'

'No, of course I don't think that. What profit could there be in them? None whatever. The only thing that troubles me is that they are dead.'

'The woman's a blockhead, it seems!' Chichikov thought to himself.

'Now, look here, ma'am, just think it over carefully: you're being ruined paying taxes for them as though they were living ...'

'Good gracious, sir, don't mention it!' she put in quickly. 'Only three weeks ago I paid more than a hundred and fifty roubles for them, besides having to grease the assessor's palm.'

'Well, there you are, ma'am. And now, take into consideration the fact that you won't have to bribe the assessor, because now I shall be paying for them – I and not you. I shall be taking all the obligations on myself. I will even pay for the title deed. Do you understand that?'

The old lady thought it over. She saw that the transaction certainly seemed profitable, but it was something a little too novel and unusual. That made her fear that the purchaser might cheat her in some way. After all, he had arrived goodness only knows from where and in the middle of the night, too.

'Well, ma'am, is it a deal?'

'Really, sir, I've never had occasion before to sell dead peasants. Living ones I did dispose of once. Three years ago I let our parish priest have two girls for a hundred roubles each. And very grateful he was for them too. They've turned out to be fine workers. They can even weave table napkins.'

'Well, it's not a question of the living. I've nothing to do with them. I'm asking for the dead.'

'Really sir, I'm very much afraid that I may be incurring some loss at first. Maybe you are deceiving me, sir – and – and I mean, maybe they're worth more.'

'Now, look here, ma'am ... Dear me, you don't seem to have any sense at all! What do you think they can be worth? Just consider: they're nothing but dust. Do you understand that? Nothing but dust. Take any useless, worthless thing you can think of, just an ordinary rag for instance, and even a rag is worth something: at least you can sell it to a paper mill. But these are of no use whatever. Now tell me yourself, what use are they?'

'Now that's quite true, sir. They're of no use whatever. But, you see, the only thi..g that makes me hesitate is that they're dead.'

'Good Lord, what a fool of a woman!' Chichikov said to himself, beginning to lose patience. 'Just try to get to terms with her! Made me sweat, the old woman did, damn her!' And, indeed, taking a handkerchief out of his pocket, he began mopping his perspiring brow. However, Chichikov need not have been angry: many a highly respected man, even a statesman, turns out to be a perfect Korobochka in practice. Once an idea has got into his head, you can't knock it out of it; however many arguments, as clear as daylight, you may put before him, they all rebound from him like a rubber ball from a wall. Having mopped his brow, Chichikov decided to try whether he could not bring her to see reason in some other way.

'Either you don't want to understand what I am talking about, ma'am,' he said, 'or you simply speak like this on purpose, just for the sake of saying something. I'm giving you money: fifteen roubles in notes. Do you understand? That's money, isn't it? You won't find it in the street, will you? Well, tell me, what did you sell your honey for?'

'Twelve roubles for forty pounds.'

'I'm afraid, ma'am, you've allowed yourself to be – er – carried away a little bit. You didn't sell it for twelve roubles.'

'Yes, I did.'

'Well, there you are! That was for honey. You had been gathering it perhaps for a whole year. It gave you a lot of trouble, worry, anxiety. You had to rush about, catch the bees, feed them in the cellar all winter. But dead souls are not something of this world at all. They require no effort whatever on your part. It was God's will that they should leave this world, bringing loss to your household. There you received twelve roubles for your work and for your trouble, but here you'll get not twelve but fifteen roubles for nothing at all, gratis, and not in silver, but all in blue notes.'

After such powerful arguments Chichikov had no doubt that the old lady would give in at last.

'I don't know,' replied the old lady. 'I'm such an inexperienced widow, you see. I think I'd better wait a little. Perhaps merchants will be coming along and I shall be able to compare prices.'

'For shame, for shame, ma'am. Why, it's simply disgraceful. Now what are you talking about? Just think. Who is going to buy them? Come, tell me what use could any of them make of them?'

'Well, perhaps they could be used for something on the farm in an emergency,' replied the old lady, and without finishing what she had to say, stared open-mouthed at him almost in terror, wondering what he would say to that.

'Dead men on a farm! What will you be saying next? Why, do you mean to scare the sparrows at night in your kitchen garden?'

'Lord have mercy upon me, what dreadful things you say!' said the old woman crossing herself.

'Where else would you like to put them? Anyway, you realize, of course, that the bones and the graves – all that will be left to you. The transfer is only on paper. Well, what about it? What do you say? Give me some answer at least.'

The old lady pondered again.

'What are you thinking about, ma'am?'

'Well, sir, I just don't know what to do. I can't make up my mind about it. I'd better sell you some of my hemp.'

'Hemp? What do I want your hemp for? Good Lord, ma'am, I'm asking you about something quite different, and you shove your hemp under my nose! There's nothing wrong with hemp. Next time I come I'll buy your hemp too. So what is it to be, ma'am?'

'Oh, dear, such strange merchandise, such an unheard of thing to sell.'

At this point Chichikov lost his patience completely and in his anger banged his chair on the floor and told her to go to the devil.

The old lady was extremely frightened of the devil.

'Oh, don't mention him!' she cried, turning pale all over. 'Leave him be. Only the night before last I kept dreaming all night of the Evil One. You see, I tried to tell my fortune at cards after prayers, and it seems God sent him to me as a punishment. Such a nasty-looking creature, too, and his horns were longer than a bull's.'

'I'm surprised you don't dream of them by the dozen. I was going to help you out of a feeling of simple Christian charity, seeing a poor widow working her fingers to the bone, trying to make ends meet. ... But to hell with you and your village – the plague take you all!'

'Gracious me, what awful language!' said the old lady, looking horrified at him.

'Well, I'm damned! Really, you're – you're – not to put too fine a point on it – like a dog in a manger. It won't eat hay itself and it won't let anyone else eat it. I was, as a matter of fact, thinking of buying all sorts of farm produce from you because, you see, I take government contracts, too.'

That was a lie, and though he had uttered it quite casually and on the spur of the moment, it turned out to be unexpectedly successful. The mention of government contracts made a strong impression on Mrs Korobochka, at least she said in an almost imploring voice:

'But why are you so angry? Had I known before that you were so short-tempered, I wouldn't have contradicted you at all.'

'Angry, am I? What is there to be angry about? The whole thing isn't worth a farthing, so why should I lose my temper over it?'

'Oh, very well, I'm ready to let you have them for fifteen roubles. Only, my dear sir, about those government contracts, if you should be wanting rye or buckwheat flour or any cereals or slaughtered animals, mind you don't forget me.'

'No, of course I won't forget you, ma'am,' he said, wiping away the perspiration that was streaming down his face. He asked her whether she had any lawyer or friend in the town whom she could authorize to draw up the deed of purchase and see to all the formalities.

'Why, of course, the son of the arch-priest, Father Kyril, who is a clerk in the law courts,' said Korobochka.

Chichikov asked her to write a letter authorizing the priest's son to act for her and, to save unnecessary trouble, even volunteered to compose the letter himself.

'It would be a good thing,' Mrs Korobochka thought to herself meanwhile, 'if he would take my flour and cattle for the government. I must be nice to him. There's some dough left over from yesterday evening and I'd better go and tell Fetinya to make some pancakes. And it wouldn't be a bad idea to make an egg pasty too. Cook does it beautifully and it doesn't take much time, either.'

The mistress of the house went out to carry out her plan about the egg pasty and very likely to add to it some other products of home baking and cooking; while Chichikov went into the drawing-room in which he had spent the night in order to get the necessary papers from the box. In the drawing-room everything had been tidied up, the magnificent featherbeds had been taken out, and the table had been laid in front of the sofa. Putting his box on the table, he sat down for a little rest, for he felt that he was wet with perspiration, as though he had fallen into a river; everything he had on, from his shirt to his socks, was soaking wet. 'Damn the old woman,' he said after a little rest as he opened his box, 'she's nearly done for me.'

The author is quite sure that there are readers so inquisitive that they would like to learn all about the plan and internal arrangement of the box. Well, why not satisfy them? Here, then, was its internal arrangement: in the very middle was a little compartment for soap, and next to it six or seven narrow partitions for razors; then came square compartments for a sand-box and an ink-pot with a little hollowed out boat for pens, sealing wax, and other things that were a little on the long side; then all sorts of little compartments with lids and without lids for things that were on the short side, full of visiting cards, funeral cards, theatre tickets, and other things kept as souvenirs. The whole of the upper drawer of the box with all its compartments could be lifted out and under it was revealed a space filled with sheets of paper; then followed a little secret drawer for money, which could be pulled out imperceptibly from the side of the box. It was always pulled out and moved back so quickly by Chichikov that it was impossible to say how much money there was in it. Chichikov got down to work at once and, having sharpened the quill, began to write. At that moment the old lady came in.

'You've a nice box there, my dear sir,' she said, sitting down beside him. 'I expect you must have bought it in Moscow.'

'Yes, in Moscow,' said Chichikov, continuing to write.

'I knew it at once: the workmanship there is excellent. The year before last my sister brought me little warm boots for the children from there: such strong material, it's still as good as new. Goodness, what a lot of stamped paper you have there!' she went on, glancing into his box. And, indeed, there was a great deal of stamped paper there. 'Couldn't you make me a present of a sheet or two? I'm always short of it, and if I should want to send in an application to the court I have nothing to write it on!'

Chichikov explained to her that it wasn't that sort of paper, that it was meant for drawing up deeds of purchase and not applications. However, to keep her quiet, he gave her a sheet worth a rouble. Having written the letter, he gave it to her to sign and asked her for a short list of her dead peasants. It turned out that the lady landowner kept neither notes nor lists, but knew them almost all by heart. He made her dictate their names to him. Some of the peasants rather surprised him by their names and even more by their nicknames, so that hearing them for the first time he paused for a moment before writing them down. He was particularly struck by one Peter Savelyev, Disrespectful-of-Troughs, and he could not help saying, 'What a long one!' Another had the nickname 'Cow's-Brick' attached to his name, another simply appeared as: 'Ivan-the-Wheel'. As he was finishing writing, he drew in the air through his nose and caught an entrancing fragrance of something fried in butter.

'Won't you have a bite of something, sir?' asked the mistress of the house.

Chichikov looked round and saw that the table was already spread with mushrooms, pies, fried eggs, curd tarts, potato cakes, pancakes, and pasties with all sorts of different fillings, some with onions, some with poppy seeds, some with curds, some with smelts and goodness only knows what else.

'Won't you have some egg pasty?' said the mistress of the house.

Chichikov moved up to the pasty and, after eating more than half of it on the spot, said how much he liked it. And, indeed, it was tasty enough by itself and after all the fuss and bother with the old woman seemed tastier still.

'Some pancakes?' said the old lady.

By way of a reply Chichikov rolled three pancakes together and after dipping them in melted butter put them into his mouth, wiping his lips and hands with a napkin. Having repeated this operation three times, he asked the mistress of the house to order his horses to be harnessed. Mrs Korobochka at once dispatched Fetinya, telling her at the same time to bring some more hot pancakes.

'Your pancakes are delicious, ma'am,' said Chichikov, applying himself to the hot ones as soon as they were brought in.

'Yes, they fry them very nicely in my house,' said the old lady. 'But the trouble is, you see, that the harvest was so bad and the flour's not very good. ... But why are you in such a hurry, sir?' she said, seeing that Chichikov had picked up his cap. 'Why, the horses aren't harnessed yet.'

'They will be harnessed, ma'am, they will be harnessed. My servants don't lose much time in harnessing horses.'

'So, please, don't forget about the contracts, sir.'

'I won't, I won't,' said Chichikov going out into the passage.

'And won't you buy any lard, sir?' said the old lady, following him into the passage.

'Buy it? Of course I'll buy it, only later.'

'I shall have plenty of lard by Christmas.'

'We'll buy it, we'll buy everything, we'll buy your lard, too.'

'You won't be wanting any feathers will you? I shall have plenty of feathers too by St Phillip's Fast.'

'Good, good,' said Chichikov.

'You see, sir, your carriage isn't ready yet,' the old lady said when they had gone out on to the steps.

'It will be, it will be ready presently. Only tell me, please, how to get to the highroad.'

'How am I to do that?' said the old lady. 'It's a bit difficult to explain. There are so many turnings, you see. Perhaps I'd better let you have a girl to show you the way. I expect you must have room for her on the box.'

'Of course.'

'Well, in that case I will let you have a girl. She knows the way. Only mind, don't you carry her off. Some merchants carried off one of mine already.'

Chichikov assured her that he would not carry off the girl and, her mind set at rest, Mrs Korobochka began scrutinizing everything in her yard; she stared at the housekeeper who was carrying out a round wooden vessel with a narrow neck full of honey from the storehouse, at a peasant who appeared at the gate, and little by little was entirely absorbed in the life of her farm. But why spend so much time over Mrs Korobochka? Whether it's Korobochka or Manilov or their well organized or disorganized households – away with them! For everything in the world is arranged in a most wonderful way: the gay will instantly turn to sadness if you dwell too long on it, and then goodness only knows what ideas may not come into your head. One might even begin to wonder whether Mrs Korobochka's station in the world is so very low on the endless ladder of human perfectibility. Is the gulf really so great that separates her from her sister, inaccessibly protected from her by the walls of her aristocratic house, with its sweet-scented wrought-iron staircases, its shining brass, mahogany, and carpets, who yawns over her unfinished book as she sits waiting for the right moment when she will be able to pay her visits to fashionable, witty society; there she would do her best to show off her intelligence and express views she has learned by heart, views which, according to fashion's decree, interest the town for a whole week, views which have little to do with what is happening in her house and on her estates, ruined and entangled in debts as a result of her ignorance of farming, views about the political revolution that is about to break out in France, or about the latest tendencies of modern Catholicism. But away, away! Why talk about it? Why is it that even in the midst of unthinking, gay, careless moments quite a different, wonderful mood suddenly descends upon one? The smile has had scarcely time to fade from a man's face, when he is suddenly transformed into another man among the same people, and his face is lit up by quite a different light. ...

'Ah, here's the carriage!' cried Chichikov, seeing his carriage draw up at last. 'Why have you been dawdling so long there, you blockhead? I can see you haven't quite sobered up yet after your drunken bout yesterday.'

Selifan made no answer to this.

'Good-bye, ma'am. But where's your girl?'

'Hey, Pelageya!' said the old lady to a girl of about eleven, standing near the steps in a frock of home-dyed linen, with bare feet so thickly covered with fresh mud that they might have been taken for boots from a distance. 'Show the gentleman the way.'

Selifan helped the girl up on the box; she lingered for a moment on the gentleman's carriage step, covering it with mud, and only then did she climb up and take her place beside Selifan on the box. Chichikov put his foot on the step after her and, tilting the carriage to the right as he did so, for he was a bit heavy, at last settled himself and said, 'Oh, everything's all right now! Good-bye, my dear lady!'

The horses set off.

Selifan was sullen all the way and at the same time most attentive to his duties, which only happened after he had done something wrong or had been drunk. The horses had been wonderfully groomed. The collar on one of them, which had hitherto been put on in a torn condition, so that the oakum always peeped out under the leather, had been skilfully sewn up. He was silent all the way, merely whipping up the horses occasionally, but without addressing any edifying speeches to them, though no doubt the dappled-grey would have liked to hear something instructive, for at those moments the reins lay rather slackly in the hands of the talkative driver and the whip passed over their backs only as a matter of form. But on this occasion only monotonous

68

and unpleasant exclamations came from his gloomy lips, such as, 'Come on, come on, you old crow, mind where you're going!' and nothing else. Even the bay and the Assessor were dissatisfied at not once hearing him address them as, 'My hearties' or 'Fine lads!' The dappled-grey felt some most unpleasant blows on his broad, plump sides. 'Look at the way he's carrying on!' he thought to himself, twitching his ears a little. 'He knows all right where to hit! He won't lash you simply across your back, but picks out the most tender spot: flicks you on the ear or lashes you under the belly.'

'To the right, is it?' was the curt question Selifan addressed to the girl sitting beside him, pointing with his whip to the road which the rain had turned into black mud between the fresh bright-green fields.

'No, no, I'll tell you when,' replied the little girl.

'Where now?' said Selifan when they got nearer.

'That way,' answered the girl, pointing with her hand.

'Well, you are a one,' said Selifan. 'Why, that is to the right. She doesn't know which is right and which is left!'

Though it was a very fine day, the ground had become so muddy that the carriage wheels, as they threw it up, were soon covered with it as with felt, which made the carriage considerably heavier. Besides, the soil was clayey and exceptionally sticky. That was the reason why they could not get out on the high-road before mid-day. Without the little girl they would have found even that difficult, for the roads crawled in all directions like crayfish shaken out of a sack, and Selifan would have been forced to drive all over the place through no fault of his own. Soon the girl pointed to a grimy building in the distance and said: 'There's the highway!'

'And what's that building?' asked Selifan.

'A pub,' said the little girl.

'Oh, well,' said Selifan, 'now we'll find our way by ourselves. You'd better run home now.'

He stopped and helped her to get down, muttering through his teeth: 'Oh, you black-footed creature!'

Chichikov gave her a brass farthing, and she set off back home, quite satisfied with having had a ride on the box.

Chapter 4

As they drew up to the inn, Chichikov told Selifan to stop for two reasons, first to give the horses a rest, and secondly to have something to eat and fortify himself. The author must confess that he is very envious of the appetite and the digestion of this sort of people. He has absolutely no use for the great gentlemen who live in Petersburg and Moscow and spend their time in deliberating what to eat tomorrow and what sort of dinner they are going to have the day after, and who toss a pill into their mouths before sitting down to dinner and swallow oysters, sea spiders, and other marvels, and then go for a cure to Carlsbad or the Caucasus. No, those gentlemen have never roused his envy. But gentlemen of the middling sort who ask for ham at one post-station and sucking pig at another and a portion of sturgeon or some smoked sausage and onion at a third, and then sit down, as if nothing had happened, to table at any time you please, and sterlet soup with pieces of burbot and soft roe hisses and gurgles between their teeth and is followed by fish and rice pie or a large fish and cabbage pie with a fat catfish tail so that it makes other people's mouths water – these are the gentlemen who have been truly blessed by heaven and are to be greatly envied! More than one of these great gentlemen would at any minute gladly sacrifice half his peasants and half his estates, mortgaged and unmortgaged, with all the improvements in foreign and Russian style, provided he could have a digestion such as that of one of the gentlemen of the middling station in life; but the trouble is that no amount of money, nor even estates with or without improvements, can procure a digestion like that of a gentleman of the middling station in life.

The grimy wooden inn received Chichikov beneath its narrow hospitable porch, standing on carved wooden posts like antique church candlesticks. The inn was something like a Russian peasant's cottage, but on a rather larger scale. It had carved figured cornices of new wood round the windows and under the roof, standing out sharply and vividly against the dark walls; jugs of flowers were painted on the shutters.

70

Going up the narrow wooden staircase into the wide entrance-hall, he met a fat old woman in a bright printed cotton gown, who had opened a creaking door and said: 'This way, please.' In the room he found the old familiar friends that are always to be found in small wooden inns, of which there are not a few built along the highways, namely a *samovar* that looked as if it were covered with hoar-frost, smoothly planed deal walls, a three-cornered cupboard with cups and teapots in the corner, gilt china eggs hanging on red and blue ribbons in front of the icons, a cat who had recently had kittens, a looking-glass that reflected four eyes instead of two and instead of a face a sort of flat cake, and, finally, bunches of fragrant herbs and pinks stuck before the icons and so dried up that anyone who tried to sniff them would only sneeze.

'Have you any sucking pig?' was the question Chichikov addressed to the old woman who was standing by the door.

'Yes, sir.'

'With horse-radish and sour cream?'

'Yes, sir, with horse-radish and sour cream.'

'Let's have it.'

The old woman went off to rummage about and brought a plate and a table napkin so stiff with starch that it stood up like dried bark, then a knife with a bone handle that had gone yellow and a blade as thin as a penknife, a two-pronged fork, and a salt-cellar which it was impossible to stand up straight on the table.

Our hero, as was his habit, immediately engaged her in conversation. He asked her whether she kept the inn herself or whether there was a proprietor, what income the inn brought in, and whether their sons lived at home with them, and whether the eldest son was a married man or a bachelor, and what kind of wife he had married, and whether she had a large dowry or not, and whether the bride's father had been satisfied, and whether their son had been angry at receiving so few wedding presents – in short, he omitted nothing. It goes without saying, that he was anxious to find out what landowners there were in the district and he did find out that there were landowners of all kinds: Blokhin, Pochitayev, Mylnoy, Colonel Cheprakov, Soba-kevich. 'Ah, you know Sobakevich, do you?' he asked, and heard at once that the old woman knew not only Sobakevich but also Mani-lov, and that she thought Manilov was a much more refined gentle-man than Sobakevich: he would order a chicken to be boiled at once, he would also ask for veal; if they had sheep's liver he would ask for sheep's liver too, and he would just taste a little of everything, while Sobakevich would only order one thing and would eat it all up and even demand a second helping for the same price.

While he was talking like that and eating the sucking pig, of which only the last piece was left, he heard the rattle of wheels of a carriage that was driving up to the inn. Looking out of the window he saw a light carriage standing in front of the inn and drawn by three good horses. Two men were getting out of the carriage: one of them was tall and fair and the other a little shorter and dark. The fair-haired man was wearing a dark blue Hungarian jacket and the dark-haired man simply a striped short Asiatic coat. Another miserable carriage was trailing along in the distance, empty and drawn by four shaggy horses with torn collars and rope harness. The fair-haired man at once went upstairs, while his swarthy companion stayed behind, fumbling for something in the carriage, talking to the servant and at the same time waving to the carriage that was following them. His voice struck Chichikov as a little familiar. While he was looking more closely at him, the fair-haired man had managed to find the door and open it. He was a very tall man with a lean, or what is called a worn face, and with a little ginger moustache. From his tanned face it might have been concluded that he knew the meaning of the smoke, if not of gunpowder, then at least of tobacco. He bowed politely to Chichikov to which the latter responded with a similar bow. They would probably have engaged in a conversation within a few minutes and have become good friends, because the ice had already been broken, and both almost at one and the same moment expressed their pleasure that the dust on the road had been completely laid by the rain of the day before and that now it was cool and pleasant for driving, when his swarthy companion came in, pulling off his cap and flinging it on the table, and dashingly ruffling his thick black hair with his fingers. He was a young fellow of medium height, of excellent build, with full rosy cheeks, snow-white teeth, and pitch-black whiskers; he was as fresh as a daisy. In fact, his face seemed to be bursting with health.

'Hullo, hullo, hullo!' he exclaimed suddenly, flinging wide his arms at the sight of Chichikov. 'Fancy meeting you here!'

Chichikov recognized Nozdryov, the man he had dined with at the public prosecutor's and who had become so familiar with him in a few minutes, though he, for his part, had given him no cause for it.

'Where have you been to?' said Nozdryov and, without waiting for an answer, went on: 'I've come from the fair, my dear fellow. Congratulate me, I've been cleaned out! I assure you, I've never been so completely cleaned out in all my life. You see, I've driven here with hired horses. Here, look out of the window!' At this point he bent Chichikov's head down so that he nearly knocked it against the window frame. 'See what trash! Barely managed to drag me here, the damned hacks! I had to get into his carriage.' Saying this, Nozdryov pointed to his companion. 'But you haven't been introduced, have you? My brother-in-law, Mizhuyev. We have been talking about you all the morning. "I bet you," I said to him, "we're going to meet Chichikov." Well, my dear fellow, if only you knew how thoroughly I've been cleaned out! Believe it or not, I've not only blewed my four fast trotters, I've lost every damn thing. You see, I have neither watch nor chain on me. ...'

Chichikov glanced at him and saw that he was indeed wearing neither watch nor chain. He even thought that one of his side-whiskers was not as large and not as thick as the other.

'And you know,' Nozdryov went on, 'if I'd only had twenty roubles in my pocket, twenty roubles, no more, I'd have won it all back. I mean, I'd not only have won it all back but, as I'm an honest man, I'd have put thirty thousand in my wallet then and there.'

'You said the same thing when I gave you fifty roubles,' said the fair man, 'but you lost them on the spot.'

'I shouldn't have lost them. I shouldn't, I tell you. Had I not done such a damn foolish thing I shouldn't have lost them. If I hadn't turned down that card and doubled my stake on that damned seven after the stakes had already been doubled, I might have broken the bank.'

'You didn't break it, though,' said the fair man.

'I didn't break it because I doubled it at the wrong moment. Do you really think that major of yours is a good player?'

'Whether he's good or bad, he beat you.'

'What does that matter!' said Nozdryov. 'I'd have beaten him too if I had been as lucky as he. Let him try to double the stakes, too, and then I'll see how good a player he is. But what a wonderful time we had during the first days, my dear Chichikov. True, the fair was really most excellent. The merchants themselves said they had never seen such crowds of people. Everything I'd brought from the village was sold at a most profitable price. Ah, my dear chap, what a terrific time we had! Even now when I think of it – oh, damn it all! I mean, I'm sorry you weren't there. There was a regiment of dragoons stationed within two miles of the town – can you imagine such luck? Believe it or not, the officers, the whole damn lot of them, forty of them, were all in the town. ... As soon as we began to drink, my dear chap ... Major Potseluyev – such a fine fellow! Such glorious moustachios, my dear chap! Calls claret simply red biddy. "Fetch me some red biddy, waiter," he says. Lieutenant Kuvshinnikov ... Ah, my dear chap, what a charming man! A real gay dog. Yes, sir. He and I were together all the time. And the wine Ponomaryov let us have! I must tell you he's a damn rogue and you shouldn't buy anything in his shop. He puts every kind of filth in the wine: sandalwood, burnt cork, and even elderberries, the dirty swine! To improve the colour, you see. But if he gets a bottle out of his back room, the room he calls his "special one", well, then, my dear chap, you'll find yourself in the empyrean. We had champagne – why, compared with it the champagne we had at the governor's was nothing but *kvass*! Just imagine, not Cliquot, but Cliquot-Matradura, which means double Cliquot. And he also got us a nice little bottle of French wine called Bon-bon. Bouquet? The fragrance of roses and anything you like. What a damned good time we had! Some prince arrived after us and sent to the shop for champagne, but there wasn't a bottle left in the whole town. The dragoon officers had drunk it all. Believe it or not, I alone drank seventeen bottles of champagne at dinner.'

'Not seventeen bottles, surely,' observed the fair man. 'You'd never manage to drink that.'

'As an honest man, I tell you I did,' replied Nozdryov.

'You can tell yourself what you like, but I tell you that you couldn't drink even ten.'

'What would you like to bet me that I could?'

'Why should I bet?'

'Well, bet me the gun that you bought in the town.'

'I don't want to.'

'Well, go on, wager it! Have a go.'

'I don't want to have a go.'

'Oh, yes, you'd have been left without a gun as you've been left without a cap. Oh, my dear Chichikov, if only you knew how sorry I was you weren't there! I know you would never have parted from

74

Lieutenant Potseluyev. How well you two would have got on together! He's not like the public prosecutor and all the other old misers in our town who tremble over every penny. That one, my dear fellow, will be only too glad to play a game of poker or faro with you. Anything you like, in fact. Oh, Chichikov, why didn't you come along? You're a pig, really you are, not to have come, you cattle-breeder, you! Kiss me, my dear chap, I do love you dearly! Look, Mizhuyev, fate, the scurvy damsel, has brought us two together! I mean, what is he to me or I to him? He has come from goodness only knows where, and I am living here. ... Oh, my dear fellow, you should have seen the carriages! Hundreds and hundreds of them! I tried my luck at roulette, won two pots of pomatum, a porcelain cup, and a guitar, then I staked once more and, damn it, lost everything and six roubles into the bargain. And what a philanderer that Kuv-shinnikov is – if you only knew! He and I went to nearly all the balls. There was a girl there all dressed up, you know, frills and furbelows and the devil knows what. All I could think to myself was, "Damn it all!" But Kuvshinnikov, that's the sort of beastly fellow he is, sat down beside her and started showering such compliments in French. ... I know you won't believe me, but he wouldn't let ordinary peasant women alone. That's what he calls "enjoying a piece of cheesecake". And you should have seen the fish and dried sturgeon there was for sale! I brought one with me. It's a good thing I thought of buying it when I still had some money. Where are you off to now?'

'Oh, I'm just going to see a certain person,' said Chichikov.

'Oh, to hell with that certain person! Forget him. Come home with me.'

'I'm sorry, I can't. I have business.'

'Business, indeed! The things he thinks of! Oh, you storyteller!'

'I really have business and important business, too.'

'I bet you're lying. Well, tell me who it is you're going to see?'

'Well, if you must know, Sobakevich.'

At this Nozdryov burst out laughing so loudly as only a man enjoying the best of health can laugh, a man who shows a row of snow-white teeth, whose cheeks tremble and quiver, so that someone living behind two doors, three rooms away, leaps up from his sleep and with his eyes starting out of his head, cries: 'What's the matter with him?'

'What's so funny about it?' asked Chichikov, somewhat displeased by such laughter.

But Nozdryov went on roaring with laughter and saying:

'Oh, don't, don't, or I'll split with laughing!'

'There's nothing funny about it. I promised to call on him,' said Chichikov.

'But if you go to see him you'll be sorry for it all your life. Why, he's an old skinflint! Why, I know the sort of man you are. You'll be cruelly disappointed if you think you'll find a good bottle of Bon-bon and a game of cards there. Listen, my dear chap, to hell with Sobakevich, come home with me! I'll treat you to such a sturgeon! Ponomaryov, the rotter, kept bowing and scraping and saying, "I got it specially for you. You can go and look all through the fair," he said, "and you won't find another one like it." The dirty rogue. I told him so to his face, "You, sir," I said, "and our government contractor are the greatest rogues in the world!" He laughed, the filthy brute, stroking his beard. Kuvshinnikov and I had lunch every day in his shop. Good Lord, my dear chap, I quite forgot to tell you! I know you'll never let me alone now, but I won't let you have it for ten thousand, I warn you. Hey, Porfiry!' he shouted, going up to the window, to his servant who was holding a knife in one hand and a crust of bread with a slice of sturgeon in the other, a slice he had had the good luck to cut off for himself while getting something out of the carriage. 'Hey, Porfiry,' Nozdryov shouted, 'bring the pup here! What a wonderful puppy,' he went on, turning to Chichikov. 'Must have been stolen, for his owner would not have parted with it for anything in the world: I offered him my chestnut mare which, you remember, I got from Khvostyrev in exchange. ...'

Chichikov, however, had never in his life seen Khvostyrev or his chestnut mare.

'Won't you have something to eat, sir?' said the old woman going up to him at that moment.

'Nothing. Oh, my dear chap, what a glorious time we had! Give me a glass of vodka, though. What sort have you got?'

'Aniseed,' replied the old woman.

'Oh, all right, let's have aniseed,' said Nozdryov.

'I think I'll have a glass too,' said the fair man.

'There was an actress at the theatre and, damn her, she sang like a canary! Kuvshinnikov, who was sitting beside me, said to me: "That's the girl, old man," he said, "I'd like to enjoy a piece of cheesecake with!" There must have been fifty booths at the fair, I should think. Fenardi, the clown, turned somersaults for four hours.' At this point he took the glass out of the hands of the old woman, who made him a low bow. 'Ah, bring him here,' he shouted, seeing Porfiry who came in with the puppy.

Porfiry was dressed like his master in a sort of Asiatic short coat, wadded and rather greasy.

'Bring him here! Put him down on the floor!'

Porfiry set the puppy down on the floor. Stretching itself out on its four paws, it began sniffing at the floor.

'Now this is a puppy,' said Nozdryov, picking it up by its back and holding it up in the air. The puppy let out a rather plaintive squeal.

'You haven't done what I told you!' said Nozdryov turning to Porfiry and examining the puppy's belly very carefully. 'You never thought of combing him, did you?'

'I did comb him, sir.'

'Why then has he got fleas?'

'I'm sure I don't know, sir. I expect, sir, they must have crawled on him from the carriage.'

'You're lying, you dirty rascal! You never thought of combing him. I shouldn't be surprised, you fool, if you haven't passed some of yours on to him. Now, just look at that, Chichikov, look at his ears, feel them, feel them!'

'Why feel them? I can see as it is. A good breed!' replied Chichikov.

'No, no, take hold of him properly. Feel his ears!'

To please him Chichikov felt the puppy's ears, adding: 'Yes, he'll make a good dog.'

'And his nose, can you feel how cold it is? Go on, feel it with your hand.'

Not wishing to offend him, Chichikov felt the puppy's nose too, saying: 'He's got a good scent.'

'A real bulldog,' Nozdryov went on. 'I must confess I have been anxious to get hold of a bulldog for a long time. Here, Porfiry, take him away.' Holding the puppy under his belly, Porfiry carried him back to the carriage.

'Look here, Chichikov, you simply must come back with me now. It's only about four miles from here. We'll be there in no time, and then, if you like, you can go and call on Sobakevich.'

'Well,' thought Chichikov to himself, 'why not? I may as well go to Nozdryov's. He is as good as anyone else, I suppose. A man like the rest of them. And he's just lost money too. One can see he'd do anything, so one might be able to get something for nothing from him.'

'All right,' he said, 'let's go. But, remember, don't keep me. My time is money.'

'Well, my dear chap, that's the stuff! That's excellent! Wait, wait, let me give you a kiss for that.' Here Nozdryov and Chichikov exchanged kisses. 'Excellent! Now we'll drive off, the three of us!'

'No, you'd better let me off,' said the fair man. 'I have to go home.'

'Nonsense, nonsense, old fellow, I won't let you go.'

'My wife will be cross, I tell you. Now you can get into the gentleman's carriage.'

'Not on your life. Don't you think of it.'

The fair man was one of those people in whose character you seem at first to discern a certain obstinacy. Before you have time to open your lips, they are ready to start arguing and it seems they will never agree to what they have so clearly set their minds against, that they will never call a fool an intelligent man and, in particular, will never agree to dance to someone else's tune; but it always ends in a weakness in their character coming to light and in their agreeing to do exactly what they have refused to do, by calling what is foolish wise and by their dancing to another man's tune, as though they have never done anything else. In short, he starts as rough as a file and ends as smooth as silk.

'Nonsense,' said Nozdryov in reply to some objection from the fair man, put the cap on his head, and – the fair man went meekly after them.

'You haven't paid for the vodka, sir,' said the old woman.

'Oh, all right, all right, my good woman. I say, my dear fellow,' he turned to his brother-in-law, 'pay for me, will you? I haven't a penny in my pocket.'

'How much is it?' asked his brother-in-law.

'Why, sir, it's only twenty copecks,' said the old woman.

'Nonsense, nonsense, give her fifteen copecks. It'll be quite enough for her.'

'It's too little, sir,' said the old woman.

However, she took the money with gratitude and ran to open the door for them. She had suffered no loss, because she had asked four times as much as the cost of the vodka.

The travellers took their seats. Chichikov's carriage drove by the side of the carriage in which Nozdryov and his brother-in-law were sitting, and they could therefore talk freely to one another during the journey. Nozdryov's miserable little carriage, drawn by the lean hired horses, followed at some distance, continually lagging behind. Porfiry was in it with the puppy.

Since the conversation which our travellers conducted with one another is of no great interest to the reader, we shall do better if we say a few words about Nozdryov himself, for he will perhaps play a not inconsiderable part in our poem.

The reader is probably to some extent familiar with Nozdryov's personality. Everyone has met quite a few people like him. They are known as smart fellows, and even in childhood and at school they have the reputation of being good comrades and yet, for all that, they quite often are the recipients of extremely painful blows. There is always something open, straightforward, and reckless in their faces. They are quick to strike up an acquaintance and before you know where you are, they are on most intimate terms with you. You think their friendship will last a lifetime, but it almost always happens that their new friend will pick a fight with them the same evening at a party. They are always great talkers, drinkers and gamblers, and dare-devils, always in the public eye. At thirty-five, Nozdryov was exactly the same as he was at eighteen and twenty: a man whose only aim in life was to have a good time. Marriage had not changed him in the least, all the more so as his wife had soon died, leaving him with two small children whom he did not want at all; the children, however, were looked after by a pretty little nurse. He never could stay for more than a day at home. His sensitive nose could smell out a fair, an assembly, or a ball for miles around: and in the twinkling of an eye he was there, arguing and causing confusion at the green table, for like all men of his type he had an uncontrollable passion for cards. As we have seen in the first chapter, his play was not altogether innocent or fair, for he knew lots of ways of shuffling cards and all sorts of other cardsharping subtleties, and that was why the game often ended in another sort of game: he would either be beaten up or have his fine, thick whiskers shuffled, so that he sometimes returned home with only one whisker and that, too, rather scanty. But his plump and healthy cheeks were so well constituted and were endowed with such vegetative powers that his whiskers soon grew again and were even better than ever. And what was most strange and what can only happen in Russia, within a short time he would again meet the friends who had given him such a thorough beating and meet them as though nothing had happened: he, as they say, didn't seem to mind and they didn't seem to mind, either.

In a certain sense Nozdryov was a 'historical' character. No gathering at which he happened to be present, went off without some 'history'. Something was quite sure to happen: either he would be conducted out of the ballroom by gendarmes, or his friends would be obliged to kick him out themselves. If that did not happen, something was quite sure to happen which never happened to anyone else: either he would get so drunk at the buffet that all he could do was to laugh, or he would tell such fantastic lies that in the end he would feel ashamed of them himself. And he would tell those lies without the slightest need: all of a sudden he would come out with a story that he had a horse with a pink or light blue coat, or nonsense of that sort, so that at last his listeners would walk away from him saying: 'Well, my dear fellow, it seems you're romancing again.' There are people who have a passion for playing dirty tricks on their neighbours, sometimes without the slightest reason. Even a man of high rank and an imposing presence with a star of St Stanislav on his breast will, for instance, press your hand warmly, talk to you about some abstruse subjects which call for thought, and a moment later play a dirty trick on you before your very eyes. And he will do it like any low-grade civil servant, like a collegiate registrar, and not at all like a man wearing a high decoration on his breast and talking to you on subjects calling for deep thought. So that you just stand amazed and all you can do is to shrug your shoulders. Nozdryov, too, had this strange passion. The more intimate you became with him, the more likely he was to do you a bad turn; he would spread such an absurd story that for sheer silliness it would be hard to beat, he would upset a wedding or a business deal and he did so without in any way considering himself your enemy; on the contrary, if he happened to meet you again, he would again treat you like a long-lost friend and would even say: 'What a horrible fellow you are! You never come to see me!' Nozdryov was a man of great versatility in many ways, that is to say, a man who could turn his hand to anything. In the same breath he would offer to go with you anywhere you liked, even to the ends of the earth, to become your partner in any enterprise you might choose, to exchange anything in the world for anything you like. A shotgun, a dog, a horse – he would be ready to exchange anything for it and not at all with any idea of making a profit out of the transaction: it all arose from some kind of restless energy and recklessness of character. If he had the good fortune to come across a simpleton at a fair and fleece him, then he would buy whatever he happened to see in the shops: horse collars, tapers, kerchiefs for the nurse, a stallion, raisins, a silver wash-basin, holland linen, fine wheaten flour, tobacco, pistols, herrings, pictures, a grindstone, pots, boots, china – for as much money as he had on him. However, it rarely happened that all this was carried home; almost on the same day it was all lost to another and luckier gambler, sometimes even with the addition of his own pipe with tobacco pouch and mouthpiece, and another time with all his four horses, carriage, and coachman, so that their former owner himself had to set off in a short Asiatic coat in search of some friend to give him a lift in his carriage. Such was Nozdryov! Perhaps he will be called a stock character and it will be said that there are no more Nozdryovs now. Alas, those who say so are wrong. It will take a long, long time for the Nozdryovs of this world to become extinct. They are to be found everywhere in our midst, except that perhaps they are wearing different clothes; but people are thoughtless and imperceptive and a man in a different coat seems a different man to them.

Meanwhile the three carriages rolled up to the front steps of Nozdryov's house. No preparations had been made for their reception. Some wooden trestles were placed in the middle of the dining-room and two peasants were standing on them and whitewashing the walls and striking up some endless song; the floor was all splashed with whitewash. Nozdryov at once ordered the peasants and the trestles out of the room and ran out into the next room to give instructions. The visitors heard him giving the cook orders for dinner; perceiving this, Chichikov, who was already beginning to feel the pangs of hunger, realized that they would not sit down to table before five o'clock. On his return, Nozdryov conducted his visitors to see everything he had on his estate and in a little over two hours he had shown them absolutely all there was to be seen, so that there was nothing left to be shown. First of all they went to inspect the stables where they saw two mares, one a dapple-grey and the other a chestnut, then a bay stallion, which was nothing much to look at, but for which Nozdryov swore he had paid ten thousand roubles.

'You didn't give ten thousand for him,' his brother-in-law observed. 'He isn't worth one.'

'I swear I did,' said Nozdryov.

'You can swear as much as you like,' answered his brother-in-law.

'Well, would you like to take a bet on it?' said Nozdryov.

But his brother-in-law had no intention of betting on it.

Then Nozdryov showed them the empty stalls in which there had once also been some good horses. In the same stable they saw a goat which, according to an old superstition, it was considered necessary to keep with the horses and which seemed to be on the best of terms with them and walked about under their bellies as though he were at home there. Then Nozdryov took them to have a look at a wolf cub which was kept tied up. 'Here's the wolf cub,' he said. 'I feed him on raw meat on purpose. I want him to be a real wild animal!' Then they went to inspect the pond in which, according to Nozdryov, there were fish of such enormous size that two men were hardly able to pull one out, about which, however, his brother-in-law did not fail to express some doubts. 'I'm going to show you a pair of fine dogs, Chichikov,' said Nozdryov. 'The strength of their haunches is simply remarkable and their muzzles are as thin as needles!' And he led them into a very beautifully built little house, surrounded by a large yard with a fence running all round it. On entering the yard, they saw dogs of all kinds, long-haired dogs, dogs with smooth coats and long hair on their tails and haunches, and of all possible shades and colours: black and tan, black and white, white with brown spots, brown with black spots, red and white, with black ears and with grey eyes. They had all sorts of names and most of them in the imperative mood: Shoot, Swear, Dash, Fire, Bully, Blast, Plague, Scorcher, Hurry, Darling, Reward, Guardian. Among them Nozdryov was just like a father among his children; with their tails (known as 'tillers' to dog fanciers) in the air, they all flew to meet and welcome the visitors. A dozen of them put their paws on Nozdryov's shoulders. 'Swear' expressed his affection for Chichikov in the same way and, getting on his hind legs, licked him right on the mouth, so that Chichikov was obliged to spit out at once. They inspected the dogs whose haunches were so amazing, and they were very excellent dogs. Then they went to have a look at a Crimean bitch which was blind and, according to Nozdryov, would soon be dead, but which two years ago had been a very good bitch. They inspected the bitch too, and, to be sure, the bitch was blind. Then they went to have a look at a water-mill, which had lost its 'flutterer' or iron ring on which the upper stone rests as it turns rapidly on its axle or 'flutters', as the Russian peasants so wonderfully express it.

'We shall soon come to the smithy,' said Nozdryov.

And, to be sure, on going on a little farther they saw the smithy; they inspected the smithy too.

'In that field there,' said Nozdryov, pointing to it, 'there's such an enormous number of hares that you can't see the ground for them. I caught one by the hind legs with my own hands.'

'Come, you'll never catch a hare with your hands,' the brother-in-law remarked.

'But I did catch one. I caught it for fun,' replied Nozdryov. 'Now,' he went on, turning to Chichikov, 'I'm going to take you to see the boundaries of my land.'

Nozdryov led his visitors across fields which in many places were covered with mounds. The visitors had to make their way between rough, fallow land and ploughed fields. Chichikov began to feel tired. In many places their feet squelched in water, so low-lying was the ground. At first they took care and stepped gingerly over the puddles, but afterwards, seeing that it made no difference, they walked straight on without bothering to see whether the ground was muddy or not so muddy. Having covered a considerable distance, they did, in fact, catch sight of the boundary which consisted of a small wooden post and a narrow ditch.

'This is the boundary,' said Nozdryov. 'Everything you see on this side is mine and even on the other side too; all that forest which you see looking blue in the distance and everything beyond it is all mine.'

'Since when has that forest become yours?' asked the brother-in-law. 'You haven't bought it recently, have you? It used not to be yours, you know.'

'Yes, I bought it recently,' replied Nozdryov.

'How did you manage to buy it so quickly?'

'Oh, I bought it the day before yesterday and I paid a lot for it, damn it.'

'But you were at the fair then!'

'You are a Simple Simon, aren't you? Can't a man be at a fair and buy land at the same time? All right, I was at the fair and while I was away, my agent bought it for me.'

'Oh well, of course, if it was your agent!' said the brother-in-law, but even then he looked doubtful and shook his head.

The visitors returned home by the same execrable route. Nozdryov took them to his study, in which, however, there were no signs of what is usually to be found in studies, that is, books or papers; on the walls there hung only swords and two guns, one worth three hundred and the other eight hundred roubles. Having examined them, the brother-in-law merely shook his head. Then they were shown some Turkish daggers, on one of which there had been engraved by mistake, 'Made by Savely Sibiryakov'. Then the visitors were shown a hurdy-gurdy. Nozdryov at once turned the handle and played a tune for them. The hurdy-gurdy played not unpleasantly, but something seemed to go wrong in the middle, for the mazurka ended up with the song *Marlbrook s'en va-t-en guerre* and *Marlbrook s'en va-t-en guerre* finished quite unexpectedly with an old familiar waltz. Nozdryov had stopped turning the handle for some time, but one of the pipes in the hurdy-gurdy was quite incorrigible and simply refused to be put down and it kept whistling away by itself for a long time. Then they were shown all sorts of pipes, some made of wood, some of clay, and some of meerschaum, smoked and unsmoked, wrapped in chamois leather and not wrapped up, a chibouk with an amber mouthpiece recently won at cards, a tobacco pouch embroidered by some countess who had fallen head over ears in love with Nozdryov at some posting-station and whose hands, according to him, were *subtilement superflues*, words that apparently meant the height of perfection to him. After a snack of cured sturgeon, they sat down to table at about five o'clock. Dinner, it was clear, was not Nozdryov's main interest in life; the dishes did not seem to be of any particular importance, some were burnt, others quite uncooked. It was obvious that the cook was guided by some kind of inspiration and put in the first thing that his hand happened to light upon: if pepper happened to be near, he put in some pepper, if cabbage turned up, he shoved in cabbage, he poured in milk, added ham, peas; in short, he just pitched in everything he laid his hands on, so long as it was hot, in the hope that it would be sure to have some sort of flavour. On the other hand, Nozdryov was very particular about wines: even before the soup was served he had poured out for each of his guests a large glass of port and another of Haut Sauterne, for in provincial and district towns no ordinary Sauterne is to be found. Then Nozdryov sent for a bottle of Madeira no field-marshal ever drank better. The Madeira certainly burnt their mouths, for the merchants, being well-versed in the tastes of the local landowners who are fond of good Madeira, doctored it mercilessly with rum and sometimes poured even ordinary vodka into it in the belief that Russian stomachs could digest anything. Then Nozdryov ordered a special bottle to be fetched which, so he said, was a mixture of burgundy and champagne. He kept filling most zealously both glasses to his right and left, those of his brother-in-law and Chichikov. Chichikov, however, noticed out of the corner of his eye that Nozdryov did not refill his own glass as often as he did theirs. This put him on his guard and whenever Nozdryov happened to turn to speak to his brother-in-law or refill his glass, he immediately emptied his own glass into his plate. After a short time a rowanberry liqueur was put on the table which, according to Nozdryov, tasted exactly like cream, but which, to their surprise, tasted strongly of raw brandy. Then they drank some sort of balsam which had a name difficult to remember and, indeed, their host himself called it by a different name afterwards. The dinner had long been over and all the wines tasted, but the guests still sat at table. Chichikov was not at all anxious to discuss his main business with Nozdryov in front of his brother-in-law; after all, the brother-in-law was a stranger and the subject he had to discuss called for a friendly chat in private without any third person being present. Still, the brother-in-law could hardly be dangerous, for he seemed to have drunk more than he could carry and, as he sat in his chair, he kept nodding every minute. Realizing himself that he was a little the worse for drink, he began at last to talk of going home, but in a voice so listless and languid, as though, to use a Russian expression, he were pulling on a horse's collar with a pair of pincers.

'I won't hear of it,' said Nozdryov. 'I won't let you go.'

'Please don't make it difficult for me, my dear fellow,' the brother-in-law said. 'I must go. Really I must. You will make a lot of trouble for me, you know.'

'Nonsense, nonsense, we'll have a game of cards.'

'Please have one yourself, my dear fellow. I can't. My wife will be very angry with me. Really, she will. I must tell her all about the fair.

You see, my dear fellow, I simply must do something to please her. No, please don't keep me.'

'Oh, to hell with your wife! As if you had anything important to do with her.'

'Oh, no, no, my dear fellow. She's a very good and faithful wife. Does so many things for me. Believe me, it makes me cry. No, please don't keep me. I'm an honest man and I must go. Honestly I must. I assure you.'

'Let him go,' Chichikov said softly to Nozdryov. 'What's the use of keeping him?'

'You're quite right,' said Nozdryov. 'I can't stand these namby-pamby sentimentalists.' And he added in a loud voice: 'Oh, to hell with you! Go and make love to your wife, you —!' *

'No, my dear fellow, don't call me a —. I owe my life to her. She's such a nice, sweet woman. She's so sweet to me. She makes me cry. I'm sure she'll ask me what I saw at the fair and I must tell her all about it. You see, she really is a darling.'

'Oh, go. Tell her a pack of lies. Here's your cap.'

'No, you oughtn't to talk like that about her, my dear fellow. You see, you really are insulting me by such talk. She is such a darling.'

'Well, then, get out and go to her quickly!'

'Yes, my dear fellow, I'm going. I'm sorry I can't stay. I'd be glad to, but I can't.'

The brother-in-law went on repeating his apologies without noticing that he had been sitting in his carriage for a long time and had been driven out of the gates hours ago and that for hours there was nothing before him but open fields. It is to be assumed that his wife did not hear a lot about the fair.

'What a rubbishy fellow!' said Nozdryov, standing before the window and watching the carriage as it drove away. 'Look at him rolling along! His trace horse isn't bad: I'd long wanted to snaffle it, but, you see, you can never agree about the price with him. He is just a —, simply a —!'

* The untranslatable word used by Gogol is *Fetyuk*, which Gogol explains in a footnote is 'a derogatory word for men, deriving from the Greek letter θ (theta), which is regarded as obscene by some people'. In Gogol's time the Russian alphabet still included the Greek letter θ, pronounced like *F* and used in names of Greek origin; the θ was regarded as 'obscene' because of its use as a female sex symbol. Tr.

They then went back to the room. Porfiry brought candles and Chichikov noticed in his host's hands a pack of cards which seemed to have materialized out of nowhere.

'Well, now, my dear fellow,' said Nozdryov, pressing the side of the pack with his fingers and slightly bending it so that the paper wrapping split and fell off, 'to pass the time I shall put three hundred roubles in the bank.'

But Chichikov pretended not to have heard what Nozdryov had said and observed, as though he suddenly remembered something:

'Oh, before I forget, I have something I want to ask you.'

'What is it?'

'Promise first that you will do it.'

'But what is it?'

'You must promise first!'

'All right.'

'On your word of honour?'

'On my word of honour.'

'Now, this is what it is. I expect you must have lots of dead souls who have not yet been struck off the census register?'

'Yes, I have. What about it?'

'Transfer them to me. To my name.'

'What do you want them for?'

'Oh, well, I want them.'

'But what for?'

'Well, I just want them. That's my business. In short, I need them.'

'Ah, I expect you must have something up your sleeve. Come on, tell me. What is it?'

'What have I got up my sleeve? There's nothing I could have. It's such a trifle.'

'But what do you want them for?'

'Oh, what an inquisitive fellow you are! You have to feel any bit of rubbish with your fingers and smell it, too.'

'And why won't you tell me?'

'But what good will it do you to know? I just want to have them. It's just a whim of mine.'

'All right, then. Unless you tell me I won't do it.'

'Well then, you see that's not very fair of you. You gave me your word and now you're trying to back out.'

'Well, just as you like, but I won't do it till you tell me.'

'What am I to tell him?' thought Chichikov, and after a moment's reflection he told him that he needed the dead souls in order to obtain a better position in society, that at present he had no big estates, so for the time being at least he would like to have some worthless dead souls.

'You're lying, you're lying,' said Nozdryov, without letting him finish. 'That's a big lie, my dear fellow.'

Chichikov himself realized that his story was not particularly clever and that his pretext was rather a feeble one.

'Very well, then I'll tell you all about it,' he said, trying to make good his mistake. 'Only please, don't tell it to anyone. You see, I've decided to get married. But, you see, my fiancée's father and mother are very ambitious people. It's a damned nuisance, in fact. I'm sorry I started the whole thing. They're absolutely set on their daughter's husband having at least three hundred serfs and, as I'm some one hundred and fifty short. ...'

'Oh, you're lying, you're lying!' Nozdryov shouted again.

'This time,' said Chichikov, 'I haven't lied even that much,' and he pointed with his thumb to the tip of his little finger.

'I'll stake my life you're lying.'

'Now, this is really too much! What do you take me for? Why are you so sure that I'm lying?'

'Well, you see, I know you. You're a great rascal, sir. Let me tell you this as a friend. If I were your chief, I'd hang you on the nearest tree.'

Chichikov took offence at this remark. Any expression in the least coarse or derogatory to decorum was distasteful to him. He even disliked any sort of familiarity, except, of course, on the part of a person of very high rank. For this reason he was now deeply offended.

'Damned if I wouldn't hang you,' Nozdryov repeated. 'I tell you so frankly not because I want to insult you, but simply as one friend to another.'

'There's a limit to everything,' said Chichikov with dignity. 'If you want to make an impression by such speeches you'd better go to the barracks.' And then he added: 'If you don't want to give them to me, why not sell them?'

'Sell them? But, you see, I know you. You're a damn rogue, aren't you? You wouldn't give me a lot for them, would you?'

'You're a nice one, too. Just listen to him! They're not made of diamonds, are they?'

'There you are! I knew you'd say that!'

'Good Lord, man, what Jewish instincts you have! You really ought to make me a present of them.'

'Now, look here, just to show you that I'm not a grasping miser, I won't take anything for them. Buy my stallion and I'll throw them in.'

'Good Lord, what do I want with a stallion?' said Chichikov, really astonished at such a proposal.

'What do you mean? Why, I paid ten thousand for him and I'll sell him to you for four.'

'But what do I want a stallion for? I don't keep a stud farm.'

'But, look here, you don't understand. You see, all I want now is three thousand. The other thousand you can pay me later.'

'But I don't want your stallion. You can keep him!'

'Oh, all right. Buy the chestnut mare then!'

'I don't want the mare, either.'

'I'll let you have the mare and the grey horse you saw in the stables for two thousand.'

'But I don't want any horses.'

'You can sell them. They'll give you three times as much for them at the first fair.'

'You'd better sell them yourself if you're so sure you'll get three times as much.'

'I know it would be to my benefit, but, you see, I'd like you to benefit from it too.'

Chichikov thanked him for his kind intention and refused point blank to buy the grey horse or the chestnut mare.

'All right, then, buy some of my dogs. I'll sell you a pair that will send a shiver down your back. Pedigree borzois with huge whiskers, coats as stiff as bristles, barrel-shaped ribs such as you never saw in your life, and paws like velvet balls – never leave a mark on the ground!'

'But what do I want dogs for? I'm not a sportsman.'

'But I'd like you to have dogs. Now, listen, if you don't want dogs, buy my barrel organ. It's a marvellous hurdy-gurdy. As I'm an honest man, it cost me fifteen hundred roubles. I'll let you have it for nine hundred.'

'What do I want a hurdy-gurdy for? I'm not a German. I don't want to go trudging about the streets with it, begging.'

'But it isn't the sort of hurdy-gurdy Germans carry about. It's an organ. Take a good look at it: it's all mahogany. Let me show it to you again!' Here Nozdryov seized Chichikov by the arm and began dragging him towards the next room, and however much he dug in his heels and assured him that he knew perfectly well what the barrel-organ was like, he had to hear again how Marlborough went to the wars.

'If you don't want to pay cash for it,' Nozdryov said, 'then this is what I'll do. Listen, I'll give you the hurdy-gurdy and as many dead souls as I've got and you give me your carriage and three hundred roubles thrown in.'

'Indeed! And what am I to travel in?'

'I'll give you another carriage. Come along to the coach-house and I'll show it you. You've only to give it a coat of paint and it'll be a wonderful carriage.'

'Good Lord, the man's obsessed!' thought Chichikov to himself, and he decided to have nothing whatever to do with any kind of carriages, barrel-organs, or any sort of dog no matter how barrel-shaped their ribs or velvety their paws.

'But don't you see? I'm giving you the carriage, the hurdy-gurdy, and the dead souls all in one lot!'

'I don't want them,' Chichikov said once more.

'Why don't you want them?'

'Because I simply don't want them and that's all there is to it.'

'What a damned awkward customer you are! I see one can't deal with you as one does with good friends and comrades. What a fellow! One can see at once that you're two-faced.'

'What do you think I am – a fool? I mean, why should I buy something that's absolutely of no use to me?'

'You'd better save your breath to cool your porridge. I understand you very well now. A damn rascal – that's what you are. Now, listen, let's have a nice little game of cards. I'll stake all my dead souls on a card and the hurdy-gurdy, too.'

'Staking it all on a card means leaving it all to chance,' Chichikov said, throwing a furtive glance at the cards in Nozdryov's hand. Both the packs seemed to him as though they had been tampered with and the very specks on the back looked suspicious.

'Why to chance?' said Nozdryov. 'What's chance got to do with it? It's luck: if luck's on your side, you can win a hell of a lot. There it is. There's luck for you!' he exclaimed as he began to deal in the hope of rousing Chichikov's gambling instinct. 'There's luck for you! See, see! Simply knocking at your door. There's that damned nine I lost everything on! I felt that it would let me down and, half-closing my eyes, I thought to myself: "To hell with you, let me down, damn you!"'

While Nozdryov was saying this, Porfiry brought in a bottle. But Chichikov absolutely refused either to drink or to play.

'Why won't you play?' Nozdryov asked.

'Oh, because I don't feel like it. And, to tell you the truth, I'm not particularly keen on cards.'

'Why aren't you?'

Chichikov shrugged his shoulders and added:

'Oh, because I'm not.'

'You're no damn good.'

'Well, I'm afraid I can't do anything about it, can I? I'm just as God made me.'

'You're simply a —! I did think at first that you were a decent sort of fellow, but it seems you've no idea of how to behave like a gentleman. One can't speak to you as one would to a friend. … No straightforwardness, no sincerity about you. A perfect Sobakevich. Just as big a scoundrel as he!'

'Why are you calling me names? Is it my fault that I don't play? Sell me your souls by themselves, if you're the sort of man who gets worked up over such nonsense.'

'You won't get a damn thing from me. I was going to let you have them for nothing, but now you shan't have them. I wouldn't give 'em to you. Not if you were to offer me three kingdoms for them. A damned rogue, a filthy chimney sweep, that's what you are! From now on I won't have anything to do with you. Porfiry, go and tell the stable boy not to give his horses any oats. Let them eat hay.'

Such a conclusion Chichikov certainly did not expect.

'I wish I'd never set eyes on you,' said Nozdryov.

In spite of this slight disagreement, however, the host and his guest had supper together, though this time there were no wines with fanciful names on the table. There was only one bottle of Cyprian wine which was as sour as vinegar. After supper Nozdryov said to

Chichikov, taking him into an adjoining room where a bed had been made up for him: 'There's your bed. I don't want even to say good night to you.'

After Nozdryov had gone, Chichikov was left in a most disagreeable frame of mind. He was annoyed with himself and swore at himself for coming there and wasting his time. But he swore at himself even more for having spoken to Nozdryov about his business and for having acted as carelessly as a child, as a fool, for his business was not at all of a kind that could be safely confided to a man like Nozdryov. ... Nozdryov was a good-for-nothing fellow, Nozdryov could go and tell all sorts of lies, he could add something of his own, he could spread goodness only knows what kind of stories, and it might lead to all sorts of scandalous tales – it was bad, bad. 'I'm simply a fool,' he said to himself. He passed a bad night. Some small and very lively insects kept biting him very painfully, so that he kept scratching the affected spot with all his fingers, saying as he did so, 'The devil take you and Nozdryov too!' He woke up early in the morning. The first thing he did after putting on his dressing-gown and his boots was to walk across the yard to the stable to tell Selifan to harness the horses at once. On his way back across the yard, he came across Nozdryov, who was also in his dressing-gown and had a pipe between his teeth. Nozdryov greeted him in a very friendly fashion and asked him whether he had slept well.

'So-so,' Chichikov replied rather dryly.

'As for me, my dear chap,' said Nozdryov, 'such abominations kept haunting me all night that are too horrible to relate, and after what happened yesterday my mouth this morning felt as though a whole squadron of cavalry had spent the night there. What do you think? I dreamt that I was being birched! Yes, indeed! And do you know by whom? You'll never guess. By Major Potseyulev and Kuvshinnikov.'

'Ay,' thought Chichikov to himself, 'what a pity they didn't really give you a good thrashing.'

'Yes, indeed! And it hurt like hell! And when I woke up, damn it, I really was itching all over – those damn witches of fleas, I suppose. Oh, well, you'd better go and get dressed. I'll come along in a minute. I must go and give that rascal of an agent of mine a good talking to.'

Chichikov went back to his room to wash and dress. When, after that, he went into the dining-room a tea service and a bottle of rum were already set on the table. There were still traces in the room of the dinner and supper of the previous day. It looked as though the room had never been swept. Bread crumbs were still lying on the floor and tobacco ash even on the tablecloth. The master of the house, who was not late in making his appearance, wore nothing under his dressing-gown, displaying a bare chest with something like a beard growing on it; holding a long-stemmed Turkish pipe in his hand and sipping his tea from a cup, he would have made a very good model for a painter who detested sleek gentlemen with their hair curled as on hairdressers' signboards or those who have their heads cropped short.

'Well,' said Nozdryov after a short pause, 'what about it? Won't you play for my dead souls?'

'I've told you, my dear fellow, that I don't play. I'll buy them if you like.'

'I don't want to sell them. It wouldn't be acting like a friend. I don't want to make a profit out of any damn thing. Now, a game of cards is a different matter. Let's have just one game, anyway!'

'I've told you already I won't.'

'And you won't exchange them for anything?'

'No.'

'Well, look here, let's have a game of draughts. If you win, they're all yours. You see, I've got lots who should have been struck off the census register. Hey, Porfiry, bring the draught board here.'

'You needn't trouble, I'm not going to play.'

'But this is not cards: there's no question of luck or cheating here. It's all a matter of skill, you know. In fact, I must warn you that I can't play at all. You really should give me a piece or two.'

'Well,' Chichikov thought to himself, 'why not sit down and have a game of draughts with him? I used to play draughts quite well, and it will be difficult for him to get up to any tricks at draughts.'

'All right, so be it. I'll have a game of draughts with you.'

'The souls against a hundred roubles!'

'Why a hundred? Fifty's enough.'

'No, what sort of stake is fifty? I'd better throw in a middling puppy or a gold seal for your watch chain.'

'Oh, very well,' said Chichikov.

'How many pieces will you give me?' asked Nozdryov.

'Whatever for? I won't give you anything.'

'You might at least let me have the first two moves.'

'I won't. I'm a poor player myself.'

'We know you,' said Nozdryov, moving a piece. 'We know what sort of a poor player you are.'

'Haven't touched a draughtsman for I don't know how long,' said Chichikov, also moving a piece.

'We know you, we know the sort of a poor player you are,' said Nozdryov, moving another piece and at the same time pushing forward another with the cuff of his sleeve.

'Haven't touched a draughtsman for ages,' said Chichikov. 'Hullo, hullo! What's that, my dear fellow? Put it back.'

'Put back what?'

'Why, that piece there,' said Chichikov, and, at the same time, saw almost under his very nose another which seemed to have got almost far enough to become king; where it had come from goodness only knows. 'No, sir,' said Chichikov, getting up from the table, 'it's quite impossible to play with you. One doesn't play like that with three pieces all at once.'

'Why with three? I'm sorry, I made a mistake. One was moved accidentally. I'll put it back if you like.

'And where did that other one come from?'

'What other one?'

'Why, the one which is going to be a king.'

'Good Lord, don't you remember?'

'No, my dear fellow, I don't. I've counted every move and I remember them all. You've only just placed it there. That's where it should be!'

'What? There?' said Nozdryov, reddening. 'I can see, my dear fellow, you like imagining things.'

'No, my dear fellow, it's you who seem to be imagining things, only not very successfully.'

'Who do you take me for?' said Nozdryov. 'You're not suggesting that I'm cheating, are you?'

'I don't take you for anyone, but I will never play with you again.'

'No, you can't refuse,' Nozdryov said, getting excited. 'The game's begun!'

'I have a right to refuse because you don't play as an honourable man should.'

'You're lying, you can't say that.'

'No, sir, you're lying yourself.'

94

'I haven't been cheating, and you can't refuse to go on. You must finish the game.'

'You can't make me do that,' said Chichikov coolly, and going up to the board, he swept all the pieces together.

Nozdryov flushed and walked up so close to Chichikov that the latter stepped back a couple of paces.

'I'll make you play! You may have mixed up the pieces, but that doesn't matter. I remember all the moves. We'll put them back as they were.'

'No, sir, that's the end. I'm not going to play with you again.'

'So you won't play?'

'You realize yourself that it's quite impossible to play with you.'

'No, sir, you tell me straight, are you going to play or not?' said Nozdryov advancing still closer.

'I won't,' said Chichikov, raising, however, both his hands nearer to his face to be on the safe side, for things were really getting too hot for him.

This precaution was very timely, for Nozdryov swung his arm and – it might very well have happened that one of our hero's agreeable and plump cheeks would have been covered with dishonour that nothing could have wiped off, but luckily warding off the blow, he seized Nozdryov by his a trifle too eager arms and held him firmly.

'Porfiry, Pavlushka!' shouted Nozdryov in a fury, struggling to free himself.

Hearing this call, Chichikov, to avoid making the domestic serfs witnesses of this interesting scene, and realizing at the same time that it was useless to hold Nozdryov, let go his arms. At the same moment Porfiry came in, followed by Pavlushka, a stalwart country lad with whom it would have been distinctly unprofitable to have anything to do.

'So you won't finish the game?' said Nozdryov. 'Answer me straight.'

'It's quite impossible to finish the game,' said Chichikov and glanced out of the window. He saw his carriage standing quite ready and Selifan apparently waiting for a wave of his hand to drive up to the steps; but there was no possibility of getting out of the room; two stalwart fools of serfs were standing in the doorway.

'So you won't finish the game?' Nozdryov repeated with a face burning, as though on fire.

'If you played as an honourable man should, but as it is I can't.'

'Oh, so you can't, you dirty dog! As soon as you see that you're losing you can't. Come on, thrash him!' he shouted in a frenzy, turning to Porfiry and Pavlushka, while he caught hold of his long-stemmed cherrywood pipe.

Chichikov turned as pale as a sheet. He tried to say something, but he felt his lips move without uttering a sound.

'Thrash him!' shouted Nozdryov, rushing forward with the cherrywood pipe, hot and perspiring, just as though he were attacking an impregnable fortress. 'Thrash him!' he shouted in a voice in which some desperate lieutenant shouts 'Forward, lads!' to his men at the time of a great assault, an officer whose madcap bravery has already acquired such notoriety that a special order has been issued to hold him back in the heat of a battle. But the lieutenant is carried away by martial ardour, his head is in a whirl, he sees the image of General Suvorov before him and is eager to perform some heroic deed. 'Forward, lads!' he shouts, dashing forward, without realizing that he is ruining the plan laid down for the general attack, that thousands of guns are levelled at him in the embrasures of the impregnable fortress walls that reach to the clouds, that his helpless company will be blown sky high, like feathers carried by a strong wind, and that already the fatal bullet is whistling through the air that will still his clamant throat for ever. But if Nozdryov looked like a desperate, rash, and thought-less lieutenant attacking a fortress, the fortress he was attacking was far from an impregnable one. On the contrary, the fortress was so frightened that its heart was in its mouth. Already the chair with which he had intended to defend himself had been wrenched from his hands by the serfs, already, half-closing his eyes and more dead than alive, he was preparing himself to have a taste of his host's Circassian pipe, and goodness only knows what might not have happened if the Fates had not decided to spare the sides, the shoulders, and all the well-bred parts of our hero. Suddenly, and in a most unexpected way, as though from the clouds, came the jingling of harness bells, there was a distinct sound of the rattle of the wheels of a trap careering up to the steps, and even in the room could be heard the heavy snorts and laboured breathing of the overheated horses of the *troika* that came to a stop at the front steps. Everyone involuntarily glanced out of the window: a man with a moustache, in a semi-military uniform, was getting out of the trap. After making a few inquiries in the hall, he entered the room at the very moment when Chichikov, still unable to recover from his terror, was in the most wretched condition a mortal man had ever found himself in.

'Which is Mr Nozdryov here?' said the stranger, looking in some bewilderment at Nozdryov, standing with his long pipe in his hand, and at Chichikov, who had scarcely begun to recover from his parlous position.

'Won't you tell me first whom I have the honour of addressing?' said Nozdryov walking up to him.

'I'm the captain of police.'

'And what do you want?'

'I've come to inform you that you are under arrest until the court has given a decision in your case.'

'What nonsense,' said Nozdryov. 'What case?'

'You are implicated in the assault on the landowner Maximov who was thrashed while drunk.'

'You're lying, sir. I've never set eyes on a landowner called Maximov.'

'Sir, may I point out to you that I'm an officer. You can speak like that to your servants, but not to me!'

Without waiting to hear what Nozdryov's reply to that would be, Chichikov grabbed his hat and slipped out of the room behind the police officer's back and out on to the steps, got into his carriage, and told Selifan to drive as fast as he could.

Chapter 5

Our hero was certainly frightened out of his wits. Although the carriage was going along at a spanking pace and Nozdryov's village had long ago passed out of sight, hidden behind fields, the sloping ground, and the hillocks, he still kept looking back in terror, as though expecting every minute to be overtaken by his pursuers. He was breathing heavily and when he tried to lay a hand on his heart he felt it fluttering like a quail in a cage. 'Dear, oh dear, he has scared me out of my wits. What a fellow!' And he went on to wish Nozdryov all sorts of terrible misfortunes; and indeed a few strong words were uttered. And who is to blame him? After all, he was a Russian and in a rage, too. Besides, it was no joking matter. 'Say what you like,' he said to himself, 'but if the captain of police had not turned up in the nick of time I might never have seen the light of day! I should have disappeared like a bubble on the water, without a trace, leaving no descendants and bequeathing neither fortune nor good name to my future children!' Our hero was very much concerned about his descendants.

'That gentleman was no good,' Selifan thought to himself. 'I never seen such a gentleman in my life. I mean, I'd gladly spit at him. Better give a man nothing to eat than not feed the horses, for a horse likes his oats. It's his victuals. What grub is to us is oats to him. It's his victuals.'

The horses too seemed to have a poor opinion of Nozdryov: not only the bay and the Assessor, but even the dappled-grey seemed disgruntled. Though the worst of the oats always fell to his share and Selifan never filled his manger without first exclaiming: 'Oh, you dirty rascal!', still they were oats and not just hay. He munched them with satisfaction and often thrust his long muzzle into his companions' mangers to see what their provender was like, especially when Selifan was not in the stable, but all they had was hay – it was too bad! Everyone was disgruntled.

But their expressions of dissatisfaction were soon cut short in a sudden and quite unexpected manner. All of them, not excluding t driver, only came to themselves and realized what had happened when a carriage drawn by six horses was right on top of them and they heard almost over their heads the screams of the ladies in the carriage and the threats and oaths of the other coachman: 'Oh, you scoundrel: I shouted to you at the top of my voice "Turn to the right," you gaping fool! Are you drunk or what?' Selifan realized that he was in the wrong, but as no Russian likes to admit before others that he is to blame, he at once retorted, drawing himself up with dignity: 'And why was you galloping like that? Pawned your eyes in a pub, have you?' He then tried to back the horses so as to extricate them from the harness of the other carriage, but it was all to no purpose, for everything had got into a terrible tangle. The dapple-grey sniffed with interest at the new friends whom he found on each side of him. Meanwhile, the ladies in the carriage looked on with an expression of horror on their faces. One was an old lady and the other a young girl of sixteen with golden hair very skilfully and charmingly arranged on her little head. The pretty oval of her face was rounded like a fresh egg and was as transparently white as when, fresh and new-laid, it is held up to the light by the dark-skinned hands of the housekeeper who is testing it and the rays of the bright sun show through it; her delicate little ears were also suffused with the warm light that pierced them. The terror on her parted lips and the tears in her eyes were all so charming that our hero stared at her for several minutes without paying any attention to the uproar that was going on among the horses and the drivers. 'Back, back, back! Why don't you back, you Nizhny-Novgorod nitwit?' yelled the other driver. Selifan tugged at the reins, the other driver did the same, the horses backed slightly, then stepping over their traces, got themselves entangled again. In this situation the dapple-grey was so pleased with his new acquaintance that he refused to do anything to get out of the predicament in which an unforeseen destiny had placed him, and laying his muzzle upon the neck of his new friend, seemed to whisper something in his ear, probably some awful nonsense because the strange horse kept twitching his ears unceasingly.

Peasants from a village, which fortunately was not very far off, soon arrived on the scene of the accident. Since a spectacle like that is a real godsend to a peasant, just as a newspaper or a club is to a German, there was a great crowd of them soon gathered round the carriages and there was no one left in the village except old women and little children. They undid the traces, a few buffets on the nose of the dapple-grey forced him back; in short, the horses were separated and led away. But the newly arrived horses, whether it was because they felt annoyed at having been separated from their friends or simply through foolishness, would not move however much the driver whipped them, and stood as if rooted to the ground. The interest of the peasants reached an incredible pitch. Each one of them vied with the other in volunteering some piece of advice: 'You, Andrushka, get hold of the trace horse, the one on the right side, and let Uncle Mityay get on the shaft horse. Come on, get on it, Uncle Mityay!' Uncle Mityay, a lean, lanky peasant with a red beard, scrambled up on the shaft horse and looked exactly like a village belfry or, better still, like the crane with which they draw water from the well. The driver whipped the horses, but nothing happened. Mityay was no help at all. 'Wait, wait!' the peasants shouted. 'You get on the trace horse, Uncle Mityay, and let Uncle Minyay get on the shaft horse!' Uncle Minyay, a broad-shouldered peasant with a coal-black beard and a belly that looked like a gigantic *samovar* in which spiced honey drinks are brewed for a marketful of frozen people, mounted willingly enough the shaft horse who almost sank to the ground under his weight. 'Now it'll be all right!' shouted the peasants. 'Give him hell, give him hell! Give the light-bay a crack of the whip! What has he got stuck there for like a daddy-long-legs?' But, seeing that no progress was being made and that no amount of whipping was of any avail, Uncle Mityay and Uncle Minyay both mounted the shaft horse, while Andrushka was put on the trace horse. At last the driver, his patience exhausted, chased away both Uncle Mityay and Uncle Minyay, and it was a good thing he did so, for such a steam rose from the horses as if they had raced from one stage to another without stopping to take breath. He gave them a minute to rest, after which they set off of their own accord. While all this was going on, Chichikov was gazing attentively at the young girl. He made several attempts to start a conversation with her, but somehow nothing came of it. Meanwhile the ladies drove off and the pretty little head together with the delicate features and the slender waist vanished almost like a vision, and once more all that was left was the highway, the carriage, the three horses the reader knows so well, Selifan, Chichikov, and the flat emptiness of the fields around. Everywhere in life, whether among its coarse, rough, poor and untidily mouldering lower orders or among its monotonously frigid and tediously tidy higher orders, everywhere a man will be sure to meet at least once in his life something that is unlike anything he has happened to see before, something that for once will awaken in him a feeling that is unlike any feeling he is destined to experience for the rest of his life. Everywhere across whatever sorrows of which our life is woven, some radiant joy will gaily flash past, just as sometimes a magnificent carriage with golden harness, gorgeous steeds, and brilliantly sparkling windows suddenly flashes by unheralded past some poor village in the wilds of the country, a village which till then has seen nothing but country carts, and long afterwards the peasants stand, hat in hand, gaping open-mouthed, though the wonderful carriage has long since sped away and vanished out of sight. In the same way, the fair-haired girl has appeared quite unexpectedly in our story and as unexpectedly vanished again. Had some boy of twenty – a hussar, a student, or any young man who had just entered upon his career in life – been in Chichikov's place – good Lord, what would not have awakened, what would not have stirred, what would not have spoken in him! For a long time he would have stood insensibly on the same spot with his eyes fixed vacantly on the far away horizon, oblivious of the road, the reprimands and scoldings that awaited him for his delay, oblivious of himself, his duty, the world, and everything in it.

But our hero was a middle-aged man and of a circumspect and unemotional character. He, too, grew thoughtful and pondered, but his thoughts were more practical, not so irresponsible, and, to some extent, extremely sound. 'A nice little wench!' he said, opening his snuff-box and taking a pinch of snuff. 'But what is it that is so particularly nice about her? Well, what is so nice about her is that she has evidently only just come out of some boarding school or institute for young ladies, that there is so far nothing, as they say, of the female about her, that is to say, nothing of what makes women so distasteful. She is like a child now; everything about her is simple, she says what comes into her head, she laughs when she feels like laughing. You could make anything out of her. She might become something wonderful and she might turn out worthless, and quite likely she will turn out worthless. Wait till the mummies and aunties get to work on her. In one year they will stuff her full of all kinds of female frippery so that her own father won't recognize her. Quite unexpectedly haughtiness and primness will make their appearance; she will begin to carry herself according to the instructions she has learned, she will rack her brains and try to think with whom, how and how much to talk, and how and at whom to look, every minute she will be afraid of saying more than she ought, she will get so confused at last that she will end by telling lies all her life and goodness only knows what she will become!' At this point he paused for a short while and then added: 'It would be interesting to know, though, who she is and what her father is, whether he is a wealthy landowner of respectable character, or simply a right-thinking man with a fortune made in the service. Why, supposing the girl has a nice little dowry of two hundred thousand! That would certainly make her a very tasty little morsel. She might, so to say, make the happiness of a decent sort of man.' The two hundred thousand gradually assumed such an attractive shape in his mind that he began inwardly to be annoyed with himself for not having found out who the ladies were from the postilion or the driver during the confusion with the carriages. Soon, however, the sight of Sobakevich's village distracted his thoughts and made them turn to the subject that constantly occupied his mind.

The village seemed to him to be a fairly large one; two woods, a pinewood and a birchwood, lay to the right and left of it, like two wings, one of darker and the other of lighter colour; in the middle was a wooden house with a mezzanine, a red roof, and dark-grey or, more correctly, natural-coloured walls, the sort of house that is built in Russia for military settlements or German colonists. It was clear that, while it was being built, the architect was constantly in conflict with the owner's tastes. The architect was a pedant and was all in favour of symmetry, while the owner wanted comfort above all and consequently boarded up all the windows on one side and had one tiny window cut in their place, which he probably required for a dark storeroom. The pediment, too, was not quite in the centre of the house in spite of the architect's efforts, because the owner had ordered one of the columns at the side to be removed so that instead of four columns, as was planned, there were only three. The courtyard was enclosed by a strong and exceedingly thick wooden fence. The landowner was apparently greatly concerned about solidity. Beams, heavy and thick enough to last for centuries, had been used for the stables, barns, and kitchens. The peasants' cottages were also marvellously well built: there were no smoothly planed walls, no carvings or other fanciful ornaments, but everything was solidly and properly built.

Even the well was made of the strong oak usually kept for flourmills and ships. In short, whatever he looked at was firm and unshakeable in a sort of strong and clumsy fashion. As he drove up to the front steps, he noticed two faces peering out of the window almost at one and the same moment: a woman's face in a bonnet, as long and narrow as a cucumber, and a man's, round and broad as the Moldavian pumpkins, the so-called flagons, out of which balalaikas are made in Russia, light two-stringed balalaikas, the pride and joy of the smart twenty-year-old peasant lad, a dandy and a gay Lothario, winking and whistling at the white-breasted and white-throated village maidens who gather round to listen to his soft strumming. No sooner had the two faces peeped out than they vanished. A footman in a grey livery with a light blue stand-up collar came out on to the front steps and conducted Chichikov into the hall, where the master of the house was already waiting for him. On seeing the visitor, Sobakevich said abruptly: 'Please,' and led him into the inner apartments.

When Chichikov looked sideways at Sobakevich, he struck him this time as being very much like a medium-sized bear. To complete the resemblance, the frock-coat he was wearing was of exactly the colour of a bear's coat, his sleeves were long, his trousers were long, he walked flat-footedly, lurching from side to side, and was continually treading on other people's toes. His complexion was of a hot red colour, such as you find on a copper penny. There are, of course, many faces in the world over the finish of which nature has taken no great pains, has used no fine tools, such as files, gimlets, and the like, having simply gone about it in a rough and ready way: one stroke of the axe and there's a nose, another and there are the lips, the eyes gouged out with a great drill, and without smoothing it, nature thrusts it into the world saying: 'It will do!' Just such a rugged and quite marvellously rough-hewn countenance was that of Sobakevich: he held it lowered rather than erect, he never turned his neck at all and in consequence of this rigidity he rarely looked at the person he was talking to, but invariably stared either at the corner of the stove or at the door. Chichikov stole another glance at him as they passed through the dining-room: 'A bear, a regular bear!' What a strange resemblance – he was even called Mikhail Semyonovich, the name Russian peasants give to a bear. Knowing his habit of treading on people's feet, Chichikov moved his own feet very cautiously and made way for him and let him go first.

The master of the house was apparently aware of this failing of his, and at once asked: 'I haven't incommoded you, have I?' But Chichikov thanked him and said that so far he had no cause for complaint.

As he entered the drawing-room, Sobakevich pointed to an arm-chair and again said: 'Please!' Sitting down, Chichikov glanced at the walls and the pictures hanging on them. They were all portraits of gallant warriors, all of them Greek generals portrayed full-length: Mavrocordato in red trousers and uniform, with spectacles on his nose, Miaoulis, Kanaris. All these heroes had such thick calves and incredible moustaches that they sent a shiver down one's spine. Among these mighty Greeks, goodness only knows why and for what reason, was a portrait of General Bagration, lean, gaunt, with tiny flags and cannons underneath in a very narrow frame. Then followed the portrait of the Greek heroine Bobelina, whose one leg seemed to be larger than the whole body of one of those dandies who fill our drawing-rooms nowadays. The master of the house, being himself strong and healthy, seemed to have intended that his room, too, should be adorned with strong and healthy people. Near Bobe-lina, right beside the window, hung a cage out of which peered a thrush of a dark colour speckled with white who was also very much like Sobakevich. The host and his guest had barely been silent for two minutes, when the drawing-room door opened and in came the lady of the house, a very tall woman in a cap with home-dyed ribbons. She entered looking very dignified and holding her head as erect as a palm-tree.

'This is my Feoduliya Ivanovna,' said Sobakevich.

Chichikov went up to kiss Feoduliya Ivanovna's hand which she almost thrust at his lips. As he did so, he had an opportunity of noticing that her hands had been washed in cucumber brine.

'Let me introduce you, my love,' Sobakevich went on. 'Pavel Ivanovich Chichikov. I had the honour of making his acquaintance at the governor's and the postmaster's.'

Mrs Sobakevich asked him to sit down, also saying: 'Please,' motioning her head like actresses in the parts of queens. Then she sat down on the sofa, wrapped her merino shawl round her, and sat without moving an eye or an eyebrow.

Chichikov again lifted up his eyes and again saw Kanaris with his thick calves and endless moustaches, Bobelina, and the thrush in the cage.

For almost five minutes they all remained silent. The only sound in the room was the tapping of the thrush's beak on the wood of the cage as he fished for grains on the bottom of it. Chichikov once more glanced round the room at everything in it – everything was solid and clumsy to the last degree and everything had a strange kind of resemblance to the master of the house; in a corner of the drawing-room stood a paunchy walnut bureau on four ridiculous legs – a regular bear! The table, the armchairs, the chairs, all of them were of the most heavy and most uncomfortable shape, in short, every object, every chair, seemed to be saying: 'I'm a Sobakevich too!' or 'I, too, am very like Sobakevich!'

'We were talking about you at Ivan Grigoryevich's, I mean, the President of the Court of Justice,' said Chichikov at last, seeing that no one had any intention of starting the conversation. 'Last Thursday it was. We spent a very pleasant evening there.'

'I'm afraid,' replied Sobakevich, 'I wasn't at the president's that day.'

'A splendid man.'

'Who's that?' said Sobakevich, staring at the corner of the stove.

'The president.'

'Well, I suppose you must have imagined it: he may be a free-mason, but he's the biggest fool on earth.'

Chichikov was a little taken aback by this rather harsh characterization, but recovering himself after a little while he went on:

'Of course, every man has his weakness, but you must admit that the governor is a most delightful person.'

'The governor a delightful person?'

'Yes. Don't you think so?'

'He's the biggest brigand on earth!'

'The governor a brigand?' said Chichikov, who was entirely at a loss to understand how a governor could be a brigand. 'I must say,' he went on, 'I'd never have thought it. His behaviour, though, if you don't mind my saying so, does not suggest anything of the kind: on the contrary, there's a great deal of softness in him.' And as proof of his assertion, he even mentioned the purses embroidered by the governor's own hands and spoke appreciatively of the amiable expression of his face.

'He has the face of a brigand too!' said Sobakevich. 'Put a knife in his hand and let him loose on the highway and he'll cut your throat.

Cut your throat for a few coppers, he will. He and the vice-governor make a fine pair. Gog and Magog, that's what they are.'

'He isn't on good terms with them,' Chichikov thought to himself. 'I'd better talk to him about the chief of police. I believe he's a friend of his.'

'For my part,' he said, 'I must confess that I liked the chief of police best of all. He's such a straightforward, open character. There's something warm-hearted in his face.'

'A swindler!' said Sobakevich very coolly. 'He'll betray you and cheat you and then have dinner with you! I know them all! They're all rogues. The whole town is like that: one rogue sits on another rogue and uses a third rogue for a whip. They're all Judases. There's only one decent man among them, the public prosecutor, and even he, to tell the truth, is a dirty swine.'

After these laudatory, though somewhat brief, biographies, Chichikov realized that it would be a waste of time to mention any other officials and he remembered that Sobakevich did not like speaking well of anyone.

'Well, my love, I suppose we'd better go in to dinner,' said Mrs Sobakevich to her husband.

'Please!' said Sobakevich.

Whereupon the host and his guest went up to the table which was laid with snacks and, as is the custom, drank a glass of vodka each and had some snacks as is done throughout the whole length and breadth of Russia, in the towns as well as the villages, that is to say, they tasted all sorts of salt pickles and other stimulating delicacies and then proceeded to the dining-room, the mistress of the house walking in front of them like a staid goose. The small table was laid for four. The fourth place was very soon taken by a lady, it was difficult to say for certain whether it was a married woman or a girl, a relative, a housekeeper, or simply someone living in the house: a thing without a cap, about thirty years of age, in a brightly coloured kerchief. There are persons who exist in the world not as objects, but as extraneous specks or spots on an object. They sit in the same place, they hold their heads in the same way, you are almost tempted to take them for pieces of furniture and you cannot help thinking that their lips have never uttered a word; but somewhere in the maids' workroom or in the pantry – oho – ho!

'The cabbage soup is very good today, my dear,' said Sobakevich, after swallowing a spoonful of cabbage soup and helping himself to an enormous portion of the famous dish which is served with cabbage soup and consists of a sheep's stomach stuffed with buckwheat, brains, and sheep's trotters. 'You won't find a dish like this in town,' he went on, turning to Chichikov. 'There they serve you with the devil only knows what!'

'The governor, however, doesn't keep a bad table,' said Chichikov.

'But do you know what it is all made of? You wouldn't eat it, if you knew.'

'I don't know what it's made of. I'm afraid I'm no judge of that, but the pork chops and the boiled fish were excellent.'

'You just imagined it. You see, I know what they buy in the market. That scoundrel of a cook of theirs, the one who's been trained by a Frenchman, he'd buy a cat, skin it, and serve it up for a hare.'

'Why, what horrible things you say,' said Mrs Sobakevich.

'Well, my love, that's the way they do things and I'm not to blame for it, am I? All the scraps that our Akulka throws away, if you don't mind my mentioning it, into the refuse bin, they put into the soup. Yes, into the soup. In it goes!'

'You will talk about such things at table, dear,' Mrs Sobakevich protested again.

'Well, my love,' said Sobakevich, 'it isn't as if I were doing it myself, is it? But I tell you straight I'd refuse to eat such filth. Coat a frog all over with sugar and I won't put it into my mouth. And I wouldn't touch oysters either: I know what oysters are like. Do help yourself to some mutton,' he went on, addressing Chichikov. 'It's a saddle of mutton with buckwheat stuffing! This is not the sort of fricassee they make in gentlemen's kitchens out of mutton which has been lying about in the market-place for four days. That's all been invented by the French and German doctors. I'd have 'em all hanged for it, every man Jack of them! It's they who've invented dieting and the starvation cure! Because they have got weak German constitutions, they imagine that they can cope with a Russian stomach! No, sir, it's all wrong. It's all their silly inventions, it's all …' Here Sobakevich shook his head angrily. 'They talk of enlightenment, enlightenment, and this enlightenment is just a lot of – balderdash! I'd have used another expression, but it would be improper at table. It's not like that in my house. If I have pork, then put the whole pig on the table, if it's mutton, then fetch the whole sheep, if it's goose, the whole goose!

I'd rather eat only two dishes, but have a good helping of each, just as much as I like.'

Sobakevich confirmed this in practice: he plumped half a saddle of mutton on his plate, ate it all, gnawing it and sucking it to the very last bone.

'Yes,' thought Chichikov, 'this fellow certainly knows what's good for him.'

'No, sir, it's not like that in my house,' said Sobakevich, wiping his hands on a napkin. 'I don't do things like some Plyushkin: he's got eight hundred souls and he lives and eats worse than my shepherd.'

'Who is this Plyushkin?' asked Chichikov.

'A rogue,' replied Sobakevich. 'You can't imagine the sort of miser he is. Convicts in prison live better than he: he's starved all his household serfs to death.'

'Has he now?' Chichikov exclaimed with great interest. 'And do you actually mean that his serfs have died in large numbers?'

'They die like flies.'

'Like flies! And may I ask how far he lives from here?'

'About four miles.'

'Four miles!' exclaimed Chichikov and he even felt his heart beginning to beat a little faster. 'But is it to the right or to the left as one drives out of your gates?'

'I wouldn't advise you even to find the way to that dirty dog!' said Sobakevich. 'It would be more pardonable to visit a house of ill fame than to visit him.'

'Oh, I didn't ask for any special reason, but simply because I'm interested to know all sorts of places,' was Chichikov's reply.

The saddle of mutton was followed by curd cheesecakes, each one of which was much larger than a plate, then by a turkey as big as a calf, stuffed with all sorts of good things: eggs, rice, liver, and goodness knows what other things that lie heavy on the stomach. With this the dinner came to an end; but when they had got up from the table, Chichikov felt about three stones heavier. They went into the drawing-room where a saucer of preserves was already waiting for them – no pears, no plums, no berries – and neither the host nor his guest touched it. The mistress of the house went out of the room to put some more preserves on other saucers. Taking advantage of her absence, Chichikov turned to Sobakevich who, lying in an armchair, was merely grunting after such an ample meal, uttering some inarticulate sounds, crossing himself, and putting his hand over his mouth every minute. Chichikov addressed him with these words:

'I'd like to talk to you about a little business matter.'

'Here's some more preserves,' said the lady of the house, returning with a saucer. 'It's horse-radish cooked in honey.'

'We'll have some of it later,' said Sobakevich. 'You go to your room now and Mr Chichikov and I will take off our coats and have a little nap.'

The lady of the house expressed her readiness to send for feather-beds and pillows, but Sobakevich said: 'Don't bother, we'll have our rest in our armchairs,' and she left the room.

Sobakevich bent his head slightly, preparing to hear what the business might be.

Chichikov began somewhat remotely. He touched upon the Russian empire in general, spoke with great appreciation of its vast extent, said that even the ancient Roman empire was not so large and that foreigners were quite right in being amazed at it. ... Sobakevich went on listening to him with his head bent low. And furthermore that, according to the existing state of affairs of this empire, than which there is no equal in fame, souls on the census list who were no longer among the living were still registered, as though they were alive, till the next census was taken, so as not to impose too heavy a burden on government offices by a multitude of petty and unimportant inquiries and so increase the complexity of an already complex administrative machinery. (Sobakevich was still listening with bowed head.) And that, on the other hand, while this measure was absolutely justified, it was to a certain extent imposing an unfair burden upon many landowners, compelling them to pay taxes as though for living serfs, and that, feeling a personal respect for Sobakevich, he was partly – he was prepared partly to relieve him of his heavy obligation. About the main subject of his remarks, Chichikov expressed himself very cautiously. He never spoke of the souls as dead, but always as non-existent.

Sobakevich still listened to him as before with a bowed head and without a trace of anything resembling an expression appearing on his face. It seemed as though his body had no soul at all, or that if it had, it was not where it ought to have been but, as with the immortal sorcerer Kashchey, it was somewhere beyond the mountains and covered with so thick a shell that whatever stirred at the bottom of it produced not the slighest movement on the surface.

'And so …?' said Chichikov, waiting not without some excitement for an answer.

'You want dead souls?' asked Sobakevich very simply, without the slightest surprise, as though they had been talking about corn.

'Yes,' replied Chichikov, and again he softened the expression by adding: 'Non–existent ones.'

'I daresay I can find some,' said Sobakevich. 'Why not?'

'And I suppose if you do find some, you will no doubt be – er – glad to get rid of them, won't you?'

'Of course, I'm quite ready to sell them,' said Sobakevich, raising his head a little, and realizing that the purchaser would no doubt get some profit out of the transaction.

'Damn it,' thought Chichikov to himself, 'he's selling them before I have even hinted that I'd like to buy them!' And he said aloud:

'And what might your price be? Though, mind you, it's a sort of merchandise that – er – it's strange to speak of the price. …'

'Well, not to ask you too much, a hundred roubles apiece,' said Sobakevich.

'A hundred!' cried Chichikov, opening his mouth and staring at him, as though he were not sure whether he had misheard him or whether Sobakevich's tongue, being so heavy, had turned the wrong way and he had blurted out one word instead of another.

'Why, is that too dear for you?' asked Sobakevich, and then added: 'And what may your price be?'

'My price! I'm afraid we must be making some mistake or have forgotten what we're talking about. For my part, and laying my hand on my heart, I think that eighty copecks a soul is a very fair price.'

'Good Lord, eighty copecks!'

'Well, in my opinion, and I'm trying to be as fair as can be, they are not worth more.'

'But I'm not selling you bast shoes.'

'But you must admit that they are not men, either.'

'Do you really think you'd find anyone fool enough to sell you a registered soul for eighty copecks?'

'But, my dear sir, why do you call them registered? They've been dead a long time. Nothing is left of them but a mere impalpable sound. However, not to go too deeply into the matter, I'll give you a rouble and a half, but I can offer you no more.'

'You ought to be ashamed to mention such a sum! You're bargaining. Tell me your real price.'

'I can't, my dear sir. On my conscience I can't. What can't be done, can't be done,' Chichikov was saying; he added another half rouble, however.

'Why are you so stingy?' said Sobakevich. 'It really isn't dear. A rogue would cheat you, sell you some rubbish instead of souls. Mine are as sound as a bell, all first-class: if not a craftsman, then a fine, sturdy peasant. Now, just have a look. Take Mikheyev, the wheelwright, for instance. He never made a carriage that wasn't on springs. And it wasn't like some of Moscow workmanship, made to last an hour. No, sir, it was all solid throughout and he'd do all the upholstery and varnishing himself!'

Chichikov was about to open his mouth to point out that Mikheyev had been dead for some time, but Sobakevich, as they say, had been carried away by his own eloquence, though goodness only knows where he got this unceasing flow of words from.

'And Stepan Probka, the carpenter. I'll stake my life you'd never find another peasant like him. Why, he was as strong as a horse. If he'd served in the guards goodness only knows what they'd have given him. Over seven feet tall he was!'

Chichikov was again about to remark that Probka had long been dead, but Sobakevich, it seems, was now carried away by his enthusiasm: such torrents of speech flowed from him that one had no choice but to listen.

'Milushkin, the bricklayer, could build a stove in any house you like. Then there was Maxim Telyatnikov, the cobbler: he had only to put the awl through the leather and a pair of boots was ready, and what boots! And he never took a drop of liquor. Not a drop! And what about Yeremey Sorokoplyokhin! Why, he was worth the whole bunch of them. Used to trade in Moscow and paid me as much as five hundred roubles in labour exemption tax alone. That's the sort of people they are. That's not what a Plyushkin would sell you.'

'But,' said Chichikov at last, amazed at such an abundant flood of words to which there seemed to be no end, 'why are you enumerating all their qualifications? They're no good at all now, you know.

They're all dead. You can't even prop up a fence with a dead body, as the proverb has it.'

'Why, of course they're dead,' said Sobakevich, as though thinking better of it and remembering that they really were dead, and then he added: 'Though, mind you, who among the men now living are any good? What sort of men are they? They're flies, not men.'

'Still they exist, whereas the others are just a figment of the imagination.'

'Why no, sir! They're not a figment of the imagination. Let me tell you you'll never find a man like Mikheyev today. A regular machine of a man, so huge that he couldn't have walked into this room. No, sir. He was no figment of the imagination! He had more strength in his huge shoulders than a horse. I'd like to know in what other place you could find a figment of the imagination like that.'

The last words he uttered addressing the portraits of Bagration and Kolokotroni, as usually happens with people who are talking when for some unknown reason one of them suddenly addresses himself not to the person for whom his words are meant, but to some third person who happens to be present, even a total stranger from whom he knows perfectly well he will get neither an answer nor an opinion nor a confirmation, but on whom he will nevertheless fix his eyes as though inviting him to be an arbitrator; and the stranger, a little embarrassed at first, does not know whether to answer him about something of which he has heard nothing or whether to remain for a few minutes out of politeness and then walk away.

'No, I can't give you more than two roubles,' said Chichikov.

'Look here, sir, I don't want you to think I'm asking too much or won't show you any consideration. You can therefore have them for seventy-five roubles a soul to be paid in notes, and believe me I'm only doing it out of friendship.'

'What does he think I am – a fool?' Chichikov thought to himself, and he added aloud:

'I do think the whole thing's rather odd. I have a feeling as though we are taking part in some theatrical performance, a comedy or something. I simply can't explain it to myself otherwise. .... I think you are a very intelligent man and you show every sign of being an educated one. Why, the whole thing is not worth talking about! What are they worth? Who wants them?'

'But you are buying them, which means that they are wanted.'

At this point Chichikov bit his lip and could think of no appropriate answer. He was beginning to say something about some sort of private family circumstances, but Sobakevich answered quite simply:

'I have no wish to know anything about your circumstances. I do not interfere in family affairs. That's your business. You want dead souls, I'm selling them to you. And you'll be sorry if you don't buy them.'

'Two roubles,' said Chichikov.

'Really, my dear sir, you're just like the magpie in the proverb who keeps repeating one and the same thing over and over again. You've got those two roubles on the brain and you can't get rid of them. Give me your real price.'

'Oh well, damn him,' Chichikov thought to himself. 'I'll offer the cur another half rouble and I hope it chokes him.'

'Very well, I'll add another half rouble.'

'Very well, and I'll give you my final word, too: fifty roubles! It's really selling at a loss, for you wouldn't buy such fine fellows more cheaply anywhere.'

'What a *kulak!*' Chichikov said to himself, and then said aloud with some vexation:

'Honestly, you talk as if we were discussing some serious business. Why, I could get them for nothing anywhere else. I'm sure anyone else would be glad to have them off their hands just to get rid of them. Only a fool would want to keep them and go on paying the tax on them!'

'But, you know, my dear sir, that transactions of this kind, and I say this strictly between ourselves as one friend to another, are not always permissible, and were I or someone else to mention it, such a man would never inspire any confidence with regard to contracts or, indeed, any profitable commercial deal.'

'So that's what he's driving at, the blackguard,' thought Chichikov, and at once said with an air of the utmost unconcern:

'Just as you like. I'm not buying them out of any necessity as you think, but simply because it's the sort of thing that appeals to me. If you won't take two and a half roubles – good-bye.'

'There's no budging him,' thought Sobakevich. 'He's stubborn!'

'Oh, well, give me thirty and you can have 'em!'

'No, I can see you don't want to sell them – good-bye!'

'Now, look here, look here!' said Sobakevich without letting go of his hand and treading on his foot, for our hero had forgotten to exercise due care and had, as a punishment, to draw in his breath and jump about on one leg.

'I'm so sorry. I seem to have incommoded you. Please sit down. Please.'

And he made him sit down in an armchair and he did it not without a certain dexterity, like a bear who has been thoroughly trained and can turn somersaults and perform all sorts of tricks when he is asked such questions as : 'Come now, Misha, show us how peasant women steam themselves in the bath-house,' or 'How do little children steal peas, Misha?'

'I'm sorry, but I'm wasting my time here and I'm afraid I am in a hurry.'

'Do stay a little longer, my dear sir. I'm going to say something you'd like in a moment.' Here Sobakevich sat down beside him and whispered in his ear, as though it were a secret, 'Will you accept a quarter?'

'You mean twenty-five roubles? Not a hope. Wouldn't even give you a quarter of a quarter. Not a penny more.'

Sobakevich was silent. Chichikov too was silent. The silence lasted for about two minutes. Bagration with his aquiline nose gazed down from the wall with the greatest attention at this transaction.

'What then is your final price?' Sobakevich said at last.

'Two and a half.'

'Really, my dear sir, your soul's like a boiled turnip. You might at least offer me three roubles.'

'I'm sorry, I can't.'

'Oh well, I can see there's nothing to be done with you. All right. It's a loss, but there – I'm just like a dog. I can't help wanting to make a fellow creature happy. I expect you'd want me to make out a deed of purchase so that everything should be in order, wouldn't you?'

'Of course.'

'I thought so. I suppose I shall have to go to town in that case.'

So the deal was settled. They both decided to be in the town next day to complete the deed of purchase. Chichikov asked for a list of the peasants. Sobakevich readily agreed, went to his bureau at once, and began writing out with his own hand not only their names, but also a testimonial of their remarkable qualities.

Chichikov, having nothing to do and finding himself behind Sobakevich, amused himself by scrutinizing his ample frame. Looking at his back, broad as a thick-set Vyatka horse, and at his legs, which looked like the iron posts stuck at the side of pavements, he could not help exclaiming inwardly: 'Dear me, God has been good to you. It's just as the saying is: badly cut but strongly sewn! Were you born such a bear, or have you been turned into a bear by your life in the wilds, by the work on the land, by your dealings with the peasants, and is it through all this that you've become what they call a fist of a man, a *kulak*? But no, I think that you would be just the same even if you had had a fashionable education, had been let loose in society and lived in Petersburg instead of in the wilds. The only difference is that now you gorge yourself on half a saddle of mutton with buckwheat stuffing and follow it up with a curd cake the size of a plate, while in Petersburg you'd have eaten some cutlets with truffles. And now, you have peasants in your power: you get on well with them and, of course, you won't maltreat them because they're yours, and you'd be worse off if you did; while in Petersburg you'd have had civil servants under you whom you would occasionally give a good dressing down, for you would have grasped the fact that they were not your serfs; or you would have robbed the treasury. No, if a man's a *kulak*, you can never make him unclench his fist! For if he were to unclench one or two fingers, it would make it all the worse. If he did acquire a superficial knowledge of some branch of science, he would afterwards, as soon as he occupied a prominent position, make those who really knew something of that branch of science feel it. And maybe he would say afterwards: "Let me just show them the stuff I'm made of!", and invent so wise a regulation that many people would be sorry they were ever born. ... Oh, if all men were *kulaks!* ...'

'The list is ready,' said Sobakevich, turning round.

'Ready? May I have it?'

He ran his eyes over it and was astonished at its accuracy and precision: not only were the trade, the calling, the age, and the family circumstances minutely entered, but there were even special notes in the margin as to their conduct and sobriety; in short, it was a pleasure to look at it.

'And now, if you don't mind, let me have an advance, please,' said Sobakevich.

'What do you want an advance for? I'll let you have the money in town in a lump sum.'

'It's usual, you know,' replied Sobakevich.

'I don't know if I can give it to you. I haven't brought enough money with me. Oh well, I've got ten roubles.'

'Ten roubles? Give me fifty at least.'

Chichikov was about to protest that he hadn't got it, but Sobakevich declared with such conviction that he had the money that he took out another note, saying: 'Here's another fifteen roubles for you, making twenty-five roubles in all. Please let me have a receipt.'

'What do you want a receipt for?'

'It's always better to have a receipt. Who knows, anything might happen.'

'All right. Let me have the money first!'

'The money? Here it is in my hand! As soon as you write out the receipt you'll have it.'

'But, my dear sir, I can't write a receipt, can I? I must see the money first.'

Chichikov let the money drop out of his hand for Sobakevich, who, coming up to the table and covering the notes with his left hand, with his other wrote on a scrap of paper that an advance of twenty-five roubles in government notes on the purchase of souls had been paid in full. After writing out the receipt, he examined the notes once more.

'This note is an old one,' he said, holding one of them up to the light. 'A bit torn, but there – it doesn't matter between friends, does it?'

'A *kulak*, a *kulak*,' Chichikov thought to himself, 'and a brute into the bargain.'

'You wouldn't be wanting any of the female sex, would you?'

'No, thank you.'

'I wouldn't charge you so much for them: only a rouble apiece, for our friendship's sake.'

'No, thank you, I don't want females.'

'Well, if you don't we needn't discuss it, need we? There's no accounting for taste: one man loves the priest and another the priest's wife, as the proverb says.'

'I'd also like to ask you to keep this transaction strictly between ourselves,' Chichikov said as he was taking leave.

'Why, of course, it's no use bringing a third party into it, is it? What takes place between good friends should remain between them as a true token of their mutual friendship. Good-bye, sir. Thank you for your visit. Don't forget to call on me again. If you have an hour to spare come and have dinner with us and pass the time of day. Perhaps we may be able to be of service to each other again one day.'

'Not if I can help it,' thought Chichikov to himself as he got into his carriage. 'Extorted two and a half roubles a dead soul from me, the damned *kulak!*'

He was displeased with Sobakevich's behaviour. After all, say what you like, he was an acquaintance of his, they had met at the governor's and at the house of the chief of police, and yet he had treated him as a complete stranger and had taken money for a lot of rubbish. When the carriage had driven out of the yard, he looked back and saw that Sobakevich was still standing on the steps, apparently watching to see which way his guest was going.

'The scoundrel! Still standing there!' he muttered through his teeth and he told Selifan to turn towards the peasants' cottages and drive away so that the carriage could not be seen from the mansion. He wanted to pay a visit to Plyushkin whose serfs, according to Sobakevich, were dying like flies, but he did not want Sobakevich to know about it. When the carriage had reached the end of the village he beckoned to the first peasant he saw, who was carrying on his shoulders a large log he had picked up somewhere on the way and, like some indefatigable ant, was dragging it to his cottage.

'Hey there, grey-beard, how do I get to Plyushkin's from here without passing your master's house?'

The peasant seemed to be a little perplexed by the question.

'Don't you know?'

'No, sir, I don't.'

'Well, well! Grey hairs in your beard, too! Don't you know the miser Plyushkin, the one who feeds his peasants badly?'

'Oh, the — in tatters!' cried the peasant.

He had added a noun before the words 'in tatters', and a very apt one, too, but one that cannot be used in polite conversation, and so we omit it. However, we should not be wrong in assuming that it was a very neat expression because although the peasant had long been out of sight and they had covered many miles, Chichikov was still chuckling to himself as he sat in his carriage. The Russian common people are very fond of strong expressions! And if they do bestow a nickname on someone, it will stick to him all through his life and will pass on to posterity, he will carry it with him into the service and into retirement and to Petersburg and to the ends of the earth. And however much he may try to enoble his nickname, even if he may get the writing fraternity for a consideration to trace it back to an ancient, princely house, nothing will be of any use: like the loud cawing of a crow it will raise its own croaking voice and proclaim clearly where the bird has flown from. A neatly uttered word is like a word that has been written down and that, according to the Russian proverb, cannot be cut out with an axe. And how wonderfully apt are the sayings that come out of the depths of Russia where there are neither Germans nor Finns nor any other foreign tribes, but everything is indigenous, living and ready Russian wit, which does not fumble for a word or brood over it like a sitting hen, but comes out with it at once and sticks it on at once to be carried like a passport all one's life, and there is no need to add a description of your nose or your lips – you have been drawn from head to foot with one stroke!

Just as a countless multitude of churches and monasteries with their cupolas, domes, and crosses is scattered all over holy, pious Russia, so a countless multitude of tribes, generations, peoples appears in colourful crowds, rushing hither and thither over the face of the earth. And each of these peoples, bearing within itself the pledge of its powers, full of its own creative and spiritual faculties and of its own visibly marked idiosyncrasies and other divine gifts, has distinguished itself in its own original fashion by its own word, which, whatever the subject it describes, reflects in its description a part of its own character. A knowledge of the heart and a wise comprehension of life will find expression in the sayings of a Briton; the Frenchman's short-lived phrase will flash like a gay dandy and then be lost for ever; the German will invent his involved, thinly intellectual sayings which are not understood by everyone; but there is not a word that is so sweeping, so vivid, none that bursts from the very heart, that bubbles and is tremulous with life, as a neatly uttered Russian word.

Chapter 6

BEFORE, long ago, in the days of my youth, in the days of my childhood, which have passed away like a dream never to return, I felt happy whenever I happened to drive up for the first time to an unfamiliar place: it mattered not whether it was a little hamlet, a poor little provincial town, or a large village, or some suburb, the inquisitive eyes of a child found a great deal of interest there. Every building, everything that bore the mark of some noticeable peculiarity – everything made me pause in amazement. Whether it was a brick government building of an all too familiar architecture with half of its frontage covered with blind windows, standing incongruously all alone among a mass of rough-hewn, timbered one-storied artisan dwellings, or a round regular cupola covered with sheets of galvanized iron, rising above the snowy whitewashed new church, or a market-place, or some provincial dandy who happened to be taking a stroll in the centre of the town – nothing escaped my fresh, alert attention, and thrusting my nose out of my travelling cart, I gazed at the cut of some coat I had never seen before or at the wooden chests of nails, or sulphur whose yellow colour I could discern from a distance, of raisins and of soap, glimpses of which I caught for a moment through the door of some grocer's shop together with jars of dried-up Moscow sweets; I stared, too, at some infantry officer, walking by himself, who had been cast into this dull provincial hole from goodness only knows what province, or at a merchant in his close-fitting, pleated Siberian coat, driving past in a trap at a spanking pace, and I was carried away in my thoughts after them, into their poor lives. If some district official happened to pass by, I immediately began to wonder where he was going, whether it was to a party given by a colleague of his, or straight home to sit on the front steps of his house for half an hour till darkness had fallen, and then sit down to an early supper with his mother, his wife, his wife's sister, and the rest of his family, and I tried to imagine what they would be talking about, while a serf-girl with her coin necklace or a serf-boy in his thick tunic brought in a tallow candle in an ancient candlestick after the soup. Whenever

I drove up to the village of some landowner, I would gaze with curiosity at the tall, narrow, wooden belfry, or at the dark, vast, old wooden church. The red roof and the white chimneys of the manor house beckoned invitingly to me from a distance through the green foliage of the trees, and I waited impatiently for the orchards which surrounded it to fall back on either side so that I might get a full view of its, in those days, alas, far from vulgar exterior; and from its appearance I tried to guess what sort of a man the landowner was, whether he was stout, and whether he had sons or a whole bevy of daughters, six in all, with loud, happy, girlish laughter, and their games, and the youngest sister, of course, the most beautiful of them all, and whether they had black eyes, and whether he was a jovial fellow himself or as gloomy as the last days of September, looking perpetually at the calendar and talking everlastingly about his rye and wheat, a subject so boring to young people.

Now it is with indifference that I drive up to every unknown village and it is with indifference that I gaze at its vulgar exterior; there is a cold look in my eyes and I feel uncomfortable, and I am amused no more, and what in former years would have awakened a lively interest in my face, laughter, and an uninterrupted flow of words, now slips by me without notice and my motionless lips preserve an apathetic silence. Oh, my youth! Oh, my freshness!

While Chichikov was thinking to himself and inwardly chuckling at the nickname the peasants had given Plyushkin, he did not notice that he had driven into the middle of a spacious village with a great number of peasants' cottages and streets. Soon, however, a tremendous jolt caused by a roadway made of logs, compared to which the town cobbles were as nothing, made him sit up and take notice. These logs went up and down like the keys of a piano, and the traveller who took no care got either a bump on the back of his head or a bruise on his forehead, or it might even happen that he would bite the tip of his tongue very painfully. Chichikov noticed some peculiar signs of decay about all these village buildings: the beams of the cottages were old and dark; many roofs let in the air like sieves; on some nothing was left but the ridge pole on the top and the rib-like poles at the sides. It looked as though the owners themselves had stripped them of the laths and shingles, arguing, and, of course, quite rightly, that as cottages cannot be roofed in the rain and as in fine weather it does not rain anyhow, there was no need to coddle oneself in them when there is plenty of room in the pub and on the highway – wherever one chose, in fact. The windows in the cottages had no panes, some of them were stopped up with a rag or an old coat; the little balconies with railings which, for some incomprehensible reason, are built below the roofs on some Russian cottages, had all gone lop-sided and had grown grimy without even looking picturesque. In many places behind the cottages huge stacks of corn stretched row after row, and it was quite clear that they must have been standing there for years; they resembled in colour an old, badly baked brick and all kinds of weeds were growing on top of them and bushes sprouted at the side. The corn evidently belonged to the landowner. Behind the stacks of corn and the dilapidated roofs two village churches rose in the air, standing side by side. Chichikov caught sight of them as the carriage turned in one direction or another, first to the right and then to the left: one was wooden and deserted and the other of brick with stained and cracked yellow walls. Then the landowner's mansion came into view, at first in parts and then the whole of it, where the chain of cottages was broken and gave place to an open space made by a kitchen garden or a cabbage patch surrounded by a low, and in places broken, fence. This strange castle looked like a decrepit invalid; it was so long, so immensely long. In places it was of one story and in others of two; on its dark roof, which did not everywhere protect it from old age, there were two belvederes facing each other, both of them lop-sided and deprived of the paint that had once covered them. The walls of the house showed in places the bare laths under the plaster and had evidently suffered a great deal from all kinds of intemperate weather, rains, gales, and the changes of autumn. Only two of the windows were uncovered, the rest were shuttered or even boarded up. Even the two windows were half-blind; one of them had a triangular patch of dark-blue sugar paper stuck on it.

A large, old garden that stretched at the back of the house and came out behind the village and then, overgrown and neglected, lost itself in the fields, seemed the one refreshing feature of the large village and was the only thing that was truly picturesque in its wild beauty. The tangled tops of the trees spreading out in uncontrolled freedom lay in green clouds and irregular canopies of trembling foliage against the horizon. The gigantic white trunk of a birch-tree, its top snapped off by a gale or a thunderstorm, rose up from this green jungle and stood up in the air like a regular, round, shining marble column; the slanting, jagged top, in which it ended instead of a capital, looked dark against the snowy whiteness of its trunk like a cap or a black bird. Hops smothered the bushes of elder, mountain-ash, and hazel below and, running along the whole top of the palisade, finally climbed upwards and twined round half of the broken birch-tree. Having reached the middle of the tree, they hung down and were already beginning to twist round the tops of other trees or were suspended in the air, their delicate, clinging tendrils twisted into rings and swaying lightly in the breeze. Here and there the green thickets, lighted up by the sun, fell apart and revealed an unlit chasm between them, yawning like the open mouth of some huge wild animal; it was plunged in shadow and in its dark depths could be dimly discerned: a narrow path disappearing in the distance, broken-down railings, a tumbledown summer-house, a decaying willow trunk, full of holes, and from behind the willow-tree a dense grey caragana thrust out its thick stubble of twigs and leaves, tangled and intertwined and withered from growing in this terrible thicket; and, finally, the young branch of a maple-tree, stretching sideways its green claw-like leaves, under one of which a shaft of sunlight suddenly transformed it, goodness only knows how, into a transparent, fiery leaf, gleaming wonderfully in that dense darkness. On one side, at the very edge of the garden, a few tall aspens growing about the level of the other trees bore enormous rooks' nests on their tremulous tops. Broken, but not entirely severed, branches hung down from some of them together with their withered leaves. In short, it was all beautiful, as neither nature nor art could contrive, but as only happens when they unite together, when nature's chisel puts its final touch to the often unintelligently heaped up labour of man, relieves the heavy masses, destroys the all too crudely palpable symmetry and the clumsily conceived gaps through which the unconcealed plan reveals itself so nakedly, and imparts a wonderful warmth to everything that has been created by the cold and carefully measured neatness and accuracy of human reason.

After driving round one or two corners, our hero found himself at last in front of the house which now looked even drearier. A green mould covered the rotting wood of the fence and of the gates. The yard was crowded with buildings such as the servants' cottages, barns, cellars used as storehouses, and they were all quite obviously falling into decay; beside them, on the right and on the left, were gates leading to other yards. Everything seemed to show that once upon a time a large farming industry had gone on here and that today everything appeared desolate. There was nothing to relieve the scene – no opening doors, no servants coming out, no animated hustle and bustle of a household. Only the main gates were open and that, too, only because a peasant had just driven through with a loaded cart covered with matting, and he seemed to have appeared as though expressly for the purpose of bringing some life into the dead place; at other times they were locked, for a huge padlock hung in the iron staple. At one of the buildings Chichikov soon noticed some strange figure engaged in an argument with the peasant who had arrived in the cart. For a long time he could not make out whether the figure was that of a man or a woman. Its clothes were quite nondescript, very much like a woman's dressing-gown; on its head was a cap such as is worn by serf-women in the country; only the voice seemed a little too husky for a woman. 'Oh, it's a woman,' he thought to himself and at once added, 'Oh, no, it can't be!' and, at last, looking at it more closely, he said, 'Of course, it's a woman!' The figure, for its part, was also staring intently at him. It seemed as though a visitor were an unusual thing for it, for it scrutinized not only him, but also Selifan and the horses from tail to head. From the fact that a bunch of keys was hanging from its belt and that it scolded the peasant in rather abusive language, Chichikov concluded that it must be the housekeeper.

'I say, my good woman,' he said, getting out of the carriage, 'is your master –?'

'He's not at home,' interrupted the housekeeper, without waiting for him to finish the question and then added a moment later: 'What do you want?'

'I have business.'

'Go in, please,' said the housekeeper, turning away and displaying a back covered in flour and a large tear in the skirt.

He stepped into a dark, wide entrance hall from which a cold breeze was blowing as though from a cellar. From the hall he got into a room which was also dark and which was only barely lit by a light coming from a big crack at the bottom of the door. Opening this door, he at last found himself in the light, and was amazed at the disorder which confronted him. It looked as though they were having a spring-cleaning in the house and that all the furniture were piled up in this room. There was even a broken chair on one of the tables and next to it a clock with a stationary pendulum on which a spider had already spun its web. Next to it stood a cupboard leaning sideways against the wall with old silver decanters and china in it. On the bureau, inlaid with a mosaic of mother-of-pearl which had fallen out in places, leaving brown grooves filled with glue, lay a large number of all sorts of things: a heap of closely written scraps of paper, covered with a marble egg-shaped paperweight, green with age, some kind of ancient book in a leather binding with a red edge, a dried up lemon no larger than a hazel nut, a broken off arm of a chair, a wine-glass containing some liquid and three flies, covered with an envelope, a bit of sealing wax, a rag that had been picked up somewhere, two ink-stained quills, dried up as though from consumption, a toothpick yellow with age, which the master must have used to pick his teeth with before the French occupation of Moscow.

Several pictures were hung on the walls very close together and without any attempt at order: a long engraving, yellow with age and without a glass, depicting some battle with huge drums, yelling soldiers in three-cornered hats, and drowning horses, put in a mahogany frame with thin strips of bronze and bronze discs at the corners. Next to it, taking up almost half the wall, was an enormous blackened oil painting, depicting flowers, fruit, a cut water melon, a boar's head, and a duck with his head hanging down. From the middle of the ceiling hung a chandelier in a linen cover, so thick with dust that it looked like the cocoon of a silkworm. On the floor in a corner of the room lay a heap of coarser articles unworthy to be placed on a table. It was difficult to make out exactly what was in the heap, for it was so thickly covered with dust that the hands of anyone who touched it began to look like gloves; the most conspicuous objects in the heap were a piece of a broken wooden spade and the old sole of a boot. It would have been quite impossible to say that a living creature was inhabiting this room, if an old threadbare skull-cap lying on the table had not indicated his existence. While Chichikov was examining these strange objects, a side door opened and the same housekeeper he had met in the yard walked in. But now he saw that it was a steward rather than a housekeeper: at least a housekeeper did not shave, while this person did, though apparently very rarely, because his entire chin with the lower parts of his cheeks resembled the currycombs made of wire with which horses are groomed in a stable.

Chichikov, assuming a questioning expression, waited impatiently for the steward to speak. The steward, for his part, waited to see what Chichikov had to say to him. At last, astonished at such strange perplexity, Chichikov made up his mind to ask:

'Where's your master? Is he in his room?'

'The master's here,' said the steward.

'Where?' repeated Chichikov.

'Why, my dear sir, are you blind?' said the steward. 'Good Lord, I'm the master!'

At this our hero involuntarily stepped back and looked intently at him. He had met a great number of all sorts of people, even such as neither the reader nor I myself are very likely to meet; but he had never met anyone like this before. His face was not anything out of the ordinary; indeed, it was practically like that of the faces of many gaunt old men, except that his chin jutted out rather a lot, so that he had always to cover it with his handkerchief to avoid spitting on it; his tiny eyes had not yet gone dim with age and kept darting about under his beetling brows like mice when, poking their sharp noses out of their dark holes, pricking up their ears and twitching their whiskers, they look around carefully to see whether a cat or a mischievous boy is lying in wait for them, and suspiciously sniff the air. His clothes were far more remarkable: by no possible methods and by no effort could one discover what his dressing-gown was made of; the sleeves and the upper parts of the skirt were so greasy and shiny that they looked like the soft leather of which Russian boots are made; at the back instead of two tails there were four out of which cotton wool hung in tufts. There was also something tied round his neck. It was impossible to make out whether it was a stocking, a garter, or an abdominal band, but it certainly could not be a neck-tie. In short, if Chichikov had met him dressed like that somewhere at a church door, he would probably have given him a copper. For, to our hero's credit be it said, he had a compassionate heart and could not resist giving a poor man a copper. Before him, however, stood not a beggar but a landowner. This landowner had more than a thousand serfs and, try as one might, one could not find another who had so much corn, grain, flour heaped simply in stacks and whose storehouses and granaries and drying sheds were filled with such great quantities of linen, cloth, cured and uncured sheepskins, dried fish, all sorts of vegetables and comestibles. If anyone had looked into his work yard, where he had stacks of various woods and utensils which were never used, he might have imagined that he had been transported to the timber market in Moscow where efficient mothers-in-law repair daily with their cooks in tow to replenish their household stocks and where every kind of wooden article, turned, dove-tailed, glued together and wattled, lies about in white heaps, barrels, half-barrels, tubs, wooden buckets with covers, wooden jugs with and without spouts, round wooden vessels, bast baskets, wooden baskets in which women keep their spinning materials and all sorts of odds and ends, baskets of thin bent aspen wood, baskets of plaited birch-bark, and many other articles used by rich and poor alike in Russia. What, one might ask, did Plyushkin want with such a mass of things? He could not have used them all in his lifetime even on two such estates as his, but all this was not enough for him. Not satisfied with it, he wandered about the streets of his village every day looking under the bridges, under the planks thrown over puddles, and everything he came across, an old sole, a bit of a peasant woman's rag, an iron nail, a piece of broken earthenware, he carried them all to his room and put them on the heap which Chichikov had noticed in the corner. 'There goes the fisherman angling again!' the peasants used to say when they saw him going in search of booty. And, indeed, there was no need to sweep the street after him: if an officer who rode through the village happened to drop a spur, the spur immediately found its way to the same heap; if a peasant woman, daydreaming at the well, forgot her pail, he carried off the pail too. When, however, a peasant caught him in the act he did not argue and gave up the plundered article; but once it had been deposited on his pile, nothing could be done about it: he would swear that the article had been bought by him on a certain day from a certain man or that it had come down to him from his grandfather. In his room he picked up everything he saw on the floor: a piece of sealing wax, a scrap of paper, a feather, and laid them all on the bureau or on the window-sill.

And yet there had been a time when he was a very careful manager of his estate. He was married and had a family and a neighbour would drive over to dine with him, to listen to him and to learn from him how to manage an estate with wise economy. Everything on his estate was done in a brisk fashion and took its proper course; his flour-mills and fulling mills ran regularly, his cloth factories, carpenters' shops, spinning mills, were all busily at work; the master's sharp eye was everywhere, looking into everything, and like an industrious spider he used to run about busily but efficiently from one end to another of his industrial web. His features did not express any strong emotions, but his eyes showed intelligence; his speech revealed experience and knowledge of the world, and his guests were glad to listen to him; his wife, friendly and talkative, was famed for her hospitality; his visitors were met by his two pretty daughters, both fair and fresh as roses; his son, a bright boy, used to run in and kiss everyone without bothering about whether the visitor was pleased or not. All the windows in the house were open; in the attic were the rooms of the French tutor who shaved wonderfully and was fond of shooting: he often brought home a woodcock or wild ducks for dinner, but sometimes only sparrows' eggs of which he would have an omelette made for himself, for no one else in the house would touch them. His compatriot, the governess of the two daughters, also lived in the attic. The master of the house came to dinner in a somewhat shabby but tidy frock-coat with no holes in the elbows and no visible patches anywhere. But the kind mistress of the house died; some of the keys and with them all the petty worries of the household passed on to him. Plyushkin became more restless and, like all widowers, more suspicious and niggardly. He could not entirely depend on his eldest daughter, Alexandra Stepanovna, and indeed he was right, for Alexandra Stepanovna soon eloped with a major of goodness only knows what cavalry regiment and hastily married him in some village church, knowing that her father did not like army officers because of some curious conviction that they were all gamblers and spendthrifts. The father sent his curse after her, but he did not bother to pursue her. The house grew emptier still. The master's miserliness became more noticeable and was made more apparent by the increasing greyness of his rough hair, for grey hair is always a faithful companion of avarice, and the greyer he became the more avaricious he grew. The French tutor was dismissed because the time had come for his son to join the service. The French governess was packed off because she had not been altogether blameless in the elopement of Alexandra Stepanovna. His son, sent to the chief town of the province to take up a post in the department of justice which, in his father's opinion, was a more substantial branch of the service, obtained an army commission instead and only after receiving it wrote to his father asking for money for his equipment; quite naturally, all he got was what is commonly known as a fig; at last the second daughter, who had remained with him at home, died, and the old man found himself the sole keeper, guardian, and master of all his riches. His solitary life provided ample food for his avarice which, as we all know, has a wolfish appetite, and the more it feeds on the more insatiable it becomes. The human feelings which had, anyhow, never been very deep in him, grew shallower every minute, and every day something more fell away from that decrepit ruin. As though in confirmation of his opinion of army officers, it happened just at that moment that his son lost heavily at cards. He sent him his fatherly curse from the bottom of his heart and was never again interested to know whether his son was alive or not. Every year more windows were boarded up in the house, and at last only two remained, one of which, as the reader has seen already, was pasted up with paper; every year he lost sight of the more important parts of the management of his estate, and his petty attention was more and more directed to scraps of paper and feathers which he used to collect in his room; he grew more uncompromising with the dealers who came to buy his produce; the dealers bargained and bargained and in the end gave him up as a bad job, saying that he was a devil, not a man; the hay and the corn rotted, the stores and haystacks turned to pure manure only good for growing cabbages on, the flour in the cellars turned to stone and had to be chopped with an axe; it was frightful to touch the cloth, linen, and household materials, for they crumbled to dust. By then he had himself forgotten how much he had of anything and only remembered the place in the cupboard where he had put a decanter with the remains of some liqueur in it and the mark he had made on it, so that no one should help himself to any of it without his permission, and also where he kept his quill and his piece of sealing wax. And meanwhile the revenue from the estate was collected as before: the peasant had to pay the same tax as before, if he wished to work for himself, every peasant woman had to bring in her usual share of nuts, and every peasant woman who worked as a weaver had to furnish as many pieces of linen as before – all this was put away in the storehouses and got mouldy and full of gaping holes and in the end he himself became a kind of gaping hole in humankind. Alexandra Stepanovna came to see him once or twice with her little son in the hope of getting something from him; evidently army life with her cavalry major was not as attractive as she had imagined it before her marriage. Plyushkin forgave her, however, and even presented his little grandson with a button that was lying on the table to play with, but he gave her no money. Another time Alexandra Stepanovna came to see him with two small children and brought him a cake for tea and a new dressing-gown, for her father was wearing a dressing-gown which was not merely awful to look at, but made her feel ashamed of him. Plyushkin fondled his two grandsons and putting the one on his right and the other on his left knee, rocked them exactly as if they were on horseback. He accepted the cake and the dressing-gown, but gave his daughter absolutely nothing; with that Alexandra Stepanovna departed.

And so this was the sort of landowner who stood before Chichikov! It must be said that people like him are rare in Russia, where everyone would rather expand than contract, and it is all the more astonishing because right there in the neighbourhood you could come across a landowner who was squandering his possessions with all the wanton recklessness of a Russian aristocrat, who, as the saying is, burns the candle at both ends. A traveller, who had never seen anything like it before, would stop in amazement at the sight of his mansion, wondering what great prince had suddenly taken up his residence among those small, obscure landlords: his white stone buildings with their multitudes of belvederes, chimneys, and weather-vanes look like palaces, and are surrounded on all sides by numerous wings and all sorts of buildings for his guests. What has he not got there? Theatrical performances, balls; and all through the night his gardens are brilliantly lit by lights and lampions and resound to the thunder of music. Half the province is there, all dressed up and promenading gaily under the trees, and nothing in this unnatural illumination strikes anyone as incongruous and menacing, not even when a branch, bathed in artificial light and robbed of its bright green colour, leaps out dramatically from the thicket of trees, and the night sky above appears darker, more austere, and a hundred times more menacing, and the tree-tops, rustling high up with their leaves and retreating deeper and deeper into the impenetrable darkness, express their indignation at the tawdry brilliance that lights up their roots underneath.

Plyushkin had been standing for several minutes without uttering a word, while Chichikov, distracted both by the appearance of the master of the house himself and by all the things in his room, could not bring himself to start the conversation. For a long time he could not think of words in which to explain the reason for his visit. He was about to express himself something in this vein, that having heard of his great virtues and the rare qualities of his heart and mind, he had deemed it his duty to pay his homage personally, but he quickly recollected himself, feeling that that would be going a little too far. Casting another sidelong glance at all the things in the room, he felt that the words 'virtues' and 'rare qualities of heart and mind' could very well be replaced by the words 'economy' and 'good order'; and therefore, changing his speech accordingly, he said that having heard of his economy and his rare ability in managing his estate, he had deemed it his duty to make his acquaintance and pay his respects in person. He could, of course, have given another and better reason, but he could think of nothing else at the moment.

To this Plyushkin muttered something between his lips, for he had no teeth, but what it was is not certain. The gist of it probably was: 'To hell with you and your respects!' But as hospitality is so popular with us that even a miser cannot bring himself to transgress its laws, he added a little more distinctly: 'Won't you take a seat, sir?'

'I haven't had visitors for a long time,' he said, 'and, to tell the truth, I don't see much use in them. We've introduced a most unseemly custom of visiting one another and as a consequence there's a terrible neglect in the management of our estates and – er – besides, they expect you to provide hay for their horses, too. I had my dinner a long time ago and my kitchen is, anyway, rather mean and in a very bad state, the chimney, too, has practically fallen to pieces: light the stove and you'll burn the place down.'

'So that's how it is!' Chichikov thought to himself. 'It's a good thing I had a cheese cake and a good helping of saddle of mutton at Sobakevich's.'

'And the worst of it is that there isn't a wisp of hay on the whole estate,' Plyushkin went on. 'And, indeed, how are you to save any? I've only a few acres of land, the peasant is lazy, hates work, only thinks how quickly he can get to a pub, and if I'm not careful I'll go begging in my old age.'

'But I've been told,' Chichikov remarked modestly, 'that you've over a thousand serfs.'

'And who told you that, sir? You should have spat in the face of the man who told you that. He must have been a practical joker.

Wanted to pull your leg. A thousand serfs! Just go and count them and I warrant you, sir, you won't find anything of the kind. That damned fever has carried off a terrible lot of my peasants.'

'You don't say so! And have many died?' Chichikov exclaimed with sympathy.

'Yes, lots of them are in their graves.'

'And may I ask how many?'

'About eighty.'

'No?'

'I wouldn't tell you a lie, my dear sir.'

'Do you mind if I ask you another question? I suppose you count that number since the last census was taken, don't you?'

'That wouldn't have been so bad,' said Plyushkin. 'The trouble is, you see, that since then about a hundred and twenty have died.'

'Really? A hundred and twenty?' exclaimed Chichikov and even gaped slightly in astonishment.

'I'm too old, my dear sir, to tell lies – I'm over three score and ten,' said Plyushkin.

He seemed to have taken offence at Chichikov's almost joyful exclamation. Chichikov realized that such lack of sympathy with another man's troubles was not quite decent and he therefore hastened to heave a sigh and say that he sympathized deeply.

'But sympathy is not a thing you can put in your pocket,' said Plyushkin. 'Now, a neighbour of mine, a captain – damned if I know where he comes from – he keeps kissing my hand, and when he starts sympathizing he sets up such a howl that he gives me an ear-ache. He has such a red face – must be from swilling raw spirits, I expect. Being an army officer, he must have gambled away his money, or some actress filched it from him, so he comes to me with his sympathy now!'

Chichikov did his best to explain that his sympathy was not at all of the same kind as the captain's, and that he was ready to prove it not in empty words but in deeds, and coming straight to the point and without beating about the bush, he declared that he was ready to take on himself the obligation of paying the tax for all the peasants who had so unfortunately died. His offer seemed to have completely astounded Plyushkin. He stared goggle-eyed at him for a long time and finally asked:

'You haven't served in the army by any chance, sir?'

'No, sir,' replied Chichikov, rather slyly. 'I was in the Civil Service.'

'In the Civil Service?' Plyushkin repeated, and began munching his lips, as though he were eating something. 'But how do you mean? Won't you lose money on it?'

'I don't mind if I lose some money to make you happy.'

'Oh, my dear sir, my benefactor!' cried Plyushkin, without noticing in his joy that a bit of snuff not unlike coffee grounds was most unpicturesquely emerging from his nose and that the skirts of his dressing-gown had flown open, revealing a garment not quite proper for inspection. 'You have comforted an old man! Oh, Lord, oh, holy Saints!' Plyushkin was unable to utter another word. But not a minute had passed before the joy that appeared so instantaneously on his wooden face, disappeared as instantaneously, as if it had never been there, and his face once more assumed a worried expression. He even wiped his face with his handkerchief rolled into a ball, and began rubbing his upper lip with it.

'But, if you don't mind my saying so, sir, for I don't want to offend you, how are you going to do it? Do you undertake to pay the tax for them every year? And will you pay the money to me or into the Treasury?'

'This is what we'll do: we'll draw up a deed of purchase just as though they were alive and you were selling them to me.'

'Yes, a deed of purchase,' said Plyushkin, thinking it over and again beginning to munch his lips. 'But, you see, a deed of purchase is – er – well, an expense. The clerks are such unscrupulous fellows. Before, you could get off with half a rouble in copper and a sack of flour, but now you have to send them a whole cartload of grain and a red ten-rouble note thrown in – such money-grubbers! I don't know how our clergy don't look into it. They ought to preach sermons about it: for, say what you like, there's no resisting God's word.'

'Well, I should think you would resist it all right!' Chichikov thought to himself, and he immediately declared that out of respect for him he was ready to take even the expenses of the deed of purchase upon himself.

Hearing that Chichikov was even taking the expenses of the deed of purchase on himself, Plyushkin concluded that his visitor must be an utter fool and was only pretending to have been in the Civil Service and had most probably been an army officer and gadded about with actresses. For all that, he could not conceal his joy and called down all sorts of blessings not only on him but also on his children, without inquiring whether he had any or not. He went up to the window, tapped on the pane and shouted: 'Hey, Proshka!' A minute later someone could be heard rushing hurriedly into the hall, bustling about there for a long time and making a noise with his boots. At last the door opened and Proshka, a boy of thirteen, came in: he was wearing a pair of boots that were so large that he almost stepped out of them when he walked. Why Proshka had such big boots can be explained at once: Plyushkin kept only one pair of boots for all his household serfs, however many there might be, and they had always to be in the hall. Every house serf summoned to his master's apartments, usually had first to skip across the yard on his bare feet, but on entering the hall had to put on the boots and only then to come into the room. On leaving the room, he once more left the boots in the hall and set off again on his own soles. If anyone had looked out of the windows in the autumn, and especially in the morning when the ground was covered with hoarfrost, he would have seen all the household serfs cutting such capers as the most agile dancer could scarcely manage to execute at the theatre.

'Just look at his stupid face, my dear sir,' said Plyushkin to Chichikov, pointing at Proshka's face. 'As stupid as a block of wood, but try putting anything down and he'll steal it in a twinkling! Well, what have you come for, you fool? Tell me that!' Here he paused for a moment and Proshka too responded with silence. 'Set the *samovar*, do you hear? And take this key and give it to Mavra. Tell her to go to the pantry: on a shelf there she'll find a rusk of the Easter cake Alexandra Stepanovna brought. Tell her to serve it for tea. Wait, where are you off to? You damn fool – dear, oh dear, what a damn fool! Is the devil tickling your feet or what? Listen carefully first: I expect the rusk must have gone a little mouldy on the top, so let her scrape it with a knife, but tell her not to throw away the crumbs, let her take them to the hens. And, mind, don't you go into the pantry, my boy, or I'll – you know what, don't you? I'll give you a good birching, I will, to improve your appetite! You've got a fine appetite, haven't you? Well, that will improve it! You just try going into the pantry – I'll be watching from the window here. ... One can't trust them with anything,' he went on, turning to Chichikov,

133

after Proshka had taken himself off with his boots. Then he began looking suspiciously at Chichikov. He was beginning to find such extraordinary generosity quite incredible and he thought to himself: 'Why, damn him, he may be just a braggart, like all those wastrels: promise you all sorts of things just to have a talk with you and drink your tea and then go away!' Therefore, as a precaution and at the same time wishing to test him a little, he said that it would not be a bad idea if they completed the deed of purchase as soon as possible, for one could never be sure of anything when dealing with a man: he may be alive today and dead tomorrow.

Chichikov expressed his willingness to complete it at that very moment and only asked for a list of all the peasants.

This reassured Plyushkin. It could be seen that he was thinking of doing something, and so he was, for, taking the keys, he went up to the cupboard and, unlocking the door, rummaged for a long time among the cups and glasses and at last said:

'What do you think of that? I just can't find it and yet I had an excellent liqueur here, if only they have not drunk it all up, the thieves. Peasants are such thieves, sir. But it isn't this, is it?' Chichikov saw in his hands a small decanter, all covered in dust as though in a woollen sweater. 'My late wife made it,' Plyushkin went on. 'That rascally housekeeper shoved it into a corner and didn't even put a stopper in it, the dirty slut! Insects and all kinds of rubbish had got into it, but I took it all out and now it's quite clean. Let me pour you out a glass.'

But Chichikov tried to decline so excellent a liqueur saying that he had already eaten and drunk.

'Eaten and drunk already, have you?' said Plyushkin. 'Why, of course, you can recognize a well-bred man anywhere: he does not eat but has had a good meal already, not like one of those dirty little thieves who're never satisfied however much you feed them. Take that captain, for instance. "Let's have a bite of something, Uncle," he says. And I'm no more his uncle than he's my grandfather. He has nothing to eat at home, I expect, so he comes running round here! You want a list of all those parasites, sir, don't you? Well, sir, as a matter of fact I wrote them all down on a special bit of paper to make quite sure they're all struck off at the next census.'

Plyushkin put on his spectacles and began rummaging among his papers. Undoing all sorts of bundles, he regaled his visitor with such a cloud of dust that Chichikov sneezed. At last he pulled out a piece of paper which had been scribbled all over. Peasants' names covered it as thick as flies. There were all sorts of names there: Paramonov and Pimenov and Panteleymonov, and there was even one Grigory Never-Get-There. There were over a hundred and twenty altogether. Chichikov smiled on seeing such a multitude of names. Putting it into his pocket, he remarked to Plyushkin that they would have to go to the town to complete the purchase.

'To the town? But how can I? How can I leave the house? You see, sir, my peasants are either thieves or swindlers: in one day they would strip me so that there wouldn't be a nail left to hang a coat on.'

'Haven't you anyone there you know?'

'Anyone I know? All my friends have either died or don't want to know me. But, good Lord, sir, I have one, of course I have one!' he cried. 'You see, the president himself is a good friend of mine. He used to come and see me in the old days. We used to play together when we were boys. We used to climb the fences together! Of course, I know him! One of my best friends! Should I write to him, do you think?'

'Why, of course write to him.'

'An old friend of mine, sir! Of course! We were good friends at school!'

And all of a sudden a sort of ray of warm light passed across that wooden face, there was an expression not so much of feeling as a sort of pale reflection of a feeling, something like the unexpected appearance of a drowning man on the surface of the water, giving rise to a shout of joy in the crowd on the bank. But in vain do his rejoicing brothers and sisters throw him a rope from the bank and wait for another glimpse of the back or the arms exhausted with struggling – that appearance was the last. Everything is still and the quiet surface of the mute element becomes all the more terrible and more desolate than before. So Plyushkin's empty face, after the feeling that passed over it for a moment, looked more callous and more banal than ever.

'There was a sheet of clean notepaper lying on the table,' he said, 'but I don't know where it could have got to – my servants are such good-for-nothing rogues!' He then began looking on the table and under the table, rummaged about everywhere, and at last shouted: 'Mavra! Mavra!'

At his call appeared a woman with a plate in her hand on which was the rusk already familiar to the reader. And the following conversation took place between them:

'Where did you put that paper, you thief?'

'Haven't seen it, sir. Honestly, I haven't, except the little bit of paper you covered the wine-glass with.'

'I can tell from your face that you've pinched it.'

'But what do I want to pinch it for, sir? It's no use to me, is it? I can't write.'

'You're lying. You took it to the sacristan. He knows how to scribble, so you took it to him.'

'But the sacristan can get paper for himself, sir, if he wants it. He's never seen your bit of paper.'

'You wait, my good woman, at the Day of Judgement the devils will roast you on gridirons for this. You'll see how they'll roast you!'

'But why should they roast me, sir, when I've never touched your notepaper? I may have some other womanly failings, but no one never accused me of theft.'

'The devils will roast you all right. They'll say, "Take that for deceiving your master, you wicked woman!" and they'll roast you on red hot irons.'

'And I'll say to them, I shall, "I done nothing, I swear I done nothing. I didn't take it!" But look, sir, there it is! Right there on the table. Always blaming me for nothing!'

Plyushkin did, indeed, see the sheet of notepaper. He paused for a moment, chewing his lips. Then he said:

'Well, what are you carrying on like that for? What a quarrelsome harridan! Good heavens, say one word to her and she answers you back with a dozen! You'd better go and bring me a light to seal a letter. But wait, wait! You'll bring me a tallow candle, tallow melts, it burns up and there's nothing left of it. Pure loss. You'd better bring me a splinter of wood!'

Mavra went out and Plyushkin sat down in an armchair, picked up a quill, and kept turning the sheet of paper over and over in his hand, wondering whether he could save half of it, but satisfying himself at last that it was quite impossible, he dipped the quill into an inkstand with some mouldy liquid and a multitude of flies at the bottom and began writing, forming the letters like musical notes, continually holding back his hand which was galloping all over the paper, setting down one line after another in a niggardly fashion and thinking, not without regret, what a lot of blank space would be left.

And to what depths of worthlessness, pettiness, and nastiness a man can sink! How could he have changed so much? And is this really true to life? Yes, it is all true to life. Anything can happen to a man: the fiery youth of today would recoil in horror if one were to show him his portrait in old age. So, as you pass from the tender years of youth into harsh and embittered manhood, make sure you take with you on your journey all the human emotions! Don't leave them on the road, for you will not pick them up afterwards! Old age, inevitable and inescapable, is terrible and menacing, for it never gives anything back, it returns nothing! The grave is more merciful than old age. On the tomb is written: 'Here Lies a Man', but you can read nothing on the cold and callous features of inhuman old age.

'And do you happen to know,' said Plyushkin, folding the letter, 'if any of your friends would like runaway peasants?'

'Why, have you runaway peasants too?' Chichikov asked quickly, pricking up his ears.

'Yes, that's the trouble. I have. My brother-in-law made a few inquiries, but he says there's no trace of them to be found anywhere. But then, he's an army man, only good at clinking his spurs, but if one has to take some matter up in the courts ...'

'And how many of them would there be?'

'Oh, I expect about seventy.'

'Not really?'

'Yes, indeed. Not a year passes without some of them running away. The peasants, you see, sir, are a terribly greedy lot. Their idleness has led them into the habit of drinking, while I've nothing to eat myself ... I'd take anything I could get for them. So do tell your friend about it, for if he can only find a dozen of them, he'll get a lot of money for them. You see, a registered serf is worth fifty roubles.'

'No, we shan't let any friend of ours get even a sniff at them,' said Chichikov to himself, and then he went on to explain that it would be quite impossible to find such a friend and that the expense of the business would be more than it was worth, considering that one had better cut off the skirts of one's coat in order to get away from the courts as fast as possible; but if he really was pressed for money, then he was ready out of sympathy alone to give ... but it was such a trifle that it was scarcely worth talking about.

'And how much would you give?' asked Plyushkin, suddenly feeling so greedy that his hands trembled like quicksilver.

'I'd give you twenty-five copecks a soul.'

'And how would you buy them? Cash down?'

'Yes, cash down.'

'Only, my dear sir, in view of my poverty you ought to give me forty copecks each.'

'My dear sir,' said Chichikov, 'I'd gladly give you not forty copecks but five hundred roubles! I'd pay it with pleasure because I can see that you're a most worthy and kind-hearted old man whose misfortunes are due entirely to his own good nature.'

'Yes, sir, that's true, indeed it is,' said Plyushkin, lowering his head and nodding sadly. 'It's all because of my good nature.'

'There, you see, sir, I grasped your character at once. So why not give you five hundred roubles a soul, my dear sir? Because, you see, I haven't got the money. Now, five copecks I'm ready to add so that each soul would work out at thirty copecks.'

'Well, sir, as you wish, but won't you add another two copecks?'

'Why, of course, I don't mind adding two copecks. By all means. How many of them have you got? You said seventy, didn't you?'

'No, altogether there are seventy-eight.'

'Seventy-eight, seventy-eight at thirty-two copecks apiece, that makes...' At this point our hero thought for one second, not more, and said at once: 'That makes twenty-four roubles, ninety-six copecks.' He was good at arithmetic.

He made Plyushkin write out a receipt at once and handed over the money, which Plyushkin took in both hands and carried to his bureau with as much care as though he were carrying some liquid and was afraid of spilling it. On reaching the bureau, he examined the money again and with the same care put it away in one of the drawers, where no doubt it was destined to be buried until Father Karp and Father Polikarp, the two priests of his village, came to bury him to the indescribable joy of his son-in-law and his daughter, and perhaps of the captain who claimed to be a relative of his. Having put away the money, Plyushkin sat down in his armchair, apparently unable to find a further subject of conversation.

'Why, are you going already?' he said, noticing that Chichikov had made a slight movement, though it was only to get his handkerchief out of his pocket.

This question reminded Chichikov that there was really no reason why he should be staying there any longer.

'Yes, it's time I went!' he said, reaching for his hat.

'And what about tea?'

'No thank you, sir, I'd rather have a cup of tea with you some other time.'

'But I ordered the *samovar*. To tell you the truth, I don't really care for tea very much myself: it's an expensive beverage and, besides, the price of sugar has gone up cruelly. Proshka, we don't want the *samovar!* Take the rusk back to Mavra, do you hear? Tell her to put it back in the same place. But, no. You'd better give it to me: I'll put it back myself. Good-bye, my dear sir, and God bless you. Please don't forget to give my letter to the president. Yes, let him read it. He's an old friend of mine. Yes, indeed, we were schoolboys together.'

And then this strange phenomenon, this wretched old man, saw him off across the yard, after which he ordered the gates to be immediately locked; he then made the round of all his storehouses to make sure that the watchmen, who were stationed at every corner and had to beat with wooden spades on empty barrels instead of a sheet of iron, were all in their proper places; after that, he looked into the kitchen where, on the pretext of finding out whether his servants were being properly fed, he had a good helping of cabbage soup and buckwheat porridge himself and, after scolding each one of them for stealing and bad behaviour, returned to his room. Left by himself, it actually occurred to him that he ought to have thanked his visitor for his unexampled generosity. 'I shall make him a present of my watch,' he thought to himself. 'It's a good silver watch, not one of your pinchbeck or bronze ones. There's something wrong with it, it is true, but he can get it repaired. He's still a young man, so he wants a watch to impress his bride-to-be! Or, no,' he added after a moment's reflection, 'I'd better leave it him in my will so that he may remember me.'

But even without the watch our hero was in excellent spirits. Such an unexpected acquisition was a real gift. And, indeed, say what you like, he had got not only dead souls but runaway ones too, altogether more than two hundred! Of course, even on the way to Plyushkin's estate he had a presentiment that he was on to a good thing, but such a bargain he had never expected. He was quite unusually cheerful all the way, whistling, putting his lips to his fist and blowing through it as if it were a trumpet, and at last broke into a song so extraordinary that Selifan listened and listened and then, shaking his head a little, said: 'Fancy, so that's the way the master sings!' Night had already fallen when they drove into the town. The light and shadows were so completely intermingled that it seemed as though the objects themselves had become intermingled too. The striped black and white turnpike assumed a sort of indefinite colour; the moustache of the soldier on sentry duty seemed to be on his forehead and much higher than his eyes, while his nose seemed to have completely disappeared. The loud rattle and jolting made it clear that the carriage was driving over the cobbled roadway. The street lamps were not yet lighted, and only here and there was there a light in the windows of the houses, while in the back streets and lanes such scenes and conversations were taking place as are to be expected at that hour in all towns where there are many soldiers, cabmen, workmen, and peculiar kinds of creatures in the shape of ladies in red shawls and shoes without stockings, who dart about like bats at the street corners. Chichikov did not notice them and he did not even observe a large number of very slender civil servants with elegant canes who were probably on their way home after a walk in the country. From time to time exclamations in apparently women's voices reached his ears: 'You're lying, you dirty drunkard, I never let him take such liberties with me!', or 'Don't you hit me, you ruffian! You'd better come along to the police station and I'll show you there ...' In fact, the sort of words that are like a bucket of cold water poured over some dreamy twenty-year-old youth returning from the theatre with his head full of a street in Spain, a moonlight night, and a ravishing woman with a guitar and beautiful hair. What wonderful visions are passing through his head! He is in the seventh heaven and has just been on a visit to Schiller, when suddenly the fatal words burst upon him like a clap of thunder, and he sees that he is back on earth, and even in the haymarket and near a pub, and once more life in its workaday clothes goes flaunting itself before him.

At last the carriage, with a violent jolt as though dropping into a hole, passed through the gates of the inn, and Chichikov was met by Petrushka who with one hand held up the skirts of his coat, for he hated to see them fly apart, and with the other helped his master out of the carriage. The waiter ran out too with a candle in his hand and a napkin over his shoulder. Whether Petrushka was pleased at his master's arrival is hard to say, but he and Selifan, at any rate, winked at each other and his usually sullen looks seemed to brighten somewhat this time.

'You've been away a long time, sir,' said the waiter, as he lighted Chichikov up the stairs.

'Yes,' said Chichikov, after he had mounted the stairs, 'and how have you been getting on?'

'I've nothing to complain of, sir,' replied the waiter, bowing. 'An army lieutenant arrived yesterday and took room 16.'

'A lieutenant?'

'Yes, sir. I don't know who he is. From Ryazan, bay horses.'

'Very well, very well, do your best in future, too,' said Chichikov and he went into his room. As he went through the anteroom he wrinkled his nose and said to Petrushka: 'You might at least have opened the windows!'

'But I did open them, sir!' said Petrushka, and he told a lie.

However, his master knew that he was lying, but did not want to have an argument about it. He felt very tired after his journey. Ordering a very light supper, consisting only of sucking pig, he undressed immediately after it, and getting under the bedclothes fell fast asleep, fell into a sound sleep, into that wonderful sleep which only happy mortals enjoy who know nothing of haemorrhoids, or fleas, or strongly developed intellectual faculties.

Chapter 7

Happy is the traveller, who after a long and wearisome journey with its cold and slush and mud, sleepy station-masters, jingling bells, repairs, altercations, drivers, blacksmiths, and all sorts of villains of the road, at last beholds the familiar roof and the lights rushing to meet him, and then the familiar rooms appear before him, he hears the joyful cries of the servants running out to meet him, the noise and the pattering footsteps of his children, and the soothing, gentle words interspersed with passionate kisses that have the power to blot out all sad thoughts from his memory. Happy the family man who has a home of his own, but woe to the bachelor!

Happy is the writer who without dwelling too long on tedious and repulsive characters, which impress us by their distressful reality, feels drawn to characters which reveal the high dignity of man, the writer who from the great whirlpool of human figures that pass daily before his mind's eyes, selects only the few exceptions, who has never once been untrue to the major key of his lyre, who has never descended from his pinnacle to his poor, insignificant fellow-creatures and, without touching the earth, has immersed himself completely in his own exalted images that are so far removed from it. His rare lot is doubly to be envied: he is among them as among his own family, and yet his fame spreads far and wide. He clouds men's eyes with enchanting incense; he flatters them marvellously, concealing the sad facts of life and showing them the noble man. Applauding, all run after him, all rush after his triumphal chariot. They call him a great, universal poet, soaring high above all the other geniuses of the world as an eagle soars over the other high-flying birds. Young, ardent hearts are thrilled at his very name; responsive tears gleam in every eye. ... He has no equal in power – he is a god. But quite different is the lot, quite different is the destiny of the writer who has dared to bring into the open everything that is every moment before men's eyes and that remains unseen by their unobservant eyes – all the terrible, shocking morass of trivial things in which our life is entangled, the whole depth of frigid, split up, everyday characters with whom our often dreary and bitter earthly path swarms, and who dares with the strong power of his relentless chisel to display them boldly and in the round before the eyes of all! Not for him the applause of the people, not for him to behold the grateful tears and the unanimous rapture of the souls he has moved so deeply; no girl of sixteen flies to meet him with her head turned and full of heroic enthusiasm; he will not find oblivion in the sweet enchantment of the sounds he has himself evoked; and, lastly, he will not escape the judgement of his contemporaries, hypocritical and callous public opinion, which will brand his cherished creations as low and insignificant, will allot him an ignoble place in the ranks of writers who have affronted humanity, will attribute to him the qualities of the heroes he himself has created, will rob him of heart and soul and the divine fire of genius. For contemporary public opinion does not acknowledge that the glasses through which suns are beheld and through which the movements of microscopic insects are studied are equally marvellous; for public opinion does not admit that great spiritual depth is required to illumine a picture drawn from ignoble life and transform it into a pearl of creation; for public opinion does not admit that lofty rapturous laughter is worthy to stand beside lofty lyrical emotion and that there is all the difference in the world between it and the antics of a clown at a fair. Public opinion does not admit that and it will turn everything into a reproach and a sneer against the unrecognized writer; without fellow feeling, without response, without sympathy, he is left standing alone in the middle of the road like a homeless wayfarer. Hard is his calling in life, and bitterly he feels his solitude.

And for a long time to come am I destined by the mysterious powers to walk hand in hand with my strange heroes, viewing life in all its immensity as it rushes past me, viewing it through laughter seen by the world and tears unseen and unknown by it. And the time is still far off when the terrible storm of inspiration will rise up in another stream out of a head encircled with a halo, inspiring sacred terror and, abashed and in trepidation, men will hear the majestic thunder of other words. ...

But on with our journey! On with the journey! Away with the wrinkles that have furrowed our brow and the gloomy shadow that has fallen over our face! Let us plunge all at once into life with all its muffled rattle and jingling bells, and let us see what Chichikov is doing.

Chichikov woke up, stretched his arms and legs, and felt that he had had a good sleep. After lying for two minutes on his back, he snapped his fingers and remembered with a face beaming with joy that he had now almost four hundred serfs. He jumped out of bed at once and did not even look at his face, of which he was genuinely fond and in which he apparently found the chin most attractive, for he very often boasted about it in front of one or another of his friends, especially while he was shaving. 'Just look,' he would usually say, stroking his chin, 'what a chin I've got – it's quite round!' But now he looked neither at his chin nor at his face, but, just as he was, put on his morocco boots with inlaid patterns of many colours, in which the town of Torzhok does a roaring trade thanks to the Russian's fondness for a life of ease and idleness and, Scottish-fashion, wearing nothing but his shirt, forgetting his dignity and the decorum of middle-age, took two leaps across the room, striking himself very deftly on the back with a heel. Then he at once set to work: he rubbed his hands in front of his box with the same sort of pleasure with which an incorruptible district magistrate, who has just arrived for a preliminary inquiry, is about to partake of a snack lunch, and he immediately took some papers out of it. He wanted to settle the whole business as soon as possible without putting it off for a single day. He made up his mind to draw up the deeds of purchase himself, to write them out and make a fair copy of them, so as not to have to pay the lawyers' clerks. He was well versed in the business of drawing up official papers and he put down in a bold hand and in large letters: 'One thousand, eight hundred and –' the exact date, then in small letters: 'So-and-so, landowner,' and everything as it should be. In two hours it was all finished. When afterwards he looked at the sheets of paper, the names of the peasants who really had once been peasants, had worked, ploughed, drunk hard, driven cabs for hire, cheated their masters, or perhaps been simply good peasants, he was seized by a strange feeling, a feeling he found it hard himself to understand. Each list seemed to have a character of its own and through it the peasants themselves seemed to acquire a character of their own. The peasants belonging to Korobochka almost all had additional descriptive nicknames. Plyushkin's list was distinguished by the brevity of its style: often only the initial letters of the names and patronymics were written down, followed by two dots. Sobakevich's register was remarkable for its extraordinarily full and circumstantial details: not one of the peasants' qualities was omitted; of one it was stated that he was 'a good carpenter', and of another it was added that 'he knows his work and does not touch intoxicating liquor'. It was stated as circumstantially who their fathers and their mothers were and what their conduct was like; of only one, a peasant by the name of Fedotov, it was stated: 'Father unknown, born of the serf-girl Kapitolina, a maidservant, but of good character and no thief'. All these details added a sort of special touch of freshness to it all: it seemed as though the peasants had been alive only yesterday. After gazing for a long time at their names, Chichikov felt deeply touched and, heaving a sigh, he said: 'My dear, dear fellows, how many of you are crammed here! What did you do in your day, my darlings? How did you get along?' And his eyes involuntarily rested on one name: it was the notorious Peter Savelyev Disrespectful-of-Troughs, who once belonged to Korobochka. Again he could not refrain from saying: 'Oh, what a long one, sprawled all over the line! What were you? Were you a craftsman or just an ordinary peasant? And how did you die? Did you die in a pub or did some clumsy cart run over you while asleep in the middle of the road? Stepan Probka, a carpenter, a man of exemplary sobriety! Ah, here he is, Stepan Probka, here is the tall man of great strength who might have made a fine guardsman! I suppose he must have gone through all the provinces with an axe in his belt and his boots slung over his shoulders, eating a farthing's worth of bread and two farthings' worth of dried fish, though, I shouldn't wonder, he used to bring home a hundred roubles in his purse every time, or perhaps sewed up a thousand-rouble note in his hempen trousers or stuck it inside his boot. Where did you meet your death? Did you perch under the church cupola for a bigger wage or perhaps even tried to reach the cross and, slipping down from the crossbeam, hit the ground and some Uncle Mikhey, who happened to be standing not far from where you fell, merely scratched the back of his head and said, "Poor old Vanya, now he's gone and done it!" and tying a rope round himself, clambered up to take your place. Maxim Telyatinkov, cobbler. A cobbler, indeed! "Drunk as a cobbler", the proverb says. I know you, I know you, my dear fellow! If you like, I can tell you the whole story of your life. You were apprenticed to a German who used to feed you all together, beat you on the back with a strap for carelessness, and did not let you out in the streets to lark about, and you were a real marvel and not just a cobbler, and the German could find no words to praise you when talking to his wife or to a fellow countryman of his. And as soon as your apprenticeship was over you said to yourself, "I'll set up business in a house of my own now, and I shan't be like the German who saves a penny a time, but I'll get rich all at once." And so, having let your master have a goodly sum in lieu of tax, you set up a small business, collected a large number of orders, and set to work. You got hold of some very cheap, rotten leather and, to be sure, made twice as much on each boot, but within a week or two your boots burst at the seams and your customers heaped the coarsest abuse upon you. And no one went into your shop any more and you took to drinking and loafing about the streets, saying, "Aye, life's hard! There's no decent living to be made by a Russian. The Germans are always in our way." But what peasant is this? Yelizaveta Vorobey! Good Lord, a woman! How did she get here? That scoundrel Sobakevich has swindled me again!' Chichikov was right: it was indeed a woman. How she got there was a mystery, but her name was so skilfully written down that from a distance she could have been taken for a peasant, and even her name had a masculine ending: Yelizavet instead of Yelizaveta. However, he refused to take it into consideration, but crossed her out at once. 'Grigory-Never-Get-There! What kind of a fellow were you? Were you a carrier by trade and, having got yourself a team of three horses and a waggon with a cover of matting, gave up your home for ever, your native lair, and went trailing off with merchants to the fairs? Did you give up your soul to the Lord on the road, or did your own pals stick a knife into you over some fat red-cheeked soldier's wife, or did some forest tramp like the look of your leather mittens and your three squat but powerful horses? Or, perhaps, lying on the plank-bed under the ceiling, you started thinking and thinking and then for no rhyme or reason went to a pub and from there straight to a hole in the ice, and that was the last they ever saw of you! Dear, oh dear, what a strange people the Russians are! They don't like to die a natural death! And what about you, my dear fellows?' he went on, casting his eyes on the scrap of paper on which the names of Plyushkin's runaway serfs were written down. 'You may still be alive, but what's the use of you? You might as well be dead. And where are your nimble legs carrying you now?

Did you have a bad time with Plyushkin or are you roaming about the forests and robbing the travellers of your own accord? Are you in prison or have you got yourselves other masters and are tilling the land? Yeremey Koryakin, Nikita Volokita, his son Anton Volokita – Koryakin, the footslogger, Volokita, the womanizer – one can see by their nicknames that they are first-class runners. Popov, a house-serf, must be a literate peasant: I suppose he never went so far as to threaten people with a knife, but did his thieving in a most gentlemanly fashion. But one day a captain of police caught you without a passport. You stand your ground well at a confrontation. "Who do you belong to?" asks the captain of police, taking advantage of the occasion to call you a few unprintable names. "I belong to landowner so-and-so," you answer boldly. "What are you doing here?" says the police captain. "I've been allowed to go on payment of tax," you reply without a moment's hesitation. "Where's your passport?" "My master, artisan Pimenov, has it." "Call Pimenov. Are you Pimenov?" "Yes, sir." "Did he give you his passport?" "No, sir, he never gave me no passport." "Why are you lying?" says the police captain with the addition of some strong language. "It's quite true, sir," you reply boldly, "I ain't given him none 'cause I came home late, but I gave it to Antip Prokhorov, the bell-ringer, for safe keeping." "Call the bell-ringer. Did he give you his passport?" "No, sir, I ain't got no passport from him." "Why are you lying again?" says the police captain, fortifying his words with more strong language. "Where is your passport?" "I did have it, sir," you reply promptly, "but I expect I must have dropped it on the road." "And why," asked the police captain, swearing at you again, "why have you carried off a soldier's greatcoat and a box-full of coppers from the priest's?" "I never took it, sir," you say, quite unmoved. "I never been mixed up in no burglaries." "Then why was the coat found in your possession?" "Don't know, sir. Someone else must have brought it." "Oh, you damn rogue, you!" says the police captain, shaking his head, with his arms akimbo. "Put the stocks on his feet and take him to jail." "As you like, sir, I'll go with pleasure," you reply. Then, taking your snuff-box out of your pocket, you offer it amicably to the two old soldiers who are putting the stocks on you, and you ask them how long ago they left the army and what wars they were in. And so you live in jail till your case is heard in court. And the court's verdict is that you are to be taken from Tsarevo-

Kokshaysk to a jail in some other town, and from there the court orders you to be sent to some place called Vessyegonsk, and you move about from prison to prison, and say when you've had a good look at your new place of residence: "No, sir, the Vessyegonsk jail is much better! There's room there for a game of skittles and there's more company!" Abakum Fyrov! What about you, my dear fellow? Where, in what places, are you roaming about now? Have you got as far as the Volga? And have you got attached to a life of freedom and joined the Volga boatmen?' At this point Chichikov paused and fell into a reverie. What was he thinking about? Was he thinking about Abakum Fyrov's lot or was he just thinking about nothing in particular as all Russians of whatever age, rank, or condition do when they start thinking of a riotous life in wide open spaces. And, indeed, where is Fyrov now? He leads a gay, rollicking life on some corn wharf, bargaining with merchants for a better wage. Flowers and ribbons on their hats, the whole gang of Volga boatmen make merry as they say good-bye to their mistresses and wives, tall slender women wearing coin necklaces and ribbons; there is singing and dancing, the whole square is full of life, while in the midst of all this shouting, swearing, and cries of encouragement, stevedores hooking a couple of hundredweights on their backs pour peas and wheat noisily into the deep holds of the barges, pile up bags of oats and corn, and all over the square piles of sacks can be seen, stacked in a pyramid like cannon balls, and the whole arsenal of grain looks enormous until it is all loaded into the deep Sura river barges and the endless flotilla sails away in single file with the melting spring ice. That will be the time for you, Volga boatmen, to work with a will! And you will set to work all together just as before you made merry and ran wild, toiling and sweating, towing the barges to the sound of a song as endless as Russia herself.

'Dear, oh dear, twelve o'clock!' said Chichikov at last, looking at his watch. 'Why have I been wasting my time like this? It's not as if I'd been doing something useful. I've just been talking a lot of nonsense for no rhyme or reason and then fallen to dreaming. Oh, what a fool I am, honestly!' Having said this, he changed his Scottish costume for a European one, tightened the buckle over his round belly, sprinkled himself with eau-de-Cologne, picked up his warm cap, and with the papers under his arm, set off to the court dealing with the transfer of properties to complete the deeds of purchase. He was in a hurry, not because he was afraid of being late – he was not afraid of being late, for the president of the court was a good friend of his and could prolong or shorten the sitting just as he liked, like Homer's Zeus, who lengthened the days or made the nights pass more quickly when he had to cut short the battle of his favourite heroes or give them an opportunity to fight to a finish – but he himself was anxious to get the business settled as quickly as possible. Until it was done, he felt uneasy and uncomfortable. The thought that the serfs were not real serfs was never absent from his mind and he felt that in a case like this it was always best to get a load of that sort off his mind as quickly as possible. He had barely walked out into the street, thinking of all this and, at the same time, pulling on his shoulders a heavy bearskin overcoat covered with brown cloth, when at the very next turning he ran into another gentleman, also wearing a bearskin overcoat covered with brown cloth, and a warm cap with ear-flaps. The gentleman uttered a cry of astonishment: it was Manilov. They immediately embraced each other and remained clasped in each other's arms for about five minutes. The kisses they exchanged were so powerful that their front teeth ached for the rest of the day. Manilov was so overjoyed that only his nose and his lips remained on his face, his eyes having completely disappeared. For a quarter of an hour he held Chichikov's hand clasped in both of his until it grew terribly hot. In the most agreeable and refined turns of phrase he described how he had flown to embrace his dear friend; his speech concluded with a compliment which was only suitable for a young lady one has invited to a dance. Chichikov opened his mouth, still uncertain how to thank him, when Manilov suddenly produced from under his fur coat a piece of rolled-up paper tied round with a pink ribbon. He offered it to Chichikov very deftly with two fingers.

'What is that?'

'The peasants.'

'Oh!' He at once unfolded it, glanced through it, and expressed his admiration at the neatness and beauty of the handwriting. 'It's beautifully written,' he said. 'There's no need to copy it. And what a lovely border round it! Who made it so artistically?'

'Oh,' said Manilov, 'you really mustn't ask.'

'You?'

'My wife.'

'Good heavens, I'm really ashamed to have given you so much trouble.'

'No trouble at all if it's for Mr Chichikov.'

Chichikov bowed in acknowledgement. Learning that he was on his way to the court to complete the deed of purchase, Manilov expressed his readiness to accompany him. The friends took each other's arms and set off together. Whenever they came to any rise in the ground, any hillock or step, Manilov supported Chichikov and almost lifted him off the ground, adding with an agreeable smile that he could not possibly let Mr Chichikov hurt his feet. Chichikov, at a loss how to express his gratitude, felt a little ashamed, realizing that he was a little heavy. Exchanging these mutual attentions, they at last reached the square in which the government offices were to be found: a large, three-storied brick house as white as chalk, no doubt to symbolize the purity of soul of those who performed their duties there; the other buildings in the square did not compare in size with this huge brick house. They were: a sentry box at which a soldier was standing with a rifle, two or three cab-stands and, lastly, long fences with the usual kind of inscriptions and drawings scrawled on them in chalk and charcoal. There was nothing else in this desolate or, as it is usually described among us, picturesque square. From the windows of the second and third stories the incorruptible heads of the votaries of Themis occasionally poked out and immediately disappeared again; most probably their chief entered their office at that moment. The friends ran rather than walked up the stairs, because Chichikov, trying to avoid being supported by Manilov, quickened his steps, while Manilov, for his part, rushed forward in order to prevent Chichikov from getting tired, so that in the end both were out of breath when they set foot in the dark corridor. Neither the corridors nor the rooms struck them as being particularly clean. In those days people did not bother about cleanliness and what was dirty remained dirty, without any attempt being made to make the place look more attractive. Themis received her visitors very simply, just as she was, in négligé and dressing-gown. The offices through which our friends passed should have been described but for the fact that our author finds himself completely overawed in government offices. Even if he has happened to pass through them when they were at their most brilliant and dignified, with polished floors and tables, he has tried to run through them as quickly as possible with eyes humbly fixed on the floor, and because of this he has no idea whatever how flourishing and prosperous things are there. Our heroes saw a prodigious number of papers, rough drafts and fair copies, bent heads, thick necks, dress-coats, frock-coats of provincial cut, and even a light-grey tunic which stood out sharply and which, head bent on one side and almost touching the paper, was copying in a bold hand and with a flourish some official report of a successful lawsuit concerning the misappropriation of land or the inventory of an estate fraudulently seized by some peaceful country gentleman, who was spending the last years of his life on it even while its ownership was being contested in the courts, having during that time begotten, reared, and brought up children and even children's children; and brief sentences uttered by snatches in a hoarse voice were audible from time to time, such as 'Please, be so good as to pass me Case No. 368, Fedosey Fedoseyevich!' or, 'You're always mislaying the cork of the office ink-pot!' At times a more majestic voice, belonging no doubt to one of the chiefs, rang out peremptorily: 'Here, copy that out again or else I'll have your boots taken off and you'll stay here for six days without anything to eat!' There was a great deal of pen-scratching and the noise of it was like the passage of several carts loaded with brushwood through a wood a quarter of a yard deep in dead leaves.

Chichikov and Manilov went up to the first desk where two clerks of tender age were sitting and inquired:

'Please, could you tell us where the deeds of purchase are dealt with here?'

'Why? What do you want?' said both the clerks, turning round.

'I should like to make an application.'

'Why, what have you bought?'

'If you don't mind, I'd first of all like to know where the deeds of purchase are dealt with, here or in some other office?'

'You'd better tell us first what you bought and at what price, and then we shall tell you where. We can't tell you otherwise.'

Chichikov saw at once that, like all young civil servants, the clerks were merely curious and wished to add more weight and importance to their work and themselves.

'Now look here, my dear fellows,' he said, 'I know perfectly well that all business relating to deeds of purchase is dealt with in one and the same office, whatever the price paid, and I should therefore be glad if you would kindly tell me where it is. But, of course, if you don't know what is going on in your own office, we will ask someone else.'

The two officials made no reply to that: one of them merely jerked a finger towards the corner of the room where an old man was sitting at a desk making notes on some official papers. Chichikov and Manilov walked between the desks and went straight up to him. The old man was deeply absorbed in his work.

'Will you please tell me,' said Chichikov with a bow, 'whether the deeds of purchase are dealt with here?'

The old man raised his eyes and said with deliberation:

'No, sir, they are not dealt with here.'

'Where then?'

'In the sales section.'

'And where is the sales section?'

'At Ivan Antonovich's desk.'

'And where is Ivan Antonovich?'

The old man jerked his finger towards the other end of the room. Chichikov and Manilov set off to Ivan Antonovich's desk. Ivan Antonovich had already cast a glance behind him and stolen a sidelong look at them, but at once became immersed even more deeply in his writing.

'Please can you tell us,' said Chichikov with a bow, 'whether you deal with the deeds of purchase here?'

Ivan Antonovich did not seem to hear the question and was completely immersed in his papers, making no reply whatever. It was instantly apparent that he was a man of a discreet age and no young chatterbox and gadabout. Ivan Antonovich was well over forty; his hair was thick and black; all the middle of his face seemed to be thrust forward and concentrated in his nose; it was, in short, the sort of face that is commonly known as a 'jug-snout'.

'Please tell us,' said Chichikov, 'whether this is the section dealing with the deeds of purchase?'

'Yes, sir,' said Ivan Antonovich, turning his jug-snout and carrying on with his writing.

'My business is as follows: I've bought peasants from various landowners of this district intending to settle them in another place. I've got the deeds of purchase here and have only to complete the formalities.'

'And are the sellers here?'

'Some are here, and from others I have an authorization.'

'And have you brought an application?'

'I have. I'm afraid I'm in rather a hurry. I'd be glad to – er – I mean, isn't it possible to complete the formalities today?'

'Today? No, sir, I'm afraid it can't be done today,' said Ivan Antonovich. 'I shall have to make some inquiries and make sure there aren't any injunctions taken out against it.'

'Perhaps it may help to speed up things if I may mention that Ivan Grigoryevich, the president, is a great friend of mine.'

'Ivan Grigoryevich is not the only one,' Ivan Antonovich said sternly. 'There are others, too.'

Chichikov took the hint thrown out by Ivan Antonovich and said: 'The others will not be overlooked, either. You see, sir, I've been in the service, too, and I know how things are done.'

'You'd better go and see Ivan Grigoryevich,' said Ivan Antonovich in a somewhat mollified voice. 'Let him give the order to the right quarter and we shall do our best.'

Chichikov took a note out of his pocket and put it down in front of Ivan Antonovich, who completely failed to notice it and instantly put a book over it. Chichikov was about to point it out to him, but Ivan Antonovich gave him to understand with a movement of his head that it was not necessary.

'This gentleman will show you to the president's office,' said Ivan Antonovich with a nod of his head, and one of the votaries who was standing near and who had been offering up sacrifices to Themis so zealously that both his sleeves had burst at the elbows and the lining had for some time past been sticking out of the holes, for which he had been rewarded with the rank of collegiate registrar, offered his services to our friends in the same way as Virgil had once offered his services to Dante. He took them to the president's office, in which there was only one spacious armchair and in it, at a desk with a triangular piece of glass on which Peter the Great's edicts were inscribed and two thick volumes, sat the president in solitary majesty, like the sun. In this place the new Virgil was so overawed that he did not venture to set foot in it, but turned back, displaying his back worn as threadbare as a bit of matting and with a hen's feather sticking to it. On entering the office, they saw that the president was not alone. Sobakevich was sitting with him, completely hidden by the triangular piece of glass. The arrival of the visitors was greeted with an exclamation, and the presidential armchair was pushed back noisily. Sobakevich, too, got up from his chair and became visible with his long sleeves from all sides. The president clasped Chichikov in his arms and the presidential office resounded with kisses. They inquired after each other's health, and it turned out that both had a pain in the small of the back which was immediately ascribed to a sedentary life. The president seemed to have been already informed of the purchase by Sobakevich, for he began congratulating Chichikov, which at first rather embarrassed our hero, especially when he saw Sobakevich and Manilov, the two vendors with whom the business had been transacted in private, now standing facing each other. However, he thanked the president and turning at once to Sobakevich, asked:

'And how are you?'

'Nothing to complain of, thank God,' said Sobakevich.

And, indeed, he had nothing to complain of: a lump of iron would sooner catch cold and start coughing than that wonderfully constituted landowner.

'Why, you've always been famous for your good health,' said the president. 'Your late father was also a strong man.'

'Yes, he used to tackle a bear singlehanded,' replied Sobakevich.

'I believe you too could knock a bear down if you cared to tackle him,' said the president.

'No, I couldn't,' replied Sobakevich. 'My late father was stronger than me.' And he added with a sigh: 'No, sir, people aren't what they used to be. Take my life, for instance. What sort of life is it? Not much to it.'

'And what's wrong with your life?' said the president.

'It's all wrong, all wrong,' said Sobakevich shaking his head. 'You see, my dear sir, I'm over fifty and I've never been ill. Not a sore throat, not a boil, not a carbuncle. ... A bad sign. I shall have to pay for it some day.' Here Sobakevich sank into melancholy.

'What a man!' Chichikov and the president thought at one and the same time. 'Found something to grumble about!'

'I have a letter for you,' said Chichikov taking Plyushkin's letter out of his pocket.

'Who from?' asked the president and, opening it, exclaimed: 'Oh, from Plyushkin. Still carrying on his stupid, aimless existence, is he?

Poor fellow, used to be a most intelligent man and very wealthy and now ...'

'A dog,' said Sobakevich. 'A scoundrel. Starved his peasants to death.'

'Of course, of course,' said the president, after reading the letter, 'I'm glad to act for him. When would you like to complete the purchase, now or later?'

'Now,' said Chichikov. 'In fact, I'd like to ask you to have it completed today, if possible, because I'm thinking of leaving the town tomorrow. I've brought the deeds of purchase and my application.'

'That's all very well, only say what you like, we're not going to let you go so soon. The purchase shall be completed today, but you must stay with us a little longer all the same. I'll give the order at once,' he said and opened the door of the general office filled with civil servants resembling industrious bees scattered all over their combs if, indeed, a honeycomb can be compared to a government office. 'Is Ivan Antonovich there?'

'Yes, sir,' said a voice from within.

'Ask him to come in, please.'

Ivan Antonovich, the jug's snout already familiar to the reader, made his appearance in the president's office and bowed respectfully.

'Will you please take this gentleman's deeds of purchase, Ivan Antonovich? ...'

'And don't forget, Ivan Grigoryevich,' interposed Sobakevich, 'we shall have to have witnesses, at least two for each party. Send at once to the public prosecutor. He's not a busy man and is probably at home. Zolotukha, the attorney, the worst money-grubber in the world, does all his work for him. The health inspector is also a gentleman of leisure and is probably at home, if he has not gone off somewhere for a game of cards, and there are lots more within easy reach – Trukhachevsky, Begushkin, all of them burden the earth without being of any use to anybody.'

'Quite right, quite right,' said the president and at once sent a messenger to fetch them all.

'I'd also like to ask you,' said Chichikov, 'to send for the agent of a lady landowner with whom I've also concluded a deal, the son of Father Kyril, the head priest. I believe he's employed here.'

'Why, of course, we shall send for him too,' said the president.

'Everything shall be done, and please, I beg you, don't give anything to the clerks. My friends should not have to pay.'

Having said this, he at once gave some order to Ivan Antonovich which evidently did not please him. The purchase deeds seemed to have made a good impression on the president, especially when he saw that the total purchases amounted to almost a hundred thousand roubles. For some time he gazed into Chichikov's eyes with an expression of great satisfaction and at last said:

'So that's how it is! So that's how you do things! Now you've become a man of property, my dear Chichikov.'

'Yes, I have.'

'Excellent, excellent. Yes, sir!'

'Yes, indeed, sir, I see myself that I couldn't have done anything better. Say what you will, but a man's task in life has not been fulfilled till at last he stands with a firm foot on a sound foundation and not on some free-thinking chimera of youth!' And here he most appropriately chided all young people for their liberalism, and not without good reason, either. But it was curious that there was a sort of lack of conviction in his words, as though he were saying to himself: 'Good Lord, my dear fellow, what nonsense you talk!' He did not even glance at Sobakevich or Manilov for fear of detecting something in their faces. But he need not have been afraid: not a muscle stirred on Sobakevich's face, while Manilov, fascinated by his high-sounding phrases, merely nodded his approval with delight, while assuming an attitude common enough among lovers of music whenever a soprano outdoes the violin itself and emits so shrill a note that even a bird's throat could not produce it.

'But why don't you tell Ivan Grigoryevich,' Sobakevich said, 'what it is you have bought? And you, sir,' he turned to the president, 'why don't you ask him what acquisition he has made? You should have seen the peasants he's bought! Real gems! Why, I've sold him my coachman Mikheyev.'

'Have you now? Not Mikheyev?' said the president. 'I know Mikheyev the coachbuilder, an excellent craftsman. He repaired my trap for me. But, look here, what do you mean? Didn't you tell me that he was dead?'

'Who? Mikheyev dead?' said Sobakevich without looking in the least embarrassed. 'It's his brother who's dead. He's alive and kicking and healthier than ever. Only the other day he made me a carriage better than anything they make in Moscow. He really should be working solely for the Emperor.'

'Yes, Mikheyev is an excellent craftsman,' said the president, 'and I'm surprised you should have parted with him. ...'

'But it isn't only Mikheyev! There's Stepan Probka, the carpenter, Milushkin, the bricklayer, Maxim Telyatnikov, the cobbler. They're all gone, I've sold them all.' And when the president asked why he had let them go, considering that they were craftsmen who were indispensable to the house, Sobakevich replied with a wave of his hand: 'Oh, I suppose I must have done it in a moment of folly. Well, I said to myself, let's sell them, and I sold them like a fool!' Then he hung his head as though he were really sorry for what he had done and added: 'I may be a grey-haired old man, but I've still got no sense.'

'But may I ask you, sir,' said the president, turning to Chichikov, 'how is it that you're buying peasants without land? Is it for re-settlement?'

'Yes, for resettlement.'

'Oh, well, that's a different matter. And in what part of the country?'

'Oh – er – in the Kherson province.'

'Ah, there's excellent land there!' said the president, and expressed his great appreciation of the fine growth of the grass in that province. 'And have you sufficient land there?'

'Yes, as much as I shall want for the peasants I've bought.'

'Is there a river or a pond?'

'A river. However, there's a pond there, too.'

As he said this, Chichikov happened to glance at Sobakevich and, though, as before, not a muscle moved on Sobakevich's face, he could not help feeling that he could read in it: 'Oh, you are lying! I don't believe there is a river there or a pond or any land at all.'

While the conversation went on, the witnesses began to arrive, one by one: the public prosecutor, whom the reader has met already, with his twitching eye, the public health inspector, Trukhachevsky, Begushkin, and the others who, as Sobakevich put it, only burdened the earth. Many of them Chichikov did not know at all: their number was made up by some of the civil servants from the office. Not only the son of the chief priest, Father Kyril, but the chief priest himself was fetched. Each of the witnesses signed his name with all his titles and ranks, some writing the letters backhand, others slantwise, and others almost upside-down, such as had never been seen in the Russian alphabet. Ivan Antonovich got through the business efficiently: the purchase deeds were registered, initialled, dated, entered in a book and wherever else was necessary, a half percent being deducted and a charge made for publication in the official gazette. Chichikov had to pay practically nothing. The president even gave orders that only half of the dues should be taken from him, the other half in some mysterious way being put down to the account of some other applicant.

'And so,' said the president when it was all over, 'all that remains to do now is to sprinkle your little deal.'

'Certainly,' said Chichikov, 'you have only to fix the time. It would be unforgivable on my part if I did not uncork two or three bottles of bubbly for such agreeable company.'

'You've got it all wrong,' said the president. 'We shall provide the bubbly ourselves. It's our duty, our obligation. You're our guest and it is for us to entertain you. Now do you know what, gentlemen? For the time being we'd better do this: let's all go just as we are to the chief of police. He's our miracle worker. He's only to wink as he walks through the fish market or past a wine merchant's shop, and we shall have a grand feast! And we might even use the occasion for a game of whist.'

No one could refuse such a proposal. The mere mention of the fish market gave the witnesses an appetite. They all at once picked up their hats and caps and the official business was at an end. As they walked through the general office, Ivan Antonovich, the jug's snout, bowing courteously, said quietly to Chichikov:

'You've bought a hundred thousand roubles' worth of peasants and only given me twenty-five roubles for my trouble.'

'But what sort of peasants are they?' Chichikov replied, also in a whisper. 'A good-for-nothing, wretched lot. They aren't worth half the money.'

Ivan Antonovich realized that he was dealing with a man of strong character who wouldn't give more.

'And how much did you pay Plyushkin for each soul?' Sobakevich whispered in his other ear.

'And why did you stick in Vorobey?' Chichikov retorted.

'Which Vorobey?' said Sobakevich.

'Why, the peasant woman Yelizaveta Vorobey, and you gave her name a masculine ending, too.'

'No, sir, I did not stick in any Vorobey,' said Sobakevich and he went off to rejoin the other members of the party.

The visitors at last arrived in a crowd at the house of the chief of police. The chief of police was, indeed, a miracle worker: as soon as he heard what it was all about he called a policeman, a smart fellow in lacquered top-boots, and apparently only whispered a couple of words in his ear, merely adding: 'Understand?' and at once, while the guests were playing whist, on the table in the next room there appeared a white sturgeon, ordinary sturgeon, salmon, pressed caviare, fresh caviare, herrings, stellated sturgeon, cheeses of all sorts, smoked tongue, and dried sturgeon – all this came from the fish market. Then there appeared all sorts of supplementary dishes from the kitchen: a pie made of the head, gristle, and cheeks of a three-hundred-pound sturgeon, another pie stuffed with mushrooms, fried pastries, dumplings cooked in melted butter, and fruit stewed in honey. The chief of police was in a sense the father and benefactor of the town. He treated the citizens as if they were members of his own family and he paid visits to the shops and the merchants' arcade as if they were his own larder. All in all, he was, as the saying is, the right man in the right place, and he understood the duties of his position to perfection. It was, in fact, hard to say whether he had been created for his job or his job for him. He had arranged things so cleverly that his income was double that of any of his predecessors and at the same time he had won the affection of the whole town. The merchants, in particular, liked him tremendously just because he was not proud; and, to be sure, he stood godfather to their children, was on familiar terms with them, and though occasionally he did fleece them terribly, he managed to do so very dexterously: he would slap a man on the back and laugh, treat him to tea, promise to come and play draughts with him, inquire about everything, how his business was and how he was getting on in general. If he learned that a child had fallen sick, he would recommend a medicine – in short, he was an excellent fellow. If he drove through the town in his light four-wheeled carriage to see that law and order was preserved, he would at the same time drop a word here and there to some of the shopkeepers: 'Well, Mikheyich, we really ought to finish our rubber one of these days.' 'Yes, sir,' the shopkeeper replied, taking off his hat, 'we ought to.' 'I say, my dear

Ilya Paramonych, come and have a look at my trotter. I'm sure he'll beat yours in a race and don't forget to put yours in a racing-fly, we'll try him out.' The merchant, who was mad on trotting horses, would smile at this with particular relish, as they say, and, stroking his beard, say: 'Yes, sir, we'll certainly try him.' Even the shop assistants, who usually stood cap in hand at this time, looked delightedly at one another and seemed about to say: 'The chief of police is an excellent fellow!' In short, he had managed to gain universal popularity and it was the opinion of the merchants that though the chief of police 'does line his pockets he will never let you down'.

Noticing that the savouries had been set out, the chief of police suggested to his visitors that they should finish the game of whist after lunch, and they all went to the room from which an agreeable smell had for some time been titillating their nostrils and into which Sobakevich had for some time been peeping, having noticed from a distance the huge sturgeon lying on a big dish set on one side of the table. After drinking a glass of vodka of a dark olive colour, which one only finds in the transparent Siberian stones of which seals are carved in Russia, the guests crowded round the table on all sides with forks in their hands and, as they say, began to exhibit each his character and inclinations: one concentrated on the caviare, another on the salmon, and a third on the cheese. Sobakevich, ignoring all these trifles, stationed himself by the big sturgeon and while the others were drinking, talking, and eating, he dispatched it in a little over a quarter of an hour, so that when the chief of police remembered it, and saying: 'And what is your opinion, gentlemen, of this work of nature?' went up to it, fork in hand, with the others of the company, he saw that only the tail was left of the work of nature; Sobakevich, meanwhile, kept quiet, just as though he had had nothing to do with it, and going up to a dish a little distance from the rest prodded some little dried fish with his fork. Having made short work of the sturgeon, Sobakevich sat down in an armchair, and ate and drank nothing more, but just screwed up his eyes and blinked. The chief of police, apparently, did not like to stint the wine; there was no end to the toasts. The first toast was, as the reader will probably guess by himself, drunk to the health of the new Kherson landowner, then to the prosperity of his peasants and their successful transmigration, then to the health of his beautiful bride-to-be, which brought an agreeable smile to our hero's face. They surrounded him on all sides and began to plead with him earnestly to remain with them for at least another fortnight.

'No, sir, no,' they told Chichikov, 'say what you will, but to go off like this means only to let the cold draught into the cottage. You can't just come in and go out again. You must stay a little longer with us. We'll marry you off! Isn't that so, Ivan Grigoryevich? We'll marry him off, won't we?'

'We will, we will!' put in the president. 'You may jib at it as much as you like, but we'll marry you off! No, my dear sir, once you're here, it's no good your complaining. We're not to be trifled with.'

'Well, why jib at it?' said Chichikov with a smile. 'Matrimony isn't such a bad thing after all, provided of course there's a bride.'

'There'll be a bride, of course there'll be a bride! There'll be everything, everything you want!'

'Oh, well, in that case …'

'Bravo, he's staying!' they all cried. 'Hurrah, Chichikov! Hurrah!'

And they all went up to clink glasses with him. Chichikov clinked glasses with everyone. 'Again, again!' cried those who were more enthusiastic and they clinked glasses once more; then they went up to clink glasses for a third time, and they clinked glasses yet again. In a short time they were all quite extraordinarily merry. The president, who was a most charming man when in a merry mood, embraced Chichikov several times, exclaiming with deep feeling: 'My darling boy, my poppet,' and even, snapping his fingers, started to dance round him singing the well-known song 'Oh, you so-and-so, you Kamarinsky peasant lad!' After the champagne, they uncorked some bottles of Tokay, which put still more spirit into them and made the whole party merrier than ever. The whist was entirely forgotten; they argued, shouted, and talked about everything, politics, military affairs, gave expression to free-thinking ideas for which at any other time they would have thrashed their own children. They settled a multitude of the most difficult questions. Chichikov had never felt himself in such a happy frame of mind. He imagined himself already a real Kherson landowner, talked of the various improvements he was going to introduce, the rotation of crops system, the happiness and bliss of two kindred souls, and began to recite to Sobakevich Werther's letter in verse to Charlotte, which only made Sobakevich blink as he lay back in his armchair, for after the sturgeon he felt a great inclination for sleep. Chichikov realized himself that he was getting a little too expansive, so he asked for a carriage and availed himself of the public prosecutor's trap. The public prosecutor's driver was, as it turned out on the way, an experienced fellow, for he drove with one hand and supported the gentleman with the other thrust out behind him. In this way Chichikov reached the inn in the public prosecutor's trap. In his room he kept talking all sorts of nonsense about a fair-haired bride with rosy cheeks and a dimple in her right cheek, his Kherson estates, his great fortune. He even gave Selifan some orders about the management of his estates, such as collecting all the newly settled peasants and taking a roll-call of them. Selifan listened for a long time in silence and then went out of the room, saying to Petrushka: 'You'd better go and undress the master.' Petrushka began pulling off his boots and almost pulled his master on to the floor with them. But at last the boots were off, the master was properly undressed and, turning over a few times on the bed, which creaked unmercifully, he fell asleep like a genuine Kherson landowner. Meanwhile Petrushka carried out into the passage his master's trousers and his gleaming cranberry-coloured dress-coat, and spreading them out on a wooden hat-stand began beating them with a riding crop and brushing them, filling the whole corridor with dust. As he was about to take them down, he looked over the gallery and saw Selifan coming back from the stables. Their eyes met and they understood each other without uttering a word: the master was fast asleep and they could go and look in somewhere. Taking the coat and the trousers back into the room, Petrushka at once went downstairs and they set off together without uttering so much as a word about the destination of their journey and cracking jokes on the way about quite different matters. They did not go far: in fact, they only crossed the road and went into a house opposite the inn. They went through a low, grimy glass door, which led down into a basement where many people were already sitting at wooden tables: some shaven and some unshaven, some in sheepskins and some simply in shirt-sleeves and one or two had frieze overcoats. What Petrushka and Selifan did there, God only knows, but an hour later they came out arm-in-arm, observing complete silence, showing the utmost attention to each other and steering each other clear of corners. Arm-in-arm, without letting go of each other, they took a whole quarter of an hour to get up the stairs, but at last they got the better of them and reached the top. Petrushka stopped for a moment before his low bed, trying to think how to lie down on it more decently, and in the end sprawled right across it so that his feet were pressed against the floor. Selifan lay down on the same bed with his head on Petrushka's belly, forgetting that he should be sleeping not there but in a different place, in the servants' quarters perhaps, if not in the stable near the horses. They both fell asleep at the same moment, raising a snore of incredible richness, to which the master responded from next door with a thin, nasal whistling. Soon afterwards everything grew quiet, and the whole inn was wrapped in deep slumber; only in one window a light could still be seen: it came from the room in which was staying the recently arrived lieutenant from Ryazan who was evidently a great lover of boots for he had already ordered four pairs and kept trying on a fifth. He went up to his bed several times to take them off and to lie down, but he could not bring himself to do so: the boots were, indeed, well-made and for a long time he kept raising his foot and examining the cleverly and wonderfully shaped heel.

Chapter 8

CHICHIKOV's purchases became a topic of general conversation. All sorts of discussions took place in the town, views and opinions were expressed as to whether it was profitable or not to purchase serfs for resettlement. Many of those who took part in these debates showed a perfect grasp of the subject. 'Of course,' some said, 'there can be no doubt at all about it: the land in the southern provinces is indeed good and fertile, but what will Chichikov's peasants do without water? You see, there is no river there.'

'That there's no water there wouldn't matter so much, my dear sir. The trouble is that resettlement is a very risky business. You know perfectly well what a Russian peasant is like: settle him on new land and set him to till it, with nothing prepared for him, neither cottage nor farmstead, and, well, he'll run away, as sure as twice two makes four. He'll take to his heels and you won't find a trace of him.'

'No, sir, I'm sorry, but I don't agree with what you say about Chichikov's peasants running away. A Russian is capable of anything and he can get used to any climate. Send him to Kamchatka and give him a pair of warm mittens, and he'll clap his hands, pick up his axe, and off he'll go to cut some timber to build himself a new cottage.'

'But, my dear sir, you've lost sight of one important point. You haven't asked yourself what sort of peasants Chichikov has got. You seem to have forgotten that no landowner ever sells a good man. I'm willing to bet you anything you like that Chichikov's peasants are thieves, confirmed drunkards, bone idle, and rowdy.'

'That may be so. I quite agree that it's true that no one will sell good men and that Chichikov's serfs are drunkards, but you must take into consideration the fact that a moral is involved here, that the whole thing must be considered from a moral point of view: they are rogues, every one of them, but settled on new land they may well become excellent subjects. There are hundreds of such instances, both in history and in our world of today.'

'Never, never!' said the superintendent of government factories.

'Believe me, that can never be. For Chichikov's peasants will have two great enemies now. The first enemy is the proximity of the Ukrainian provinces, where, as you all know, the sale of vodka is unrestricted. I assure you that within a fortnight they'll be as drunk as lords. Their other enemy is the habit of vagrancy which peasants invariably acquire during their migration. The only way to prevent it is that they should always be before Chichikov's eyes and that he should rule them with a rod of iron, punish them for every trifle. And he must remember not to rely on anyone else, but to give them a punch on the nose or a cuff on the ear when necessary with his own hands.'

'But why should Chichikov have to bother about it himself and go on handing out cuffs on the ears? He may get a good estate manager.'

'Oh, yes, just try and find a good estate manager! They're all rogues.'

'They're rogues because the masters don't attend to their business themselves.'

'That's true,' many people assented. 'If the master had some notion of farming himself and if he could pick the right man, he'd always have a good estate manager.'

But the superintendent of factories declared that one couldn't find a good estate manager for less than five thousand roubles. The president retorted that one could find one for three thousand. But the superintendent said: 'Where are you going to find him? Not in your nose?' But the president said: 'No, not in my nose, but in this district. I mean Peter Samoylov. He's the manager that Chichikov's peasants need!'

Many persons were deeply concerned about Chichikov's position and the difficulty of transporting so vast a number of peasants alarmed them greatly; they began to be extremely perturbed by the possible outbreak of a mutiny among so turbulent a rabble as Chichikov's peasants. But the chief of police observed that there was no need to be afraid of a mutiny, that there was a rural captain of police to see to it that it did not occur, and that even if the rural captain of police did not go there himself but sent his cap, the sight of this cap alone would be sufficient to drive the peasants to their new places of residence. Many persons offered suggestions for eradicating the turbulent spirit of Chichikov's peasants. These suggestions were of all kinds: some of them smacked a little too much of military harshness and severity, which was perhaps not altogether necessary in such a case; but there were others which were imbued with the spirit of leniency. The postmaster observed that Chichikov was now faced with the sacred duty of becoming, as he expressed it, a kind of father to his peasants and even of introducing some beneficent educational reforms and on this occasion spoke with great approval of Joseph Lancaster's system of education.

That was how they argued and talked in the town and many people, moved by sympathy, offered Chichikov some of this advice and even proposed that he might find an escort of soldiers useful to ensure the safe conveyance of his peasants to their new places of residence. Chichikov thanked them for their advice, assuring them that he would not fail to take advantage of it in case of need, but he flatly turned down the idea of a military escort, saying that it was quite unnecessary because the peasants he had bought were of an extremely docile character and were themselves favourably disposed to the idea of resettlement and there could be no question of any mutiny among them.

All these arguments and discussions, however, produced so favourable a result that Chichikov could not possibly have expected anything better; that is to say, rumours soon spread that he was neither more nor less than a millionaire. The people of the town had, as we have seen in the first chapter, taken a great liking to Chichikov anyhow, but after such rumours they took an even greater liking to him. To tell the truth, they were all kind-hearted people, got on well together, treated each other in a most friendly fashion, and their talk was characterized by a special kind of good nature and intimacy: 'My dear friend, Ilya Ilyitch!,' 'Now, look here, my dear fellow, Antipator Zakharyevich,' 'Aren't you going a little too far, Ivan Grigoryevich, old man?' When addressing the postmaster, who was called Ivan Andreyevich, they always added: '*Sprechen sie Deich*, Ivan Andreich?' – in short, they were all one happy family. Many of them were not without some education: the president knew Zhukovsky's *Lyudmila* by heart, a poem which was then still a novelty, and he used to recite many passages in a quite masterly fashion, particularly the line: 'The pine forest sleeps, the valley slumbers,' and the word: 'Hark!', so that they really seemed to see the valley slumbering: to make it all the more realistic, he even closed his eyes as he said it. The postmaster was more addicted to philosophy and he used to read very diligently even at night Young's *Night Thoughts* and Eckartshausen's *Key to the Mysteries of Nature*, from which he used to copy out very long passages, though no one knew what they were about. He was, however, a wit, flowery in his speech and fond, as he expressed it, of larding his speech. And he larded his speech with a multitude of all sorts of short auxiliary phrases, such as, 'My dear sir, sort of, you know, you understand, you can imagine, relatively speaking, to a certain extent,' and so on, which he scattered about in sackfuls; he also larded his speech fairly successfully by winking and screwing up one eye, which lent a very sardonic expression to many of his satirical allusions. The others, too, were all more or less educated people, one read Karamazin, another the *Moscow News*, and a third actually read nothing at all. Some were of a kind known as 'bags', that is to say, men who could only be aroused by a kick in the pants; others were simply sluggards, lying all their lives on one side, and it was a sheer waste of time even to attempt to rouse them: they wouldn't have got up under any circumstances. As for decorum, they were all, as we know, highly solid people, and there were no insignificant looking persons among them. They were all the sort of people upon whom wives in their intimate exchanges and endearments in private bestowed such names as 'Dumpling', 'Fatty', 'Tubby', 'Blackie', 'Kiki', 'Zouzou', and so on. But, generally speaking, they were good-natured people, full of hospitality, and anyone invited by them to dinner, anyone who spent the evening playing whist with them, was treated as one who was near and dear to them, and that was particularly true of Chichikov who with his charming qualities and manners really knew the great secret of pleasing people. They had grown so fond of him that he could think of no way of escaping from the town. All he heard was: 'Come, stay another week with us, just one more week, dear Mr Chichikov!' In short, they made a fuss of him, as the saying is. But incomparably more remarkable was the impression (a subject of absolute astonishment) which Chichikov made on the ladies. To explain it to some extent one would have to say a great deal about the ladies themselves, about their society, to describe, as is said, in vivid colours their spiritual qualities; but that the author finds a very difficult thing to do. On the one hand he is restrained by his unbounded respect for the wives of the high officials, and on the other hand – on the other hand, it is simply too difficult. The ladies of the town of N. were – No, I'm afraid I just can't go on: I feel too shy. The most remarkable thing about the ladies of the town of N. was that – It is really strange how my pen simply refuses to move, just as though it were weighted down with lead. So be it: it seems I must leave it to someone else to say something about their characters, to someone whose colours are more vivid and who has a greater assortment of them on his palette, while I will merely say a word or two about their looks and that, too, in a most superficial manner. The ladies of the town of N. were what is called very presentable and in this respect they can fearlessly be held up as an example to all others. So far as deportment was concerned, the maintenance of good tone, the observance of etiquette, and a multitude of the most refined rules of propriety, and especially the strict conformance to fashion in its minutest details – indeed, in all these things they left even the ladies of Petersburg and Moscow far behind. They dressed with great taste and drove about the town in carriages, as the latest fashion prescribed, with a footman perched behind in a livery with gold galloons. A visiting card, even if written on a two of clubs or an ace of diamonds, was a very sacred thing. It was because of such a card that two ladies, great friends and even relations, had a violent quarrel, simply because one of them had for some reason failed to return a call. And in spite of all the efforts of their husbands and relations to reconcile them afterwards, it was all in vain, for it seemed that one can do anything else in the world, but that one thing is impossible – to reconcile two ladies who have quarrelled because one of them had failed to return a call. And so the two ladies remained, as members of the high society of the town expressed it, in a state of mutual indisposition. There were also a great many extremely violent scenes over the question of precedence, which sometimes inspired in their husbands highly chivalrous and generous conceptions of their duty in taking their wives' parts. Duels, of course, did not take place because the gentlemen were all civil servants, but, on the other hand, they tried their best to play each other dirty tricks whenever possible, and that, as everyone knows, is sometimes much more painful than any duel.

So far as morals were concerned, the ladies of the town of N. were severe and full of noble indignation at every kind of vice and every form of temptation, and they were merciless in their punishment of every kind of weakness. If something that can be described as an *affair* did happen, it happened in secret, so that not the slightest hint was given of anything improper having taken place; appearances were preserved and the husband himself was so well coached that even if he did get wind of the *affair* or heard of it, he briefly and sensibly quoted the Russian proverb: 'What business is it of yours that your godmother was speaking to your godfather?' One ought also to mention the fact that the ladies of the town of N., like many Petersburg ladies, were distinguished by their extraordinarily careful and dignified choice of words and expressions. They never said, 'I blew my nose', 'I perspired', or 'I spat', but 'I relieved my nose', or 'I made use of my handkerchief'. In no circumstance might one say 'this glass or that plate stinks'. One could not even say anything that might give the slightest hint of this, but said instead 'I'm afraid this glass isn't quite nice', or something of the kind. To ennoble the Russian tongue even more, almost half its words were banished from their conversation, and because of that they had very often to have recourse to French; but in French it was quite a different matter: in that language they permitted themselves words far coarser than those mentioned above. This is all one can say about the ladies of the town of N., speaking, of course, superficially. If we were to look a little more deeply many other things would of course be discovered; but it is highly dangerous to look too deeply into the hearts of ladies. And so, confining ourselves to a superficial view, let us continue. The ladies had for some reason talked very little about Chichikov so far, though they did give him full credit for his agreeable behaviour in society; but as soon as rumours had been spread of his being a millionaire, they discovered other qualities in him, too. The ladies, however, were not at all mercenary-minded: the word 'millionaire' alone was to blame, not the millionaire himself, but just the word alone; for quite apart from the money bags, there is something in the mere sound of that word which alike affects people who are scoundrels, people who are neither the one thing nor the other, and good people; in short, it affects everyone. The millionaire has the advantage of observing baseness that is utterly disinterested, baseness pure and simple, baseness that is not based on any personal motives: many people know perfectly well that they won't get anything out of him and have no right to expect it, but they will do their best to anticipate his wishes, to laugh at his jokes, to take off their hats, to do all they can to obtain an invitation to a dinner to which they know the millionaire has been invited. It cannot be said that any tender inclination towards baseness was felt by the ladies; in many drawing-rooms, however, they began to say that Chichikov was of course not as handsome as all that, but that he was what a real man ought to be, and that if he had been a little fatter or stouter, it would be a great shame. And apropos of this something rather derogatory was added about thin men, namely that they were more like toothpicks than men. All sorts of additional touches appeared in the dresses of the ladies. There was a crowd, almost a crush, in the shopping arcade; there were so many carriages driving up to it that they looked almost like a procession. The shopkeepers were amazed to see that several rolls of cloth which they had brought from the fair and could not get off their hands because of the price, which seemed too high, were suddenly in great demand and were snapped up in no time. At mass in church one of the ladies was observed to have such a *rouleau* at the bottom of her skirt that it spread and covered half the church, so that the police inspector, who happened to be present, ordered the peasants to move farther back, that is, nearer to the porch, that they might not crush her ladyship's dress. Even Chichikov himself could not help noticing such extraordinary attention. One day, on returning home, he found a letter lying on his table. He could not find out who had brought it or from whom it came. The servant at the inn merely said that it had been brought by someone with orders not to reveal the name of the person who sent it. The letter began in a most emphatic fashion: 'Yes, I must write to you, my darling!' Then something was said about there being 'a mysterious affinity of souls'; this truism was confirmed by a number of dots which covered almost half a line. Next followed a number of reflections so remarkable for their justice that we think it almost incumbent upon us to quote them: 'What is our life? – A vale of sorrows. What is high society? – A crowd of people without feelings.' Then the lady correspondent mentioned the fact she was bedewing the lines with tears for a tender mother, who had departed this life twenty-five years before; Chichikov was invited to betake himself to the desert and to forsake forever the city where men, confined between stifling walls, could not breathe the fresh air; the letter ended on a note of absolute despair and concluded with the following verse:

> Two turtle doves will show thee
>   Where my cold ashes bide,
> Their languid murmurings will tell thee,
>   How, weeping, I died.

The last line did not scan, but that did not matter: the letter was written in the spirit of those days. There was no signature, either: neither Christian name, nor surname, nor even the date. But in a postscript it was added that his own heart ought to divine who his woman correspondent was, and that she would be present at the governor's ball that was to take place the next day.

This interested him greatly. There was so much that was thrilling and that excited his curiosity in the anonymous letter that he read it through a second and a third time and said at last: 'It would be interesting, though, to find out who the woman is!' In short, things were apparently taking a serious turn; he kept thinking about it for over an hour and at last, spreading out his hands and inclining his head, said: 'The letter is certainly very, very flowery!' Then, needless to say, the letter was folded up and put away in his box next door to some playbills and an invitation to a wedding, which had been lying there in the same place and in the same position for the last seven years. Shortly afterwards an invitation was indeed brought him for the governor's ball – quite an ordinary occurrence in a provincial town: where there's a governor there's a ball, for otherwise he would not enjoy the respect and love of the nobility.

Everything that had no relation to the ball was immediately put aside and dismissed from his mind, his entire attention being concentrated on getting ready for the ball; for, indeed, there were many stimulating and exciting reasons for it. No man since the creation of the world perhaps spent so much time on dressing up. A whole hour was devoted solely to the examination of his face in the looking-glass. He tried to assume a multitude of various expressions: one moment he tried to look grave and important, another moment respectful but with the ghost of a smile, then simply respectful without a smile; a number of bows were made to the looking-glass, accompanied by inarticulate sounds remotely resembling French, though Chichikov did not know French at all. He even gave himself a number of pleasant surprises, winking an eye and twitching a lip, and even did something with his tongue; in short, one is liable to do all sorts of odd things when left alone, feeling, moreover, that one is a handsome fellow and being perfectly sure that no one will be looking through a crack. At last he chucked himself slightly under the chin and said: 'Oh, you silly old face!' and began dressing. He felt perfectly happy and contented all the time he was dressing; pulling on his braces or tying his cravat, he bowed and scraped with particular adroitness, and though he had never danced in his life, he executed an *entrechat*. This *entrechat* produced a small and harmless effect: the chest of drawers shook and the brush fell from the table.

His arrival at the ball created an extraordinary sensation. Everyone there turned round to look at him. One man with cards in his hands, someone else at the most interesting point in the conversation, having just uttered the words: 'And the lower district court's answer to this...'; but what the district court's answer was he tossed aside and hurried to greet our hero. 'Mr Chichikov! Good heavens, Mr Chichikov! Dear Mr Chichikov! Most honourable Mr Chichikov! My dear Mr Chichikov! So here you are at last, Mr Chichikov! There he is, our dear Mr Chichikov! Bring him here and let me give him a big kiss, my dear, dear Mr Chichikov!' Chichikov felt himself embraced by several people all at once. He had barely time to extricate himself from the president's embrace, when he found himself in the arms of the chief of police; the chief of police handed him over to the inspector of public health, the inspector of public health to the government contractor, the government contractor to the architect ... The governor, who was at that moment standing beside some ladies, holding a raffle ticket in one hand and a lap dog in the other, dropped both ticket and lap dog on to the floor on seeing him, the dog yelping piteously; in short, Chichikov spread an atmosphere of joy and quite extraordinary gaiety. There was not a face that did not express pleasure or at least a reflection of the general pleasure. So it is with the faces of civil servants when the offices entrusted to their charge are being inspected by the chief of a government department: after their first panic has passed off they see that there is a great deal that has pleased him, and when at last he has graciously condescended to joke, that is to say, to utter a few words with a pleasant smile, the civil servants crowding round him laugh twice as much in reply; those who have hardly heard what he said laugh with all their might too, and finally a policeman standing at the door an appreciable distance away, who has never laughed in his life and who has a minute earlier been shaking his fist at the people outside, even he, according to the unalterable laws of reflection, shows some kind of smile on his face, though it looks more as though he were about to sneeze after a pinch of strong snuff. Our hero responded to all and each and he felt extraordinarily at his ease; he bowed to right and to left, a little to one side, as was his habit, but without the slightest constraint, so that everyone was enchanted by him. The ladies at once crowded round him in a glittering garland, bringing with them whole clouds of every kind of scent: one exuded roses, another brought with her the scent of spring and violets, a third was saturated through and through with mignonette; Chichikov just kept lifting up his nose and sniffing. Their dresses displayed an infinite variety of taste: muslins, satins, chiffons were of the pale fashionable shades for which even a name could not be found (such a degree of refinement has modern taste reached). Bows of ribbon and bunches of flowers fluttered about here and there in most picturesque disorder, though much thought had been given to the creation of this disorder. A light head-dress was supported only by the ears, and seemed to be saying, 'Look out, I'm going to take flight and I'm only sorry I can't carry the beautiful creature away with me!' The waists were tightly laced and had the most firm and agreeable shape for the eyes to enjoy (it must be noted that, in general, the ladies of the town of N. were rather plump, but they laced themselves so skilfully and carried themselves so charmingly that it was quite impossible to notice how plump they were). They had thought out and foreseen everything with most extraordinary care: necks and shoulders were bared just as much as was necessary and not an inch more; each one of them bared her possessions only as far as she thought them capable of ruining a man; the rest was all hidden away with extraordinary taste: either some light ribbon of a neck-band or a scarf that was lighter than a puff pastry known as 'a kiss', ethereally encircled the neck, or tiny fringed pieces of fine cambric known as 'modesties' were let in from under the dress over the shoulders. These 'modesties' concealed in front and at the back what could not possibly bring about a man's ruin and yet made one suspect that it was there that final disaster lay. The long gloves were not drawn up as far as the sleeves, but purposely left bare those alluring parts of the arm above the elbow that in many of the ladies were of an enviable plumpness; some ladies had even split their kid gloves in the effort to pull them up as far as possible – in short, it was as if everything had been inscribed with the legend: 'No, this is not a provincial town! This is a capital city! This is Paris itself!' Only here and there a bonnet of a shape never seen on earth before, or some feather that might have been a peacock's, was thrust out in defiance of all fashion and in accordance with individual taste.

But you can't help that, for such is the nature of a provincial town: it is bound to trip up somewhere. Standing before them, Chichikov thought: 'Who could be the authoress of the letter?' He thrust out his nose, but a whole row of elbows, cuffs, sleeves, ends of ribbons, perfumed chemisettes, and dresses brushed past his very nose. The galop was at its height: the postmaster's wife, the police captain, a lady with a pale blue feather, a lady with a white feather, the Georgian prince, Chipkhaykhilidzev, an official from Petersburg, an official from Moscow, a Frenchman called Coucou, Perkhunovsky, Berebendovsky, all were whirling madly in the dance.

'Look at them! The whole provincial administration in full swing!' said Chichikov to himself, stepping back, and as soon as the ladies had resumed their seats, he again started trying to find out whether he could tell from the expression of a face or a look in some eyes who the writer of the letter was; but it was utterly impossible to recognize either from the expression of the face or the look in the eyes who the writer was. Everywhere something could be detected that seemed to be on the point of betraying some secret, something elusively subtle – oh, how subtle! ... 'No,' Chichikov said to himself, 'women are a subject such as ...' Here he dismissed it with a wave of the hand: 'What's the use of talking! Just try and describe or put into words everything that is flitting over their faces, all the subtle twists of meaning, all the hints – and you simply won't be able to put it into words. Their eyes alone are such a vast realm that if a man ventured to enter it he'd be as good as done for! You won't drag him out of there by hook or by crook. Just try describing, for instance, their glitter alone: moist, velvety, sugary. Goodness only knows what else you may not find there. Harsh and soft, and quite languishing, or as some say, voluptuous or not voluptuous but a hundred times worse than voluptuous – and it clutches at your heart and plays upon your souls, as though with a violin bow. No, one simply can't find the right words: the "ever so refined" half of the human species, and that's all there is to it!'

I'm terribly sorry! I believe a rather colloquial expression has escaped from the lips of my hero. But what's to be done about it? Such is the sad predicament of a writer in Russia. However, if a very colloquial expression has got into the book, it is not the author's fault; it is the fault of the readers and, above all, of the readers who belong to the best society: it is from them more than from anyone that you will never hear a single decent Russian word, but they just can't help being over-generous with French, German, and English words, so that you get sick and tired of them, and they will even let you have them in every possible pronunciation: they speak French through their nose and with the Parisian 'r', English they chirp like a bird and even try to look like a bird, and they even laugh at anyone who is unable to make his face look like a bird; but they will never let you have anything Russian, except perhaps out of patriotism build a country cottage in the style of a Russian peasant's cottage. That is what the readers of high society are like, and they are aped by all who like to think that they belong to high society. And yet how fastidious they are! They insist that everything should be written in the most correct, pure, noble language; in short, they would like the Russian language to drop from the sky perfectly polished, so that they have nothing to do but open their mouths and let it drop straight on to their tongues. Of course, the female half of the human species is not so easy to understand; but our estimable readers, it must be confessed, are sometimes even more difficult to understand.

Meanwhile Chichikov was completely at a loss to decide which of the ladies was the authoress of the letter. Having tried to look more intently, he perceived on the ladies' part, too, an expression that seemed to hold out the promise of both hope and sweet torment to a poor mortal's heart and he said at last, 'No, it's quite impossible to find out!' That, however, did not in the least diminish his cheerful mood. He exchanged a few agreeable words with some of the ladies in a most unconstrained and adroit manner, going up first to one and then to another with short, quick, or as they say, mincing steps, as is usual with little doddering old dandies with high heels, known as 'mousey little stallions', when they strut about nimbly in front of ladies. Having taken one or two rather nimble mincing steps to right and to left, he scraped with one foot as though drawing a short tail or a comma on the floor. The ladies were very pleased with him and not only discovered in him a host of agreeable and amiable qualities, but began to discern a majestic expression on his face, even something martial and military which, as we all know, women find extremely attractive. They even began quarrelling a little over him: noticing that he usually stood near the door, some tried vieing with one another by hastening to secure a seat nearer the door, and, when one of them succeeded in getting there first, it nearly gave rise to an unpleasant scene, and such forwardness appeared a little revolting to many of those who had been trying to do the same.

Chichikov was so absorbed in his conversation with the ladies, or rather the ladies so absorbed and overwhelmed him with their conversation, adding hundreds of the most ingenious and subtle allegorical remarks which had all to be interpreted and which even made the sweat stand out on his brow, that he forgot to observe the rules of decorum and first of all pay his respects to his hostess. He only remembered it when he heard the voice of the governor's wife who had been standing before him for some minutes. With a charming shake of her head, the governor's wife said in a rather affectionate and arch tone of voice: 'Oh, Mr Chichikov, so that's how you are engaged!' I cannot reproduce the governor's wife's words with any accuracy, but something extremely polite was said in the manner in which ladies and gentlemen converse in the works of our society novelists who are so eager to describe drawing-rooms and boast of their knowledge of aristocratic manners, something in the style of: 'Have they so taken possession of your heart that there's no longer any place in it, not even the tiniest corner, for those you have so mercilessly forgotten?' Our hero at once turned round to the governor's wife and was on the point of making a reply, probably no worse than those uttered in our modern novels by the Zvonskys, the Linskys, the Lidins, the Gremins, and all similarly accomplished army officers when, chancing to raise his eyes, he stopped all of a sudden as though felled by a blow on the head.

It was not the governor's wife alone who stood before him: on her arm was a young, sixteen-year-old girl, a sweet looking, fair-haired girl, with delicate and graceful features, a pointed chin, an enchantingly rounded oval face, such as a painter might have taken as a model for his Madonna, and such as is only rarely found in Russia, where everything, whatever it may be, likes to assume large dimensions: mountains, woods, steppes, faces, lips, and feet. It was the same fair-haired girl whom he had met on the road on his way back from Nozdryov when, owing to the stupidity of the drivers or the horses, their carriages had so strangely collided and their harness had become entangled and Uncle Mityay and Uncle Minyay had volunteered to disentangle them. Chichikov was so taken aback that he could not utter a single sensible word, and goodness only knows what he mumbled, something that certainly no Gremin, Zvonsky, or Lidin would have said.

'You don't know my daughter, do you?' said the governor's wife. 'She's only just left boarding school.'

He replied that he had already by chance had the good fortune of making her acquaintance; he tried to add something more, but the something more did not come off. The governor's wife said a few more words and then walked away with her daughter to the other end of the ballroom to talk to other guests, while Chichikov was still standing motionless on the same spot, like a man who, having gone out gaily for a walk with eyes disposed to look at everything, suddenly stops dead, having remembered that he has forgotten something, and there can be nothing sillier than such a person: in an instant the careless expression disappears from his face, he is trying hard to remember what he has forgotten   his handkerchief? – but his handkerchief is in his pocket; his money? – but his money too is in his pocket. He seems to have everything, and yet some unseen spirit keeps whispering in his ear that he has forgotten something. And so there he stands, looking confusedly and vaguely at the moving crowd before him, at the carriages dashing past, at the shakos and rifles of the regiment marching by, at some signboard, and is unable to see anything distinctly. In the same way Chichikov suddenly became indifferent to everything that was going on round him. At that moment a great many hints and questions full of the most polite and refined subtleties were fired at him from the fragrant lips of the ladies. 'May we poor dwellers on the earth make so bold as to ask you what you are dreaming of?' 'What are those happy regions where your thoughts are now wandering?' 'May we know the name of her who has plunged you into this sweet vale of reverie?' But Chichikov paid no attention whatever and the agreeable phrases vanished into thin air. He was even so uncivil as to walk away from them hurriedly to the other end of the room, anxious to find out where the governor's wife had gone with her daughter. But the ladies were not apparently willing to let him go so quickly; every one of them was inwardly determined to make use of all the weapons that are so perilous to our hearts and put everything best fitted to that end into action. It must be observed that some ladies – I say 'some', which is not the same as saying all – have a little weakness: if they notice anything particularly attractive about themselves, whether brow or mouth or arms, they immediately assume that the most attractive part of their faces will be the first to be noticed by everyone and that everyone will at once exclaim in one voice: 'Look, look, what a beautiful Grecian nose she has!' or 'What an enchanting, regular forehead!' A woman who has lovely shoulders is convinced in advance that all the young men will be absolutely in raptures over them, will continually be repeating when she passes: 'Oh, what marvellous shoulders she has!' and will not even glance at her face, her hair, her nose, her forehead, or if they do, they will regard it as something that has nothing whatever to do with her. This is what some ladies think. Every lady vowed to be as ravishing as possible when dancing and to show off in all its splendour what she regarded as her best asset. When she waltzed, the postmaster's wife put her head on one side so languorously that she really gave the impression of something not of this earth. One very amiable lady who had come with no idea of dancing at all because, as she herself expressed it, of a slight *incommodité* in the shape of a corn on her right foot as a result of which she was even obliged to put on plush boots, could not, however, resist joining in the dance and taking a few turns in her plush boots to make sure that the postmaster's wife did not take it into her head to think too much of herself.

But all this did not produce the desired effect on Chichikov. He did not even look at the circles described by the ladies, but kept rising on tiptoe to look over other people's heads in the hope of seeing where the ravishing fair-haired girl had gone; he also kept stooping down and peering between the shoulders and backs, and at last his efforts were rewarded and he saw her sitting with her mother, on whose head a sort of oriental turban with a feather was nodding majestically. It looked as if he meant to take them by storm; whether it was the effect of spring or whether someone was pushing him from behind, he pressed forward determinedly, regardless of everything; the government contractor received so violent a push from him that he staggered and only just succeeded in balancing himself on one leg, or he would, no doubt, have brought a whole row of people down with him; the postmaster, too, stepped back and stared at him with astonishment mingled with rather subtle irony; but he did not look at them; all he saw was the fair-haired girl in the distance, pulling on a long glove, and no doubt burning with desire to go flying over the parquet floor. And already four couples were dashing off a mazurka, their heels crashing down on the floor, and an army major was working so hard with arms and legs, body and soul, executing steps such as no one had ever executed even in his wildest dreams. Chichikov darted past the mazurka dancers, almost treading on their heels, and made straight for the place where the governor's wife was sitting with her daughter. He approached them very timidly however; he did not mince so jauntily and foppishly. Indeed, he even looked confused and there was a kind of awkwardness in all his movements.

It is impossible to say with any certainty whether the feeling of love had awakened in our hero's heart; it is indeed doubtful whether gentlemen of his kind, that is to say, not too fat and yet not too thin either, are capable of falling in love; but for all that there was something of the kind here, something strange, something which he could not have explained to himself: he could not help feeling, as he admitted to himself afterwards, that the entire ball with all its noise and conversation had for a few moments seemed to become very remote; the fiddles and trumpets seemed to be playing somewhere far, far away and everything seemed to be covered with a mist, like some carelessly painted background in a picture. And out of this misty, roughly sketched background only the delicate features of the ravishing fair-haired girl emerged clearly: her rounded oval little face, her slender, slender figure, which is so characteristic of young girls during the first months after they have left school, her white almost plain dress which lightly and elegantly draped her graceful young limbs, setting off her pure lines. She was like some toy beautifully carved out of ivory; she alone stood out white and brightly translucent against that crowd.

It seems that things do happen like that. It seems that even the Chichikovs are for a few moments transformed into poets; but the word 'poet' is perhaps an exaggeration. At all events, he felt quite like a young man, almost a hussar. Seeing an empty chair beside them, he at once took it. Conversation flagged at first, but afterwards it picked up and he even began to show-off, but – here to our great regret we must observe that sedate gentlemen occupying important posts are somehow a trifle ponderous in their conversation with ladies; it is young lieutenants who are excellent at this sort of thing and no officers of a rank higher than that of captain are any good at it. Goodness only knows how they manage it; they don't seem to be saying anything very clever, but the young lady keeps on rocking with laughter on her chair. A State Councillor, on the other hand, will talk to her about all sorts of important matters, or he will enlarge on the fact that Russia is a vast empire, or will pay her a compliment, which has of course been not unwittily thought out, but unfortunately it has a terribly bookish flavour; even if he does say something funny, he will laugh at it himself much more than the girl listening to him. We have pointed this out here so that the reader may see why the fair-haired girl was beginning to yawn while our hero was talking to her. Our hero, however, did not seem to notice it at all and he went on talking about a great number of highly agreeable things which he had already noted on similar occasions in all sorts of places: to wit, in the Simbirsk province, at Sofron Ivanovich Bespechny's, where there were at the time his daughter Adelaida and her three sisters-in-law Maria, Alexandra, and Adelheida; at Fyodor Fyodorovich Perekroyev's in the Ryazan province; at Frol Vassileyvich Pobedonosny's in the province of Penza, and at his brother's, where there were his sister-in-law Katerina and her second cousins Rosa and Amelia; in the province of Vyatka, at the house of Peter Varsonofyevich, where there were: his sister-in-law Pelageya and her niece Sofia and her two half-sisters Sofia and Maklatura.

All the ladies were highly displeased with Chichikov's behaviour. One of them deliberately walked past him in order to draw his attention to it, and even rather carelessly brushed with the thick *rouleau* of her dress against the fair girl and so cleverly managed her scarf, which was fluttering round her shoulders, that its end flapped right into the young girl's face; at the same time, one of the ladies behind him let fall together with the scent of violets a rather biting and caustic observation from her lips. But either he really did not hear, or he pretended not to hear. He made a bad mistake, though, for one must attach importance to the opinion of the ladies: he came to regret it, but only afterwards when it was too late.

A look of absolutely justifiable indignation appeared on many faces. However high may have been Chichikov's position in society, though he might be a millionaire, though there might be an expression of majesty and even of something martial and military in his face, yet there are things that ladies can forgive in no one, whoever he may be, and when that happens you might as well give him up as beyond redemption. There are cases in which a woman, however weak and helpless in character compared with a man, suddenly becomes harder not only than a man, but than anything on earth. The disrespect shown by Chichikov, however unintentional it might have been, restored among the ladies that harmony which had been on the brink of destruction through their competition for a seat next to him. They discovered sarcastic allusions in the few indifferent and ordinary words he had uttered at random. To make things worse, one of the young men composed some satirical verses on the dancers without which, as we all know, no provincial ball is ever complete. These verses were immediately attributed to Chichikov. The indignation grew, and in different parts of the ballroom the ladies began to speak of him in a most unfavourable way, while the poor schoolgirl was utterly annihilated and already sentence had been passed on her.

Meanwhile a most unpleasant surprise was in store for our hero: while the fair young lady was yawning and he was telling her all sorts of amusing stories that had happened to him at different times and even referred to the Greek philosopher Diogenes, Nozdryov appeared from one of the back rooms. Whether he had torn himself away from the buffet or from the little green drawing-room, where the play was more hazardous than ordinary whist, whether he had come of his own free will or whether he had been thrown out, he appeared looking gay and in the best of spirits, holding on to the arm of the public prosecutor, whom he must have been dragging along with him for some time, for the poor prosecutor was turning round his beetling eyebrows in all directions, as though trying to find a way of escape from this amicable arm-in-arm promenade. It was, indeed, quite an intolerable situation. Nozdryov, having gulped down a great amount of conviviality with two cups of tea which were, of course, laced with rum, kept telling the most outrageous stories. Catching sight of him from a distance, Chichikov even decided to make a sacrifice, that is to say, to give up his enviable position and beat a hasty retreat; this encounter boded no good to him. But, as ill-luck would have it, the governor turned up at that very moment and expressed his great delight at having found Mr Chichikov. He stopped him and asked him to arbitrate in an argument he was having with two ladies as to whether a woman's love was lasting or not; meanwhile Nozdryov had seen him and came straight towards him.

'Ah, the Kherson landowner, the Kherson landowner!' he shouted as he came up, roaring with laughter so that his cheeks, fresh and pink as a spring rose, quivered and shook. 'Well? Have you bought up a lot of dead souls? You see, your Excellency,' he shouted at the top of his voice, turning to the governor, 'he deals in dead souls, he does, cross my heart! Listen, Chichikov, you're – I tell you this as a friend, for we're all your friends here and his Excellency is here too – I'd hang you, I'm damned if I wouldn't!'

Chichikov simply did not know whether he was standing on his head or on his heels.

'Would you believe it, sir,' Nozdryov continued, addressing the governor, 'when he said to me "Sell me your dead souls", I nearly burst my sides with laughing. When I arrived here, I was told that he had bought three million roubles worth of serfs for resettlement. For resettlement! Why, he was bargaining with me for dead ones. Look here, Chichikov, you're a dirty beast, I'm hanged if you aren't! His Excellency is here, too – isn't he, public prosecutor?'

But the public prosecutor and Chichikov and the governor himself were thrown into such confusion that they were completely at a loss what to say, and meanwhile Nozdryov, without taking the slightest notice of them, carried on with his half-tipsy speech.

'Now, look here, my dear fellow, I mean, you'd better – I – I won't leave you till I find out why you're buying dead souls. Now, listen, Chichikov, you really ought to be ashamed of yourself. You know perfectly well that you haven't got a better friend than me. And here's his Excellency, too. Isn't that so, prosecutor? You can't imagine, your Excellency, how attached we are to one another! I mean to say, if you just said, I mean here I am, and if you were to say, "Nozdryov, tell me honestly which is dearer to you, your own father or Chichikov?" I'd say "Chichikov". Damn me if I wouldn't … Now, my dear fellow, let me imprint a leetle kiss on your chaste cheek. You won't mind me kissing him, your Excellency, will you? No, no, Chichikov, don't you try to resist, just let me imprint one leetle kiss on your snow-white cheek!'

Nozdryov was given so violent a push with his 'leetle kiss' that he was almost hurled to the floor: everyone recoiled from him and refused to listen to him any more; but, all the same, his words about the purchase of dead souls had been uttered at the top of his voice and were accompanied by such loud laughter that they attracted the attention even of those who were at the farthest ends of the room. This piece of news struck everyone as so strange that they all stood gaping with a kind of wooden, stupidly interrogative expression. Chichikov noticed that many of the ladies glanced at each other with a kind of spiteful, sarcastic smile and the faces of some of them expressed something so ambiguous that it increased his confusion still more. That Nozdryov was an inveterate liar was a fact they all knew and it was nothing unusual to hear him talk the most absurd nonsense; but mortal man being what he is, and it is really difficult to understand what mortal man is made of, however silly a piece of news may be, so long as it is news, he will consider it his duty to communicate it to another mortal, if only for the sake of saying, 'Just think what lies people are spreading!' And the other mortal will lend his ear eagerly, though afterwards he too will say, 'Yes, of course, it's a perfectly stupid lie, not worth the slightest attention,' and having delivered himself of that opinion, he will at once go in search of a third mortal so that after telling the story, both of them may exclaim together with righteous indignation, 'What a stupid lie!' And it will most certainly make the round of the town and all the mortals, be there ever so many of them, will talk about it till they're sick and tired of it, and will then freely admit that it does not deserve being taken seriously and is not worth while discussing.

This apparently absurd incident appreciably upset our hero. However stupid a fool's words may be, they are sometimes sufficient to upset an intelligent man. He began to feel uncomfortable and ill at ease; exactly as if he had stepped into a filthy, stinking puddle with a beautifully polished boot; in short, it was bad, very bad! He tried not to think of it, he did his best to distract himself, to amuse himself. He sat down to whist, but everything went wrong, like a crooked wheel: he revoked twice and, forgetting that the third player should not trump, he flung down his card and, like a fool, picked it up again. The president just could not understand how Chichikov, who had such a good and, one might even say, such a subtle understanding of the game, could make such mistakes and had even trumped his king of spades, on which, to use his own expression, he had relied as upon God. Of course, the postmaster and the president and even the chief of police himself, as is the custom, bantered our hero, asking whether he was in love, adding that they knew perfectly well that Chichikov's heart had been smitten and that they knew who it was who had shot the arrow; but all that did not comfort him in the least, however much he tried to laugh it off and pretend that it was all a joke. At supper, too, he was not able to show off to advantage in spite of the fact that the company at table was agreeable and Nozdryov had been thrown out long ago; for even the ladies had observed that his behaviour was becoming a bit too scandalous. In the middle of the cotillion, he had sat down on the floor and begun grabbing hold of the dancers' skirts which, as the ladies put it, was really outrageous. The supper was a very happy affair: all their faces, appearing and disappearing before the three-stemmed candelabras, the flowers, the sweets, and the bottles, were beaming with the most unconstrained contentment. Officers, ladies, frock-coats – everything became polite to the point of mawkishness. The gentlemen jumped up from their chairs and ran to take the dishes from the servants to offer them with quite extraordinary adroitness to the ladies. One colonel handed a lady a plate of sauce on the tip of his drawn sword. The men of discreet years, among whom Chichikov was sitting, were arguing loudly, following up each sensible word with a bit of fish or beef, mercilessly smothered in mustard; they were discussing the subjects in which he was always interested, but he was more like a man wearied or utterly exhausted and shaken by a long journey who cannot think of anything and who is quite incapable of taking any interest in anything. He did not even stay to the end of supper and went back to the inn much earlier than he was in the habit of doing.

There in the little room so familiar to the reader, with the door blocked up by the chest of drawers and the cockroaches peering out of the corners, his thoughts and his mind were as uncomfortable as the armchair in which he was sitting. He felt confused and sick at heart, there was a kind of oppressive emptiness in it. 'Oh, to hell with all those who invented these balls!' he said furiously. 'What were they so pleased about, the fools? The harvests in the province are bad, prices are rising, and here they're all for balls! A nice thing. Dress themselves up in their female finery! The ridiculous things a woman covers herself with for a thousand roubles. And all at the expense of the peasants' taxes, or, what's even worse, of the consciences of their husbands. We all know why they take bribes and act against their consciences: it's to get their wives a shawl or all kinds of crinolines, the devil take them, whatever they're called. And what is it all for? That some slut of a woman won't say that the postmaster's wife is wearing a better dress, and, because of her, bang goes a thousand roubles. They shout: "A ball, a ball, gaiety!" A ball's just a stupid thing! It isn't in the Russian spirit at all. It isn't in the Russian national character. Damn it, just think of it: a grown-up man, an adult person, suddenly darts out, all in black, looking silly, his waist pulled tight as a little devil's, and off he goes, working away with his legs. Even while standing beside their partners, someone will start talking to someone else about some important business and at the same time he will be capering like a kid to right and left. ... It's all because they're trying to ape other people. Because a Frenchman at forty is as much of a child as he was at fifteen, we must be the same. Yes, indeed, after every ball one feels as though one had committed a sin; one doesn't like even to remember it. One's head is as empty as after a talk with a man-about-town: he will talk about everything, touch lightly upon everything, say everything he has got out of books, brightly, wittily, but he hasn't retained anything of it in his head, and you realize afterwards that a talk with a common or garden merchant who knows nothing but his own business, but knows that thoroughly and by experience, is much better than all this clever society prattle. What can you get out of it, out of a ball like this? Suppose some writer were to take it into his head to describe all that scene just as it was. Why, it would be just as stupid in a book as it is in life. What is it, moral or immoral? Goodness only knows what it is. You'd simply feel disgusted and close the book.' So unfavourably did Chichikov express himself about balls in general; but it would seem there was another reason for his indignation. His chief annoyance was not with the ball, but with the fact that his enjoyment of it was suddenly cut short, that he had been made to look like goodness knows what in front of everybody, that he had played a somewhat strange and ambiguous part. Of course, looking at it as a sensible man, he saw that it was all nonsense, that a foolish word was of no significance, especially now when the chief business had been successfully concluded. But man is a strange creature: what hurt his feelings so painfully was the ill will of those very people whom he did not respect and whom he criticized so severely for their vanity and their fine dresses. This vexed him all the more because when he analysed the matter clearly he saw that to some extent he was the cause of it himself. He was not, however, angry with himself, and there, of course, he was quite right. We all have a little weakness for sparing ourselves and we try to find someone we know on whom to vent our spleen, for instance, a servant or one of our subordinates at the office, who happens to turn up at the wrong moment, our wife, or even a chair which can be sent flying against the door so violently that its arms and back are snapped off: let it see, as it were, what our anger can be like. So Chichikov, too, soon found someone upon whose shoulders he could put everything his vexation suggested to him. This was Nozdryov; and, needless to say, he was belaboured by Chichikov at every point and on every side as soundly as some rascally village elder or driver is belaboured by some much-travelled and experienced army captain and sometimes even by a general who, in addition to the many expressions that have become classics, adds others, unfamiliar, for the invention of which he is solely responsible. All Nozdryov's family tree was pulled to bits and many members of his family in ascending line were severely dealt with.

But while Chichikov was sitting in his hard armchair, troubled by his thoughts and sleeplessness and vigorously berating Nozdryov and all his relations, while a tallow candle glimmered in front of him and was on the point of going out any minute because its wick had for a long time been covered by a black cap of soot, while the blind, dark night was staring at him from the window, ready to turn blue with the approaching dawn, and while in the distance cocks were crowing, and in the slumbering town perhaps some poor wretch in a frieze overcoat, of unknown class and rank, trudged along the highway he knew only too well, worn away, alas, by all the vagabonds of Russia – at that very moment an event was taking place at the other end of the town that was destined to increase the unpleasantness of our hero's situation. To wit, through the remote streets and alleys of the town a very strange carriage was rattling along, a carriage so strange that it is difficult to find a name for it. It was not like a four-wheeled wooden cart with seats on either side, nor a carriage, nor a chaise. It was more like a full-cheeked, rounded water-melon on wheels. The cheeks of this water-melon, that is to say, the doors, bore traces of yellow paint and shut very badly owing to the poor condition of the handles and locks which were tied up rather in-expertly with string. The water-melon was filled with cotton cushions in the shape of tobacco pouches, bolsters, and ordinary pillows, stuffed with sacks of bread, fancy loaves, doughnuts, griddle cakes, and bread rings made of boiled dough. Ordinary chicken pies and chicken pies stuffed with buckwheat, chopped eggs, and pickles peeped out at the top. On the footboard at the back of the carriage stood a man whose face proclaimed the footman, in a tunic of brightly coloured homespun with an unshaven chin slightly touched with grey, a person who is generally referred to as a 'fellow'. The clanking and the creaking of the iron clamps and rusty screws woke a policeman at the other end of the town who, picking up his halberd, shouted half-awake with all his might: 'Who goes there?' but seeing that no one was going anywhere and only hearing the distant rattling of a cart, caught some sort of beast on his collar, and going up to a lamp-post, executed it there and then with his nail. After which, putting aside his halberd, he fell asleep again in accordance with the rules of his order of chivalry. The horses kept stumbling, for they had not been shod, and, besides, the quiet cobbled roads of the town were apparently unfamiliar to them. After turning several times from one street into another, this heavy and unwieldy carriage turned into a dark side-street past the small parish church of St Nicholas and stopped in front of the gates of a house belonging to the head priest's wife. A maidservant with a kerchief on her head and wearing a warm jacket clambered out of the carriage and began knocking with both fists on the gates so violently that a man might have envied her (the fellow in the brightly coloured cotton tunic was afterwards dragged down by his legs for he had been fast asleep). Dogs began barking and the gates, opening wide at last, swallowed, though with difficulty, this clumsy travelling contraption.

The carriage drove into the narrow yard filled with stacks of logs, chicken coops, and all sorts of little sheds; an old lady got out of it: this old lady was none other than Korobochka, landowner and widow of a Collegiate Assessor. Soon after our hero's departure the old lady had got into a terrible state of anxiety at the thought that he might have cheated her. After three sleepless nights she decided to drive into the town, in spite of the fact that the horses were not shod, so as to find out for certain what the price of dead souls was and whether she had, God forbid, made a mistake by selling them perhaps at a third of their proper price. What effect this arrival of Mrs Korobochka was to have, the reader will be able to learn from a conversation which took place between two ladies. This conversation – but this conversation had better be kept for the next chapter.

Chapter 9

IN the morning, earlier than the hour usually fixed for visits in the town of N., a lady in a smart check cloak ran out of the door of an orange-coloured wooden house with a mezzanine and light-blue columns. She was accompanied by a footman in a coat with many collars and gold braid on his round, glossy hat. With quite extra-ordinary haste the lady flew up the lowered steps of a carriage that stood at the door. The footman at once slammed the carriage door, pulled up the steps, and, catching hold of the straps at the back of the carriage, shouted to the driver: 'Drive on!' The lady was the bearer of a piece of news she had just heard and which she felt an irresistible desire to communicate as soon as possible. She kept looking out of the window every minute, seeing to her unspeakable vexation that she was still half-way to her destination. Every house seemed longer than usual; the white brick alms-house with its narrow windows seemed to stretch for miles so that in the end she could not resist exclaiming: 'Damn the building, there's no end to it!' Twice already the driver had received the order: 'Faster, faster, Andrushka! You're in-sufferably slow today.' At last she reached her destination. The car-riage stopped in front of a one-storied wooden house of a dark-grey colour with little white bas-reliefs above the windows and a high trellis wooden fence in front of them and a little, narrow front garden in which the spindly trees had grown white with the dust of the town that never came off them. In the windows could be seen pots of flowers, a parrot swinging in a cage and clinging with his beak to a ring, and two lap-dogs asleep in the sun. In this house lived the best friend of the lady who had just arrived. The author is at his wits' end how to name the two ladies in such a way as to avoid making people angry with him, as they were in the past. To call them by a fictitious name is dangerous: whatever name you think of, there's sure to be in some corner of our empire, seeing how vast it is, someone of the same name who is quite certain to become terribly angry and declare that the author has deliberately paid a secret visit to his town in order to find out what he is like, what sort of sheepskin he wears, what

Agrafena Ivanovna he visits regularly, and what food he enjoys best. If you were to give them, which God forbid, their ranks, it is even more dangerous. For nowadays people of all ranks and classes in our country are so sensitive that they think everything in a book refers to them personally: this sort of thing seems to be in the air. It is enough to say that in a certain town there is a stupid man and it is already interpreted as a personal reference to someone. A gentleman of respectable appearance will suddenly jump up and scream out: 'Why, I am a man too, so it seems I am stupid too!' In short, he grasps at once what it is all about. So to avoid all this, I will name the lady on whom the visitor has called, as she was almost unanimously called in the town of N., that is to say, a lady agreeable in all respects. This appellation she acquired quite legitimately. For indeed she did all she could to be obliging in the extreme, though, of course, through her agreeable manners one could catch a glimpse of – oh, so tart a liveliness of female character! and though even in her most agreeable words there was hidden – oh, so sharp a pin! And God help the woman who had somehow pushed herself in front of her, for heaven knows what feelings would seethe in her breast against such a woman. But all this would be wrapped up in the most delicate and refined good manners such as could only be found in provincial towns. Every gesture of hers was made with the utmost good taste, she was even fond of poetry and sometimes even knew how to hold her head dreamily, and everyone agreed that she was indeed a lady agreeable in all respects. The other lady, that is, the visitor, had not so versatile a character and we will therefore call her the simply agreeable lady. The arrival of the visitor woke the lap-dogs who were asleep in the sun: the shaggy haired Adèle, who was continuously getting entangled in her own coat, and the spindly-legged Potpourri. Both rushed barking with their tails in the air into the hall where the visitor divested herself of her cloak, appearing in a dress of fashionable cut and colour with long pieces of material trailing from her neck; a scent of jasmine pervaded the whole room. As soon as the lady agreeable in all respects learnt of the arrival of the simply agreeable lady, she ran out into the hall. The ladies clasped each other by the hands, kissed each other, and uttered little screams, as girls do on meeting again after leaving their boarding schools and before their mothers have had time to explain to them that the father of one of them is poorer and of a lower rank than the other one's. They kissed so noisily that the dogs started barking again, for which they were flicked with a handkerchief, and both ladies went into the drawing-room, which was, of course, pale-blue, with a sofa, an oval table, and even a little screen with ivy winding round it; shaggy Adèle and tall Potpourri on his spindly legs ran in growling after them. 'This way, this way, let's sit down in this little corner!' said the hostess, making her visitor sit down in the corner of the sofa: 'So, so, here's a cushion for you,' saying this, she stuffed a cushion behind her back, on which a knight was embroidered in wool, as such knights always are embroidered on canvas, the nose looking like a ladder and the lips a square. 'I'm so glad it's you, my dear. ... I heard someone drive up and I wondered who it could be so early. Parasha said it was the vice-governor's wife, and I said "Dear, oh dear, the silly creature is coming to bore me again," and I was just on the point of telling Parasha that I was not at home. ...'

The visitor was about to get down to business and communicate her piece of news, but an exclamation uttered at that moment by the lady agreeable in all respects gave another turn to the conversation.

'What a gay little cotton print!' exclaimed the lady agreeable in all respects, looking at the dress of the simply agreeable lady.

'Yes, it is gay, isn't it? Praskovya Fyodorovna, however, finds that it would have been much better if the checks had been smaller and the spots pale-blue and not brown. Her sister was sent a piece of that material. Oh, my dear, it's so delightful that I simply can't describe it. Just think, little narrow stripes, as narrow as one can well imagine, a pale-blue ground, and in between the stripes little spots and sprigs, spots and sprigs, spots and sprigs. ... Oh, it's quite wonderful! I'm quite sure there has never been anything like it in the world.'

'But, my dear, isn't it too gaudy?'

'Oh, no, it isn't a bit gaudy.'

'Oh, I'm sure it must be gaudy.'

It must be noted that the lady who was agreeable in all respects was a bit of a materialist, disposed to doubt and scepticism, and there were a great many things in life she refused to acknowledge. At this point the simply agreeable lady exclaimed that it was not at all gaudy and then exclaimed:

'Oh, yes, I must tell you something I know will please you: frills are no longer worn.'

'No longer worn?'

'Little festoons are worn instead.'

'Oh, little festoons aren't nice at all.'

'Yes, my dear, little festoons. It's all festoons. Pelerines are made of festoons, festoons on the sleeves, little epaulettes made of festoons, festoons below, festoons everywhere.'

'It won't look nice at all, my dear, all these festoons.'

'Why, no, my dear, it's so incredibly charming. It's made with two seams: wide arm-holes and above ... But, my dear, this will really astonish you, this will really make you say that ... Well, never mind. You see, the under-bodice has become longer, coming to a point in front, and the busk is more prominent than ever; the skirt is gathered all round just as in the old-fashioned farthingale and they even stick on a little cotton-wool padding at the back to make you a perfect *belle femme*.'

'Well, really, my dear, that's going a bit too far,' said the lady agreeable in all respects, tossing her head with a feeling of dignity.

'Yes, my dear, that *is* going too far!' replied the simply agreeable lady.

'Do what you like, but I shall never follow that fashion.'

'I shan't, either. ... Really, when you think what extremes fashion will go to sometimes. It's quite fantastic! I asked my sister to send me the pattern just for fun. My Melanya has started to make up the dress.'

'Why, have you really got the pattern?' cried the lady agreeable in all respects, not without perceptible excitement.

'Why, of course, my sister brought it.'

'Darling, you simply must let me have it!'

'But, my dear, I've already promised it to Praskovya Fyodorovna. Perhaps after she's finished with it.'

'But, my dear, who's going to wear it after Praskovya Fyodorovna? It's really horrid of you to show preference to strangers before your own friends.'

'But she's a cousin of mine.'

'Some cousin, I must say. A cousin by marriage. No, my dear, I won't hear of it. It's just as if you'd wanted to insult me. I suppose you must be tired of me. I can see you want to bring our friendship to an end.'

Poor simply agreeable lady did not know what to do. She felt that she was between the devil and the deep blue sea. She would keep on bragging and this was the result of it! She felt like biting off that stupid tongue of hers.

'Well, and how's that fascinating gentleman of ours?' the lady agreeable in all respects asked.

'Oh dear, I don't know what I'm doing sitting here like this! What a fool I am! Do you know what I've come to you about?' Here the visitor was almost breathless with excitement, the words were ready to go chasing after one another like hawks and one had to be as inhuman as her dearest friend to venture to interrupt her.

'You may praise him up to the skies and say all sorts of nice things about him,' she said with greater animation than usual, 'but I tell you straight, and I'll say it to his face, that he's a good-for-nothing fellow, good-for-nothing, good-for-nothing!'

'But please listen to what I have to tell you ...'

'They spread rumours that he is a nice man, but he isn't at all nice, not at all, and his nose is – er – a most unattractive nose.'

'But please, darling, do let me tell you! Please! You see, it's a whole story, quite a scandalous story, you understand, *c'est qu'on appelle une histoire*,' the visitor was saying in an imploring voice, with an expression almost of despair and dismay.

It may as well be pointed out here that the conversation of the two ladies was interlarded with a great number of foreign words and sometimes even with whole French sentences. But great as the author's reverence is for the exceptional benefits which the French language has bestowed on Russia and great as is his reverence for the praiseworthy custom of our upper classes to express themselves in this language at all hours of the day out of their profound love for their motherland, of course, yet he cannot bring himself to introduce sentences in any foreign language into this Russian poem of his. And so let us continue in Russian.

'What story?'

'Why, darling, if you could only imagine the position in which I found myself. Just think, the wife of our head priest, Father Kyril, came to see me today, and what do you think? That modest gentleman of ours, whom we received in our houses, what do you think he's been up to, eh?'

'Good heavens, you don't mean to say he's been making love to the priest's wife?'

'Oh, my dear, if it were only that, it wouldn't matter so much.

Just listen to what the priest's wife told me. She said Mrs Korobochka, a lady estate owner, arrived at her place in a panic and pale as death and told her – oh, my dear, the things she told her! Just listen, a perfectly romantic story! Suddenly, in the middle of the night, when everyone in the house was asleep, there came a knocking at the gate more awful than anything you could imagine. "Open up!" they shouted. "Open up, or we shall break down the gates!" How do you like that? A nice, charming fellow after that, isn't he?'

'Why, what is Korobochka like? Is she young and good-looking?'

'Not at all. She's an old woman.'

'Dear me, that *is* charming. So he's running after old women now, is he? Well, I can't say much for the taste of our ladies after that. Found a nice person to fall in love with!'

'But, my dear, it's not at all what you think. Just imagine, he arrives armed from head to foot like some Rinaldo Rinaldini and demands: "Sell me all your souls who are dead." Korobochka answers him very reasonably: "I can't sell them because they are dead." "No," he says, "they are not dead. It's my business to know whether they are dead or not. They're not dead," he shouts. "Not dead, not dead!" In short, he made a most fearful scene. All the village came running round, the children were crying, everyone was shouting, nobody could understand anyone, it was simply *horreur, horreur, horreur*! Well, my dear, you simply can't imagine how frightfully alarmed I was when I heard all this. "Mistress, darling," my Mashka said to me, "just look in the looking-glass! How pale you are!" "I've no time for looking-glasses now," I said to her, "I must go at once and tell my best friend all about it." I ordered the carriage at once; Andrushka, my driver, asked me where to drive, but I couldn't utter a word. I just stared at his face like a fool. I do believe he thought I had gone mad. Oh, my dear, if you could only imagine how frightfully alarmed I was.'

'It does sound a little odd,' said the lady agreeable in all respects, 'don't you think? What can the meaning of these dead souls be? I must say I simply can't make it out at all. This is the second time I've heard of these dead souls, but my husband said Nozdryov was just talking a lot of nonsense. There must be something in it. I'm sure of it.'

'But just imagine, my dear, what I felt like when I heard of it. "And now," Korobochka says, "I don't know," she says, "what I am to do. He made me sign some forged document and threw down fifty roubles in notes. I'm a helpless and inexperienced widow," she says. "I know nothing about it." So that's the sort of thing that's happening! Oh, if you could only imagine how alarmed I was.'

'But, say what you will, I'm sure it's not a question of dead souls at all. There's something else behind it all.'

'I must say I think so, too,' said the simply agreeable lady not without an air of surprise, and was at once aware of a strong desire to find out what could be behind it. She even said with slow deliberation: 'And what do you think is behind it?'

'Well, what do you think?'

'What do I think? I must say I'm completely at a loss.'

'All the same, I'd like to know what you really think about it.'

But the simply agreeable lady could think of nothing to say. She only knew how to be alarmed, but she did not possess enough reasoning powers to form any sensible idea as to what it was all about, and that was why she more than anyone else was in need of tender friendship and advice.

'Well, let me tell you what these dead souls are,' said the lady agreeable in all respects, and at these words her visitor was all attention: her ears seemed to prick up of their own accord, she raised herself so that she was hardly touching the sofa at all, and though she was rather heavily built, she seemed to become suddenly much thinner and as light as a feather which might float up into the air at a puff of wind.

So a Russian gentleman, a dare-devil rider to hounds, might ride up to a wood out of which a hare, roused by the beaters, will any moment leap, and with his horse and raised crop become transformed in one frozen instant, into powder to which a lighted match might at any moment be applied. His eyes fixed steadily on the murky air, he is about to overtake the animal and slay it ruthlessly, though the entire whirling snowy waste of the steppe may rise up against him, scattering silvery stars on his lips, his moustache, his eyes, his brows, and his beaver cap.

'The dead souls ...' said the lady, agreeable in all respects.

'What, what?' her visitor asked in great excitement.

'The dead souls ...'

'Oh, go on, for heaven's sake!'

194

'They've been merely invented to cover up something else. What he is really after is this: he wants to abduct the governor's daughter.'

This conclusion was indeed quite unexpected and in every way extraordinary. The agreeable lady, on hearing it, was petrified. She turned pale, she turned pale as death, and was certainly alarmed in good earnest.

'Oh dear,' she exclaimed, throwing up her hands, 'that I would never have suspected.'

'And I realized what it was all about as soon as you opened your mouth,' replied the lady who was agreeable in all respects. 'But what is one to think of boarding school education after this, my dear? So this is their innocence!'

'Innocence, indeed! I've heard her say things I'd never dare repeat.'

'It simply breaks one's heart, you know, my dear, to see to what lengths depravity can go.'

'And the men are crazy about her, though so far as I'm concerned I can't see anything in her. Her affectation is quite intolerable.'

'Oh, my dear, she's a statue, a real statue! If only she had some kind of expression in her face.'

'Oh, she's so affected, so affected! My goodness, how affected she is. Who taught her that I don't know, but I've never seen a girl give herself such airs.'

'Why, darling, she's just a statue and as pale as death.'

'Oh, don't say that, my dear, she rouges shamelessly.'

'How can you say that, my dear? She's chalk, chalk, pure chalk.'

'My dear, I was sitting beside her: the rouge was as thick as my finger and it kept peeling off in bits like plaster. I expect her mother must have taught her. She's a flirt herself and the daughter will out-shine the mother yet.'

'But really, my dear, I'm ready to take any oath you like. May I lose my children, my husband, my entire estate this minute, if there's a single drop, the tiniest particle, a shadow of rouge on her face.'

'Oh, what are you saying, my dear?' said the lady agreeable in all respects, clasping her hands.

'Really, my dear, you surprise me,' said the agreeable lady and also clasped her hands.

The reader mustn't think it strange that the two ladies were not agreed about what they had seen at one and the same moment. There are, indeed, many things in the world which have the property of appearing to be absolutely white when one lady looks at them, and as red as a cranberry when another lady looks at them.

'Well, here's another proof that she is pale,' the agreeable lady continued. 'I remember, as though it were now, how I was sitting beside Manilov and said to him: "Look how pale she is!" Really, one must be as stupid as our men are to admire her. And as for our charming gentleman ... Oh, how revolting I thought him. You can't imagine, my dear, how revolting I thought him.'

'Well, but there were some ladies who were not indifferent to him.'

'You don't mean me, my dear, do you? You can never say that about me. Never, never!'

'But I'm not talking about you at all. Aren't there others beside you?'

'Never, never, my dear. Let me tell you I know myself very well indeed. There might have been something on the part of certain ladies who pretend to be unapproachable.'

'I'm sorry, my dear, but there have never been any such scandalous stories spread about me. About anyone else perhaps, but not about me. That much I must say.'

'Why are you so offended? There were other ladies there as well, weren't there? There were even some who rushed to get hold of the chair near the door so as to sit near him!'

Well, after these words uttered by the agreeable lady, a storm might have been expected to blow up, but surprisingly enough both ladies suddenly quieted down and nothing whatever followed. The lady agreeable in all respects remembered that the pattern of the new fashionable dress was not yet in her possession, and the simply agreeable lady realized that she had not yet succeeded in getting all the details about the discovery made by her bosom friend, and as a result peace was very quickly restored. Neither of the ladies, however, could be said to be naturally disposed to be disagreeable to people, and indeed there was nothing spiteful in their characters. It was simply that in the course of conversation there arose in them an unconscious desire to stick pins into one another. It was simply that each derived a certain pleasure from saying something hurtful to the other on some occasions: 'Take that!' 'Go on, swallow it!' There are all sorts of impulses in the hearts of the masculine as well as the feminine sex.

'What I can't understand, though,' said the simply agreeable lady, 'is how a stranger like Chichikov could make up his mind to undertake such a bold step. I'm sure he must have accomplices.'

'Why, you don't suppose he hasn't, do you?'

'And who do you think could be helping him?'

'Well, Nozdryov for one.'

'Not Nozdryov!'

'Why not? It's just the sort of thing he would do. Don't you know he once tried to sell his own father or rather gambled him away at cards?'

'Goodness, what interesting things I'm learning from you! I could never have imagined Nozdryov mixed up in this affair.'

'And I always thought it possible.'

'Good gracious, the things that are happening in the world! Who would have thought that when Chichikov first arrived in our town, you remember, he would have caused such a strange upheaval in the world. Oh, my dear, if only you knew how terrified I feel! If it were not for your friendship and kindness, I – I – er – I should really have been on the very brink of disaster. Who else could I turn to? My Mashka saw that I was as pale as death. "Mistress darling," she says to me, "you're as pale as death." "Mashka," I said, "I haven't time for that now." So that's what it is! And Nozdryov's mixed up in it too! Well, I must say!'

The agreeable lady was very anxious to find out further details about the abduction, that is, at what hour it would take place and so on, but she wanted to know too much. The lady agreeable in all respects frankly declared that she did not know. She was incapable of telling a lie: to put forward a theory was a different matter, but in that case even the theory must be based upon inner conviction; if she felt such an inner conviction she knew how to stand up for herself, and let any advocate famed for his gift of changing other people's opinions try to contend with her in this matter and he would soon see what an inner conviction means.

That both ladies were at last absolutely convinced of the truth of what they had at first regarded as a mere supposition is nothing extraordinary. We men who pride ourselves upon our cleverness behave almost in the same way, and our learned discussions are a proof of it. To begin with, a scholar approaches them in a most blackguardly fashion: he begins timidly, moderately, he begins by asking a most modest question: 'Is it not from there? Does not a certain country derive its name from that particular place?' Or, 'Does not this document date from another and later age?' Or, 'Are we sure that such a people does not mean quite another people?' He immediately quotes such and such ancient writers, and as soon as he detects some kind of a hint or something that he believes to be a hint, he at once becomes emboldened and self-confident, talks to the writers of antiquity like an old friend, puts questions to them and supplies the answers himself, forgetting completely that he has begun with a timid supposition; he already believes that he can see it all, that everything is clear and his argument is concluded with the words: 'So that is how it was; so this is the people we have to assume it is; so it is from this point of view that we look at the subject!' Then he proclaims it *ex cathedra*, for all to hear, and the newly discovered truth is sent travelling all over the world, gathering followers and disciples.

While the two ladies were so cleverly and successfully unravelling this involved affair, the public prosecutor with his perpetually immobile countenance, beetling eyebrows, and blinking eyes, came into the drawing-room. The ladies immediately began telling him about all these circumstances, interrupting each other as they told him of the purchase of the dead souls and of the plot to abduct the governor's daughter, and threw him into such confusion that he was quite unable to understand anything, in spite of the fact that he stood on the same spot for some time, winking with his left eye and flicking his beard with his handkerchief to brush the snuff from it. The two ladies left him in this state of bewilderment and set off each in her own direction to rouse the town. This they succeeded in doing in little over half an hour. The town was decidedly roused. Everything was in a ferment and yet not one had the slightest idea what it was all about. The ladies succeeded in so thoroughly befogging the senses of everyone, that all, and especially the government officials, were for a time completely dumbfounded. Their position was at first similar to that of the schoolboy who wakes up to find that his classmates, who were awake before him, have stuffed a *hussar*, a piece of paper filled with snuff, into his nose while he was asleep. Having inhaled the snuff with all the force of a sleeping person, he wakes, jumps out of bed, looks round him like a fool with eyes popping out of his head, and cannot grasp where he is or what has happened to him, and only a little later does he become aware of the walls lit by the slanting rays of the sun, the laughter of his classmates hiding in the corners of the dormitory, and the dawn peeping through the windows, with the awakened woods resounding with the songs of a thousand birds, and the flashing stream, twisting and turning among the thin rushes, covered densely with naked boys calling to their friends to come for a swim, and only then realizes at last that a *hussar* has been put in his nose. This was exactly the situation in which the inhabitants of the town and the government officials found themselves at first. Everyone of them stopped dead like a sheep with his eyes starting out of his head. Dead souls, the governor's daughter, and Chichikov were all mixed and intermingled in their heads in a most extraordinary way; it was only afterwards, after recovering from their stupefaction, that they were apparently able to distinguish and separate them one from another, and they began to demand an explanation and to be annoyed that the affair did not seem to have any proper explanation. What did it all mean really? What was the meaning of these dead souls? There was no logic in dead souls. How could one buy dead souls? Who would be such a fool? And what sort of defaced coinage would one pay for them? And what would be the purpose of it? What could one use those dead souls for? And what had the governor's daughter to do with it? If he wanted to carry her off, why did he have to buy dead souls? And if he wanted to buy dead souls, why carry off the governor's daughter? Was he going to make her a present of the dead souls? What sort of nonsense do they spread about the town? What are things coming to when before you have time to turn round such a scandalous story is being spread about? If there had been any sense in it! ... But the story was spread abroad so there must be some reason for it. But what reason could there be for dead souls? There's absolutely no reason for them. It's just a lot of nonsense, a lot of drivel, a lot of meaningless noise! It's goodness knows what! In short, the story became the subject of general discussion, and all the town was talking of dead souls and the governor's daughter, of Chichikov and dead souls, of the governor's daughter and Chichikov, and the whole place was in a ferment. The town that till then seemed to be peacefully asleep was suddenly awakened as if by a whirlwind. All the sluggards and lie-a-beds who had for years been lying about in their dressing-gowns at home putting the blame on the shoemaker for making their boots too narrow, or on the tailor, or the drunken coachman, crawled out of their holes, all who had long dropped their friends and whose only acquaintances were Squire Lie-a-bed and Squire Take-a-Nap (well-known terms very popular in Russia and originating from the verbs to lie-a-bed and to take-a-nap, just as the phrase 'pay a visit to Mr Snooze and Mr Snore', signifying to sleep like the dead on the side or on the back or in any other position to the accompaniment of snoring, nasal whistling, and suchlike activities); all those who could not be lured out of their homes even by an invitation to taste a fish soup costing five hundred roubles with a six-foot long sturgeon and all sorts of fish pies which melt in the mouth; in short, it seemed that the town was both populous and large and full of all sorts of inhabitants. A Sysoy Pafnutyevich and a Macdonald Karlovich, who had never been heard of before, suddenly made an appearance in public; a very long and lanky gentleman with an arm in a sling, taller than anyone who had ever been seen before, suddenly became a daily visitor in the drawing-rooms. All sorts of closed chaises, hitherto unknown traps, carriages that rattle and carriages with creaking wheels, appeared in the streets, and there was a hell of a to-do. At another time and in other circumstances such rumours would perhaps not have attracted attention, but the town of N. had been for a long time without any news at all. Indeed, for the last three months there had not been in the town what in Petersburg is called *commérages* which, as everyone knows, is as important for a town as the timely arrival of food supplies. In all this confused talk in the town, two diametrically opposed points of view became at once apparent and two diametrically opposed parties were at once formed: a male party and a female party. The male party, the most muddle-headed, concentrated their attention on the dead souls. The female party were preoccupied exclusively with the abduction of the governor's daughter. In this party, to the credit of the ladies be it said, there was far more discipline and circumspection. It was apparently their vocation in life to be good housewives and organizers. With them everything soon assumed a lively and definite shape, everything was clothed in clear and precise form, everything was explained and crystal clear; in short, a finished picture emerged. It turned out that Chichikov had been in love for some time, that he had been meeting the governor's daughter in the garden by moonlight, that the governor would gladly have given him his daughter's hand, because Chichikov was as rich as a Jew, had it not been for his wife, whom he had abandoned (how they had found out that Chichikov was married no one could say), and that his wife, who was hopelessly in love with him and was brokenhearted, had written a most touching letter to the governor, and that Chichikov, seeing that the father and the mother would never give their consent, made up his mind to abduct the girl. A different version of the story was told in other houses, namely that Chichikov had no wife, but that being an extremely clever man who never did anything unless he was sure of success, he had made up his mind, in order to win the daughter's hand, to lay siege to her mother, and that he had had a secret liaison with her, and it was only afterwards that he had made a proposal for the hand of the daughter; but the mother, horrified at the thought that a crime might be committed which was repugnant to religion and suffering from pangs of conscience, had categorically refused, and that was why Chichikov had made up his mind to abduct the girl. All sorts of other explanations and amendments had become attached to these versions as the rumours at last penetrated to the more remote back streets of the town. In Russia the lower orders are very fond of discussing the scandals that occur in the upper classes, and so all this began to be talked about in the slum dwellings where they had never set eyes on Chichikov or knew anything about him and, naturally enough, new details and explanations were added to the story. Indeed, the subject became more interesting every minute and assumed more and more definite forms every day, and at last was brought to the ears of the governor's wife herself in its final version. As the mother of a family, as the first lady of the town, and, finally, as a lady who had no suspicions of anything of the kind, the governor's wife felt deeply offended by all these stories and was greatly indignant, and her indignation was absolutely justified. The poor, fair-haired schoolgirl had to put up with the most painful *tête-à-tête* that a sixteen-year-old girl had ever had to endure. A whole torrent of questions precipitated itself over her head, followed by interrogations, reprimands, threats, reproaches, admonitions, so that the girl burst into tears and fell to sobbing and could not understand a single word of what had been said to her. The porter was given the strictest orders not to admit Chichikov at any time or under any circumstances.

Having done their worst so far as the governor's wife was concerned, the ladies began to apply pressure to bear upon the men's party and tried to bring them over to their side, maintaining that the dead souls were a fiction intended to divert suspicion and to assure the success of the abduction. Many of the men were indeed led astray and made to join the ladies' party, in spite of the fact that they were subjected to severe censure by their male friends who called them 'silly old women' and 'petticoats' – names, as we all know, most offensive to the male sex.

But, however much the men defended themselves and however strongly they resisted, there was not by any means the same discipline in their party as in the female one. Everything with them was somehow crude, unpolished, unsuitable, improper, inharmonious, wrong, a muddle, a chaos, confusion, untidiness in their heads and their thoughts, in short, everything showed the emptiness and crudeness of man's nature, incapable of domestic management or heartfelt convictions, lacking in faith, lazy, full of endless doubts and everlasting fears. They maintained that it was all nonsense, that the abduction of the governor's daughter was the sort of thing a hussar and not a civilian would do, that Chichikov would never do that, that the silly women were talking a lot of nonsense, that a woman is like a sack that carries about anything you put in it, that the dead souls were the main thing to concentrate on, though what on earth it was all about it was impossible to say, but that there was certainly something very nasty and evil about it. Why the men believed that there was something very nasty and evil about the purchase of the dead souls we shall know in a minute. A new governor-general had been appointed for the province, an event which is well known to throw civil servants into a state of great alarm, for such an appointment might be followed by transfers, reprimands, castigations, and all sorts of official treats with which a chief regales his subordinates. 'What if he should find out', thought the civil servants, 'that these stupid rumours are going about the town? Why, he may fly into a rage and that might be a matter of life and death.' The public health inspector suddenly turned pale, he imagined goodness only knows what: might not the words 'dead souls' refer to the patients who had died off in great numbers in the hospitals and in other places of an epidemic fever against which no proper measures had been taken, and might not Chichikov be an official of the governor-general's office sent specially to make a secret investigation? He mentioned this to the president. The president replied that it was nonsense, and then he suddenly turned pale himself, having asked himself the question whether the serfs bought by Chichikov were really dead, and he had allowed the deed of purchase to be drawn up and had even acted for Plyushkin in the matter, and what would happen if this were to come to the governor-general's knowledge? He just happened to mention this to one or two other officials, and they immediately turned pale too; fear is more contagious than the plague and is instantly communicated. They all at once discovered in themselves transgressions they had never even committed. The words 'dead souls' had such a nebulous association that they began to wonder whether they might not refer to some corpses buried in haste as a result of two incidents which had happened a short while before. The first incident concerned some Solvychegodsk merchants who had come to town for the fair and, after selling their goods, had thrown a party for their friends, the Ustsysolsk merchants, a banquet on a true Russian scale with all sorts of German improvements: orgeats, punches, balsams, and so on. The party ended as usual in a fight. The Solvychegodsk merchants assaulted and killed their Ustsysolsk guests, but not without suffering some broken ribs in their turn, as well as blows in the solar-plexus, which testifies to the tremendous size of the fists of their deceased opponents. One of the conquering heroes even had his 'snout', as the combatants expressed it, smashed to a pulp, that is to say, his nose was so completely bashed in that there was hardly half a finger's breadth left on his face. At their trial the merchants pleaded guilty, saying that they were sorry to have misbehaved a little; there were rumours that when pleading guilty they each had slipped in four thousand-rouble notes. The whole case, however, was rather obscure. From the different official inquiries and investigations it appeared that the Ustsysolsk lads had died of charcoal fumes and as such they were buried. The other incident which had happened only the other day was as follows: the crown peasants of the village of Lousy-Swagger together with the peasants of the village of Hoggy, otherwise Dirty-Bully, were charged with having swept from the face of the earth the local rural police in the person of a fat assessor, a certain Drobyazhkin; it was also asserted that the rural police, that is to say, the assessor Drobyazhkin, had taken to visiting their village a little too frequently, which in some cases is as bad as an epidemic, the reason for it being that the rural police, having a certain weakness for the fair sex, was chasing the village girls and women. Nothing was known for certain, however, though in their depositions the peasants stated quite clearly that the rural police was as lecherous as a tomcat and that they had warned him several times and, indeed, on one occasion they had kicked him stark naked out of a cottage into which he had contrived to enter. The rural police, of course, deserved to be punished for his weakness for the fair sex, but the peasants of Lousy-Swagger and Dirty-Bully could not be acquitted of taking the law into their own hands, if they really did have a hand in the murder. But the whole case was obscure. The rural police was found on the road, the uniform or coat on the rural police was in a worse state than any rag, and his face was quite unrecognizable. The case went through the courts and came up at last before the higher provincial court, where it was at first heard *in camera*, its verdict being as follows: whereas it was not known which of the peasants had taken part in the murder, whereas there were a great many of them, and whereas Drobyazhkin, being as dead as a doornail, could not possibly benefit even if he won the case, and whereas in view of the fact that the peasants were still alive, it was of the utmost importance that a decision should be given in their favour, it was therefore decided that Drobyazhkin was himself responsible for his death, since he had been unjustly oppressing the peasants of Lousy-Swagger and Dirty-Bully, and that he had died of an apoplectic stroke while returning home in his sledge. The case, it would appear, had been rounded off perfectly, but the civil servants, for some unknown reason, began to wonder whether the dead souls had anything to do with it. Now, as ill-luck would have it, it so happened that just when the officials were in this difficult position, two communications to the governor arrived simultaneously. One of them was to the effect that according to the evidence and the information in the hands of the authorities, a forger of counterfeit notes was hiding in their province under various aliases, and that a very thorough search for him should be instituted at once. The other document was a dispatch from the governor of a neighbouring province concerning a brigand, a fugitive from justice, asking that if any suspicious person who could produce no passport or identification papers of any kind were to be found in their province he should be apprehended immediately. These two documents produced a shattering effect on everybody. Their previous theories and surmises were thrown into utter confusion. Of course, it could not possibly be supposed that any of these documents had anything to do with Chichikov; as they turned the matter over in their minds, however, all of them recalled that they had no idea who Chichikov really was, that he had been extremely vague about himself, that he had indeed said that he had suffered in

the cause of justice, but that was all rather vague, and when they remembered in this connexion that he even had said that he had many
enemies who had attempted his life, they began to wonder even more;
his life, then, was in danger, he was, therefore, being pursued, he must,
therefore, have done something wrong – and, anyway, who was he
really? Of course, there could be no question of his forging counterfeit notes and still less of his being a brigand: he certainly looked a
law-abiding citizen; but, for all that, who was he really? And so the
officials asked themselves the question which they should have asked
themselves in the first chapter of our poem. It was decided to make
a few more inquiries among those from whom the dead souls had
been bought, so as to find out at least what sort of business deal it
was and what was to be understood by these dead souls, and whether
he had perhaps revealed to someone by chance, by some casual remark, what his real intentions were, and whether he had not told
someone who he really was. First of all, they turned to Mrs Korobochka, but they did not get much out of her: he had bought them
for fifteen roubles, she said, and he was also going to buy birds'
feathers, and had promised to buy a great many things, and he also
bought lard for the government, and he was therefore most certainly
a rogue, for she already had dealings with a man who was buying
birds' feathers and lard for the government and he had deceived them
all and cheated the priest's wife of over a hundred roubles. Everything
else she said was merely a repetition of the same thing, and the officials
realized that she was simply a silly old woman. Manilov replied that
he was always ready to answer for Chichikov as for himself, that he
was ready to give up his whole estate for a hundredth part of Chichikov's admirable qualities, and altogether spoke of him in most flattering terms, adding a few reflections about friendship with a starry-
eyed expression on his face. These reflections, of course, revealed most
satisfactorily the tender emotions of his heart, but they did not reveal
to the officials what was behind this business. Sobakevich replied that
in his opinion Chichikov was a good man and that he had sold him
a most excellent selection of peasants who were alive in every sense
of the word; but that he could not answer for what might happen in
the future and that it would not be his fault if they died during their
transportation owing to the hardships of the journey, and that it was
all in God's hands, considering that there were so many fevers and
fatal illnesses in the world, and that there were, indeed, instances of

whole villages dying out. The officials resorted to one other method, which was not very honourable, it is true, but which is sometimes employed, that is to say, they questioned Chichikov's servants indirectly through their various acquaintances among the servants to find out whether they knew anything of their master's past life and circumstances, but again they learnt very little. From Petrushka they got only the smell of a stuffy room and from Selifan they got the information that his master had been in government service, in the Customs and Excise Department – and nothing more. People of his class have a very strange habit. If you ask them a direct question about something, they are never able to remember anything, they never take it all in, or they simply reply that they do not know, but if you ask them about something else, they at once answer your first question in such detail that you do not want to hear any more. All the investigations set on foot by the officials merely disclosed the fact that they did not know what Chichikov was, but that Chichikov certainly must be something. They finally decided to discuss the subject thoroughly and at least make up their minds what they were to do, how they were to do it, and what measures they were to take, and what sort of person he was: whether he was the sort of man who was to be seized and detained as an undesirable character, or whether he was the sort of person who might seize and detain them all himself as undesirable characters. For this purpose it was proposed to hold a special meeting at the house of the chief of police, who is already known to the reader as the father and benefactor of the town.

Chapter 10

W HEN they assembled at the house of the chief of police, who is already known to the reader as the father and benefactor of the town, the officials had a chance to remark to one another that they had grown thinner as a result of all these troubles and worries. Indeed, the appointment of a new governor-general and the documents of so serious a character they had received, and these goodness only knew what rumours – all this left perceptible marks on their faces, and the frock-coats of many of them had become noticeably looser. Everything showed signs of deterioration: the president had grown thinner, the chief of the health department had grown thinner, the public prosecutor had grown thinner, and a certain Semyon Ivanovich, who was never called by his surname and who wore on his first finger a solitaire which he used to show to the ladies, he, too, had grown thinner. Of course, there were some bolder spirits, as there are everywhere, who did not lose their presence of mind, but there were very few of them: there was only the postmaster. He alone remained unchanged in his invariably equable temper and on such occasions he was always in the habit of saying: 'We know all about your governor-generals! There may be three or four of them coming and going, but I, my dear sir, have been sitting in one and the same place for thirty years!' To which the other civil servants usually replied: 'You're all right, *sprechen-sie-Deitch*, Ivan Andreich, all you have to worry about is the post office, receiving and dispatching the mails. The worst you can do is to cheat the public by closing the post office an hour earlier or overcharge some merchant for accepting a letter at the wrong time, or send off a parcel that should not have been sent off – who wouldn't be a saint in your place? But what if some devil were to make it a habit of getting in your way every day, so that even if you are loath to accept anything, he keeps shoving it under your nose? You, of course, don't care a damn. You've only got one son. But the good Lord, my dear sir, has been extremely generous to my dear wife, so that not a year passes without her presenting me with a little girl or a little boy. Ay, if you were in my shoes, you'd sing a different tune!' That was what the civil servants said, but whether or not it is possible to withstand the blandishments of the devil is not for the author to say. The council, which assembled on this occasion, was conspicuous for the absence of the essential thing known among the common people as common sense. In general, we somehow don't seem to be made for representative assemblies. In all our assemblies, from the meetings of the village communes to all kinds of scientific and other committees, there is pretty terrible confusion, unless there is some person at the head who can take charge of the proceedings. It is indeed hard to say why this should be so; our people seem to be made like that, and only those meetings are successful which are called to arrange some drinking dinner or party, such as clubs and all sorts of pleasure gardens in the German style. And yet we are always ready for anything. As the wind blows, so we suddenly organize charitable, philanthropic, and goodness only knows what other societies. The intention may be excellent, but nothing ever comes of it for all that. Perhaps it is because at the very beginning we suddenly feel satisfied and think that everything has already been done. For instance, after organizing some charitable society for the benefit of the poor and subscribing a considerable sum, we at once give a dinner to the prominent dignitaries of the town in honour of so laudable an undertaking and, needless to say, spend half of the subscribed funds on it; with what is left of the money we at once rent magnificent offices with heating facilities and porters for the members of the committee, and all that is left for the poor is five and a half roubles, and even over the distribution of this sum the members cannot agree and everyone keeps recommending some relation of his own. However, the conference that assembled on this occasion was of a quite different kind: it was called as a result of necessity. It was not a question of any poor or strangers; it was a question that concerned every official personally; it concerned the disaster that threatened them all alike, and so the conference should have willy-nilly been more unanimous and more united. But for all that the whole thing was a fiasco. Quite apart from the differences of opinion that are characteristic of all conferences, a sort of incomprehensible indecision became apparent in the views of all those present: one kept saying that Chichikov was a forger of government notes and then added: 'But perhaps he isn't a forger'; another maintained that he was an official of the governor-general's office, and immediately corrected himself by saying: 'Still, damn him, it's not written on his forehead, is it?' None of them was in favour of the theory that he was a brigand in disguise; it was considered that quite apart from his appearance, which was highly respectable, there was nothing in his conversation that betrayed a man of violent deeds. All of a sudden, the postmaster, who had for some minutes been absorbed in thought, whether because of some sudden inspiration or because of something else, cried quite unexpectedly:

'Do you know who he is, gentlemen?'

The voice in which he uttered this question concealed an implication so stupendous that it made everyone cry out with one voice:

'Who?'

'Why, gentlemen, it is none other than Captain Kopeikin!'

And when they at once asked with one voice:

'Who is this Captain Kopeikin?'

The postmaster said:

'Why, don't you know who Captain Kopeikin is?'

They all answered that they did not know who Captain Kopeikin was.

'Captain Kopeikin,' said the postmaster, opening his snuff-box only a little way for fear that someone near him might take a pinch with fingers in whose cleanliness he had but little faith, being, indeed, in the habit of saying 'We can't tell, my good sir, where your fingers have been, and snuff's a thing that must be kept clean' – 'Captain Kopeikin,' said the postmaster as he took a pinch of snuff, 'why, if I were to tell you, it would make a most entertaining story for some writer. Indeed, it's an epic poem of a sort.'

Everyone present expressed the wish to hear this story, or, as the postmaster put it, this epic poem of a sort that any writer would consider most entertaining, and he began as follows:

The Tale of Captain Kopeikin

'After the campaign of 1812, my good sir,' so began the postmaster, although there was not one but six gentlemen in the room, 'after the campaign of 1812, Captain Kopeikin was one of the wounded sent back home to Russia. Whether it was at Krasny or at Leipzig, I don't know, only I regret to say he had an arm and a leg blown off. Well, you see, in those days there were no – er – instructions of any kind issued about – er – the wounded; that – er – so-called pension fund for crippled soldiers was, as you probably know, in a way, established much later. Well, Captain Kopeikin realized that he would have to find some work, but he had only one arm, you see, the left one. So he went back home to his father, but his father said to him, believe it or not, "Sorry, son," he said, "I can't keep you," he said, "I can hardly get a crust of bread for myself." So, poor old Captain Kopeikin, my good sir, decided to go to Petersburg to ask the Emperor whether he'd grant him some pension from the privy purse. "See how things are with me, I've sacrificed my life in a manner of speaking, shed my blood ..." Well, in one way or another, getting lifts on army transports or military wagons, in short, my good sir, somehow or other he managed to get to Petersburg at last. Well, sir, you can imagine what an ordinary army captain, Captain Kopeikin, that is, felt when he suddenly found himself in a capital city the like of which, in a manner of speaking, is not to be found anywhere in the world. Suddenly there was the great world before him, a – er – a vast arena of life, a Scheherazade fairyland. Suddenly, you understand, he found himself in a place like Nevsky Avenue or – er – you know, Gorokhovaya Street. Damn it all! Or some such place as Liteyny Street; there's some – er – some sort of high spire in the air; bridges, you understand, suspended in the air and kept from falling by some magic, I mean, without any visible supports – in short, a Semiramis, my good sir, and that's all you can say about it! The poor fellow dragged himself about in search of some lodgings, but the rents they asked were so terribly high: curtains, blinds – every damned thing, you see, carpets – in a word – Persia! Trampling on millions, in a manner of speaking. Well, I mean to say, you just walk along a street and your nose simply keeps inhaling the smell of thousands and thousands of roubles. And all poor Captain Kopeikin's capital, sir, the whole of his banking account, consisted of barely ten blue five-rouble notes. Well, somehow or other, he did manage to get himself a room in a cheap hotel – Revel Hotel its name was – for a rouble a day, including cabbage soup and minced beef for dinner. He realized, of course, that his money wouldn't last him for ever. He made inquiries where he had to apply. He was told there was a high commission of some sort, you understand, and at the head of it was a full-ranking general. And the Emperor, you must know, wasn't in the capital at the time. The troops, you see, had not yet returned from Paris. They were all abroad. Well, so old Kopeikin got up a little earlier, scratched his beard with his left hand, for to pay a barber would, you see, be like running up a bill or something, pulled on his tattered uniform, and dragged himself off on his wooden leg – poor fellow! – to see the head of the commission, the great man himself. He inquired where the general lived. "There," they told him, pointing to a house on Palace Embankment. Well, you see, it turned out to be quite a peasant's little cottage: the window panes, believe it or not, were ten feet of smooth, highly polished glass, so that the vases and everything in the rooms looked as if they were outside – you could, in a manner of speaking, take them out with your hand from the street; precious marbles on the walls, metal bric-à-brac, a door-knob, you know, of a kind that first you would have to rush into a grocer's shop, buy yourself a farthing's worth of soap and rub your hands for two or three hours with it and only then make up your mind to take hold of it – in short, such polish on everything as would, in a manner of speaking, take your breath away. The porter alone looked like a generalissimo: a gilt mace, a face like a count's, like some fat, overfed pug, cambric collars – the dirty dog! ... Poor old Kopeikin just managed to drag himself on his wooden leg to the waiting room, squeezed himself into a corner so as not, you see, to stick his elbow into some America or India – some gilt porcelain vase, you understand. Well, I need hardly tell you, he had to stand about there for hours for, as you may well imagine, he had arrived at a time when the general had, in a manner of speaking, barely got out of bed and his valet had perhaps just brought him some silver basin for his various ablutions, you see. So old Kopeikin waits for about four hours, and then an aide-de-camp or some other official on duty comes in at last. "The general", he says, "will be coming into the waiting-room presently." And there were already as many people in the room as beans on a plate. And they were not just poor miserable underlings like ourselves, but all of the fourth or fifth rank, colonels, with here and there some fat star glittering on an epaulette – some high-ranking general, in short. All of a sudden there was, you understand, a barely perceptible movement in the room, just like some light flutter of a breeze. Here and there people uttered a surprised "Sh-sh" and at last there was an awful silence. The great man entered. Well – you can imagine what he was like – a statesman! In his face – I mean to say – in conformity with – er – his rank, you understand – high rank and – and such an air, you understand. Everyone in the room, needless to say, stood to attention immediately, waiting, trembling, all ready, in a manner of speaking, for their fate to be decided. The minister or the great man goes up to one man, then another: "What have *you* come for? What do *you* want? What's *your* business?" At last, my good sir, he goes up to Kopeikin. Plucking up his courage, Kopeikin says: "This is how it is, your Excellency. I've shed my blood, lost, in a manner of speaking, an arm and a leg. Can't work any more. I make bold to beg his Majesty's favour." The minister sees the man has got a wooden leg and his right sleeve is empty and pinned up to his uniform. "All right," he says, "come and see me again in a couple of days." Poor old Kopeikin is almost beside himself with joy. I mean to say, the mere fact that he had been deemed worthy of an audience with such an important statesman! And, furthermore, there was the fact that at last the question of his pension would, in a manner of speaking, be decided. Well, being in such high spirits, you understand, he was fairly skipping along the pavement. He dropped into the fashionable Palkinsky public house for a glass of vodka, had his dinner, my good sir, at the famous London restaurant, ordered cutlets with caper sauce, a chicken with all sorts of fancy trimmings, asked for a bottle of wine, too; in the evening he went to the theatre – in short, you understand, he went on the razzle. As he was walking along the pavement, he saw a tall and slender Englishwoman coming towards him, like a swan, yes, sir, like a real swan, in a manner of speaking. Poor old Kopeikin – his blood, you see, was on fire – started running after her, his wooden leg clip-clopping on the pavement. "But, no," he said to himself, "I'd better leave that for later, when I get my pension. Now I'm afraid I'm over-doing it a little." So, my good sir, three or four days later Kopeikin went to see the minister again and waited for him to come out. "This is how it is, sir," he says. "I've come," he says, "to hear your Excellency's order with respect to my illnesses and the wounds I've sustained. ..." And a lot more to the same effect, you understand, all in official style. The great man – believe it or not – recognized him at once. "Oh," he says, "very well," he says, "I'm sorry, but this time I can only tell you that you must wait until the Emperor's return. Then I'm sure orders will be issued concerning the wounded, but without, so to speak, his Majesty's command I'm afraid I can do nothing." A bow, you understand, and – good-bye! Kopeikin, as you can well imagine, went away not knowing what to think. You see, he had thought that he would get the money the very next day. "Here you are, my dear fellow, drink and make merry!" But instead of that he was told to wait and no date fixed, so he went down the steps looking miserable, like a poodle, you understand, over whom a cook had emptied a bucket of water, his tail between his legs and his ears hanging down. "No, sir," he said to himself, "I'm not giving up as easily as that. I'll go there again and explain that I'm eating my last morsel. If you don't help me, I must, in a manner of speaking, starve to death." Well, to cut a long story short, my good sir, he went to the Palace Embankment again, but he was told: "You can't come in. He's not receiving. Come tomorrow." The next day it was the same; the porter would not even look at him. Meanwhile, you understand, he had only one blue five-rouble note left in his pocket. While he had been having cabbage soup and some boiled beef before, he now bought himself a salted herring in some shop, or a salted cucumber and a ha'penny worth of bread – in short, the poor fellow was beginning to go hungry, and yet his appetite was simply wolfish. Every time he passed some restaurant – the chef there, as you can well imagine, would be a foreigner, some Frenchman with a large, open face, wearing fine linen, an apron as white as snow, and preparing some spicy sauce *aux fines herbes*, cutlets with truffles – in short, some delectable delicacy to make your mouth water and, I mean to say, give you such an appetite that you'd be glad to devour yourself. Every time he went past the Milyutinsky stores he'd catch sight of a huge salmon staring out of the window at him, in a manner of speaking, lovely cherries at five roubles apiece, an enormous water-melon, as big as a mail-coach, poking out of the window, looking, as it were, for some fool to pay a hundred roubles for it – in short, such temptation at every step that his mouth watered, but all he heard was "tomorrow, tomorrow". So you can easily imagine what his position was like: here, on the one hand, in a manner of speaking, was the salmon and the water-melon, and on the other, they kept presenting him with the same dish: "tomorrow". At last the poor fellow could bear it no longer, and he decided that, come what may, he'd have to take the place by storm, you understand. So he waited at the front door till another petitioner came along and then slipped through with his wooden leg into the waiting room in the wake of some general. The great man came out as usual. "What have *you* come for? What have *you* come for? Ah," he said, catching sight of Kopeikin, "haven't I told you that you have to wait for a decision?" "But, for pity's sake, your Excellency, I haven't a piece of bread left. ..." "I'm afraid I can't help that. I'm very sorry, but I can't do anything for you. Try to help yourself in the meantime. Look for some means yourself." "But, your Excellency, judge for yourself. What means can I find without an arm and leg?" "But I hope you will agree, sir," said the state dignitary, "that I can't be expected to provide for you at my own expense, as it were. I have lots of wounded and they all have equal rights. ... Arm yourself with patience. I give you my word of honour that as soon as the Emperor arrives, his Majesty won't let you go without conferring some favour upon you." "But I can't wait, your Excellency," said Kopeikin, and he said it, you understand, somewhat rudely. The great man, of course, was rather annoyed. And, indeed, here were generals waiting all round for decisions and orders – all, as it were, important affairs, affairs of state, in a manner of speaking, every minute counted, and here he was being pestered by some damned importunate fellow. "I'm sorry," he said, "I'm very busy. I've much more important affairs than yours to attend to." He was, of course, hinting in this rather subtle way, you see, that it was high time he was gone. Well, poor old Kopeikin – I expect hunger must have spurred him on – says: "Do what you like, your Excellency," he says, "but I shall not budge from this place until you give an order." Well, you may well imagine that to reply in such a manner to a great man who has only to say a word for you to be sent flying so that the devil himself won't find you is – er – I mean to say, if any civil servant were to say something of the kind to another civil servant who was one grade higher, it would be considered rude. But here – why, look at the vast difference, the vast difference: a high-ranking general and some Captain Kopeikin! Ninety roubles and – and zero! All the general did, you understand, was just to give one look, but that look of his was like a fire-arm: you're left with no heart, it has already gone into your boots. But old Kopeikin, you understand, never moved an inch, but stood there rooted to the spot. "Well, sir," said the general and, as they say, delivered a k.o. However, to tell the truth, he treated him fairly kindly: someone else would have given him such a fright that for three days the street would have been spinning round and round before his eyes, but he only said: "Very well, if you find it too expensive to live here and you cannot wait quietly in town for the decision about your future, I shall have to send you back at the government's expense. Call the courier! Let him be sent back to his place of permanent residence!" And the courier, you under-

214

stand, was standing there already: a huge, six-foot giant of a man whose enormous hand nature herself had fashioned specially for the purpose of cuffing coachmen, in short, a fellow who'd knock your teeth out better than any dentist. ... So, my good sir, they seized the miserable sinner and put him into a cart, with the courier beside him. "Well," Kopeikin thought, "at any rate, I shan't have to pay my fares. Thanks for that at least." So, my good sir, he was driven home with the courier as his guard and, driving along with the courier, he, in a manner of speaking, kept saying to himself: "All right," he said, "the general told me to look for means of helping myself – so I will," he said, "find the means!" Well, nothing is known about how he was taken to his place of permanent residence and where exactly he was taken to. It was thus, you understand, that the rumours about Captain Kopeikin were swallowed up in the river of oblivion, in this – er – Lethe, as the poets call it. But I hope you won't mind, gentlemen, my pointing out to you that it is here that, in a manner of speaking, the thread or the plot of the story begins. And so, where Kopeikin got to is not known but, believe it or not, two months had not elapsed before a band of robbers made their appearance in the forests of Ryazan, and the chief of that band, my good sir, was none other than –'

'But, look here, Ivan Andreyevich,' said the chief of police suddenly, interrupting him, 'you said yourself that Captain Kopeikin had lost an arm and a leg, while Chichikov has –'

At this point the postmaster uttered a cry and slapped himself violently on the forehead, calling himself a silly ass in public before them all. He could not understand how a circumstance like that had not occurred to him at the beginning of the story and he confessed that the saying, 'a Russian is wise after the event', is fully justified. However, a minute later he tried to be a little too clever and attempted to get round it by pointing out that mechanical devices had reached such a point of perfection in England that, as it would appear from the newspapers, someone had invented a pair of artificial legs which the moment a hidden spring was touched would carry off a man goodness only knows where, so that he could not be found anywhere afterwards.

But they were all very doubtful whether Chichikov really was Captain Kopeikin and they thought that the postmaster had gone a little too far. Still, for their part, they did their best not to disgrace themselves and, inspired by the postmaster's clever conjecture, went even further than he. Among a number of rather shrewd suggestions there was, strange to say, one to the effect that Chichikov might be Napoleon in disguise, that the English had long been envious of the vastness and greatness of Russia, and that there were, in fact, several cartoons published in which a Russian was shown talking to an Englishman. The Englishman was holding a dog on a rope behind him, and the dog was meant to be Napoleon: 'You'd better look out,' the Englishman was saying, 'if anything is not to my liking, I'll set the dog on you!' And now perhaps they had let him out from the island of St Helena, and he was now wandering all over Russia in the guise of Chichikov, though he was not really Chichikov at all.

Of course, the officials did not really believe it, but it did make them wonder and, thinking it over each for himself, they found that Chichikov's face, when he turned round and stood sideways, was very much like a portrait of Napoleon. The chief of police, who had served in the campaign of 1812 and had seen Napoleon personally, could not but admit that he was not an inch taller than Chichikov and that Napoleon could certainly not be said to be too fat, though he was not too thin, either. Some readers will perhaps call it a little too improbable; the author, too, is quite ready to oblige them by calling all this improbable; but unfortunately it all happened exactly as it is related here, and what makes it all the more astonishing is that the town was not far away in the wilds, but, on the contrary, quite near our two capital cities. Still, one ought to remember that all this took place shortly after the glorious expulsion of the French. At that time all our landowners, civil servants, merchants, shop assistants, and everyone who was literate and, indeed, the illiterate peasant as well became for at least eight years inveterate politicians. The *Moscow News* and the *Son of the Fatherland* were read with quite extraordinary avidity and reached the last reader in shreds that were no longer of any use for anything. Instead of such questions as, 'How much did you sell the measure of oats for, sir?' or 'What did you do in yesterday's first fall of snow?' they used to say, 'What are they writing in the papers? They haven't let Napoleon out of the island again, have they?' The merchants were very much afraid of this for they had implicit faith in the predictions of a prophet who had been for three years in prison; the prophet had come from no one knew where in bast-shoes and an uncovered sheepskin smelling terribly of stinking fish, and announced that Napoleon was Antichrist and was kept on a stone chain behind six walls and seven seas, but that later on he would break his chain and gain possession of the whole world. The prophet was very properly put in prison for his prediction, but he had done his work all the same and completely unsettled the merchants. Long afterwards, even while negotiating most profitable transactions, the merchants, on their way to some tavern to clinch the deal over a cup of tea, kept talking about Antichrist. Many civil servants and members of the nobility as well could not help thinking about it too and, infected by mysticism, which was, as everyone knows, very fashionable just then, thought every letter of Napoleon's name to be of some special significance; some even discovered Apocalyptic numbers in them. So there is nothing surprising in the fact that the civil servants could not help thinking about it; soon, however, they recollected themselves, realizing that they had let their imaginations run away with them and that all that had nothing to do with the matter under discussion. They thought and thought, they talked and talked, and at last decided that it would not be a bad idea to question Nozdryov thoroughly again. Since he was the first to make public the story of the dead souls, and since he was, as the saying is, on the most intimate terms with Chichikov, he would undoubtedly know something about the circumstances of his life and it was worth while trying again to find out what Nozdryov would say.

Civil servants are certainly a queer lot, as indeed are people of other professions: they knew perfectly well that Nozdryov was a liar, that one could not believe a word he said, even if it were of no importance whatever, and yet it was to him that they turned. What is one to do with man? He doesn't believe in God, but he believes that if the bridge of his nose itches he will die; he will ignore a poet's work that is as clear as daylight, harmonious through and through and pervaded by the spirit of the sublime wisdom of simplicity, but he will pounce eagerly upon the work of some bounder who confuses, traduces, twists, and distorts nature, and he will like it very much and he will start crying: 'This is it! This is true knowledge of the mysteries of the human heart!' All his life he does not care a pin for doctors and ends up by running for advice to some wise woman who cures by muttering spells and by spittle, or, better still, he himself invents some decoction of goodness only knows what rubbish, which for some mysterious reason he regards as the only remedy for his ills. One could, of course, excuse the officials to some extent because of the really difficult

217

situation in which they found themselves. A drowning man, they say, will clutch at a straw and his mind is at the time incapable of reflecting that a fly could perhaps have a ride on a straw, but that he weighs eleven or twelve stone; this consideration does not occur to him at that moment and he clutches at the straw. So, our gentlemen too clutched at Nozdryov. The chief of police immediately wrote a note to him, inviting him to an evening party, and a policeman in top boots and with engagingly rosy cheeks ran off that very minute, holding up his sword as he skipped along towards Nozdryov's lodgings. Nozdryov was engaged on some highly important business; for four days he had not left his room, admitting no one and having his meals passed to him through the window; in fact, he had actually grown thinner and green in the face. His business demanded the utmost concentration: it consisted of the selection from several hundreds of cards of two packs which would never let him down and on which he could rely as on a trusty friend. There was still another fortnight's work ahead of him and all this time Porfiry had to keep the mastiff puppy's navel clean with a special brush and wash it with soap three times a day. Nozdryov was very angry at having his solitude disturbed; to begin with, he sent the policeman to the devil, but when he read in the note that he might be able to win a lot of money because they were expecting a greenhorn at the party, he became mollified at once, quickly unlocked the door of his room, dressed himself anyhow, and set off. Nozdryov's statement, his testimony and theories were so diametrically opposed to those of the officials that even their latest conjectures were confounded. He was most certainly a man for whom doubt did not exist; and there was as much incertitude about their suppositions as there was firmness and certitude in his. He replied to all their questions without the slightest hesitation. He declared that Chichikov had bought several thousand roubles' worth of dead souls and that he himself had sold them to him because he saw no reason why he shouldn't. To the question whether he was a spy and whether he was trying to find out something, Nozdryov replied that he was a spy, that even at school where he, Nozdryov, was with him, he had been called a tell-tale for which his classmates, including Nozdryov himself, had given him a going over, so that they had had to apply two hundred and forty leeches to his temple, that is, what he meant was forty, but the two hundred had somehow slipped out by themselves. To the question whether Chichikov was a forger of counterfeit notes, he replied that he was indeed, and incidentally told an anecdote of Chichikov's extraordinary dexterity: how, when the police discovered that he had counterfeit notes for two million roubles in his house and sealed it up and put a guard of two soldiers at every door, Chichikov changed all the notes in a single night so that when they removed the seals next day the notes were found to be all genuine. To the question whether Chichikov really planned to abduct the governor's daughter and whether it were true that he, Nozdryov, had himself undertaken to assist him and to take part in this affair, Nozdryov replied that he had and that but for him nothing would have come of it. At this point he recollected himself, realizing that he had told a lie quite unnecessarily and that he might get himself into trouble, but he was no longer able to control his tongue. Besides, it was rather difficult to do so because there were so many interesting details bobbing up of their own accord, that it was quite impossible to give them up: he even mentioned by name the village in the parish church of which it was proposed that the wedding should take place, to wit, the village of Trukhmachevka, the priest, Father Sidor, who was to be paid seventy-five roubles for the wedding and who would not have agreed to do it even for that if he, Nozdryov, had not frightened him by threatening to report him for marrying the corn-chandler Mikhailo to the godmother of a child to which he had stood godfather, that he had even placed his carriage at their disposal and had got ready relays of horses at all the posting stations. His details became so authentic that he began even to mention the names of the drivers. They tried dropping a hint about Napoleon, but they were sorry themselves to have done so, for Nozdryov began to talk nonsense that not only had no semblance of truth, but had no semblance of anything at all, so that the officials just walked away with a sigh. Only the chief of police went on listening to him in the hope that there might be something at least in what he would say later, but in the end he, too, gave it up, saying: 'Damned if I can make head or tail of it!' And they all agreed that 'you can't make a silk purse out of a sow's ear', and the officials found themselves in a worse predicament than ever, and the upshot of the matter was that, try as they might, they could not discover who Chichikov was. And it became abundantly clear what sort of creature man is: wise, clever, and sensible in all things that concern others but not himself. The discreet and firm advice he gives in difficult moments of life! 'What a resourceful fellow,' cries the crowd. 'What a steadfast character!' But let some misfortune befall that resourceful fellow and let him be put in a difficult position himself and what becomes of his character! The steadfast man goes all to pieces and proves a miserable little coward, a weak, insignificant child, or simply a —, as Nozdryov called it.

All these discussions, opinions, and rumours for some unknown reason produced their greatest effect on the poor public prosecutor. They had such an effect on him that on returning home he began to think and think and suddenly, without rhyme or reason, as they say, dropped dead. Whether he had a stroke or some other sort of seizure, but, as he was sitting on a chair, he flopped down and fell on his back. As is usual on such occasions, they threw up their hands and cried, 'Good God!', sent for the doctor to bleed him, but soon saw that the public prosecutor was just a soulless corpse. It was only then that they realized with regret that the late public prosecutor really had a soul, though, being a modest man, he had never shown it. And yet the appearance of death was as terrible in a small man as in a great man: he who had only recently been walking about, moving about, playing whist, signing all sorts of papers, and was so often seen among the civil servants with his beetling brows and his winking eye, was now lying on the table, his left eye winking no more, but one eye-brow still raised with a sort of questioning expression. What the dead man was inquiring about, why he died, or why he had lived – God only knows.

But this is absurd! This is quite at variance with ordinary facts! It's impossible that officials could so frighten themselves, could make up such nonsense, could depart so far from the truth, when even a child could have seen what was wrong. So many of my readers will say, and will blame the author for all sorts of improbabilities, or will call the poor officials 'fools', because man is very lavish in the use of the word 'fool' and is ready to apply it twenty times a day to his neighbour. It is sufficient if out of a dozen sides of his character he has one foolish one for a man to be put down as a fool in spite of his eleven good ones. Readers can find it easy to criticize, looking down from their comfortable corner on the heights from which the whole horizon lies open at everything that is taking place below, where man can only see the object nearest to him. And in the universal chronicle of mankind there are many entire centuries which he could apparently cross out and suppress as unnecessary. Many errors have been made in the world which today, it seems, even a child would not have made. How many crooked, out-of-the-way, narrow, impassable, and devious paths has humanity chosen in the attempt to attain eternal truth, while before it the straight road lay open, like the road leading to a magnificent building destined to become a royal palace. It is wider and more resplendent than all the other paths, lying as it does in the full glare of the sun and lit up by many lights at night, but men have streamed past it in blind darkness. And how many times even when guided by understanding that has descended upon them from heaven, have they still managed to swerve away from it and go astray, have managed in the broad light of day to get into the impassable out-of-the-way places again, have managed again to throw a blinding mist over each other's eyes and, running after will-o'-the-wisps, have managed to reach the brink of the precipice only to ask themselves afterwards with horror: 'Where is the way out? Where is the road?' The present generation sees everything clearly, it is amazed at the errors and laughs at the folly of its ancestors, unaware that this chronicle is shot through with heavenly fires, that every letter in it cries out aloud to them, that from everywhere, from every direction an accusing finger is pointed at it, at the present generation; but the present generation laughs and proudly and self-confidently enters on a series of fresh errors at which their descendants will laugh again later on.

Chichikov knew nothing of what was going on. As luck would have it, he had caught a slight chill at the time and had a swollen face and a slight inflammation of the throat, in the distribution of which the climate of many of our provincial towns is extremely generous. To make sure that his life, God forbid, was not cut short without posterity, he decided that it would be wiser not to leave his room for two or three days. During those days he gargled continually with a mixture of milk and figs which he afterwards ate, and carried a little bag with camomile and camphor tied round his cheek. Not wishing to waste his time, he made several new and detailed lists of all the peasants he had bought, read a volume of the French novel *La Duchesse de la Vallière*, which he dug out of his trunk, looked through the various objects and notes he kept in his box, read something over a second time, and was terribly bored by it all. He could not understand why none of the officials of the town had even once called on him to inquire after his health when only a short while before all sorts of carriages had been standing before the door of his inn – either the postmaster's or the public prosecutor's or the president's. He only shrugged his shoulders as he paced about the room. At last he felt better and was greatly overjoyed when he realized that he could at last go out for a breath of fresh air. Without any further delay he at once began to get ready, opened his box, poured some hot water into a glass, took out his shaving brush and his soap and proceeded to shave, which, incidentally, he should have done long ago, for feeling his chin with his hand and looking into the glass he exclaimed, 'Dear me, what a jungle!' And, indeed, though it was no jungle, there was quite a thick growth all over his cheeks and his chin. Having shaved, he began to dress with such great speed that he all but jumped out of his trousers. At last he was dressed, sprinkled with eau-de-Cologne, and, warmly wrapped up, made his way out into the street, keeping his cheek tied up as a precaution. Going out was for him, as for every convalescent, like a holiday. Everything he came across – houses, passing peasants, who looked rather glum, one of them having already managed to box another one's ears – assumed a gay, laughing air. He intended to pay his first call on the governor. On the way all sorts of ideas came into his head; the fair-haired young girl kept coming into his mind again and again, his imagination even beginning to indulge in all sorts of playful scenes till he began to joke and laugh at himself a little. In such a frame of mind he found himself before the governor's front door. He was about to fling off his overcoat hurriedly in the entrance hall, when the porter completely confounded him by the utterly unexpected words:

'I've orders not to admit you, sir.'

'What did you say? Good heavens, man, don't you know me? Have a good look at me!' Chichikov said to him.

'Of course I know you, sir,' said the porter. 'It's not the first time I've seen you. But, you see, sir, it's you, sir, I've orders not to admit. I may admit anyone else.'

'Well, I must say! Why? What on earth for?'

'Them's my orders, sir, so I suppose that's how it should be,' said the porter, and only added the words, 'Yes, sir'. After that he stood facing him, completely unembarrassed and without the obsequious air with which he had hastened to help him off with his coat before. He seemed to be thinking as he looked at him: 'Oho, if gentlemen are showing you the door, you must be a low-born rascal.'

'Can't understand it! Can't understand it!' Chichikov thought to himself and set off at once to pay a call on the president, but the president was thrown into such confusion on catching sight of him that he could not say two words that made any sense and talked such drivel that they were both ashamed. On leaving him, Chichikov tried his utmost to make some sense of what the president was getting at and what his words could be referring to, but he could make nothing of it. Then he went to see the others: the chief of police, the vice-governor, the postmaster, but either they refused to receive him or received him so strangely, talked in so constrained and incomprehensible a manner, looked so embarrassed, and altogether everything was in such a confusion and muddle that he began to have doubts as to whether their brains were quite in order. He tried to pay one or two more visits in order to find out at least the cause of it all, but he could not discover any real cause. Like a man half-awake, he wandered aimlessly about the town, unable to decide whether he had gone out of his mind or the officials had gone out of theirs; whether it was all a dream or whether reality was more absurd than any dream. It was late, almost dusk, when he returned to the inn which he had left in such high spirits, and feeling very depressed he ordered tea to be sent up. He began pouring out the tea, musing and wondering rather vacantly at the strangeness of his situation, when suddenly the door of his room was flung open and Nozdryov quite unexpectedly stood before him.

'As the proverb says, "For a friend five miles is just like walking across the street",' he said, taking off his cap. 'I was passing and saw a light in your window, so I said to myself, Why not drop in, he's probably still up. Oh, good! I see you've got tea on the table. I'm dying for a cup of tea. Eaten all sorts of rubbish at dinner today and I'm beginning to feel a rumbling in my stomach. Tell your man to fill a pipe, will you? Where's your pipe?'

'I don't smoke a pipe,' said Chichikov dryly.

'Nonsense, as if I don't know you're a smoker. Hey, there! What's your valet's name? Hey Vakhramey, come here!'

'It's not Vakhramey but Petrushka.'

'How's that? I could have sworn you had a Vakhramey before.'

'I never had a man called Vakhramey.'

'Why, of course, it's Derebin whose man is called Vakhramey. Just imagine, what luck that fellow Derebin has: his aunt has quarrelled with her son because he has married a serf-girl, and now she has left him all her property. I thought to myself, if only I had an aunt like that I shouldn't have to worry about the future. But, my dear fellow, why have you been avoiding everyone? Why aren't you to be seen anywhere? I know of course that you sometimes study all sorts of learned subjects, that you're fond of reading.' (Why Nozdryov should have concluded that our hero was studying learned subjects and was fond of reading, we confess, we cannot tell and still less could Chichikov.) 'Why, Chichikov, old fellow, if you'd only seen – it would have been a subject fit for your satirical turn of mind.' (Why Chichikov had a satirical turn of mind is also unknown.) 'Would you believe it, my dear fellow, we were having a game of cards at the merchant Likhachov's and we had great fun, I can tell you! Perependev, who was there with me, said, "Now, if only Chichikov were here, he too would have enjoyed himself!"' (Chichikov had never known anyone called Perependev in his life.) 'But you must admit, my dear fellow, you did treat me disgracefully over that game of draughts. Remember? I won it, you know. ... Yes, my dear fellow, you did diddle me all right, but then, dammit, I can't be cross. The other day at the president's ... Oh, yes, I forgot to tell you. Everyone in the town has turned against you. They think you forge counterfeit notes. They've been pestering me about you, but, my dear fellow, I stood up for you like a rock, told them that I'd gone to school with you and knew your father. Well, I don't want to boast, but I did spin them a beauty of a yarn.'

'I forge notes?' cried Chichikov, getting up from his chair.

'But why did you give them such a scare?' Nozdryov went on. 'Damme, man, they're terrified out of their wits: they've made you out to be a brigand and a spy ... The public prosecutor, you know, has died of fright. His funeral is tomorrow. Will you be coming? To tell the truth, they're afraid of the new governor-general, in case they get into trouble over you. You know what I think of the governor-general? If he turns up his nose and starts giving himself airs, he won't get far with the nobility. The nobility, my dear fellow, demands to be treated with cordiality. They must be entertained, mustn't they? Of course, he can shut himself up in his study and not give a single ball, but what good will that do? He won't gain anything by that, will he? But you know, Chichikov, you've undertaken a very risky business.'

'What risky business?' Chichikov asked uneasily.

'Why, abducting the governor's daughter. I did expect it, though. Damned if I didn't. The first time I saw you together at the ball I thought to myself, "That fellow Chichikov is surely up to something. ..." However, I can't say that I admire your choice. Can't see anything in her. Now, there is one, a relation of Bikusov's, his sister's daughter, now that's some girl, I can tell you. A lovely bit of goods!'

'What are you talking about? What nonsense is this? Abduct the governor's daughter? What on earth do you mean?' said Chichikov, staring open-eyed at him.

'Come on, out with it! What a secretive fellow you are. You see, I don't mind telling you that I came to offer you my help. I'd be glad to hold the wedding crown over your head. I'll provide the carriage and the relays of horses, but, mind, first you must promise to lend me three thousand roubles. I simply must have them!'

While Nozdryov was chattering away, Chichikov rubbed his eyes several times to make sure that he was not hearing it all in a dream. A forger of notes, abducting the governor's daughter, the death of the public prosecutor, of which he was supposed to be the cause, the arrival of the governor-general – all this alarmed him considerably. 'Well,' he thought to himself, 'if things have gone as far as this, I mustn't stay here much longer. Must get out of here as soon as possible.'

He got rid of Nozdryov as quickly as he could, at once sent for Selifan and told him to be ready at daybreak, so that they could leave the town without fail at six o'clock in the morning. He also told him to look over everything carefully, to have the carriage greased, and so on. Selifan said, 'Yes, sir,' but remained standing for some minutes at the door without stirring from his place. His master also told Petrushka to pull the trunk out from under the bed, covered as it already was with a thick layer of dust, and together they began to pack all his belongings just as they came to hand, socks, shirts, clean and dirty linen, boot-trees, calendar. ... All this was packed anyhow; he was absolutely determined to be ready by the evening so that nothing could happen to detain him in the morning. After standing two minutes at the door, Selifan at last walked very slowly out of the room. Slowly, as slowly as one can imagine, he went down the stairs leaving the imprint of his wet boots on the steps, worn hollow by people's feet, and for a long time after he kept scratching the back of his head. What did that scratching betoken? And what does it generally signify? Was it

vexation at not being able to keep his appointment on the following day somewhere in a licensed pub with his friend in the uncovered sheepskin with a belt tied round his waist, or had some little affair of the heart started in the new place and had he to give up standing in the evening at the gates and the discreet holding of little white hands at an hour when dusk is falling upon the town, and a huge fellow in a red shirt twangs on a balalaika before a gathering of house-serfs, and a mixed crowd of working people carry on a quiet exchange of words after their work? Or was he simply sorry to leave the snug place in the servants' kitchen under a sheepskin coat near the stove, the cabbage soup with the soft town-made pie, to go once more trailing along through rain and slush and all the hardships of the road? Goodness only knows. It is hard to say. Scratching the back of the head can mean all sorts of things to a Russian peasant.

Chapter 11

However, nothing happened as Chichikov had intended. To begin with, he woke later than he expected. That was his first disappointment. As soon as he got up, he sent a man to find out whether the horses were harnessed and whether everything was ready, but he was informed that the horses had not been harnessed and nothing was ready. That was his second disappointment. He flew into a rage and was even prepared to give our friend Selifan something in the nature of a thrashing, merely waiting impatiently to hear what excuse Selifan would give to justify himself. Selifan soon appeared in the doorway and his master had the pleasure of listening to the sort of speech one usually hears from servants when one is in a hurry to set off on a journey.

'But the horses will have to be shod first, sir.'

'Oh, you damned fool, you blockhead! Why didn't you say so before? You've had plenty of time, haven't you?'

'Yes, sir, I've had plenty of time, sir. ... Then, of course, you see, there's the wheel too, sir. The iron rim has to be properly tightened, because, you see, sir, the road is very bumpy with all those terrible potholes we've got now. And if you don't mind me saying so, sir, the front part of the carriage has become very rickety, so that I'm not sure, sir, if it will last for two stages.'

'You're a scoundrel!' cried Chichikov, throwing up his hands, and he went up so close to him that Selifan stepped back a little, afraid of getting a present from his master. 'Do you want to murder me, eh? Cut my throat? Planning to cut my throat on the highway, are you? You dirty brigand, you! You sea monster! Eh, eh? We've been here for three weeks, eh? And you never said a word to me, you dissolute fellow, you! And now at the last minute you come out with it! Just when everything's almost ready for me to get in and set off, eh? And now you come along and make a mess of it all, eh? Eh? You knew it before, didn't you? You knew, didn't you? Answer me, eh?'

'I did, sir,' replied Selifan, hanging his head.

'Why didn't you tell me then?'

To this question Selifan made no reply, but, hanging his head, seemed to be muttering to himself: 'Fancy it turning out like that! I knew it all right, but didn't say nothing.'

'You'd better go now and fetch a blacksmith and see that everything's ready in two hours' time. Do you hear? In two hours and not a minute more, and if it isn't, I'll – I'll – I'll – show you who's the master here! I'll make you rue the day you were born!' Our hero was very angry indeed.

Selifan turned to the door as if intending to go and carry out his master's orders, but he stopped and said: 'And there's another thing, sir. That dapple-grey horse of ours, sir, ought to be sold, because he's a regular rascal, he is. God preserve me from having to do with such a horse again. He's just a lot of trouble.'

'So I'm to chase off to the market to sell him, am I?'

'But, God's my witness, sir, he just looks all right, but he's really a crafty horse. Aye, very crafty he is. You won't find such another horse anywhere else, sir.'

'Idiot! When I want to sell him I'll sell him. Starting an argument, are you? Now you'd better listen to me. If you don't fetch the blacksmith at once and if everything is not ready in two hours from now, I'll give you such a thrashing that – that you won't be able to recognize yourself. Go! Get out.'

Selifan went out. Chichikov was in a vile temper and he hurled his sword down on the floor, the sword he carried about with him when travelling so as to inspire proper terror in whomsoever it was necessary. He spent a quarter of an hour bargaining with the blacksmiths before he could come to terms with them, for the blacksmiths as usual were inveterate scoundrels, and realizing that the work was urgent and was wanted in a hurry, asked six times the ordinary price. However much he fumed, calling them scoundrels, brigands, robbers who fleeced travellers, and even hinting at the Day of Judgement, he made no impression whatever on the blacksmiths: they stood firm and not only stuck to their original price, but took five and a half hours over their work instead of two. During that time he had the satisfaction of experiencing those agreeable moments which are so well known to every traveller when everything is already packed and only bits of string and pieces of paper and all sorts of rubbish are left lying on the floor, when a man is neither on the road nor yet settled in one place, and when he looks out of the window and watches people passing by up and down the street, talking of their tuppeny-halfpenny affairs and raising their eyes with a sort of stupid curiosity to stare at him and then going on their way, which still further sours the temper of the poor traveller who is waiting in vain to start on his journey. Everything around him, everything he sees: the little shop opposite his windows and the head of the old woman living in the house opposite, going up to the window with the short curtains – all this sickens him, and yet he does not move away from the window. He stands there, one moment oblivious to everything and another again turning his dulled attention upon everything that moves or does not move before him and in his vexation swats a fly which buzzes and struggles on the window-pane under his fingers. But there is an end to everything and the longed-for minute came. Everything was ready, the front part of the carriage had been properly repaired, the wheel had a new iron rim put on it, the horses had been brought from the watering place, and the brigands of blacksmiths had departed after counting over their roubles and wishing him a good journey. At last the carriage was ready and two hot, freshly bought white loaves were put inside, and Selifan put something for himself in the pocket of the coachman's box, and our hero got into the carriage at last, while the waiter, who came out to see him off in his cotton cut-away coat, waved his cap, and hotel servants and all sorts of other footmen and coachmen gathered round to gape at the departure of someone else's gentleman, and amid the various other circumstances which usually crop up at a departure, the carriage, usually favoured by bachelors, which had been standing so long in the town and of which my readers are probably heartily sick by now, at last drove out of the gates of the inn.

'Thank God,' said Chichikov, and crossed himself. Selifan cracked his whip; Petrushka, after hanging for a while on the steps, now climbed up and sat beside him, and our hero, settling himself more comfortably on the Georgian rug, put a leather cushion behind his back, pressed the two hot white loaves against his sides, and the carriage set off again, jolting and bouncing thanks to the cobbled roadway which, as everyone knows, has wonderful bouncing properties. With a sort of indeterminate feeling Chichikov gazed at the houses, the walls, the wooden fences, and the streets, which for their part seemed to bounce about too as they slowly receded, and which God only knew whether he was ever destined to see again in his life. At a turning in one of the streets, the carriage had to stop because its whole length was occupied by an endless funeral cortège. Chichikov put his head out of the window and asked Petrushka whose funeral it was, and learned that it was the public prosecutor's. Full of unpleasant sensations, he at once hid himself in a corner, covering himself with the leather apron, and pulled the curtains over the windows. At the very moment when the carriage was brought to a halt in this way, Selifan and Petrushka, devoutly taking off their hats, were trying to see who, how, in what, and on what, were driving in the procession, counting how many people there were on foot and in the carriages, while their master, having ordered them not to recognize or greet any of their acquaintances, also began watching timidly through the little pane in the leather curtain. All the civil servants of the town walked bareheaded behind the coffin. He began to be a little afraid that his carriage might be recognized, but they all had other things to think of. They were not even indulging in the small talk which people usually indulge in at a funeral. All their thoughts were at that moment concentrated on themselves: they were wondering what the new governor-general would be like, how he would set about his duties, and how he would receive them. After the officials who were walking came the carriages out of which peeped ladies in mourning bonnets. From the movements of their lips and their hands it was evident that they were engaged in an animated conversation; perhaps they too were discussing the arrival of the new governor-general and speculating about the balls he would give and were busily chatting about their everlasting frills and furbelows. Finally, the carriages were followed by several empty cabs in single file, and at last there was nothing left and our hero was at liberty to drive on. Drawing back the leather curtains, he sighed and exclaimed from the bottom of his heart: 'Poor old public prosecutor! He lived and lived and then died! And now they will print in the newspapers that to the grief of his subordinates and of humanity at large there passed away an honoured citizen, a devoted father, an exemplary husband, and they'll write a lot more nonsense about him, adding perhaps that he was followed to the grave by the lamentations of widows and orphans. And yet taking a sober view of the matter, it appears that when all is said and done there was nothing special about you except your beetling brows.' Then he ordered Selifan to drive faster and meanwhile thought to himself: 'It's a good thing we came across a funeral. They say it's lucky to run across a corpse.'

Meanwhile the carriage had turned into more deserted streets; soon there were only long wooden fences stretching away into the distance, a sure sign that the end of the town was in sight. And now the cobbled streets came to an end, the turnpike and the town had been left behind, and there was nothing any more, and once more they were on the highroad. And once more at either side of the highroad there was a quick succession of milestones, station-masters, wells, strings of village-carts, drab villages with samovars, peasant women, and a brisk bearded innkeeper running out of his yard carrying oats, a tramp in worn bast-shoes who had trudged over five hundred miles, little towns built in a hurry with little wooden shops, barrels of flour, bast-shoes, white loaves, and all sorts of other cheap articles, striped turnpikes, bridges under repair, fields stretching for miles on either side of the highway, old-fashioned, bulky landowner's carriages, a soldier on horseback carrying a green box with grape-shot and the name of some artillery battery inscribed on it, green, yellow, and freshly ploughed black furrows flashing by on the steppes, a song struck up somewhere far away, the tops of pine-trees in the mist, the peal of church bells fading away in the distance, crows as thick as flies, and a horizon without an end ... Russia! Russia! I see you, from my wondrous beautiful afar: I see you now. Everything in you is poor, straggling, and uncomfortable: no bold wonders of nature crowned with ever bolder wonders of art, no cities with many-windowed tall palaces built upon rocks, no picturesque trees, no ivy-covered houses in the roar and the everlasting spray of waterfalls will rejoice the traveller or startle his eyes; the head will not be thrown back to gaze at the huge rocks piled up endlessly on the heights above it; through dark arches, stacked one on top of the other in a tangle of vines, ivy, and countless millions of wild roses – through dark arches he will catch no glimpse in the distance of the eternal lines of gleaming mountains soaring into bright silvery skies. Everything in you is open, empty, flat; your lowly towns are stuck like dots upon your plains, like scarcely visible marks; there is nothing to beguile and ravish the eye. But what is the incomprehensible, mysterious force that draws me to you? Why does your mournful song, carried along your whole length and breadth from sea to sea, echo and re-echo incessantly in my ears? What is there in it? What is there in that song? What is it that calls, and sobs, and clutches at my heart? What are those sounds that caress me so poignantly, that go straight to my soul and twine about my heart? Russia! What do you want of me? What is that mysterious, hidden bond between us? Why do you look at me like that? And why does everything in you turn eyes full of expectation on me? ... And while, deep in perplexity, I stand motionless, a cloud, full of menace and heavy with approaching downpours of rain, already casts its shadow over my head and thought grows numb confronted with your vast expanse. What do those immense, wide, far-flung open spaces hold in store? Is it not here, is it not in you that some boundless thought will be born, since you are yourself without end? Is not this the place for the legendary hero of Russian fable, here where there is plenty of room for him to spread himself and move about freely? And menacingly your mighty expanse enfolds me, reflected with terrifying force in the depths of me; my eyes are lighted up with supernatural power – oh, what a glittering, wondrous infinity of space the world knows nothing of! Russia! ...

'Stop, stop, you fool!' Chichikov shouted to Selifan.

'I'll slash you with my sabre!' shouted a military courier with moustaches a yard long, who was galloping towards them. 'Can't you see, the devil flay your soul, it's a government carriage?'

And like a phantom the *troika* vanished with a thunderous rattle and in a cloud of dust.

What a strange, alluring, enthralling, wonderful word it is: the open road! And how wonderful that open road is itself: a sunny day, autumn leaves, cool air – wrap your travelling cloak more tightly round you, pull your cap over your ears, snuggle up more closely and more cosily in the corner! For the last time a shiver runs through your limbs and already it is followed by a pleasant warmth. The horses go racing along. How seductively does drowsiness steal over you! Your eyelids close, and through sleep you hear the strains of the song 'No more white were the snows', and the snorting of the horses, and the rattle of the wheels, and you, too, are already snoring, pressing your fellow-passenger against the corner. You wake up: five stages have been left behind; moonlight, a strange town, churches with ancient wooden cupolas and spires standing out darkly against the sky, dark timber houses and white brick ones. Shafts of moonlight here and there: they look like white linen handkerchiefs hung on walls, the roadway, the streets; coal-black shadows cut across them slantingly; the wooden roofs, with the moonlight falling obliquely across them, shine like gleaming metal, and not a soul anywhere. Everything is asleep. Except, perhaps, for a light glimmering all by itself in some small window: an artisan mending his boots or a baker busy with his oven – who cares? And the night! … Heavens above, what a night is being enacted on high! And the air, and the tall sky, far, far away, there in its unfathomable depths, spread out so boundlessly, harmoniously, luminously! But the chill breath of the night blows fresh upon your eyes and lulls you to sleep, and already you are dozing and you fall asleep and you snore and the poor fellow-traveller, crushed against the corner, stirs angrily, feeling the weight of your body. You wake – and again fields and steppes stretch before you, nothing to be seen – everywhere emptiness and open spaces. A milestone with a number on it flashes past. Day is breaking. A pale, golden streak appears on the cold whitening horizon. The wind grows fresher and harsher: wrap yourself more closely in your warm cloak! What glorious coolness! How wonderful is the sleep that steals over you again! A jolt – and again you wake. The sun is high up in the sky. 'Gently, gently!' a voice is heard saying. A cart is coming down a steep hill. Below is a broad dam and a broad clear pond, sparkling like burnished copper in the sunlight. A village. Peasants' cottages scattered on the hillside. The cross of the village church gleams like a star on one side. The chatter of peasants and a ravenous appetite … Dear Lord, how wonderful the long, long road is sometimes! How many times have I clutched at you, lost and drowning, and every time you have magnanimously brought me ashore and saved me! And how many wonderful ideas and poetic dreams were you responsible for and how many glorious impressions have I experienced thanks to you! … But our friend Chichikov, too, was at that moment indulging in not altogether prosaic dreams. Let us see what he was feeling. At first he felt nothing, but was only looking back, anxious to make quite sure that he really had left the town behind him; but when he saw that the town had long disappeared, that neither windmills nor smithies nor anything one usually finds on the outskirts of towns were to be seen, and that even the white spires of the brick churches had long since sunk into the ground, he became entirely absorbed by the open road and kept looking only to the right and to the left as though the town of N. had never existed, as though he had passed through it a long time ago, in his childhood. At last the road too ceased to interest him and he began to close his eyes slightly and lean his head on the cushion. The author confesses that he is glad of it, for it gives him an opportunity to say a few words about his hero; for, as the reader has seen, until now he was constantly prevented from doing so either by Nozdryov, or by balls, or by ladies, or by the scandal-mongers of the town, or, finally, by thousands of trifling incidents, which only seem trifling when they are brought into a book, but when they are happening in the world are considered to be matters of the utmost importance. But let us put absolutely everything else aside and get down to business.

It is very doubtful whether the reader will like the hero of our choice. The ladies will not like him, that we can say without any fear of contradiction; for ladies demand that their hero should be perfect in every respect, and if there should be the slightest stain on his soul or body then – there's trouble. However deeply the author may peer into his soul and even if he were to reflect his image more clearly than any mirror, they will give him no credit for it. The very fact that Chichikov was stout and middle-aged will do him great harm in their eyes: they will never under any circumstances forgive stoutness in a hero and many ladies will turn away and say: 'Ugh, what a disgusting man!' Alas, the author knows it very well, and yet he cannot take a virtuous man for his hero. But – perhaps in this very novel some people will catch the sound of other hitherto untouched chords and get a glimpse of the untold riches of the Russian soul, of a man endowed with divine valour, or of a wonderful Russian girl, the like of whom cannot be found anywhere in the world, a girl possessing all the wondrous beauty of a woman's soul, full of generous instincts and self-sacrifice. And all the virtuous men of other races will seem as dead beside them as a book is dead beside the living word. And Russian emotions will rise up ... and everyone will see how deeply what merely skims over the surface of the nature of other nations has sunk into the Slav nature. ... But why speak of what is still in the future? It is unseemly for the author who has long ago attained years of discretion and who has been brought up in the hard school of spiritual life and in the refreshing sobriety of solitude to forget himself like a young man. There is a time and place for everything. All the same I have not taken a virtuous man for my hero. And I can even say why not. Because at last the time has come to give a rest to the poor virtuous man; because the words 'virtuous man' have become meaningless; because they have transformed the virtuous man into a horse and there is no writer who does not ride him, urging him on with a whip or anything else he can lay hold of; because they've exhausted the virtuous man to such an extent that there's not a shred of virtue left in him, and all that remains of him is skin and bone; because their appeal to the virtuous man is sheer hypocrisy; because they do not respect the virtuous man. No, it is high time we harnessed the scoundrel. And so let us harness the scoundrel!

Our hero's origin was humble and obscure. His parents were of the nobility, but whether they were hereditary noblemen or life noblemen – goodness only knows. He did not look like them: at least, a relative who was present at his birth, one of those short little women who are commonly known as 'lapwings', exclaimed as she took the baby in her arms: 'He's not at all what I expected! He should have been like his granny on his mother's side, that would have been much better, but he was born just as the proverb says: "Neither like his mother nor like his father, but like a tall and handsome stranger".' From the very first, life turned a sour and unfriendly countenance on him, as though gazing at him through some dim, snow-covered window: he had neither friends nor playmates as a child. A small little room with tiny windows never opened in winter or summer. His father, an invalid, in a long coat lined with lambswool and with knitted slippers on his bare feet, was always sighing as he paced up and down the room, spitting into a spittoon full of sand in a corner. He himself was always sitting on a bench with a pen in his hand and inkstains on his fingers and even on his lips, everlasting injunctions before his eyes: 'Speak the truth! Obey your elders! Cherish virtue in your heart!' The everlasting shuffling and flapping of the slippers about the room, the familiar but always stern voice: 'Playing the fool again!' every time the child, tired of the monotony of his work, added some flourish or tail to some letter; and the all too familiar and never very pleasant sensation when these words were followed by the lobe of his ear being tweaked very painfully from behind by the nails of his father's long fingers. Such is the pitiful picture of his early childhood of which he retained only a dim memory. But in life everything changes with quite striking rapidity. One day, with the first sunshine and the floods of early spring, the father, taking his son with him, set out in a little cart, drawn by a chestnut piebald nag, of the kind known among horse-dealers as 'magpies'; it was driven by a little hunchback, the progenitor of the only serf family owned by Chichikov's father, who performed almost all the duties in the house. They drove with the 'magpie' for over a day and a half. They spent a night on the road, crossed a river, had their meals of cold pie and roast mutton, and reached the town only on the morning of the third day. The streets of the town dazzled the boy with their unexpected splendour, making him gape for several minutes. Then the 'magpie' plunged with the cart into a big hole at the entrance of a narrow lane running downhill and thick with mud; it took the 'magpie' a long time to get out of it; after struggling with all her might to wade through the mud, urged on by the hunchback and by the master himself, she finally succeeded in dragging them out into a little yard standing on the slope of the hill. Two flowering apple-trees grew in front of the little old house, covered with shingle and with one narrow opaque window, and there was a small garden at the back. Here lived a relative of theirs, a wizened old woman who still went to market every morning, drying her stockings on the *samovar* afterwards. She patted the boy on the cheek and admired his plumpness. There he was to stay and go every day to the town school.

After spending a night there, his father set off home again next morning. No tears were shed by his father at parting. He was given fifty copecks in copper coins for pocket money and to buy sweets and, what was far more important, this wise admonition: 'Mind, Pavlusha, do your lessons. Don't play the fool and get into mischief. Above all, do your best to please your teachers and superiors. If you please your chief, you will be all right and you will get ahead of everyone, even if you turn out to be a bad scholar, and even if God has given you no talent. Do not make friends with your classmates. They will teach you no good. But if you do make friends with them, play with those who are better off and might be useful to you. Don't entertain or treat anyone, but behave in such a way that you may be treated by others and, above all, take care of and save your pennies: money is the most reliable thing in the world. A classmate or friend may cheat you and be the first to leave you in the lurch when you're in trouble, but money will never let you down whatever trouble you may be in. With money in your pocket you can do anything and money will see you through everything.' Having delivered himself of these precepts, the father parted from his son and dragged himself off home again on his 'magpie' and from that day his son never set eyes on him again, but his words and precepts sank deeply into his mind.

Pavlusha began attending his classes on the following day. He did not show any special aptitude for any subject and he distinguished himself most of all by his diligence and tidiness; on the other hand, he showed a great ability in another direction, in practical affairs. He grasped the situation at once and conducted himself towards his schoolfellows in such a way that they treated him, while he never treated them, and indeed he sometimes concealed the things they had given him and then sold them to them afterwards. Even as a child he knew how to deny himself everything. He did not spend a copeck of the fifty copecks his father had given him; on the contrary, that same year he increased the amount, displaying an almost extraordinary resourcefulness: he moulded a bullfinch in wax, painted it, and sold it at a great profit. After that he embarked on other speculations for some time. For instance, he would buy some rolls and cakes in the market and sit down in class near the more well-to-do boys and as soon as he noticed that one of them showed signs of queasiness, a true indication of approaching hunger, he let him see a bit of honey cake or a roll from under the desk, as if by accident, and having thus tempted him, he would make him pay a sum proportionate to his appetite. For two months he kept training a mouse at home, keeping it in a little wooden cage, and succeeded at last in making it stand on its hind legs, lie down, and get up at a word of command, and then sold it, also very profitably. When he had saved up five roubles, he sewed them up in a bag, and then started saving up in another little bag. He was even more astute in his behaviour towards his teachers. No one in class could sit so quietly on a bench. His master, incidentally, was a great stickler for silence and good behaviour and he could not stand clever and quick-witted boys; he imagined that they were laughing at him. It was enough for a boy, who had been reprimanded for being too clever, merely to stir in his seat or inadvertently twitch an eyebrow to become all of a sudden the object of his anger. He persecuted and punished him unmercifully. 'I'll knock the conceit and insubordination out of you, sir!' he used to say. 'I know you through and through. Better than you know yourself. I'll make you kneel for hours! I'll teach you what hunger is like!' And the poor boy wore out his knees and went hungry for days without knowing what it was all about. 'Gifts and abilities?' he used to say. 'It's all a lot of poppycock.

237

All I'm concerned about is conduct. I shall give full marks in all sub-jects to the boy of exemplary behaviour even if he does not know his ABC. And if I see anyone showing a bad spirit or any inclination to scoff, I'll give him a nought, even if he were a hundred times wiser than Solon!' So said the teacher who hated Krylov because he said: 'If you ask me, I'd rather have a drunkard who knows his job than a sober man who doesn't', and who always described with a look of keen gratification on his face and in his eyes how the silence in the school where he used to teach was so great that you could hear a pin drop, and that throughout the year not a single one of his pupils had coughed or blown his nose in class, and that until the bell rang it was impossible to tell whether there was anyone in the room or not. Chichikov at once grasped what his teacher was after and what his idea of good conduct was. He never blinked an eye or twitched an eyebrow in class, however much some of the boys pinched him from behind; as soon as the bell rang he dashed forward so as to be the first to hand the master his warm cap with three flaps, two over the ears and one over the back of the neck (the teacher always wore such a cap); having handed him his cap, he was the first to get out of the classroom and tried to run across the teacher at least three times on the way, taking his cap off every time. This policy was completely suc-cessful. All the time he was at school he was well thought of and on leaving he was given full marks in all the subjects, a certificate, and a book inscribed in gold letters, 'For exemplary diligence and excellent conduct'. On leaving school he turned out to be a young man of rather attractive appearance with a chin that was already in need of a razor. Just then his father died. All he inherited was four irretrievably worn-out woollen sweaters, two old coats lined with lambswool, and an insignificant sum of money. His father apparently was only good at giving advice on how to save money, for he had saved very little himself. Chichikov immediately sold the tumbledown homestead with its wretched piece of land for a thousand roubles, and brought his family of house-serfs to town, intending to settle there and join the Civil Service. About the same time the poor teacher who loved quiet and praiseworthy conduct was dismissed for stupidity or some other fault. The teacher took to drink to drown his sorrows, but at last he had nothing left with which to buy drink; ill, hungry, and without anyone to help him, he spent his time in some unheated, abandoned hovel. His former pupils, the clever and quick-witted ones whom he had always suspected of disobedience and cheeky behaviour, learning of his wretched plight, got up a collection for him and even sold many things they needed to do so; Pavlusha Chichikov alone excused himself on the ground of lack of funds, offering a mere five copecks in silver which his former classmates flung back at him saying: 'Oh, you skinflint!' The poor teacher buried his face in his hands when he heard what his old pupils had done; tears gushed from his dimming eyes, as if he were a helpless child: 'The Lord has made me weep on the brink of the grave,' he said in a weak voice and he sighed bitterly when he heard about Chichikov, adding at once: 'Oh, Pavlusha, how a man can change! He used to be such a well-behaved boy, never wild, soft as silk! He took me in! He took me in all right!'

It cannot be said, however, that our hero was so harsh and callous by nature or that his feelings were so blunted that he knew neither pity nor compassion; he was capable of feeling both, he was even eager to help provided the sum in question was not too big and provided he did not have to touch the money which he had decided not to touch; in short, he kept and profited by his father's precept: 'Take care and save every penny.' But he had no love of money for its own sake. Meanness and miserliness had no hold on him. No, those were not his ruling passions: he was dreaming of a life full of comfort and all sorts of luxuries: carriages, a well-appointed house, good dinners – these were the things that occupied his mind constantly. It was to enjoy all this some time in the future that he saved up every penny which for the time being he stingily denied to himself and others. Every time a rich man drove past him at a spanking pace in an elegant light four-wheeler drawn by a pair of trotters in costly harness, he stopped dead as if rooted to the spot, and then as though waking from a long sleep, he would say: 'Why, he was just a clerk once and wore his hair in a basin-cut like any peasant'. And everything that was suggestive of wealth and prosperity made an impression on him that he could not himself understand. On leaving school, he did not even want to take a holiday; so strong was his desire to start work as soon as possible and join the Civil Service. However, in spite of his excellent testimonials, it was with great difficulty that he was able to get a job in the Courts of Justice. Even in the most out-of-the-way provincial towns, patronage is necessary. The job he obtained was an insignificant one and his salary was only thirty or forty roubles a year. But he made up his mind to work zealously at his job and to overcome and get the better of all the difficulties. And, indeed, he displayed quite incredible selflessness, patience, and self-denial. From early morning till late at night, without allowing himself to get tired either in body or in spirit, he kept writing, immersed entirely in official papers, hardly ever going home, sleeping on a table in the office, dining sometimes with the night-watchmen, and yet succeeded in preserving a tidy appearance, in dressing respectably, in keeping an agreeable expression on his face and even a certain dignity in his movements. It must be said that the clerks at the law courts were particularly noted for their nondescript appearance and forbidding looks. Some had faces like badly baked loaves of bread: a cheek swollen on one side, a chin askew on the other, a boil on the upper lip, which had burst into the bargain; in short, far from beautiful. They all spoke somehow gruffly in a voice that sounded as if they were just going to give someone a beating. They made frequent sacrifices to Bacchus, so proving that there are still many traces of paganism in the Slav nature: quite often they came 'sozzled', as they say, to the office, which made things in the office rather unpleasant and the air far from fragrant. Among such officials Chichikov could not fail to be noticed and singled out, for he offered a complete contrast to them in everything: in his looks, in the amiability of his voice, and in his complete abstinence from strong drink. But in spite of all this, he did not find things easy. He was under the authority of a very old head clerk who seemed to be a model of stony callousness and insensibility: always the same, unassailable, he had never in his life been seen with a smile on his face, and he had never greeted anyone with an inquiry after his health. No one, either in the street or at home, had ever seen him looking different from what he always was. If only he had shown an interest in something, if only he had got drunk and laughed while in his cups, or if only he had given himself up to wild merriment such as a brigand may give himself up to when drunk, but there was not even a shadow of anything of the kind about him. There was absolutely nothing in him: neither wickedness nor goodness, and there was something terrifying in this absence of anything. His hard, marble-like face, without a trace of any irregularities, did not suggest any resemblance to anything; there was a stern, inflexible harmony in his features. Only the many pockmarks and holes which pitted his face placed it in the category of those faces on which, according to the popular saying, the devil came to thresh peas at night. It seemed as though it were beyond human power to gain the confidence of a man like that and win his favour, but Chichikov made the attempt. At first he began by trying to please him in all sorts of small, insignificant things: he examined carefully how the quills with which he wrote were sharpened and, having prepared several like them, always put them down within easy reach of his hand; he blew or brushed away the sand and snuff from his table, he got a new rag for his ink-stand; he unearthed his cap from somewhere, as horrible a cap as ever existed, and always laid it down beside him a minute or so before it was time to go home; he brushed his back when he happened to brush it against a whitewashed wall, but all this brought not the slightest sign of acknowledgement, just as though nothing of the sort had been done. At last he nosed out something about the old man's private life. He discovered that he had a grown-up daughter with a face that also looked as if the devil had been threshing peas on it at night. He decided to launch an attack from that side. He found out what church she went to on Sundays and made a point of standing just opposite her, neatly dressed, with his shirt-front stiffly starched, and his tactics were successful: the stern head clerk wavered and invited him to tea. And before anyone in his office had time to realize what was happening, things were so arranged that Chichikov had moved into the old man's house, had become a useful and indispensable person, going out to buy the flour and sugar, treating the old man's daughter as though they were engaged, addressing the head clerk as 'Papa', and kissing his hand. It was generally assumed at the law courts that at the end of February, before Lent, there would be a wedding. The stern head clerk even put in a word for him with a higher authority and in a short time Chichikov was himself appointed head clerk when a vacancy occurred. This apparently was the chief object of his relations with the old head clerk, for the next day he secretly removed his trunk and on the following day was already installed in a new flat. He stopped calling the old head clerk 'Papa' and never kissed his hand again, while the question of marriage never cropped up again, just as if nothing had happened. However, whenever he happened to meet the old man, he pressed his hand warmly and invited him to tea, so that in spite of the old man's everlasting immobility and harsh indifference, he used to shake his head each time and mutter under his breath: 'He took me in! He took me in, damn him!'

This was the most difficult obstacle for Chichikov to surmount. After that everything went more easily and more successfully. He became a man to watch. He seemed to have everything that was necessary in that world: agreeable manners and turn of speech and a brisk way of dealing with business matters. By these means he obtained in a short time what is known as a lucrative job and made the best possible use of it. It ought to be pointed out that at that very time the strictest measures were taken against bribery and corruption. He was not afraid of these measures and immediately turned them to his own advantage, displaying the truly Russian resourcefulness which manifests itself only in times of stress. The way things were done was this: as soon as an applicant arrived and put his hand in his pocket in order to pull out from it the well-known letters of introduction signed, as the saying goes among us in Russia, by Prince Khovansky, the treasurer of the State Bank: 'No, no,' he would say with a smile, restraining his hand, 'you don't think that I ... No, no, it's our duty, our obligation! We have to do it all without any recompense. So far as that is concerned you needn't worry at all: everything will be done by tomorrow. Do you mind giving me your address? You won't have to trouble at all, for everything will be brought to your house.' The delighted applicant would return home almost in a state of ecstasy, thinking to himself, 'Here at last is an honest man! We should have more like him. He's a precious jewel!' But he waited one day, then another, the papers were not brought to the house, nor were they there on the third day. He went off to the office only to find that the business had not even been started. He applied to the precious jewel. 'Oh, I'm so sorry,' said Chichikov very courteously, seizing both his hands, 'we've had such a lot of work, but tomorrow everything will be done. Tomorrow for certain. I really am quite ashamed!' And all this was accompanied by the most charming gestures. If, while talking to the applicant, a skirt of Chichikov's coat flew open, his hand would try to set things to rights and hold the skirt. But neither tomorrow nor the day after tomorrow nor the day after that were the papers brought to the house. The applicant twigged at last: surely, there must be something wrong there? He started making inquiries and was told that the copying clerks must be given something. 'Why not? I'm ready to give them a quarter of a rouble or so.' 'No, sir, not a quarter, but a white twenty-five-rouble note.' 'A twenty-five-rouble note for the copying clerks?' the applicant exclaimed. 'But why are you so astonished?' they replied. 'It will work out in the same way. The copying clerks will get twenty-five copecks each and the rest will be divided among the higher authorities.' The slow-witted applicant slaps himself on the forehead and curses for all it's worth the new order of things, the measures against bribery, and the courteous, refined manners of the civil servants. Before, at least, you knew what you had to do: you gave the head of a department a red ten-rouble note and the thing was in the bag; but now you have to give a white twenty-five-rouble note and you waste a whole week before you realize what you have to do. 'Damn the disinterestedness and the noble-minded-ness of civil servants!' The applicant, of course, is right. But, on the other hand, there are no bribe-takers now; all the heads of departments are the most honourable and noble of men, only the secretaries and copying clerks are scoundrels. Soon a much wider sphere of activity presented itself to Chichikov: a commission was set up to supervise the construction of a very important government building. He, too, managed to get on to the commission and became one of its most active members. The commission set to work at once. For the next six years they were hard at work on the building; but whether it was the climate that hindered its progress or whether the building materials were at fault, the government building never rose higher than its foundations. Meanwhile every member of the commission built himself a handsome private residence of an excellent architectural design in other parts of the town: it seemed the soil was much more favourable there. The members of the commission began to grow prosperous and to rear families. It was only at this point that Chichikov began slowly to disentangle himself from the stern rules of self-restraint and his own inexorable regime of self-denial. It was only then that his long drawn-out fast was at last broken, and it appeared that he had not always been averse to all sorts of enjoyments which he had known how to deny himself of in those years of ardent youth, when no man is absolute master of himself. Some signs of over-indulgence made their appearance: he engaged a fairly good chef and began to wear fine linen shirts. Already he had bought himself cloth such as no one else in the province wore and from that time began to favour clothes of gleaming brown and reddish colours; already he had acquired an excellent pair of horses and held one rein himself, making the side-horse turn its head to one side; already he had got into the habit of rubbing himself down with a sponge dipped in water mixed with eau-de-Cologne; already he had bought some special and very expensive soap to preserve the smoothness of the skin; already –

But suddenly a new chief was appointed to replace the weak-willed old dodderer, a military man, a stern disciplinarian, an enemy of bribe-takers and of everything smacking of injustice. On the very next day he put the fear of God in every one of them. He demanded to see the accounts, discovered defaults and sums of money missing at every step, and immediately noticed the houses of handsome architectural design. A full inquiry was at once set on foot. The officials were dismissed from their posts; the private houses of handsome architectural design were taken over by the government and turned into all sorts of charitable institutions and schools for the sons of soldiers. Everything was swept away, and Chichikov had a worse time of it than anyone else. The chief, goodness only knows why, sometimes indeed it happens for no reason at all, suddenly took a dislike to Chichikov's face in spite of its amiable appearance, and he conceived a deadly hatred for him. But as he was, after all, a military man and therefore unacquainted with all the subtleties of civilian stratagems, other officials wormed themselves into his favour in a short time thanks largely to their honest appearance and their ability to adapt themselves to all circumstances, and the general soon found himself in the hands of even greater scoundrels whom he completely failed to recognize as such. Indeed, he was quite satisfied that he had at last picked the right men and he quite seriously boasted of his flair for discerning men's true qualities. The officials suddenly grasped his temper and character. Everyone serving under him became a terrible persecutor of injustice. They persecuted it everywhere, in every case, as a fisherman hunts down some large fat sturgeon with a harpoon, and they persecuted it with such success that in a short time every one of them had found himself in possession of several thousand roubles. It was then that many of the former officials returned to the paths of righteousness and were again received into the service. But try as he might, Chichikov could not worm his way in again, and however much the general's secretary, spurred on by Prince Khovansky's letters of introduction, tried to help him and stood up for him, he could do nothing whatever for him, although he had completely mastered the art of leading the general by the nose. The general was the kind of man who, though he could be led by the nose (without his knowledge, of course), if he got an idea into his head, it stuck there like an iron nail: there was no pulling it out again. All the clever secretary could do was to contrive the destruction of Chichikov's ignominious service record, and this too he achieved only by arousing the general's compassion, painting in vivid colours the piteous fate of Chichikov's unhappy family, which fortunately did not exist.

'Oh, well,' said Chichikov, 'if you had a bite, played your fish, and the line broke, don't waste your time asking questions. It's no use crying over spilt milk. I must do something.' And so he decided to begin his career all over again, to arm himself with patience once more, to deny himself everything once more, however much he had enjoyed his freedom from worry and however pleasant it was to give free play to his talents. He had to move to another town and to get himself a good position there. But somehow things did not go well with him. He had to change two or three jobs in a very short time. The jobs turned out to be of a low and degrading character. Chichikov, it must be understood, was one of the most refined men that ever lived. Though at first he had to mix with coarse society, he was always at heart a stickler for cleanliness and he liked the tables at the office to be of polished wood and everything to be nice and decent. He never permitted himself to use any indecent words in his speech and he was always offended if he discovered an absence of proper respect for rank or calling in the words of others. I think the reader will be pleased to learn that he changed his linen every second day and during the hot weather in summer every day; the slightest offensive smell annoyed him. That was why every time Petrushka came to undress him and pull off his boots he put cloves into his nose, and in many cases his nerves were as delicate as a young girl's; and that was why it was hard for him to find himself again among those classes of people where everything smelt of strong vodka and everyone's manners left much to be desired. However much he tried to take heart, he grew thinner and even greenish in the face during this time of hardship. He was already beginning to put on weight and to assume those rotund and decorous forms in which the reader found him when he first met him, and many a time when he looked into the looking-glass he would think of all sorts of pleasant things: a young, pretty wife, a nursery, and a smile accompanied such thoughts; but now when he happened to glance at himself in the looking-glass inadvertently he could not help exclaiming: 'Dear Mother of God, how horrible I look!' And for a long while after he was not particularly anxious to look at himself. But our hero put up with it, put up with it like a man, put up with it patiently and – at last got himself a job in the Customs and Excise. It must be said that this department had long been the secret object of his schemes. He saw what stylish foreign articles the customs officers acquired, what fine pieces of porcelain and cambric they used to send to their sweethearts, aunts, and sisters. More than once he said to himself with a sigh: 'If only I could get a job there: the frontier is near, all sorts of cultured people, and think what fine linen shirts one could get hold of!' I must add that every time he thought of it he also dreamt of a special sort of French soap which imparted an extraordinary whiteness to the skin and freshness to the cheeks; what it was called, goodness only knows, but he had good reason to hope that he would most certainly find it at the frontier. And so he had for years been anxious to get into the Customs and Excise, but he had not done so because of the various advantages connected with the building commission, for he quite rightly argued that, say what you like, the Customs and Excise was still a dream, while, so far as the building commission was concerned, a bird in hand was worth two in the bush. Now, however, he made up his mind to get a job in the Customs and Excise at all costs and he got it. He applied himself to his new job with extraordinary zeal. It seemed as though fate itself had destined him to be a customs officer. Such resourcefulness, perspicacity, and shrewdness had never been seen or heard of before. In three or four weeks he had become so perfectly versed in the affairs of the customs that he knew absolutely everything about them: he did not even weigh or measure, but found out from the invoice how many yards of cloth or other material there was in each piece, and picking up a parcel in his hands he could tell at once what its weight was. As for searching travellers, in that, as even his own colleagues expressed it, he simply had the scent of a hound: one could not help being amazed at the patience with which he felt every button, and all this was done with an air of deadly calm and a quite incredible courtesy. And while those who were being searched were furious and beside themselves with rage, and felt a malicious impulse to slap his seraphic face, he would say, without the slightest change of expression or of his courteous manners, 'I'm awfully sorry to trouble you, sir, but would you mind getting up?', or 'Would you mind going into the other room, madam? There the wife of one of our officials will interview you', or 'If you don't mind, sir, I'll just slit the lining of your overcoat with my penknife', and, as he said it, he would pull out from inside the lining shawls and kerchiefs, as coolly as though he were taking them out from his own trunk. Even his superiors declared that he was not a man, but a devil incarnate: he would find contraband goods in wheels, shafts of carriages, horses' ears, and goodness only knows where else – in places in which it would never occur to any author to look for them and where only customs officials are allowed to penetrate. So that the poor traveller, having crossed the frontier, could not recover his senses for several minutes and, as he mopped the perspiration which by that time covered the whole of his body, kept crossing himself, muttering, 'Well, well!' His position was very much like that of a schoolboy who has run out of the headmaster's study after being quite unexpectedly birched instead of reprimanded. Within a very short period he made the life of the smugglers quite impossible. He became the menace and despair of all the Polish Jews. His honesty and incorruptibility were unassailable, almost unnatural. He did not even make a small fortune out of the confiscated goods and the various small articles which were not passed on to the Treasury but retained in order to avoid unnecessary correspondence. Such zealous and dis-interested service could not but become the object of universal as-tonishment and, finally, came to the notice of the higher authorities. He was promoted to a higher rank and given a rise and soon after-wards presented a project for catching all the smugglers, only asking for the means of carrying it out himself. He was immediately put in charge of the project and given full authority to carry out all sorts of searches. This was just what he wanted. Just at that time a power-ful society of smugglers had been formed in accordance with carefully laid plans; the bold enterprise stood to make a profit of millions. Chichikov had long known about it and had even refused the bribe he was offered by its emissaries, saying dryly, 'It isn't time for that yet.' But when he had been put in charge of everything, he at once sent word to the society, saying, 'Now's the time!' His calculation was only too correct. Now he could make in one year what he could not have made in twenty years of the most loyal service. He had not been willing to enter into any relations with them before because he would have been nothing but a pawn in the game and would there-fore have received very little; but now – now it was quite a different matter: he could propose any terms he liked. To make sure the busi-ness could be carried on without let or hindrance, he won another official over to his side, another official, a colleague of his, who could not resist the temptation although his hair was grey. The terms were agreed on and the society began operations. The operations started brilliantly. The reader must have heard the oft repeated story of the ingenious journey of merino sheep crossing the frontier in two sheep-skins and carrying Flemish lace to the value of millions under their fleeces. This happened just at the time when Chichikov served in the Customs. Had he not had a hand in this enterprise, no Jews in the world would have succeeded in carrying out such an undertaking. After three or four flocks of sheep had crossed the frontier, the two officials found themselves in possession of four hundred thousand roubles each. Chichikov is said to have made over five hundred thousand because he was a little smarter. Goodness knows to what an enormous figure these beneficial sums might have grown, had not some evil power brought the whole enterprise crashing to the ground. The devil deprived the two officials of their senses; or, putting it more plainly, they lost their temper and quarrelled over nothing. In some heated argument, a little the worse for drink, perhaps, Chichikov called the other official 'the son of a priest', and though he really was a priest's son, he was for some unknown reason terribly offended and answered him back forcefully and with quite extraordinary sharpness in these very words: 'No, sir, you're lying! I'm a State Councillor, it's you who are the son of a priest!' And to add insult to injury, he added: 'Yes, sir, that's what you are!' And although he had told him off pur-posely in this way, throwing the words Chichikov had called him back in his teeth and although the expression, 'Yes, sir, that's what you are!' may have been quite a forceful one, he was not satisfied with that and he sent in a secret report about Chichikov's activities. It is said, though, that they had quarrelled violently over some young woman, as fresh and firm as a juicy turnip, to use the expression of customs officers; that men had even been bribed to beat up our hero in some dark alley in the evening, but that she had made fools of both customs officials and some Major Shamsharyov had got the pretty creature in the end. What really happened, God only knows; the reader who likes this sort of story can make up his own ending. The important thing is that their secret relations with the smugglers now came to light. Though the State Councillor was himself ruined, he put his colleague into the dock too. The two officials were put on trial, all their possessions were impounded and confiscated, and all this burst like a thunderclap over their heads. They came to themselves like men recovering from coal-gas poisoning, and realized with horror what they had done. The State Councillor, as usually happens in Russia, drowned his grief in drink, but the Collegiate Councillor held his ground. He managed to conceal some of the money, however keen the scent of the officials who carried out the investigation. He made use of all the subtle resourcefulness of his mind, already thoroughly experienced and possessing a little too thorough a knowledge of people: with some he prevailed by his agreeable turns of phrase, with others by pathetic speeches, in one place he used flattery, which never quite misfires, in another he slipped in a few banknotes, in short, he managed things with quite considerable success, so that he was not left with as great a disgrace as his colleague and escaped criminal proceedings. But nothing was left of his money or of the valuable articles he had appropriated; others found excellent use for it all. All he had left was a paltry ten thousand roubles he had put away for a rainy day, two dozen linen shirts, a small four-wheeled carriage, such as bachelors prefer to drive about in, and two serfs, the driver Selifan and the valet Petrushka; and out of the goodness of their hearts the customs officers left him five or six pieces of soap for preserving the freshness of his complexion. And that was all. So that was the position in which our hero once more found himself. Such was the immensity of the calamities that had crashed down upon his head. This is what he called 'suffering in the cause of justice'. It might now have been expected that after such storms, trials and tribulations, vicissitudes and disappointments, he would retire with his hard-earned ten thousand roubles to some peaceful backwater of a provincial town and there fritter his life away in a printed cotton dressing-gown, at the window of a small, one-storied house, trying to stop the fighting that broke out between the peasants under his windows on Sundays, or, taking a stroll in the poultry yard for a breath of fresh air, feel with his own hands the hen destined for soup, and so lead not a noisy but far from useless life. But it did not turn out like that. One must do justice to the invincible strength of his character. After all this, which would have been sufficient if not to kill, at least to damp and subdue a man for ever, his indomitable passion was not quenched. He was grieved and vexed, he murmured against the entire world, he was angry at the unfairness of fate, he was indignant at the unfairness of men, and yet he could not give up making a new attempt. In short, he displayed a patience compared with which the wooden patience of a German, caused by the slow and sluggish circulation of his blood, is nothing. Chichikov's blood, on the contrary, coursed strongly through his veins, and he needed a great deal of disciplined willpower to keep in check everything that was eager to leap out and roam at large. He argued, and there was some justice in the argument: 'Why me? Why should disaster have overtaken me? Who lets his chance slip by in the Civil Service nowadays? They are all lining their pockets. I have made no one unhappy. I have not robbed the widow. I have not ruined anyone. I've merely profited from what was left over. I took where anyone else would have taken. If I had not taken advantage of it, others would have. Why, then, do others prosper, and why should I be crushed like a worm? And what am I now? What am I good for? How can I look any respectable head of a family in the face? How am I not to feel pricks of conscience when I know that I am burdening the earth to no purpose? And what will my children say afterwards? "Look," they will say, "what a dirty rotter our father was – he has left us no fortune!"'

Chichikov, as we know already, was very much concerned about his progeny. Such a touching subject! Many a man would not, perhaps, have thrust his hand so deeply into other men's pockets, if it had not been for the question, which for some unknown reason leaps to his mind by itself: 'And what will my children say?' And so the future progenitor, like a cautious tomcat, glancing out of the corner of one eye to see whether his master is watching him, grabs quickly everything within his reach: soap, candles, lard, or a canary if he can get his claws into it; in short, he misses nothing. So our hero wept and lamented, and yet his brain never for a moment stopped working: something seemed about to take shape there and was only waiting for a plan. Once more he economized, once more he began to lead a hard life, once more he denied himself everything, once more he sank from a clean and decent social position into filth and low life. And in expectation of better things, he was even forced to take up the calling of a solicitor, a calling that has not yet received general recognition among us. He was pushed about on all sides, treated with scant respect by the small fry of lawyer's clerks and even by those who employed him, condemned to grovel in outer offices, to put up with rudeness and so on, but want forced him to put up with everything. One of his jobs was to arrange for the mortgaging of several hundred peasants to the Trustee Council. The estate was completely ruined. It had been ruined by foot-and-mouth disease, dishonest rogues of agents, bad harvests, epidemics which killed off the best workers and, finally, by the stupidity of the landowner himself, who had furnished a house in Moscow in the latest fashion and had squandered on it the whole of his fortune to the last copeck, so that he had not enough left for food. It was for that reason that he had been forced to mortgage his last remaining estate. Mortgaging to the Treasury was still quite a new thing in those days and it was not without a certain apprehension that people resorted to it. Chichikov, acting as solicitor, first of all got everyone in the right frame of mind (without a preliminary action of this kind, as we know only too well, it is impossible to obtain any official information or verification, at least one bottle of Madeira has to be poured down every throat), and so after getting everyone concerned in the right frame of mind, he explained the position, namely, that half of the peasants had died, in the hope that there might be no complications afterwards.

'But,' said the secretary, 'they are still on the register, aren't they?'

'They are,' replied Chichikov.

'So what are you worrying about?' said the secretary. 'One dies, another's born, they're all as good as corn.'

The secretary evidently could talk in rhyme. Meanwhile the most brilliant idea that ever came into a man's head suddenly dawned on our hero. 'Oh, what a Simple Simon I am,' he said to himself. 'Looking for my mittens, and they're stuck in my belt all the time! Why, were I to buy up all the peasants who died before a new census is taken, were I to acquire them for, say, a thousand roubles, and the Trustee Council gave me two hundred a soul: why, there's already a fortune of two hundred thousand roubles! And now is just the right time! There's been an epidemic a short while ago and, thank God, thousands of peasants must have died. The landowners have been losing heavily at cards, they've been carousing and squandering their money right and left in the usual way, everyone is rushing off to Petersburg in search of government jobs, their estates are abandoned and managed anyhow, and they find it more and more difficult every year to pay their taxes – so that they will be only too glad to sell me their dead serfs, if only because they won't have to pay the tax on them; some of them, indeed, may even pay me something to get them off their hands. No doubt, it's a rather tricky business, a bit troublesome. And there's always the risk that I might get into trouble, get myself involved in some unpleasantness. But then man has been given a brain for something, hasn't he? And what is so good about it is that the whole thing will strike everyone as so incredible that no one will believe it. It is true, it is impossible to buy or mortgage serfs without land, but then I shall be buying them for resettlement. Land in the Taurida and Kherson provinces is distributed today free, provided you settle peasants on it. That's where I shall settle them! To the Kherson Province with them! Let them live there! And the resettlement can be carried out legally, with the approval of the courts. If they should want to get an official confirmation of the existence of the peasants, I should not mind it, either – why not? I'll present such an official confirmation with the signature of the local rural police inspector. I might call the village Chichikov Village, or after my Christian name, Pavlovsky Hamlet.' It was in this way that this strange idea took shape in our hero's head, and I don't know if my readers will be grateful to him for that, but no words can express the author's gratitude for, say what you like, if this idea had not occurred to Chichikov, this epic poem would never have seen the light of day.

Crossing himself after the Russian fashion, he set about carrying it out. Under the pretext of looking for a place to settle and under all sorts of other pretexts, he undertook to look into various corners of our empire, particularly those which had suffered more than others from all sorts of natural calamities, such as bad harvests, high rates of mortality, and so on and so forth – in short, where he could buy most conveniently and cheaply the sort of peasants he wanted. He did not approach any landowner indiscriminately, but selected those who were more to his taste or those with whom he could negotiate such deals with least difficulty, trying first to make their acquaintance and gain their confidence, so as to obtain the peasants through friendship rather than by purchase. The reader must therefore not be indignant with the author if the characters who have so far appeared are not to his taste; it is Chichikov's fault, he is complete master here, and we have to follow him wherever he thinks fit to go. So far as we are concerned, if we are to be criticized for the colourlessness and unattractiveness of the persons in our story and their characters, we can only say that at the beginning one can never see the whole broad current and the full scope of everything. The entry into any town, even into the capital, is always somehow disappointing; at first everything looks drab and monotonous: you drive past endless workshops and factories, all begrimed with smoke, and it is only afterwards that you catch sight of six-storied buildings, large shops, signboards, vast vistas of streets, full of belfries, columns, statues, towers, with the magnificence, noise, and uproar of the town, and everything that is so marvellously fashioned by the hand and brain of man. How the first purchases were made, the reader has already seen; how things will go afterwards, what successes and failures are in store for our hero, how he will manage to solve more difficult problems and overcome more difficult obstacles, how colossal characters will appear, how the hidden springs of our great novel will come into play as its horizon expands wider and wider and the whole of it assumes a majestic lyrical course – all this the reader will see afterwards. There is still a long journey ahead of our travelling party, consisting of a middle-aged gentleman, the carriage in which bachelors like to travel, the valet Petrushka, the driver Selifan, and the team of three horses, already known by name to the reader, from the Assessor to the rascally dappled-grey. So here you have our hero – just as he is! But perhaps you want a final definition of one trait of his character, namely what exactly is he so far as his moral qualities are concerned? That he is not a hero filled with all sorts of perfections and virtues is self-evident. What is he then? A villain? Why a villain? Why be so severe on people? We no longer have villains nowadays. We have right-thinking and agreeable people, but you might find only two or three men who would run the risk of disgracing themselves by thrusting out their faces to be slapped in public, and even they now talk of virtue. It would be fairer to call him a business man, a money-maker. Making money is at the root of all evil: things have been done for its sake which the world has described as *not very clean*: it is true that there is something repellent in such a character, and the very same reader who would make friends with such a man in the course of his life, would entertain him in his house and be entertained by him and spend a pleasant time with him, will be sure to look askance at him if he is made the hero of a drama or an epic poem. Wise is he who disdains no character, but, fixing a searching eye on him, explores him down to the first causes. Everything in man is rapidly transformed. Before you have time to look round, a terrible worm has grown up within and is feeding voraciously upon his vital sap. Not once only has some great passion – and not only a great passion, but some worthless passion for something petty and trivial – assumed ever larger proportions in a man born for better things and has made him forget great and sacred duties and see something great and sacred in worthless gewgaws. Countless as the sands of the sea are human passions, and not all of them are alike, and all of them, base and noble alike, are at first obedient to man and only later on become his terrible masters. Blessed is the man who has chosen the most noble passion from among them all, his immeasurable bliss grows and increases tenfold every hour and minute, and he enters deeper and deeper into the infinite paradise of his soul. But there are passions which are not of man's choosing. They are born with him at the moment of his birth and he has not been granted the powers to reject them. They are directed by a higher will and there is in them something that is for ever calling and is never silent all through one's life. They are destined to play a great part on earth, and it makes no difference whether they appear in a dark and gloomy image or flash past like a bright apparition that gladdens the world – they are equally called forth for some good unknown to man. And, perhaps, in Chichikov himself, the passion that leads him on is not part of him, and in his cold existence there lies hidden that which will one day make man fall on his knees in the dust before the wisdom of the heavens. And the reason why this particular hero has appeared in the epic poem, which is about to be published, is yet another mystery.

But what is so hard to bear is not that my readers will be dissatisfied with my hero, but that they would have been highly satisfied with the very same hero, the very same Chichikov, if the author had shown him as he appeared to the whole town and had not looked more deeply into his soul and had not stirred up in its depths the things that steal away and hide from the light, had he not exposed the most secret thoughts which no man confides to another. If he had shown him as he appeared to Manilov and the others, everyone would have been simply delighted, and would have accepted him as an interesting man. It would not have mattered that either his face or his whole personality would have passed and repassed as though alive before their eyes; for when they had finished reading, their peace of mind would not have been disturbed and they could have gone back to the card table – the solace of the whole of Russia. Yes, my gentle readers, you would rather not see the poverty of human nature exposed. Why do it? you say. Whatever for? Don't we know ourselves that there is a great deal that is stupid and despicable in life? As it is, we often have to see things which are far from comforting. You'd better show us what is beautiful and attractive. Better let us indulge in daydreams! 'Why do you tell me, my dear fellow, that my estate is in a bad way?' says the landowner to his agent. 'I know that, my dear fellow, without your telling me. Haven't you got anything else to say to me? Just give me a chance to forget it. Let me not know it, then I shall be happy.' And so the money which might to some extent have saved the situation is spent on various means for bringing about self-oblivion. The mind which might have discovered an unexpected source of great affluence is asleep; and in the meantime bang goes the estate sold at a public auction and, trying to find oblivion, the landowner goes wandering all over the world with a soul which, driven to the last extremity, is ready to commit acts of baseness from which he himself would have recoiled in horror before.

The author will also be censured by the so-called patriots who sit quietly in their homes and busy themselves with quite different matters, amassing private fortunes and making sure of their own future at the expense of others; but as soon as anything happens which in their opinion is insulting to their country, if a book appears in which sometimes some bitter truth is told, they run out of every corner like spiders at the sight of a fly that has got itself caught in their web and at once raise an awful clamour. 'Is it right to bring such a thing to light, to shout about it from the housetops? Why, everything described here is ours – is it right? And what will the foreigners say? Is it nice to hear a bad opinion of oneself? Do they think it isn't painful? Do they imagine that we are not patriots?' I must confess that I cannot find a proper answer to these sagacious remarks about the opinion of foreigners, unless perhaps it is this. In a remote corner of Russia there lived two Philistines. One of them was the head of a family called Kifa Mokiyevich, a man of a gentle disposition who lived a happy-go-lucky sort of life. He did not worry about his family; his whole existence was taken up more with abstruse matters and was devoted chiefly to the following philosophical, as he called them, questions: 'Now take for example a wild animal,' he used to say, pacing up and down his room. 'A wild animal is born naked. Why naked? Why isn't he born like a bird? Why isn't he hatched out of an egg? Dear me, it is really – er – you can't understand nature. The more you delve into it, the less you understand it!' So thought the Philistine, Kifa Mokiyevich. But that is not the point. The other Philistine was

Moky Kifovich, his son. He was what is called in Russia a legendary hero, and while his father was preoccupied with the birth of the wild animal, his own twenty-year-old, broad-shouldered nature was bursting with a desire to show what it could do. But he could not do anything by halves: somebody's arm would always crack or a lump would spring up on someone else's nose. Everyone in the house and in the neighbourhood, from the household serf-girl to the household dog, fled at the sight of him; he even knocked his own bedstead in his bedroom into smithereens. Such was Moky Kifovich, though, mind you, he was a good-natured fellow for all that. But that is not the point, either. The point is this: 'For goodness sake, Kifa Mokiyevich, sir,' the servants of his own and the neighbouring households said to the father, 'what sort of man is your Moky Kifovich? He leaves nobody alone, he's such an awful bully!' 'Yes,' his father usually replied, 'he is a little playful, isn't he? A playful little fellow. But what's to be done? I'm afraid it's too late to chastise him and, besides, if I did beat him, people would accuse me of cruelty. Moreover, he's a very vain fellow, and if I were to reproach him in front of two or three people, he'd quieten down, but then think of the publicity! That's the trouble. When the town learns about it, everyone will be calling him a cur. Do they really think I don't feel it? Am I not his father? Because I'm engrossed in philosophy and have no time to look after my family, do you think I'm not a father? No, indeed, I am a father! I am a father, damn it. Moky Kifovich is right here in my heart!' At this point Kifa Mokiyevich beat his breast violently with his fist and became terribly excited. 'If he is to remain a cur, don't let them find it out from me. Don't let me betray him.' And having displayed his parental feelings in so affectionate a manner, he left Moky Kifovich to carry on with his heroic exploits and turned his attention to his favourite subject, asking himself some such question as: 'Well, if an elephant were hatched out of an egg, the shell would, I suppose, have to be so thick that you couldn't pierce it with a cannon-ball. One would have to invent some new kind of gun.' And they went on living, these two Philistines of that peaceful corner of our country, who so unexpectedly peeped out, as out of a window, at the end of our epic poem, in order to give a modest answer to the accusation of certain ardent patriots who have till now been quietly engaged in philosophic pursuits or in increasing their fortunes at the expense of their dearly beloved country, thinking not so much about not doing wrong as about preventing people from accusing them of doing wrong. But, no. It is not patriotism, nor genuine feeling, which lies at the root of these accusations. Another feeling lies concealed under them. Why be afraid to say it? Who if not an author ought to speak the sacred truth? You are afraid of anyone looking too deeply into things. You are scared to look deeply into anything yourselves. You like to glide over everything with unthinking eyes. You will even laugh heartily at Chichikov. Perhaps you will even praise the author, saying: 'He has hit it off very cleverly! He must be a man of infinite jest.' And after saying that, you will turn to yourself with redoubled pride and a self-satisfied smirk will appear on your face and you will add: 'There's no denying that in some provinces you come across the strangest and funniest people, and they're damned rogues into the bargain, too!' But which of you, full of Christian meekness, not in public but in solitude, in moments of silent communion with yourself, will peer into his own soul and ask himself this very painful question: 'Is there not something of Chichikov in me too?' Why, of course there is! And if a friend of his, a man of neither too high nor too low a rank, were to pass by, he would at once nudge his neighbour and say to him, almost with a scornful snort: 'Look, look! There's Chichikov! There goes Chichikov!' And then, like a child, forgetting every consideration due to his age and social position, he will run after him, teasing him from behind and repeating: 'Chichikov! Chichikov! Chichikov!'

But I'm afraid we are talking too loudly, forgetting that our hero, who was asleep while we have been telling the story of his life, has awakened and could easily hear his name so frequently repeated. He is quick to take offence and he will be annoyed if anyone speaks disrespectfully of him. The reader, of course, does not care whether Chichikov is angry with him or not, but the author must not quarrel with his hero under any circumstances: they still have to go a long way hand in hand together; two long parts are still to come – that is no trifle.

'I say,' said Chichikov to Selifan, 'what are you doing? You there!'
'What?' said Selifan slowly.
'What? You damned idiot! How you are driving. Come on, faster, faster!'
And indeed Selifan had for a long time been driving with closed eyes, only from time to time shaking the reins about the sides of the

horses who were also half asleep; Petrushka's cap had fallen off long ago, goodness only knows where, and he had sunk back, his head buried in Chichikov's lap so that his master had to push it roughly away. Selifan sat up and, flicking the dappled-grey on the back with his whip a few times and making him set off at a trot, then flourishing the whip over all the three horses, he cried out in a thin, sing-song voice: 'Gee-up!' The horses roused themselves and pulled the light carriage along as though it were a feather. All Selifan did was to wave his whip and keep shouting: 'Gee-up, gee-up, gee-up!', bouncing smoothly on the box, while the *troika* flew up and down the hillocks scattered all along the highway that sloped imperceptibly downhill. Chichikov only smiled as he bounced lightly on his leather cushion, for he was very fond of fast driving. And what Russian does not love fast driving? How could his soul, which is so eager to whirl round and round, to forget everything in a mad carouse, to exclaim sometimes, 'To hell with it all!' – how could his soul not love it? How not love it when there is something wonderful and magical about it? It is as if some unseen force has caught you up on its wing and you yourself fly and everything with you flies also; milestones fly past, merchants on the coachman's seat of their covered wagons fly to meet you, on each side of you the forest flies past with its dark rows of firs and pines, with the thudding of axes and the cawing of crows; the whole road flies goodness only knows where into the receding distance; and there is something terrible in this rapid flashing by of objects which are lost to sight before you are able to discern them properly, and only the sky over your head and the light clouds and the moon appearing and disappearing through them seem motionless. Oh, you *troika*, you bird of a *troika*, who invented you? You could only have been born among a high-spirited people in a land that does not like doing things by halves, but has spread in a vast smooth plain over half the world, and you may count the milestones till your eyes are dizzy. And there is nothing ingenious, one would think, about this travelling contraption. It is not held together by iron screws, but has been fitted up in haste with only an axe and chisel by some resourceful Yaroslav peasant. The driver wears no German top-boots: he has a beard and mittens, and sits upon goodness only knows what; but he has only to stand up and crack his whip and start up a song, and the horses rush like a whirlwind, the spokes of the wheels become one smooth revolving disc, only the road quivers and the pedestrian cries out as he stops in alarm, and the *troika* dashes on and on! And very soon all that can be seen in the distance is the dust whirling through the air.

Is it not like that that you, too, Russia, are speeding along like a spirited *troika* that nothing can overtake? The road is like a cloud of smoke under you, the bridges thunder, and everything falls back and is left far behind. The spectator stops dead, struck dumb by the divine miracle: is it not a flash of lightning thrown down by heaven? What is the meaning of this terrifying motion? And what mysterious force is hidden in these horses the like of which the world has never seen? Oh horses, horses – what horses! Are whirlwinds hidden in your manes? Is there some sensitive ear, alert to every sound, concealed in your veins? They have caught the sound of the familiar song from above, and at once they strain their chests of brass and barely touching the ground with their hoofs are transformed almost into straight lines, flying through the air, and the *troika* rushes on full of divine inspiration. Russia, where are you flying to? Answer! She gives no answer. The bells fill the air with their wonderful tinkling; the air is torn asunder, it thunders and is transformed into wind; everything on earth is flying past, and, looking askance, other nations and states draw aside and make way for her.

PART TWO

Chapter 1

WHY describe poverty and poverty and the imperfections of our life, digging up people from the wilds and the remote corners of our country? What can be done about it, if that is the characteristic trait of the author and, falling ill with his own imperfections, he cannot describe anything but poverty and poverty and the imperfections of our life, digging up people from the wilds and the remote corners of our country. So here we are once more in the wilds and once more we've come upon an out-of-the-way corner.

But what a wilderness and what an out-of-the-way corner!

Like the gigantic rampart of some immense fortress full of escarpments and embrasures, the mountain peaks ran zig-zagging for over a thousand miles. They towered magnificently over the endless plains with here and there jutting-out cliffs, like sheer walls of clay and lime, scarred with fissures and ravines in some places, stretching in beautifully undulating green hills covered with young shrubs as with lambs-wool and shooting up from the stumps of cut-down trees, and in others covered with thick dark forests miraculously untouched by the axe. The river, true to its banks, twisted and turned with them, sometimes leaving them for the meadows and sometimes, after taking several serpentine turns, flashing like fire in the sun and then disappearing in a copse of birch-trees, aspens, and alders and running out of it in triumph accompanied by bridges, mills, and dams, which seemed to be pursuing it at every turn.

In one place the steep side of the rising hills was covered more densely with the green foliage of the trees. By artificial planting, thanks to the unevenness of the hilly ravine, the north and the south of the vegetable kingdom were here gathered together. The oak and the fir, the wild pear-tree, the maple, the wild cherry, and the black-thorn, Siberian pea-trees, and the mountain-ash overgrown with hops, now helping each other's growth and now stifling each other, were climbing along the side of the hill from top to bottom. At the very top, on the crest of the hill, the red roofs of the manor-house buildings mingled with the green tree-tops, and behind them could be seen the carved horses' heads and the roof-tops of the peasants' cottages as well as the upper part of the landowner's mansion with its fretted balcony and large semi-circular window, and over all this assembly of trees and roofs an ancient wooden church rose with its five gilded, flashing cupolas. Each of them had a pierced gilt cross fastened with pierced gold chains so that from a distance the gold seemed to hang in the air without any visible support, flashing like new gold sovereigns. And all this – the tree-tops, the roofs, the crosses – were reflected prettily upside down in the river where, horribly mis-shapen and full of holes, stood willow-trees on the bank and in the water, dipping their leaves and branches into it and seeming to admire this wonderful reflection where it could not be reached by the slimy fresh-water sponges with the bright-green drifting leaves of the yellow water lilies.

It was a very fine view, but the view from the top, from the upper story of the house, into the far away distance was even finer. No guest or visitor could stand unmoved on the balcony. He would be breath-less with surprise and he could only exclaim: 'Lord, what a magnifi-cent view!' Miles upon miles of open country rose before him: be-yond the water meadows, covered here and there with copses and water-mills, woods formed several green belts; beyond the woods, through the thin haze that was already rising from the ground, yellow sands could be seen, and beyond them more woods looking blue in the distance like the sea or like a mist that has spread far and wide; and beyond them more sands, paler than before but yellow still. Ridges of chalk hills lined the far distant horizon, gleaming with dazzling whiteness even in rainy weather, as though illumined by eternal sunshine. Across their dazzling whiteness, at the foot of the hills, dove-coloured patches could be seen here and there looking like puffs of smoke. Those were distant villages which could not be discerned by the human eye. Only the flashing golden cupola of the church in the sunlight showed that it was a large, populous vil-lage. All this was wrapped in imperturbable silence, unbroken even by the faint calls of the birds lost in the wide spaces of the sky. After gazing at the scene for two hours a visitor, standing on the balcony, could not but exclaim, 'Lord, what a magnificent view you get from here!'

Who was the owner of this village which, like an unassailable fortress, could not be approached from this side, but could only be reached from the other side, where the scattered oak-trees welcomed the visitor with their branches spread out wide like the open arms of a friend and accompanied him to the house itself, the very same house the top of which we have seen and which is now standing in full view with a row of peasant cottages topped by carved horses and fretted gables on one side, and, on the other, a church all aglitter with the gold of its crosses and the gold lacework patterns of chains suspended in the air? Who was the lucky man who owned this out-of-the-way corner of the world? It was owned by Andrey Ivanovich Tentetnikov, a landowner of the Tremalakansky district, a lucky young man of thirty-three and a bachelor into the bargain.

Who was he? What was he? What were his qualities and his character? You should ask his neighbours, my dear women readers. You should ask his neighbours. One of these, a member of the smart and fast-disappearing race of retired fire-eating army officers, expressed his opinion of him as follows:

'A real beast of a man!' A general, who lived some eight miles from his estate said, 'The young man is far from stupid, but he thinks too much of himself. I could have been useful to him because I have all sorts of connexions in Petersburg and even at ...' The general never finished his sentence. The rural police captain used to give the following reply: 'I don't think much of his rank and I shall be calling on him tomorrow to collect arrears of taxes.' A peasant of his village, if asked what his master was like, would make no reply. Which, in fact, means that the general opinion of him was unfavourable.

Looked at impartially, however, he was not a bad man; he was simply a man who idled away his life. But are there not quite a number of people in this world who idle away their time? Why then shouldn't Tentetnikov do the same? Here, however, as an example, is a description of a day in his life which is in every respect like any other day, and let the reader judge for himself what his character was like and to what extent his life corresponded with the beauty of his environment.

He woke up very late in the morning and, sitting up in bed, spent a long time rubbing his eyes. As his eyes were unfortunately very small the rubbing of them lasted quite an extraordinarily long time, and all this time his valet Mikhailo was standing at the door with the wash basin and a towel. Poor Mikhailo would stand waiting for an hour or two, and then would go back to the kitchen and come back again, but his master was still sitting up in bed and rubbing his eyes. At last he would get out of bed, wash, put on his dressing-gown, and go into the drawing-room to drink tea, coffee, cocoa, or even fresh, foaming milk, sipping a little of everything, crumbling his bread mercilessly and dropping his tobacco ash shamelessly all over the place. And he would sit for two hours over his breakfast like that. And that was not all: he would take a cup of cold tea and go to the window which looked out on to the yard. At the window the following scene would take place every day.

To begin with, Grigory, a serf who performed the duties of a pantry-boy, would address the housekeeper Perfilyevna almost in the following words:

'You disgusting little creature, you good-for-nothing slut! You'd better keep your mouth shut, you vile thing!'

'And you wouldn't like to get this, would you?' the good-for-nothing slut or Perfilyevna would cry, accompanying her words with an appropriate gesture. She was a hard woman in spite of the fact that she was very fond of raisins, pastilles, and all sorts of sweets which she kept under lock and key.

'Why, you storeroom trash,' Grigory bawled, 'you'll fall foul of the steward.'

'The steward is as big a thief as you are. Do you think the master doesn't know about you, too? Why, he's here and he can hear everything.'

'Where's the master?'

'Why, he's sitting at the window. He sees it all.'

And to be sure, the master was sitting at the window and he did see it all. To make the uproar more complete, one of the house-serfs, a little boy who had been slapped by his mother, was screaming at the top of his voice, and a borzoi hound was squatting on the ground and whining pitifully because the cook, who had looked out of the kitchen, had thrown some boiling water over him. In short, everyone was screaming and the din was unbearable. The master saw and heard it all, but it was not till it became so unendurable that it even prevented him from doing nothing that he sent to tell them not to make so much noise. ...

About two hours before dinner he went off to his study to apply himself seriously to a work which he planned should embrace the whole of Russia from every point of view: civic, political, religious, and philosophical. This work was to solve all the difficult problems and questions that had arisen in Russia in the course of time and to define clearly her great future; in short, all this was presented in a way that was calculated to appeal to modern man. However, this colossal undertaking had so far not advanced beyond the stage of meditation; the quill pen was bitten, all sorts of drawings appeared on the paper, and then everything was pushed aside, a book was taken up instead and was not put down till dinner-time. The book was read with the soup, the sauce, the roast, and even with the sweet, so that some dishes grew cold while others were removed completely untouched. Then followed coffee with a pipe, a game of chess with himself. What he did afterwards until supper time, it is really hard to say. Apparently he simply did nothing at all.

And so this thirty-three-year-old young man spent his time, all alone in the whole world, sitting indoors in a dressing-gown and without a cravat. He did not go out for walks, he did not feel like pacing the room, he did not even want to go upstairs to open the window to get some fresh air into the room; and the beautiful view of the countryside which no visitor could gaze upon with indifference did not seem to exist for the owner himself. From all this the reader can gather that Tentetnikov belonged to that class of people still plentiful in Russia who used to be known as loafers, lie-a-beds, lazy-bones, and whom I really don't know what to call now. Are such characters born or formed afterwards as a result of unhappy circumstances which beset a man through his life? Instead of answering this question I think I had better tell the story of his upbringing and childhood.

It would seem that everything conspired to make a man of him. As a clever, dreamy, and delicate boy of twelve he happened to go to a school the headmaster of which at that time was a most extraordinary man. The idol of the boys, a model for teachers, the incomparable Alexander Petrovich had the gift of divining a man's nature. How well he knew the qualities of a Russian! How well he knew children! How well he knew how to inspire! There was not a single mischievous boy who, having done something wrong would not have come to him of his own accord and owned up to everything. And that was not all: after being given a severe talking to, he did not go away looking crestfallen, but with his head in the air. There was something encouraging, something that said, 'Forward, you must get quickly on your feet again in spite of the fact that you have fallen.' He never talked to them of good behaviour. He usually said: 'I ask you to use your brains and nothing else. He who tries to use his brains has no time for mischief: mischief should disappear of itself.' And to be sure, it did disappear of itself. He who did not try to improve himself became an object of contempt for his fellows, the grown-up asses and fools had to put up with the most offensive nicknames from the smallest boys and they dared not lay a finger on them. 'This is too much!' many people said. 'The clever boys will grow into arrogant men.' 'No, it's not too much,' he used to say. 'I do not keep dull boys for long. One course is enough for them. But I have a different course for clever boys.' And, indeed, all the capable boys went through the special course with him. He did not restrain the boys' high spirits, for he regarded them as the beginning of spiritual development, and he used to say that it was as necessary to him as the rashes on the body to a doctor, for it made it possible for him to find out for certain what was going on inside the patient.

How the boys loved him! Never were children so attached to their parents. No, not even in their crazy years of wild enthusiasms was unquenchable passion so strong as the love of the children for him. To the grave, to the very last days, the grateful pupil would raise a glass on the birthday of his wonderful teacher though he had long been in his grave, and closing his eyes, he would weep for him. His least word of encouragement thrilled them, made them feel happy and tremble with excitement, and increased their ambitious desire to excel everyone else. He did not keep the less capable boys long; for them he had a special shorter course. But the capable boys had to go through a double course with him. And the last course, reserved only for the elect, was unlike those in other educational establishments. It was only there that he demanded of his pupils what some people stupidly demand of their children – that higher expression of intelligence which never ridicules anything, but puts up with any scornful remark: to suffer a fool gladly without getting irritated or losing one's temper, never under any circumstances to revenge oneself on anyone and to preserve a proud tranquillity and imperturbability of spirit; and he employed every method calculated to form a firm character and he kept making experiments with them to that end. Oh, how well he knew the science of life!

He did not employ many teachers. He taught most of the subjects himself, he knew how to convey the very essence of a subject without using any pedantic terms or pompous theories and opinions, so that even a small boy could grasp immediately what he needed it for. He selected only those subjects which were capable of turning a man into a useful citizen of his country; most of his lectures consisted of accounts of what the young man would expect to find on leaving school and he knew how to describe the whole sphere of his pupil's future career so well that the young man, though he was still sitting on the school bench, was in his thoughts and spirit already living in the particular branch of the Civil Service he had chosen. He concealed nothing; all the disappointments and obstacles which a man might find in his path, all the temptations and trials that were in store for him, he presented to them in all their nakedness without concealing anything. He knew everything, just as though he himself had had personal experience of all the various callings and posts. Whether it was because his ambition was strongly developed or because there was something in the eyes of this extraordinary teacher that said to the youth 'Forward!' – a word so familiar to the Russian and one that has such a miraculous influence over his sensitive nature – but from the very beginning the young man was eager to cope only with difficulties, where the obstacles were more numerous, where one had to display greater spiritual force. Very few completed this course, but those who did were men who knew the smell of powder. In service they kept their most precarious posts while many others who were much cleverer than they, unable to put up with all sorts of petty personal unpleasantness, threw up everything, or growing torpid and lazy, losing their sense of proportion and their self-respect, fell into the hands of bribe-takers and scoundrels. But his pupils did not weaken and, knowing life and man and grown wise with experience, even exercised a strong influence on evil men.

The ardent heart of an ambitious boy beat faster at the very thought of joining that course. Tentetnikov could not have had a better teacher! But as ill-luck would have it, no sooner had he joined this course of the elect – something he desired so much! – than this extraordinary teacher suddenly died. Oh, what a blow that was for him! What a terrible first loss! Alexander Petrovich was succeeded by a certain Fyodor Ivanovich. He immediately concentrated his attention on external discipline and began demanding of children what can only be demanded of grown-ups. He saw something unbridled in their free and easy manners. And as though to spite his predecessor, he declared on the very first day that intelligence and success meant nothing to him and that he would take into account only good conduct. Strange to say, what Fyodor Ivanovich was never successful in achieving was good conduct. All sorts of secret vices made their appearance. In the daytime everything was reduced to servile obedience and strict discipline was preserved, but at night there were orgies.

Something strange also happened to their studies. New teachers were engaged with new ideas and new points of view and new slants on things. They smothered their pupils with a multitude of new terms and words; in their expositions they showed both logical connexions and great enthusiasm but, alas, life was the only thing lacking in the things they taught. It all seemed dead, and learning was a dead letter in their mouths. In short, everything was turned upside down. The pupils lost their respect for their school authorities. They began to laugh both at their tutors and at their teachers, they called the headmaster by the contemptuous name of Fedka, or the bun, and all sorts of other nicknames. Depravity assumed far from childish forms: such things were committed that many boys had to be expelled. Within two years the establishment had become quite unrecognizable.

Tentetnikov was of a very gentle disposition. He could not be led astray, either by the nocturnal orgies of his classmates, who had set up a 'lady' in rooms before the very windows of the headmaster's flat, or by the sacrilegious remarks they made about religion just because their priest did not happen to be particularly intelligent. No, he was aware of the heavenly origin of his soul even in his dreams. He could not be led astray, but he lost courage. His ambition had been aroused, but there was no proper activity or vocation for him. It would have been better if it had never been aroused at all. He listened to the professors who delivered their lectures with such enthusiasm and could not help thinking of his former teacher who, without growing enthusiastic, had known how to speak so that his pupils understood him. What subjects and what courses did he not follow! Medicine, chemistry, philosophy, and even law and the universal history of mankind in so comprehensive a form that in three years the professor had only succeeded in completing his introduction and enlarging on the development of the communes in some of the German cities – and goodness only knows what subjects he did not hear. And all this stuck in his mind in shapeless bits and pieces. Thanks to his native wit he realized that that was not the way to teach, but he had no idea how it ought to be done and he often thought of Alexander Petrovich and he felt so sad that he did not know what to do with himself.

But youth is lucky in that it has a future before it. As the time of leaving school drew near, his heart began to beat faster. He said to himself: 'This isn't life yet; it is only a preparation for life; real life is to be found in the service. It is there that great things are to be done.' And without a glance at the beautiful spot which so astonished every visitor, without paying his respects to the grave of his parents, he rushed off to Petersburg, as is the custom of all ambitious youths. It is to Petersburg, as we all know, that our enthusiastic young men flock from all parts of Russia – to join the Civil Service, to shine, to gain promotion, or simply to get a smattering of the colourless, ice-cold, deceptive 'society' education. But Tentetnikov's ambitious plans were from the very outset damped by his uncle Onufry Ivanovich, a Regular State Councillor. He declared that the only thing that mattered was good handwriting and that he had better first begin with a study of calligraphy, and that without that he would never become a minister or a statesman.

With great difficulty and with the help of his uncle's connexions he at last got a job in some department. When he was conducted into a magnificent, well-lighted room with a parquet floor and polished writing desks, which looked as if the greatest statesmen of the land held their conferences and decided the fate of their country there, and he saw the legions of handsome scribbling gentlemen, scratching away with their pens with their heads leaning sideways, and when he himself had been placed at one of those desks and told to copy some documents which, as though on purpose, dealt with some trifling matter (it concerned three roubles and the correspondence about it had been going on for six months), the inexperienced youth was suddenly overcome by a most extraordinary sensation. He felt as though he had been transferred for some misdemeanour from an upper to a lower class: the young gentlemen who were sitting around him reminded him of a lot of schoolboys. To complete the similarity, some of them were reading a stupid foreign novel which they hid between the large sheets of the official documents, pretending to be busy and at the same time starting every time the head of the department entered the room. It all seemed so strange to him and his former work at school seemed so much more important than his present occupation and the preparation for entering the service so much better than the service itself. He began to be sorry he had left school and suddenly Alexander Petrovich rose up before him as though he were alive, and he nearly wept. The room began to go round and the civil servants and the tables got all mixed up and he had to make an effort not to suffer a momentary black-out. 'No,' he thought to himself when he recovered, 'I'm going to apply myself to my work however unimportant it may seem at first!' Reluctantly and with a heavy heart he decided to follow the example of the others.

Is there any place where there are no enjoyments? They are to be found even in Petersburg in spite of its stern and gloomy appearance. There is a severe frost of thirty degrees below zero in the streets; the fiend of the north, the witch of a blizzard, is howling outside, covering the pavements with snow, blinding the eyes, powdering fur collars, men's moustaches, and the shaggy muzzles of horses, but through the whirling snow-flakes a light gleams invitingly from some window on the fourth floor; in a cosy little room lit by modest stearine candles, to the singing of the *samovar*, a conversation that warms the heart and the soul is carried on, a bright page of some inspired Russian poet is being read, of a poet whom God has bestowed on Russia as a heavenly gift, and the youthful heart throbs ardently and loftily as it never does even under southern skies.

Tentetnikov soon grew used to his work at the office, but it was no longer the sole aim and object of his life as he had at first imagined, and it became something of secondary importance. It served as the best way of filling in his time and made him appreciate his hours of leisure all the more. His uncle, the Regular State Councillor, was already beginning to think that his nephew would make a career for himself, when his nephew made an unholy mess of things. Among Tentetnikov's friends, of whom he had quite a number, there were two who belonged to the class of what is called 'frustrated' men. They were those strange and uncomfortable characters who cannot endure not only injustices, but what they believe to be injustices. Fundamentally kind-hearted, but disorderly in their behaviour, demanding indulgence for themselves but full of intolerance for others, they made a very great impression on him by their fiery speeches and the way they expressed their noble indignation against society. Working upon his nerves and arousing his feeling of exasperation, they forced him to take notice of all those trivialities to which at first he had never dreamt of paying any attention. He suddenly took a dislike to Fyodor Fyodorovich Lenitsyn, the chief of one of the departments in those magnificent rooms. He began to discover all sorts of faults in him. It seemed to him that when speaking to his superiors, Lenitsyn became transformed into a kind of cloyingly sweet sugar, but when one of his subordinates turned to him for advice he was turned into vinegar; that, like all petty-minded people, he chose to reprimand those who did not come to him with their congratulations on holidays and re-venged himself on those whose names did not appear on the list of visitors in the porter's lodge; and as a result of it he felt a nervous aversion for him. Some evil spirit was egging him on to do some-thing unpleasant to Lenitsyn. He seemed to look for an opportunity of doing so with a kind of special relish and at last succeeded in finding one. One day he spoke so rudely to him that he was ordered by his superiors either to apologize or to resign. He sent in his resignation. His uncle, the Regular State Councillor, came to see him, looking terribly alarmed.

'In Christ's name,' he implored him, 'my dear fellow, what are you doing? To throw up such a promising career simply because your chief does not happen to be the sort of man you like? Good Lord, man, what are you thinking of? Why, if one were to take that line nobody would be left in the service. Come to your senses, my boy. Forget your pride and your vanity and go and talk it over with him.'

'That's not the point, uncle,' said the nephew. 'I don't mind apolo-gizing to him. I was at fault. He's my chief and I shouldn't have spoken to him like that. But, you see, the point is that I have a dif-ferent kind of work. I have three hundred serfs, my estate is in a bad way, and my agent's a fool. It will be no great loss to the state if some-one else takes my place at the office copying papers, but it will be a great loss if three hundred men don't pay their taxes. Please don't for-get that I'm a landowner. A calling not without its duties. If I concern myself with the preservation, care, and improvement of the lot of the people entrusted to me and put at the disposal of my country three hundred industrious, sober, and hard-working subjects, in what way will my work be worse than that of some chief of a department like Lenitsyn?'

The Regular State Councillor gaped at him in astonishment. He had not expected such a flood of words. After a moment's reflection he began as follows:

'But, all the same, er – er – how can you? I mean, how can you bury yourself in the country? What kind of society will you find among illiterate peasants? Here at least you can run across a general or a prince in the street. You can go for a walk and pass some – er – I mean, well, there's gas lighting here, industrial Europe, but what will you find there? The only people you will run across there will be a peasant or a peasant woman. Why, I ask you, why condemn yourself to spend the rest of your life among ignorant rustics?'

But the uncle's persuasive arguments made no impression on the nephew. He began to look on the country as a sort of free and untrammelled place of refuge, a stimulant to thoughts and ideas, the one and only calling of useful activity. He had already acquired the latest books dealing with farming and agriculture. In short, about a fortnight after his conversation with his uncle, he was already in the vicinity of the places where he had spent his childhood, not far from that beautiful spot which no guest or visitor could sufficiently admire. A new emotion stirred within him. Impressions that had long lain dormant awakened in his breast. He had forgotten many of the places altogether and he now gazed at the beautiful scenery with the interest of a man who had never seen it before. And suddenly, goodness only knows why, his heart began to beat violently. When the road passed by a narrow ravine into the heart of an immense forest that had run wild, and he saw above, below, over his head, and beneath him, oaks three hundred years old that three men could barely encompass, and between them silver firs, elm-trees, and black poplars, higher than any ordinary poplar, and when in answer to the question: 'Whose forest is this?' he was told, 'Tentetnikov's'; when, having left the forest, the road ran through meadows, past aspen copses, willows, old and young, and weeping willows, in sight of high hills stretching in the distance, and across two bridges which spanned the river in two places, having it sometimes on the right and sometimes on the left, and when in answer to the question: 'Whose meadows and water meadows are these?', he was told, 'Tentetnikov's'; when the road afterwards began rising up the hillside and then continued on a level plateau, with the still unharvested corn fields, wheat fields, oat fields, and barley fields on the one side, and on the other all the places he had already traversed and which now appeared foreshortened, and when, gradually getting darker, the road entered and passed under the shade of large spreading trees scattered here and there along a green carpet right up to the village, and he caught sight of the carved peasants' cottages and the red roofs of the landowner's brick buildings, the large country mansion and the old church, and the golden cupolas of the church gleaming in the sunlight; when his eagerly beating heart knew without being asked where it had arrived, all the emotions that had been accumulating within him, at last burst out into loud words: 'Well, haven't I been a fool? Fate has decreed that I should be the owner of this earthly paradise and I have sold myself into slavery as a scribbler of dead papers. After being educated and enlightened, and having acquired a store of knowledge needed for doing good among the people who have been put in my power, for the improvement of a whole district, for performing the duties of a landowner who is at one and the same time a judge, a manager, and a guardian of law and order, to entrust this task to an ignorant agent, and to prefer the work of settling by correspondence the affairs of people I have never seen before, people whose characters and qualities I knew nothing about, to prefer this fantastic government by red tape of whole provinces a thousand miles apart from each other, in which I had never set foot and in which I could only commit a whole lot of stupidities and errors, to the real task of managing my own estate!'

Meanwhile, another spectacle was awaiting him. Learning of the master's arrival, the peasants had gathered at the entrance of the house. He was soon surrounded by women wearing their holiday head-dresses, headbands, and kerchiefs, and by men in short coats of thick cloth and with picturesque broad and thick beards. When he heard the words, 'Dear master, you've remembered us,' and when the old men and women, who still remembered his father and his grandfather, burst into tears, he could not keep back his tears, either. And he thought to himself: 'So much love and for what? Because I've never come to see them and never bothered about them', and he vowed to share their labours and their toils.

He began to look after his estate and to issue orders. He cut down the amount of the peasants' unpaid labour, decreased the numbers of days they had to work for their master, and gave them extra time for their own work on the land. He dismissed the fool of an agent.

He himself began to take an interest in everything, to show himself in the fields, on the threshing floor, in the barns, the water-mills, on the quayside when the flat-bottomed boats were being loaded, so that the ne'er-do-well peasants began scratching their heads. But this went on only for a short time. The Russian peasant is shrewd and he soon realized that, though his master was keen and willing to do many things, he had no idea how they are done or even how to begin doing them, though he talked like an educated man he had no real knowledge. The result was that the master and the peasants did not fail to understand each other so much as fail to find a common language. They did not succeed in singing in tune. Tentetnikov began to notice that everything somehow turned out worse on his own land than on the peasants' land. His fields were sown earlier and came up later. Yet they seemed to be working well: he himself was present and even ordered them to be given a mug of vodka for their diligent work. The peasants' rye had already long been in ear, their oats were dropping, their millet was growing thickly, while his corn was only just beginning to form stems and the base of the ears had not yet begun to appear. In short, the master began to notice that the peasants were simply cheating him, in spite of the various privileges he had granted them. He tried reproaching them but the answer he got was: 'How is it possible for us, sir, not to take our master's interests to heart? You saw yourself, sir, how we did our best when we were ploughing and sowing. You even ordered a mug of vodka for us.' What could he reply to that? 'But why has everything turned out so badly then?' the master asked. 'I'm sure I don't know, sir. It must have been the worms eating it below. Besides, sir, look at the sort of summer it has been: no rain at all.' But the master saw that the worms had not eaten the peasants' corn and that the rain must have been falling in a funny sort of way, in some places and not in others: it had favoured the peasants and not a drop of it had fallen on the master's ploughed fields.

He found it even more difficult to get on with the peasant women. They were continually asking to be given leave from work, complaining of the hardships of their compulsory labour for their master. It was indeed strange. He had let them off completely from any free deliveries of linen, fruit, mushrooms, and nuts, he had halved their forced labour hours in the hope that they would employ their free time looking after their household affairs, that they would do more sewing for their families and make clothes for their husbands and enlarge their kitchen gardens. But nothing of the kind happened. Such idleness, fighting, scandal-mongering, and all sorts of squabbles spread among the fair sex that their husbands were continually coming to him, saying: 'Please, sir, do something to keep that devil of a wife of mine under control. She's a fiend incarnate, there's no living with her!' Reluctantly he was beginning to think that he'd have to take firmer measures. But how was he to be firm? The woman came, looking such a typical peasant woman, shrieking at the top of her voice, looking so sick and ailing, covered in such filthy rags that he could not help wondering where she could possibly have picked them up. 'Go away! For goodness sake, get out of my sight! Do as you like!' said poor Tentetnikov, and a minute later saw how the sick woman, once she was out of the gates, started fighting with a neighbour over some turnip and gave her a drubbing such as not even a sturdy peasant could have given her.

He tried to start a school for them, but it turned out to be such a hopeless failure that he hung his head, feeling that it would have been better not to have thought of it. A school, indeed! There was no time for sending children to school: as soon as a boy reached the age of ten, he was supposed to help his father with his work and it was there that he was educated.

In dealing with all sorts of legal and arbitration cases, he found that all the legal subtleties his philosophizing teachers had taught him at school were of no use at all. Both plaintiff and defendant would be telling lies and only the devil could make out who was right and who was wrong. And he came to realize that a simple knowledge of human nature was much more important than all the subtleties of books of law and philosophy; he also perceived that there was something lacking in himself, but what it was he did not know. And the usual thing happened: the peasant failed to understand the master and the master failed to understand the peasant; and the peasant turned his bad side to the master and the master turned his bad side to the peasant. And the landowner's zeal cooled. He no longer paid any attention to the work in the fields. When the scythes rose and fell gently during the haymaking, when the hayricks were being put up, or the corn stooked up, even when the work was proceeding near him, his eyes looked away into the distance; when the work was going on in the distance, his eyes sought out objects which were nearer at hand and looked away at some bend in the river, on the bank of which some red-beaked, red-legged gull was walking – a bird of course and not a man. He looked on with curiosity to see how, having caught a fish, the gull held it crossways in its beak, as though wondering whether to swallow it or not, and at the same time looking up the river where in the distance another gull could be seen, a gull who had not yet caught a fish but who was watching intently the gull which had already caught one. Or with eyes half-closed and his head raised upwards at the vast expanse of the sky, he inhaled the scent of the fields and listened to the marvellous voices of the songsters of the air, when from everywhere, from the sky and from the ground, they joined in one harmonious choir without jarring on one another. In the corn the quail was calling shrilly, in the grass a corncrake was creaking, linnets were twittering and chirruping as they flew above him, a lamb was bleating as it skipped in the meadow, a lark trilled as it disappeared in the sunlight, and the calls of the cranes, as they flew high in the heavens in wedge-shaped formations, descended like the ringing notes of trumpets. The entire countryside had been transformed into sounds that re-echoed from every corner. Oh Creator! How beautiful still is your world in the depths of the country, in a little village far from the foul highways and towns! But he lost interest in this too. Very soon he gave up going to the fields, never left his rooms, and refused to receive even the agent with his reports.

Some of the neighbours used to call on him before, a retired lieutenant of the hussars, an inveterate pipe smoker and reeking of tobacco, or a student of radical views who had not finished his studies and who had acquired wisdom from papers and pamphlets. But this too began to bore him. He began to find their conversations superficial, and their free and easy European manners, their way of slapping him on the knee as well as their obsequiousness and their lack of decorum began to strike him as a little too obvious and unreserved. He made up his mind to drop their acquaintance and he did so rather brusquely. So when Varvar Nikolayevich Vishnepokromov, the most agreeable of these superficial conversationalists and a representative of the now defunct type of fire-eating colonels, who was at the same time an adherent of the most advanced school of thought, called on him to have a long discussion about politics, philosophy, literature, and morals and even the financial position of England, he sent word to say that he was not at home and at the same time was incautious enough to show himself at the window. The visitor and the master of the house exchanged glances. One of them, of course, muttered through his teeth, 'The brute!' while the other called him a swine from annoyance. That was the end of their relationship. Since that day no one ever came to see him.

He was glad of that and devoted himself entirely to planning a great work on Russia. How this great work was being planned the reader has already seen. A strange, disorderly order was established in his house. It cannot be said, however, that there were not moments when he seemed to wake from his dreams. When the papers and journals arrived and he happened to come across the name of some old schoolfellow in print, a man who was making a name for himself in some important government post, or one who had made an important contribution to science or world affairs, a quiet, secret sadness crept into his heart and a mournful, dumbly-melancholy regret at his own inactivity overwhelmed him in spite of himself. Then his life seemed to him nasty and loathsome. His schooldays rose up before him with extraordinary vividness and Alexander Petrovich would suddenly appear before him as though he were alive. ... A flood of tears gushed from his eyes and his sobs lasted almost all day.

What did these sobs signify? Did his aching heart reveal in them the sorrowful secret of its sickness – that the noble inner man that had begun to be formed within him was not given a chance of developing and growing strong; that unaccustomed from childhood to struggle against failures, he had never succeeded in reaching a state of mind which would enable him to overcome and rise above obstacles and difficulties; that the rich reserve of lofty feelings, which had glowed in him like molten metal, had not been tempered like steel, that his wonderful teacher had died too soon, and that now there was no one in the whole world who could restore his strength which was being sapped by his constant wavering and by his impotent will-power, which was deprived of resilience, that there was no one to rouse his soul with the encouraging word, 'Forward', which the Russian at every stage of his development and of every class, calling, and profession, is so eager to hear?

But where is the man who could utter that all-powerful word 'Forward' and address it to the Russian soul in its native tongue, who, knowing all the strength and quality and depth of our nature, could by the mere waving of a magic wand direct us towards a higher life? With what tears and with what love would he be repaid by the grateful Russian? But century after century goes by, half a million sluggards and idlers and lie-a-beds are plunged into deep sleep, and rarely is the man born in Russia who is able to utter that all-powerful word.

There was one thing that nearly awakened him from his slumber and nearly brought about a complete transformation of his character. It was something very much like love. But this too came to nothing. In the neighbourhood, some seven miles from his estate, there lived a general who, as we have already seen, did not have too high an opinion of Tentetnikov. The general lived like a general, he entertained on a large scale and he liked his neighbours to call on him and to pay their respects to him. He himself did not pay visits. He talked in a gruff voice, read books, and had a daughter, a strange and quite unique creature. She was alive like life itself. Her name was Ulinka. Her education had been rather strange. She had been brought up by an English governess who did not know a word of Russian. She had lost her mother early in childhood. Her father had no time for her. However, as he loved his daughter passionately, he could only have spoilt her. Like any child that grows up in freedom, she was extremely wilful; anyone who had seen how sudden anger furrowed her beautiful forehead and how heatedly she argued with her father, might have thought that she was a most capricious creature. But her anger was only aroused when she heard of some injustice or of anyone, whoever it might be, behaving badly. But she was never angry and never quarrelled about anything that concerned herself, and she never attempted to justify herself. And how quickly her anger would have passed if she had seen the person she was angry with in trouble himself. At the first request for charity she was ready to throw her purse and all it contained to the man who made it, without any argument or calculation. There was something impulsive about her. When she spoke everything, everything in her seemed to be rushing after her thoughts – the expression of her face, the tone of her voice, the movement of her hands; the very folds of her dress seemed flying in the same direction, and one got the impression that any moment she herself would fly after her own words. There was nothing secretive about her. She would not have been afraid to disclose her thoughts to anyone, and no force in the world could have made her be silent when she wanted to speak. The way she walked was so fascinating, so much part of herself and so fearlessly free that everyone involuntarily made way before her. An evil man was overcome with confusion and struck dumb in her presence; and the most free and easy and glib person could not find what to say to her, while a shy person could talk to her as he never talked to anyone in his life before, and right from the beginning of their conversation he felt that he had met her before and had seen those features somewhere, that it might have happened in the long-forgotten days of their early childhood, in their own home, on some happy evening while playing happily with a lot of other children, and long afterwards the years of discretion seemed dull and boring to him.

The same thing happened with her and Tentetnikov. A new and inexplicable feeling came into his soul. His dull life was for a moment lighted up.

At first the general received Tentetnikov fairly well and amiably, but they could not get on together. Their conversations always ended in an argument and in a sort of unpleasant feeling on both sides, for the general did not like contradictions or disagreements, while Tentetnikov, for his part, was also a most touchy person. It goes without saying that much was forgiven the father for the sake of the daughter and there was no open breach between them till some relatives came to stay with the general: Countess Boldryrev and the Princess Yuzyakin, former ladies-in-waiting, who still had some connexions with the Court, for which reason the general fawned on them a little. From the very first day of their arrival Tentetnikov could not help feeling that the general had been treating him more coldly, scarcely noticing him, or when he did, never speaking to him; when he did speak to him he did so in a very slighting manner, addressing him as 'my dear sir', 'look here, my good man', or even more familiarly. This, in the end, made him furious. Very reluctantly and gritting his teeth, he had, however, the presence of mind to say in an unusually courteous and soft voice, while red spots appeared on his face and he was boiling inwardly: 'I thank you, general, for being so kind to me. By addressing me in so familiar a manner, you show your close friendship for me and oblige me to address you in the same familiar fashion. But I am afraid the difference in our ages prevents such a familiar mode of address between us.'

The general looked embarrassed. Stammering and trying to think of something to say, he began to explain, though a little incoherently, that he used the familiar mode of address not in that sense at all and that an old man could sometimes allow himself to address a young man in such a familiar fashion (he did not say a word about his rank).

Their acquaintance, of course, came to an end after that, and love was nipped in the bud. The light that had flashed for a moment was extinguished and the twilight that followed became gloomier than ever. Everything went back to the sort of life the reader has seen at the beginning of the chapter, a life spent in lying about and doing nothing. Dirt and disorder reigned in the house. The broom remained for days in the middle of the room together with the dirt. His trousers even made their way into the drawing-room. On the elegant table in front of the sofa lay a pair of greasy braces as though they had been offered as a treat to a visitor, and his life became so useless and somnolent that not only his own servants lost all respect for him, but even the hens almost pecked at him. Picking up a pen, he would scribble abstractedly for hours on a piece of paper, drawing squiggles, little houses, peasant cottages, carts, *troikas*. But sometimes, forgetting everything, his pen would unconsciously draw a little head with delicate features, with a quick penetrating glance, and a loose lock of hair, and to his surprise he would see that it had turned into a portrait of a girl whose portrait no famous artist could have painted. And he felt more cheerless than ever and, convinced that there could be no happiness on earth, he became even more depressed and despondent.

Such was the state of Tentetnikov's mind when one fine day, as he walked up to the window as usual with his pipe and a cup of tea in his hands, he noticed a certain commotion in the yard. The kitchen boy and the woman who scrubbed the floors were running to open the gates. And in the gates appeared horses exactly as they are carved or painted on triumphal arches: one head to the right, another head to the left, and a third head in the middle. Above them on the box sat a driver and a footman wearing a full frock-coat tied round the waist with a handkerchief. Behind them sat a gentleman in a cap and greatcoat, wrapped in a rainbow-coloured shawl. When the carriage pulled up before the front steps of the house it appeared that it was nothing more than a light sprung four-wheeled chaise. A gentleman of a quite extraordinarily decorous exterior jumped out on to the steps with almost the speed and agility of a military man.

For a moment Tentetnikov was alarmed. He thought he might be a government official. It must be explained that in his youth he had been mixed up in a rather foolish affair. Two philosophers – hussars – who had read all sorts of pamphlets and an aesthete who had not finished his course at the university as well as a gambler who had lost a fortune at cards, had founded a kind of philanthropic society under the leadership of an old rogue, a freemason and gambler, but who was a most eloquent man. The society was formed with a most grandiose aim – to procure enduring happiness for the whole of mankind from the banks of the Thames to Kamchatka. The funds required for this project were enormous and large subscriptions were collected from generous members. But where it all went to no one knew except the chief director. Two of his friends had drawn him into this society, friends who belonged to the class of frustrated men, excellent fellows both of them, but inveterate drunkards from offering up too many toasts to science, general enlightenment, and future benefits to be conferred on mankind.

Tentetnikov quickly came to his senses and left the group. But the society managed to get itself involved in all sorts of acts which did not redound to the honour of a nobleman, so that in the end the police became interested in its activities. ... It was therefore no wonder that though he had resigned from this society and broken off all relations with its members, Tentetnikov could not help feeling unhappy about it. His conscience was not altogether at ease. It was consequently not without a feeling of alarm that he looked at the door which was opening just at that moment.

His fears, however, vanished as soon as his visitor made his bows with incredible agility, keeping his head respectfully bent a little on one side and explaining in a few words that he had been travelling for some time across Russia both on business and out of curiosity. He went on to say that our country was rich in most remarkable things, not to mention the large variety of trades and the diversity of soils, that he had been greatly attracted by the picturesque situation of Tentetnikov's estate, that in spite of the beautiful scenery he would not have dared to disturb him by his untimely visit, had he not been involved in a slight accident to his carriage caused by the spring floods and the bad roads, but that even if nothing had happened to his carriage, he would not have been able to deny himself the pleasure of paying his personal respects to him.

Having finished his speech, the visitor with charming courtesy scraped his foot clad in a smart patent leather shoe, with mother-of-pearl buttons, and in spite of the rotundity of his body, skipped backwards a little with the lightness of an india-rubber ball. Reassured, Tentetnikov concluded that his visitor must be some inquisitive, learned professor, who was travelling about Russia to collect plants or possibly archaeological specimens. He at once declared his readiness to be of assistance to him in every way, offered him the services of his workmen, his wheelwrights, and blacksmiths, and begged him to make himself comfortable just as though he were in his own house; he made him sit down in a large Voltairian armchair and prepared to listen to his discourse on natural sciences. The visitor, however, touched on incidents of a more intimate character. Comparing his life to a ship at sea tossed by treacherous winds, he mentioned the fact that he had to change his posts very frequently, that he had suffered much in the cause of justice, that his life itself was several times endangered by enemies, and he said a great deal more which showed that he was a practical man. Concluding his speech, he blew his nose into a white cambric handkerchief so loudly that Tentetnikov had never heard anything like it before. Sometimes in an orchestra you will find such a cunning rogue of a trumpet that when it lets out a blast it seems to be coming not from the orchestra but from somewhere inside your ear. Such was the sound which resounded in the awakened rooms of the slumbering house and it was followed immediately by an agreeable whiff of eau-de-Cologne, invisibly diffused by a dexterous wave of the cambric handkerchief.

The reader will perhaps have guessed that the visitor was none other than our honoured Pavel Ivanovich Chichikov, whom we had left behind for such a long time. He looked a little older, and it was obvious that the time that had elapsed had not been free from storms and worries. Even the coat he wore seemed to be a little more worn and his carriage, his coachman, his footman, his horses, and the harness had grown a little older and shabbier. His finances, too, did not seem to be in a very flourishing state. But the expression on his face, his decorum and his exquisite manners remained the same. Indeed, he seemed to be even more agreeable in his manners and turns of speech and he crossed his legs even more deftly when sitting down in an armchair. There was a greater softness in the way he delivered his speeches and more cautious moderation in his words and expressions, more skill in the way he carried himself, and greater tact in everything he did. His collar and his shirt-front were whiter than snow and, though he had just been travelling, there was not a speck of dust on his coat – you could have invited him to a birthday party straight away. His cheeks and chin were shaved so smoothly that only a blind man could have failed to admire their pleasantly rounded curves.

A transformation took place in the house at once. Half of it, which had hitherto been in a state of total blindness with shuttered windows, suddenly regained its sight and was flooded with light. Chichikov's things were brought into the lighted rooms and soon everything assumed the following appearance: in the room which was to be his bedroom were placed the things which were considered necessary for the night toilet; and the room which was to be his study – but first of all we ought to know that there were three tables in this room: a writing table in front of the sofa, a card table between the two windows in front of the looking-glass, and a corner table in the corner between the door leading into the bedroom and the door leading into an unused drawing-room with broken furniture, which was now to become an anteroom and which for over a year no one had entered. The clothes taken from the trunk were now placed on this corner table, to wit, one pair of trousers to wear with the cut-away coat, a pair of blue trousers and a pair of grey trousers, two velvet waistcoats and two satin waistcoats, a frock-coat and two dress-coats. These were piled one on top of another in a pyramid and covered with a silk handkerchief. In another corner between the door and the window a whole row of boots was set out: one pair which was not quite new, another which was quite new, a pair of patent leather shoes, and a pair of slippers. They too were discreetly veiled with a silk handkerchief just as though they were not there at all. On the writing desk were immediately placed in excellent order Chichikov's box, a bottle of eau-de-Cologne, a calendar, and two novels, both second volumes. The clean linen was put away in the chest of drawers which was already in the bedroom; the linen which was to go to the laundry was tied into a bundle and put under the bed. The trunk, having been emptied, was also shoved under the bed. The sword which accompanied him on his journeys and which was meant to inspire fear in highwaymen was also taken into the bedroom and hung on a nail not far from the bed. Everything in the rooms acquired quite an extraordinary look of tidiness and cleanliness. Not a scrap of paper, a feather, or a speck of dust was to be seen. The very air seemed to have become more refined: it was now full of the agreeable odour of a strong healthy man who changed his linen frequently, who went regularly to the baths, and who rubbed himself down with a wet sponge on Sundays. In the anteroom there was the danger of the footman Petrushka's odour getting a firm foothold, but Petrushka was soon moved into the kitchen, which was indeed a more fitting place for him.

For the first few days Tentetnikov had fears for his independence, being apprehensive that the visitor might in some way encroach on his privacy or hamper him by introducing changes into his daily routine which he had so successfully established, but his apprehensions were groundless. Our Chichikov revealed an extraordinary flexibility in adapting himself to everything. He approved his host's philosophical leisureliness, saying that it held the promise of living to be a hundred. He expressed himself extremely felicitously about his host's secluded mode of life, saying that seclusion fostered great ideas in man. Glancing at his host's library and saying a few words in praise of books in general, he observed that they saved man from the vice of idleness. He was chary of his words, but whatever he said had weight. In his actions he showed himself even more considerate. He came in at the right time and left at the right time; he did not bother his host with all sorts of questions at an hour when he preferred to be silent; he enjoyed playing chess with him and he also enjoyed being silent. While his host was smoking his pipe and puffing out smoke rings, Chichikov, who did not smoke a pipe, did his best to occupy himself with some corresponding activity: he would, for instance, take his black and silver snuff-box out of his pocket and, holding it firmly between two fingers of his left hand, spin it round quickly with a finger of his right hand somewhat in the same direction in which the earth turns on its axis, or simply drum on it with a finger, whistling some tune at the same time. In short, he did not interfere with his host in any way. 'For the first time in my life I've come across a man with whom I could live,' Tentetnikov said to himself. 'Generally speaking, we are not very good at this art. We've lots of clever, educated, and good-natured men, but we have no men of an even temper, people with whom one could live for years without quarrelling. Such people are very rare among us. This is the first I've met.' That was what Tentetnikov thought of his guest.

Chichikov, for his part, was very glad to settle down for a time in the house of so peaceful and quiet a man. He was tired of his gypsy life. To have a rest even for only a month in a beautiful country place in view of the fields and at the time of approaching spring was beneficial even from the point of view of his haemorrhoids. It would have been hard to find a better spot for a rest. The spring which had been held back for a long time by frosts, suddenly arrived in all its beauty and everything came to life everywhere. Patches of blue could already be seen in the forest glades, and on the fresh emerald of the young grass dandelions showed yellow and the lilac-pink anemones bowed their tender little heads. Swarms of midges and clouds of insects appeared over the swamps; water spiders were already engaged in chasing them; and all kinds of birds were gathering in the dry bulrushes. And they were all assembling to have a closer look at each other. All of a sudden the earth was full of creatures, and the woods and meadows awakened. In the village the peasants had already started their round dances. There was plenty of room for festivities. What brilliance in the foliage! What freshness in the air! What excited twittering of birds in the orchards! Paradise, joy, and exaltation in everything! The countryside resounded with song as though at a wedding feast.

Chichikov went for long walks. There were plenty of opportunities for country walks. Sometimes he took his walks along the flat plateau on the top of the heights, overlooking the valleys spread out below, still covered by large lakes from the floods, with islands on which dark and still leafless woods were growing; or he would go into the thickets, into the ravines in the woods, where the trees grew densely and were thickly covered with birds' nests, the habitations of cawing rooks, which darkened the sky as they flew across it. When the ground had dried, it was possible to make one's way to the landing stage from which the first barges laden with peas, oats, barley, and wheat were casting off, while at the same time with a deafening roar the water plunged on to the wheels of the water-mill which was just resuming its work. He went off into the fields to watch the first spring labours, to see how the freshly ploughed fields cut across the green sward with black furrows, and the sower, tapping on the sieve slung from his neck over his chest, scattered the seed by handfuls without a single grain falling to one side or the other.

Chichikov had been everywhere. He conducted long conversations with the agent, the peasants, and the miller. He got to know every-thing about the work on the estate, how and what and why things were done and how the estate was managed, what they charged for their grain and what they charged in the spring and the autumn for grinding the corn, and what each peasant's name was, and which was related to which, and where they bought their corn and what they fed their pigs on – in fact, everything. He also found out how many peasants had died. There were very few of them. As an intelligent man, he could not help noticing at once how badly Tentetnikov's land was being managed. Everywhere there were signs of omissions, neglect, thieving, and a great deal of drunkenness. And he thought to himself: 'What a brute that Tentetnikov is! What a wonderful estate! And to let it go to rack and ruin! He could have had an income of fifty thousand roubles a year from it.'

More than once during these walks it occurred to him that one day – not immediately, of course, but later on when his great enterprise was accomplished and he had the means, he would become a peaceful owner of a similar estate. And it goes without saying that he im-mediately conjured up a vision of a young, fresh, fair-complexioned young woman of the merchant or any other well-to-do class, who would even be able to play music. He also pictured to himself the younger generation destined to perpetuate the name of Chichikov: a mischievous boy and a beautiful daughter or even two boys and two or even three girls, so that everyone should know that he had really lived and existed and had not passed over the earth like a shadow or a phantom, so that he shouldn't feel that he had let his country down. It also occurred to him just then that it would not be a bad idea to ob-tain a higher rank, such as the rank of State Councillor, for instance, a highly respected and honoured rank. … All sorts of ideas occur to a man during his walks, so that he is often carried away from the boring present, things that disturb, tease, and stir the imagination and give him pleasure even if he knows they will never come to pass!

Chichikov's servants also liked the village. Like him they felt at home in it. Petrushka soon got very friendly with Grigory, the pantry-boy, though at first they showed off to one another and gave themselves insufferable airs. Petrushka tried to impress Grigory with having been in all sorts of places, but Grigory at once floored him with Petersburg, a place Petrushka had never visited. Petrushka wished to recover his prestige by telling him of the great remoteness of the places he had been to, but Grigory mentioned a place which could not be found on any map and counted up journeys of twenty-five thousand miles, which made Chichikov's footman gape foolishly and he was made a laughing stock of by all the servants. It all ended in their becoming close friends, however. At one end of the village Bald Pimen, who was called Uncle by all the peasants, kept a pub, the name of which was Akulka. In that establishment they could be seen at all hours of the day. There they became *habitués* or what is known as 'regulars'.

Selifan had something else that made the place congenial to him. Every evening there was singing in the village and they kept weaving in and out in all sorts of spring country dances. Strong, well-built country wenches, such as one does not often find now in large villages, made him stand gaping for hours. It was hard to say which was the fairest; they were all white breasted and white throated, they all had eyes like turnips, languishing eyes – they moved like peacocks and their plaits reached to their waists. When he took hold of their beautiful hands and slowly moved with them in the round dance, or when in a row with other village lads he advanced like a wall on them and the loud-voiced girls, also advancing on the lads like a wall, sang out smiling: 'Boyars, show us the bridegroom!' and the dusk slowly descended on the countryside all around and the echo of the song came back like a sad refrain from far beyond the river, Selifan did not know himself what was happening to him. Awake or asleep, in the morning or at dusk, he kept imagining that he was still holding the beautiful hands of the girls and moving round with them in the dance. With a wave of the hand he would say: 'The damned girls won't leave me alone!'

Chichikov's horses also liked their new home. Both the shaft horse and the Assessor as well as the dapple-grey found their life on Tentetnikov's estate anything but dull. The oats were excellent and the stables quite unusually comfortable: each of them had a separate stall, and though it was partitioned off, it was possible to see other horses over the partitions, so that if any of them, even the one in the remotest corner of the stable, took it into his head to neigh, he could be paid back in the same coin immediately.

In short, they all felt at home. As for the business, which made Chichikov travel all over the vast spaces of Russia, that is to say, the dead souls, Chichikov became very cautious and discreet about it.

Even if he had had to deal with complete fools he would not have broached the subject suddenly. Tentetnikov, whatever you might think of him, read books, philosophized, tried to explain to himself all sorts of reasons for everything – why and wherefore? No, it would be best to start the other way round. So he thought. From his frequent talks with the household serfs, he found out, incidentally, that their master used quite often to visit their neighbour the general, that the general had a daughter, and that the master had taken a liking for his daughter and that the daughter reciprocated his feelings, but that afterwards they seemed to have fallen out for some reason and parted. He noticed himself that Tentetnikov was continually drawing with pen and pencil little heads which were remarkably like one another. One day after dinner, turning his silver snuff-box round on its axis as usual, he spoke as follows:

'You've got everything, my dear fellow, only one thing's lacking.'

'What?' Tentetnikov asked, puffing out a ring of smoke.

'A partner to share your life,' said Chichikov.

Tentetnikov made no answer. That was the end of the conversation.

Chichikov was in no way disconcerted and he chose another moment, this time before supper and, after talking of this and that, said suddenly:

'Honestly, my dear fellow, it would not be a bad thing at all if you got married.'

But Tentetnikov said not a word in reply, just as though the very mention of the subject was distasteful to him.

Chichikov was not one whit disconcerted. For the third time he chose an opportune moment, this time after supper, and he spoke as follows:

'All the same, my dear fellow, the more I consider the circumstances of your life, the more I can see that you simply must get married. Otherwise you will fall into hypochondria.'

Either Chichikov's words were this time very convincing, or Tentetnikov's mood that day was particularly predisposed towards frankness – he heaved a sigh and said, blowing tobacco smoke into the air:

'You have to be born lucky for everything, my dear sir,' and he told him the whole story of his acquaintance with the general and the reason for their rupture.

When Chichikov heard of the affair, word for word, and saw that the whole quarrel arose out of a familiar form of address, he was dumbfounded. For a minute he stared intently at Tentetnikov's face, wondering what to think of him; whether he was a complete idiot or whether he was only a bit of a fool and at last –

'My dear sir,' he said, gripping both his hands, 'what kind of an insult is that? What is there so insulting about addressing you familiarly?'

'There's nothing insulting about it. It wasn't so much the words as the tone of voice in which they were spoken. What he meant was: "Remember that you're trash. I receive you only because there's no one better, but now that Princess Yuzyakin is here you'd better know your place and stand at the door." That's what it meant,' and as the mild and gentle Tentetnikov said this his eyes flashed and there was a note of irritation and resentment in his voice.

'Why,' said Chichikov, 'even if he said it in that sense, what does it matter?'

'What does it matter? Do you mean to say that I ought to go on visiting him after such an action?'

'What kind of action?' Chichikov said coolly. 'It's not an action at all.'

'Not an action?' Tentetnikov asked in astonishment.

'It's not an action, it's merely a general's habit. They speak like this to everyone, and, besides, why not allow some honourable and distinguished man to do it?'

'That's a different matter,' said Tentetnikov. 'If he were an old man, a poor man, a man who was not proud or boastful, not a general, I'd allow him to talk to me like this and indeed would have accepted it with respect.'

'Oh, he's a perfect idiot,' thought Chichikov to himself. 'He'd allow a beggar to say it, but not a general!'

'All right,' he said aloud, 'suppose he did insult you. But you were quits with him. He was rude to you and you were rude to him. But to quarrel like that without regard to your personal affairs, that, if you don't mind my saying so, is something I – I mean, if you've once decided to get something, then you must stop at nothing. What do you care if a man is rude to you. A man is rude to others too. He's always rude to people. He is made like that. Why, I defy you to find any man in the world who isn't rude to people today!'

'What a strange fellow this Chichikov is!' thought Tentetnikov to himself in perplexity, completely put out by his words.

'What a funny fellow this Tentetnikov is!' Chichikov thought to himself at the same time.

'Look here, my dear fellow,' said Chichikov, 'let me talk to you as to a brother. You don't seem to have had a great deal of experience. Let me arrange this matter for you. I shall go to the general and explain to him that it was all a misunderstanding so far as you were concerned, due to your youth and your ignorance of people and the world.'

'I'm not going to grovel before him,' said Tentetnikov, offended, 'and I can't authorize you to do it on my behalf.'

'I'm not capable of grovelling before anyone,' said Chichikov, offended. 'I'm ready to acknowledge any other mistake I may have made, being only human, but as for grovelling – never! I'm sorry, my dear fellow. I made that proposal in good faith, but I never expected that you would interpret my words in such an offensive way.' All this was said with an expression of great dignity.

'I'm sorry,' Tentetnikov said hastily, feeling touched and seizing Chichikov's hands in his. 'I never intended to offend you. I swear I value your kind sympathy highly, but let's drop the subject. Don't let us speak of it again.'

'In that case, I shall call on the general, anyway.'

'Why?' asked Tentetnikov, looking bewildered at Chichikov.

'To pay him my respects,' said Chichikov.

'What a curious man this Chichikov is,' thought Tentetnikov.

'What a curious man this Tentetnikov is,' thought Chichikov.

'I shall go to see him tomorrow, about ten o'clock tomorrow morning,' said Chichikov. 'I think the sooner one pays one's respects, the better. As my carriage is not yet in a fit state, I'd be glad if you would let me have your carriage.'

'Good Lord, what a thing to ask. Everything here is at your disposal: my carriage and everything else.'

After this conversation, they said good night and went to bed, not without reflecting upon each other's strangeness.

A funny thing, though. Next morning when the carriage was brought round and Chichikov jumped into it with the agility of a young army officer, wearing his new dress-coat, a white tie, and waistcoat, and drove off to pay his respects to the general, Tentetnikov was thrown into a state of agitation such as he had not experienced for a long time. The whole rusty and drowsy trend of his thoughts grew restless and excited. The sluggard, whose feelings had hitherto been plunged in careless sloth, was suddenly possessed by a feeling of nervous agitation. One moment he sat down on the sofa, then got up and walked to the window, then he took up a book, or tried to think. But it was all in vain. Thoughts would not come into his head. He tried not to think, but that too was in vain, for fragments of something like thoughts, the bits and pieces of thoughts, came creeping into his head from all directions: 'What a strange condition,' he said to himself, moving nearer to the window. He looked out on the road which cut across the oak wood, at the end of which the dust raised by Chichikov's carriage was still swirling in the air. But let us leave Tentetnikov and follow Chichikov.

Chapter 2

In just over half an hour the excellent horses transported Chichikov over the seven miles, at first through an oakwood, then past corn-fields just beginning to turn green in the midst of the freshly ploughed land, then along the crest of a hill from which fresh views over the distant plains came into sight every minute, then along a wide avenue of lime-trees, whose leaves were only just beginning to open up, which brought him straight into the middle of the village. There the avenue of lime-trees took a turning to the right and, transformed into a drive of long oval-shaped poplars, protected at the base by wicker boxes, ended in wrought-iron gates, through which could be seen the ornately magnificent façade of the general's house supported by eight Corinthian columns. Everywhere there was a smell of oil paint with which everything was continually renewed and nothing was allowed to deteriorate. The yard was as clean as a parquet floor. Chichikov got out of the carriage with a feeling of respect, asked to be announced to the general, and was shown straight into his study. The general impressed him by his majestic appearance. He wore a quilted satin dress-ing-gown of a gorgeous purple colour. A candid look, a manly face, moustaches, and large grizzled whiskers, his hair at the back closely cropped, his neck thick, a neck of three stories, as it is called, that is, in three folds of fat with a crease across the middle of it; in short, he was one of those picturesque generals, who were so plentiful in the famous year of 1812. General Betrishchev, like most of us, possessed a great number of good qualities as well as a great number of bad ones. As is usual with Russians, both were mixed up in a sort of picturesque disorder. In critical moments – magnanimity, bravery, boundless generosity, and intelligence in everything he did, but, mixed up with this, capriciousness, ambition, vanity, and all other petty characteris-tics which no Russian leading a life of idleness is complete without. He did not like those who rose above him in the service and he spoke of them in biting, sardonic epigrams; the man he attacked most of all was a former colleague whom he regarded as inferior to himself in intel-ligence and abilities and who nevertheless had got ahead of him and had held two appointments as governor-general in the provinces in which, as though on purpose, General Betrishchev had his estates so that he was in a way dependent on him. By way of revenge, he taunted him at every favourable opportunity, criticized every order he was responsible for, and saw only the height of absurdity in all his measures and actions. Everything about him was somehow peculiar, beginning with education of which he was a champion and a zealot; he liked to show-off, he liked to know what others did not know, and he did not like people who knew something he did not know; in short, he loved to boast a little of his intelligence. Though his education had been half foreign, he was at the same time anxious to play the part of a grand Russian gentleman. And it is not surprising that with this unevenness of character and with such great and glaring contradictions, he was inevitably bound to meet with a great deal of unpleasantness in the service and had retired as a result of it, putting the blame on some hostile party and lacking the magnanimity to blame himself for anything. In retirement he preserved the same picturesque, majestic deportment. Whether he was wearing a frock-coat, a dress-coat, or a dressing-gown, he was always the same. Everything about him, from his voice to his slightest movement, was commanding, dominating, and inspired in those of inferior rank awe if not respect.

Chichikov felt both respect and awe. Bending his head respectfully to one side and spreading his hands, as though he were about to pick up a tray of cups, he bowed with astonishing deftness and said:

'I thought it my duty, sir, to pay my compliments to your Excellency, having the greatest respect for the magnificent exploits of the men who've saved our country on the field of battle. I considered it my duty, sir, to present myself in person to your Excellency.'

This kind of approach was quite evidently not entirely displeasing to the general. With a gracious inclination of the head he said: 'Very glad to meet you, sir. Please take a seat. Where have you served?'

'My career in the service, sir,' said Chichikov sitting down not in the middle of the armchair but on the edge of it, and gripping one arm with his hand, 'began at the Treasury. I held various other posts afterwards: I have served in the law courts and on a building commission and in the Customs and Excise. My life, sir, can be likened to a ship on a stormy sea. I was, so to speak, swaddled in patience, sir,

and indeed, if I may say so, sir, I'm the personification of patience. ...
And what I have had to put up with from my enemies, sir, who have
even attempted my life, neither words nor colours, nor even, so to
speak, a painter's brush could depict, so that I am now reduced to
looking for a peaceful spot where to spend the remnant of my days.
For the time being, I am staying with a neighbour of yours, your
Excellency. ...'

'Oh? And who is it?'

'Tentetnikov, sir.'

The general frowned.

'He is very sorry, sir, for having failed to show the respect due to –
er –'

'To what?'

'To your great merits, sir. He can't find words. He said to me: "If
only I could in some way" – er – "for," he says, "I do know how to
appreciate the great men who have saved our country."'

'Good Lord, what is he so upset about? I'm not angry with him,'
said the general, mollified. 'I'm very fond of him at heart and I'm
sure that he'll become a most useful person in time.'

'You couldn't have put it better, sir. Yes, indeed, a most useful person. He has the gift of words and he can write, too.'

'Write? Not some nonsense, I hope. Not scribbling verses, is he?'

'Why, no, sir, not nonsense. He's writing something of real importance. He – er – he's writing – er – a history, sir.'

'A history? A history of what?'

'A history ...' At this point Chichikov paused and either because
there was a general sitting before him or simply to give more importance to the subject, he added: 'A history of generals, sir.'

'Of generals? What generals?'

'Of generals in general, sir. I mean, of generals of our country.'

Chichikov was completely confused and embarrassed. He almost
spat, and thought to himself: 'Good Lord, what a lot of nonsense I'm
talking.'

'I'm sorry, but I don't quite understand. Is it a history of some
period or separate biographies? And does it deal with all of them or
only with those who took an active part in the campaign of 1812?'

'Exactly, sir. Of those who took part in the campaign of 1812.' As
he said this, Chichikov thought to himself: 'I'm hanged if I know
what I'm talking about.'

'Then why doesn't he come to me? I could supply him with a great deal of highly interesting material.'

'He's afraid, sir.'

'Afraid? What nonsense! Just because of some silly word that passed between us. ... Why, I'm not that sort of person at all, sir. I'm quite ready to call on him myself.'

'He wouldn't dream of letting you do that, sir,' said Chichikov, sitting up in his chair and feeling much more encouraged. 'What a piece of good luck,' he thought to himself. 'The generals certainly have come in handy, though they just slipped out without thinking.'

There was a rustling sound in the study. The carved walnut door of a closet opened by itself and on the other side of it a living figure appeared, clutching with her hand at the brass door-knob. If a transparent picture had suddenly been lit up from behind by lamps, it would not have caused such surprise by its unexpected appearance as that figure which seemed to have appeared for the sole purpose of lighting the room. It was as if a ray of sunshine had flown into the room with her, as if the frowning general's study had burst into laughter. At first Chichikov did not realize what exactly was standing before him. It was difficult to say in what country she was born. Such pure and noble features could not have been found anywhere, except perhaps on some old cameos: straight and light as an arrow, she seemed to tower over everything. But that was an illusion. She was not at all tall. It was due to the exceptionally harmonious symmetry of all the parts of her body. Her dress fitted her so well that it seemed as though the best dressmakers had consulted among themselves how to dress her in the best possible way. But that too was an illusion. She made her own dresses; a piece of uncut material was caught up in two or three places by a needle and it seemed to hang and drape round her in such folds and pleats that, if she were to be painted in it, all the young ladies dressed in the latest fashion would have appeared like rag dolls, something out of a junk shop. And if she were to be chiselled in marble with all her folds and pleats clinging round her body, she would have been pronounced a copy of the work of some sculptor of genius.

'Let me introduce you to my spoilt darling,' said the general, turning to Chichikov. 'But I'm afraid, sir, I don't know your surname or your Christian name or your patronymic.'

'Is there any need to know the name and patronymic of a man who has not distinguished himself by any deeds of valour?' Chichikov said modestly, bending his head to one side.

'But, all the same, sir, one ought to know it.'

'Pavel Ivanovich, your Excellency,' said Chichikov bowing almost with the smartness of an army officer, and skipping back with the lightness of an india-rubber ball.

'Ulinka,' said the general, addressing his daughter, 'Pavel Ivanovich has just told me a very interesting piece of news. Our neighbour Tentetnikov is not quite as stupid as we thought. He is engaged on a rather important work, a history of the generals of the campaign of 1812.'

'But who thought he was stupid?' she said quickly. 'Perhaps only Vishnepokromov, whom you trust, although he is an empty-headed and contemptible person.'

'Why contemptible? True enough, he's not very clever.'

'He's mean and disgusting as well as not very clever,' Ulinka said. 'Anyone who has treated his brothers as badly as he and turned his sister out of the house is a disgusting person.'

'But that is only talk.'

'People wouldn't say such things if there wasn't anything in it. I can't understand, father, how a man with a heart of gold like yours, a man as kind as you, can go on receiving a man who's the very opposite of you and who you know yourself is a bad character.'

'You see,' said the general to Chichikov with a laugh, 'that's how we always go on arguing with one another,' and turning to his daughter he went on: 'You don't expect me to kick him out, do you?'

'Why kick him out? But why be so nice to him? Why like him?'

At this point Chichikov thought it his duty to put in a word of his own.

'Everyone wants to be liked, my dear young lady,' said Chichikov. 'You can't do anything about it. Even an animal likes to be stroked. It will poke its muzzle out of a stall for you – here, stroke me, please.'

The general laughed.

'Yes, yes, it will poke out its muzzle, as though to say, Stroke me! Stroke me! Ha, ha, ha! The fellow's face is not only covered all over with soot but, as they say, he demands encouragement too, ha, ha, ha, ha!' And the general's body began to rock with laughter, his shoulders that once carried thick epaulettes shaking as if even now they were carrying them.

Chichikov also burst out laughing, but out of respect for the general, he used the letter *e*: 'Heh, heh, heh, heh!' And his body too began to rock with laughter, though his shoulders did not shake because they had never worn heavy epaulettes.

'He'd rob and clean out the Treasury and he'd expect to be rewarded for it, too, the dirty rogue. You can't carry on without encouragement, he'd say. I've worked so hard. ... Ha, ha, ha, ha!'

A painful expression appeared on the noble, sweet face of the girl.

'Oh, daddy, I can't understand how you can laugh. Such acts of dishonesty merely depress me and that's all. Whenever I see an act of dishonesty being perpetrated in the sight of all and those responsible for it escaping universal contempt, I don't know what happens to me. I grow vicious and even ugly. I think and think ...' And she nearly burst out crying.

'Now, please, do not be angry with us,' said the general. 'We've nothing to do with it, isn't that so?' he said turning to Chichikov. 'Come, give me a kiss and go back to your room. I shall be dressing for dinner presently. You, sir,' he said, looking him straight in the face, 'will dine with me, of course?'

'If only your – er – your Excellency ...'

'Without ceremony, please. Thank God, I can still afford to feed my guests. There's plenty of cabbage soup.'

Spreading out his arms very smartly, Chichikov bowed his head with such respect and gratitude that for a moment everything in the room disappeared from his sight and he could only see the tips of his own shoes. When, after remaining in that respectful attitude for a little while, he raised his head again he did not see Ulinka. She had vanished. In her place a giant of a valet had appeared with thick moustaches and whiskers, holding a silver ewer and basin his hands.

'You don't mind my dressing in your presence, do you?' said the general.

'Your Excellency may not only dress, you may do anything you like in my presence.'

Slipping off his dressing-gown and rolling up the sleeves of his shirt over his athletic arms, the general began to wash himself, splashing and snorting like a duck. Soapy water was flying all over the place.

'Yes, yes, they all love to be encouraged,' he said, drying his neck. 'Stroke him, stroke him! You see, he won't even steal without encouragement! Ha, ha, ha, ha!'

Chichikov was in quite extraordinarily good spirits. Suddenly he had an inspiration. 'The general,' he thought to himself, 'is a merry, kind-hearted fellow. Why not try?' And seeing that the valet had gone out with the wash basin, he cried:

'Since your Excellency is so kind and considerate to everyone, I'd like to ask you a great favour.'

'What is it?'

Chichikov looked round him.

'I have an uncle, sir, a very decrepit old man. He owns three hundred souls and about seven thousand acres of land and I'm his only heir. He is too old to manage the estate by himself, but he won't let me do it, either. And this is the strange reason he gives for it: "I don't know my nephew," he says, "he may be a wastrel. Let him prove that he is a reliable fellow. Let him get three hundred souls, then I'll let him have my three hundred, too."'

'Why,' said the general, 'he seems to be an utter fool of a man.'

'I shouldn't mind that, sir. He can stay a fool for all I care. But think of my position, sir. You see, sir, the old fool has got himself a house-keeper and that housekeeper has children. If I don't do something, he'll leave everything to them.'

'The silly old man has lost his senses. That's all there is to it,' said the general. 'But – but – I'm afraid I don't see how I can help you.'

'What I thought of, sir, was this: if you were to transfer to me all your dead souls just as if they were alive, I mean, the peasants who died after the last census, and if we concluded a deed of purchase, I'd show it to the old man and he'd let me have my inheritance.'

At this the general burst into a roar of laughter such as no one has ever laughed before. He collapsed in an armchair just as he was, threw back his head, and almost choked. The whole house was alarmed. His valet appeared, his daughter ran into the room looking frightened.

'Father, what's the matter?' she said in alarm, looking at him in bewilderment, but the general could not utter a sound for a long time.

'It's nothing, my dear, nothing. Go back to your room. We shall come in to dinner in a moment. Don't worry, my dear. Ha, ha, ha, ha!'

And almost choking several times, the general burst out laughing again with renewed force and could be heard from the entrance hall to the remotest room in the house.

Chichikov began to be alarmed.

'Think of your poor uncle! What a fool he'd look after that, ha, ha, ha! He'll get a lot of corpses instead of living peasants, ha, ha!'

'There he goes again,' Chichikov thought to himself. 'What a hilarious fellow.'

'Ha, ha!' the general went on. 'What an ass! Fancy anyone saying, First get three hundred souls out of the blue and then I'll give you another three hundred. What an ass!'

'A silly ass, your Excellency!'

'And your idea of making the old man a present of dead peasants isn't a bad one at all – ha, ha, ha, ha! I'd give anything in the world to see you hand him over the deed of purchase. Well, what is he like? I mean what does he look like? Is he very old?'

'About eighty.'

'But he can still move about, eh? He's in good health, isn't he? He must be still quite strong and healthy to have a housekeeper living with him.'

'Strong and healthy, sir? He's on his last legs.'

'What a damned fool! He is a damned fool, isn't he?'

'He is a damned fool, your Excellency.'

'But does he still drive about? Still pays social calls, does he? Still on his feet, is he?'

'Yes, sir, but with difficulty.'

'What a damned fool, ha, ha! Still strong enough, though. Still got his teeth?'

'Only two teeth, your Excellency.'

'What an ass! Now, don't be angry with me, my dear fellow. He may be your uncle, but he's an ass all the same.'

'Yes, sir, he's an ass all right. He may be a relative of mine and, of course, I find it embarrassing to admit it, but what's to be done about it?'

Chichikov was lying. He did not find it hard at all to admit it, particularly as he had probably never had an uncle.

'So you will let me have them, sir?'

'Let you have the dead souls? Why, my dear fellow, for such an idea I'd give them to you with the land and the houses thrown in. Take the whole cemetery, if you like, ha, ha, ha, ha! Think of the old man, ha, ha, ha, ha! What a fool you'll make of him, ha, ha, ha!' And the general's laughter went echoing through the general's apartments again.

[*The rest of the chapter is missing in the manuscript.*]

Chapter 3

'I F Colonel Koshkaryov is really mad, it's not at all a bad thing,' said Chichikov when he found himself again in the midst of open fields and wide open spaces, after everything had disappeared and only the firmament and two clouds sailing on one side of it remained. 'You there, Selifan! Are you sure you've found out the way to Colonel Koshkaryov's?'

'I'm sorry, sir, but, you see, I've been so busy looking after the carriage that I had no time. But Petrushka asked the other coachman.'

'What a fool you are, man! I told you not to rely on Petrushka! Petrushka is a block-head. Petrushka is stupid. I expect even now Petrushka is drunk.'

'Why, sir,' said Petrushka, turning half round and looking askance at him, 'it's not such a difficult thing, is it? All you have to do, sir, after going down the hill, I mean, is to drive along by the meadows. That's all there is to it.'

'And I suppose you haven't had another drop in your mouth except hard liquor? A fine fellow, I must say. Astonished all Europe by your handsome looks.' Having said this, Chichikov stroked his chin and thought to himself: 'Lord, what a difference there is between an educated citizen and the physiognomy of a coarse footman.'

In the meantime the carriage began to go downhill. Once more meadows and open country dotted with aspen copses came into view.

Rocking gently on its firm springs, the comfortable carriage went on going down cautiously an almost imperceptible slope and at last rolled on swiftly past the meadows, past the water-mills, rattling thunderously over bridges and swaying gently over the bumpy rough track of a declivity. Chichikov did not feel the slightest jolt when his carriage passed over a little mound or hillock. It was the acme of comfort, not a carriage. There were glimpses of sand in the distance. They drove quickly past willow-bushes, slender alder-trees, and silvery poplars, their twigs brushing Selifan and Petrushka across the face. Petrushka had his cap knocked off almost every minute. The surly servant would jump down from the box, curse the stupid tree and the man who planted it, but he still refused to tie his cap on or even to hold it with his hand, hoping that it was the last time and that it wouldn't happen again. Soon birch-trees and fir-trees joined the other trees, thick brushwood growing at their roots; in the thick grass grew wild blue irises and wild yellow tulips. The impenetrable darkness of the endless forest grew thicker and seemed to be turning into night. But all at once the light glittered from every direction, like bright mirrors. The trees began to thin out, the flashes of light increased, and there in front of them was a lake, a stretch of water of some three miles across; on the other shore of the lake a village of grey timbered peasants' cottages could be seen. There were shouts in the water. Some twenty men up to their waists, shoulders, or necks in water, were dragging a net to the opposite bank. There had been an accident: a big, rotund man, almost as tall as he was broad, looking like a huge water-melon or a barrel, had got entangled in the net, together with the fish. He was in a desperate fix and was shouting at the top of his voice: 'Dennis, you idiot, hand over to Kozma! Kozma, take the end from Dennis! Don't pull so hard, Big Foma – go and join Little Foma. Damn you, I tell you you'll break the net!' The water-melon was not apparently afraid for himself; being so stout, he could not very well drown, however much he tried to plunge, wishing to dive, for the water would have brought him up again; and even if a couple of men had sat on his back, he would have remained floating with them like an obstinate bubble, only groaning a little under them and blowing bubbles out of his nose. But he was very much afraid that the net might break and the fish escape, and that was why he was being dragged inside the net with the fish as well as being secured with ropes by several men on the bank.

'I expect that's Colonel Koshkaryov, sir,' said Selifan.

'Why do you think so?'

'Because, if you don't mind my saying so, sir, his body is whiter than the others and he is also well-covered like a real gentleman, sir.'

Meanwhile, they pulled the entangled gentleman much nearer the shore. Feeling that he could reach the bottom, he stood up and just then caught sight of the carriage which was coming down from the dam with Chichikov sitting in it.

'Have you had your dinner?' the gentleman shouted, coming up to the carriage still entangled in the net with the caught fish, just like a lady's hand in an open-work glove, shielding his eyes with one hand from the sun and holding his other hand a little lower like the Medici Venus stepping out of the bath.

'No, sir,' said Chichikov raising his cap and continuing to bow from the carriage.

'Well, then, thank God for that.'

'Why?' asked Chichikov with curiosity, holding his cap over his head.

'I'll tell you. Throw down the net, Little Foma, and get the sturgeon out of the basin. Hey, Kozma, you idiot, go and help him.'

The two fishermen lifted the head of some sea monster out of a tub.

'Look at the prince! Look at the prince! Must have come in from the river!' shouted the rotund gentleman. 'Drive into the yard, sir. Driver, take the lower road through the kitchen garden. And Big Foma, you idiot, run and take down the hurdle. He'll show you the way. I'll come along presently.'

The long-legged, bare-footed Big Foma ran just as he was in a shirt ahead of the carriage, across the whole village in which each cottage had creels, nets, and scoops made out of willow twigs hanging in front of it: all the peasants there were fishermen. Then he took down a hurdle outside a kitchen garden and the carriage drove through kitchen gardens to a square outside a wooden church. Behind the church in the distance could be seen the roof of the outbuildings of the manor house.

'This Koshkaryov is a bit of an eccentric,' Chichikov thought.

'And here I am!' cried a voice from behind him.

Chichikov looked round. The gentleman was already driving beside him. He had dressed: he was wearing a grass-green nankeen coat, yellow trousers, but he had no cravat round his neck and looked like a Cupid. He was sitting sideways in his trap, which he completely filled. Chichikov was about to say something to him, but the fat man had disappeared. The trap reappeared on the spot where they were pulling out the fish. Once more his voice could be heard: 'Big Foma and Little Foma, Kozma and Dennis!' But when Chichikov drove up to the front steps, the fat gentleman, to his great astonishment, was already on the steps and he received him there in his arms. How he had managed to get ahead of him Chichikov simply could not make out. They exchanged kisses three times, first on one cheek and then on the other, according to the old Russian custom. The gentleman was quite obviously of the old school.

'I've brought you greetings from his Excellency,' said Chichikov.

'From what Excellency?'

'From your relative, from General Alexander Dmitriyevich.'

'Who is this Alexander Dmitriyevich?'

'General Betrishchev,' replied Chichikov with some surprise.

'Don't know him,' the gentleman replied also with surprise.

Chichikov was still more surprised.

'How's that? I hope I have at least the pleasure of addressing Colonel Koshkaryov.'

'No, sir, don't hope that. You haven't arrived at his place but at mine. Pyotr Petrovich Petukh! Petukh, Pyotr Petrovich,' the gentleman added.

Chichikov was dumbfounded.

'How's that?' he asked turning to Selifan and Petrushka, who were also gaping open-mouthed and staring at Petukh, the one sitting on the box and the other standing at the carriage door. 'What have you done, you fools? Didn't I tell you Colonel Koshkaryov's, but this gentleman here is Pyotr Petrovich Petukh!'

'The lads have done excellently,' said Petukh. 'Off with you to the kitchen. You'll be given a glass of vodka there. Unharness the horses and go straight to the servants' quarters.'

'I'm awfully sorry,' said Chichikov. 'What a stupid mistake.'

'It's not a mistake, sir,' said Petukh, taking Chichikov's arm and ushering him into the house. 'First see what the dinner is like and then say whether it's a mistake or not. After you, sir.' They were met by two young men in summer coats, both of them as thin as willow wands and almost a yard taller than their father. 'My sons, sir. High-school boys. They're at home for the holidays. Nicholas, you'd better stay with our guest and you, Alexander, come with me.' Having said this, Petukh disappeared.

Chichikov entered into conversation with Nicholas. Nicholas, it seemed, was likely to turn out to be a bad lot. He told Chichikov at once that there was no point in studying at a provincial high school and that he and his brother wished to go to Petersburg because the provinces were not worth living in.

'I see,' thought Chichikov, 'it'll all end up with pastry-cooks' shops and the boulevards.'

'And what condition,' he asked aloud, 'is your father's estate in?'

'Mortgaged,' the father himself replied, reappearing again in the drawing-room. 'Mortgaged.'

'Bad,' Chichikov thought to himself. 'At that rate there won't be a single estate left soon: I'll have to hurry up.'

'It's a great pity,' he said with an air of regret, 'you were in such a hurry to mortgage it.'

'Oh, I don't know,' said Petukh. 'I'm told it's profitable: everyone is mortgaging his estate now. Why should I be worse than the rest? Besides, I've lived all my life here, so it's about time I tried to see what life in Moscow is like. My sons, too, are persuading me to leave. They want the sort of education that only a capital city can give.'

'The fool, the fool!' thought Chichikov. 'He'll squander all he has and turn his children into spendthrifts, too. He's got a nice estate. The peasants are well off and he's not badly off, either. But as soon as they get their enlightenment in the restaurants and the theatres there, everything will go to rack and ruin. He should have stayed in the country, the poor fish!'

'I know what you're thinking,' said Petukh.

'What?' said Chichikov looking a little embarrassed.

'You're thinking, "He's a fool, he's a fool, this Petukh. He's invited me to dinner and there's no sign of dinner so far." But dinner will soon be ready, my dear sir. It will be ready in less time than it takes a cropped wench to plait her hair.'

'Father, Platon Mikhailovich is coming,' said Alexander, looking out of the window.

'On a bay horse,' Nicholas put in, bending down to the window.

'Where, where?' cried Petukh going up to the window.

'Who is this Platon Mikhailovich?' Chichikov asked.

'A neighbour of ours, Platon Mikhailovich Platonov, an excellent fellow, a very excellent fellow,' Petukh himself replied.

Meanwhile Platonov himself entered the room. He was a handsome man, tall and fair-haired. A big ferocious looking dog called Yarb, with a large muzzle, came in after him, jingling its brass collar.

'Have you dined?' asked the host.

'Yes, I have.'

'Good Lord, man, have you come to make fun of me? What good are you to me after dinner?'

The visitor said with a smile: 'I'm afraid I had nothing at all at dinner if that's any comfort to you: I've no appetite at all.'

'What a catch we've had! You should have seen it. What a huge sturgeon we caught, what huge carp, what crucians!'

'It makes me vexed to talk to you. Why are you always so cheerful?'

'Why on earth be bored?' said their host.

'What do you mean: why be bored? Because one is bored.'

'You don't eat enough, that's the trouble. You'd better try having a proper dinner. You see, they've invented boredom only recently. No one was ever bored in the old days.'

'Don't boast! And don't you try to tell me that you've never been bored yourself.'

'Never. I don't know what it means. I haven't time to be bored. I wake up in the morning and there's the cook to see, dinner has to be ordered, then I have breakfast, and then I have to see my estate agent and then I go fishing and then it's dinner-time. You have hardly time to take a nap after dinner when it's time to see the cook again and order supper. When is there time to be bored?'

All during this conversation Chichikov was scrutinizing the visitor, who astonished him by his quite unusually handsome appearance, his picturesque stature, the freshness of his unwasted youth, the virginal purity of his face unblemished by a single pimple. No passion, no sorrows, nothing remotely resembling excitement and restlessness dared touch his virginal face and leave a wrinkle on it. But at the same time they did not enliven it, either. In spite of the ironic smile which brightened his face occasionally, it wore a sort of somnolent expression.

'If you don't mind my saying so,' said Chichikov, 'I too can't understand how a man of your appearance can possibly be bored. Of course, if you're short of money or, as it sometimes happens, you have enemies, who are ready even to attempt your life ...'

'Believe me,' the handsome visitor interrupted him, 'that for the sake of variety I'd be glad of some kind of trouble or anxiety. I mean, if someone would only make me angry, but I'm afraid even that never happens. I'm bored and that's all there is to it.'

'Haven't you got enough land on your estate? Or a small number of souls?'

'Not at all. My brother and I have over thirty thousand acres of land between us and we own over a thousand peasants.'

'Well, this is strange. I simply can't understand you, sir. But perhaps you've had bad harvests or epidemics? Have a great many of your male serfs died?'

'On the contrary, sir. Everything is in excellent order and my brother is a first-class landowner.'

'And yet you're bored,' said Chichikov, shrugging. 'Can't understand it.'

'Well,' said their host, 'we'll soon rid you of your boredom. Run quickly to the kitchen, Alexander, and tell the cook to send in the fish pies as soon as he can. But where's that loafer Yemelyan and that thief Antoshka? Why aren't they serving the savouries?'

But at that moment the door opened. The loafer Yemelyan and the thief Antoshka came in with table napkins, laid the table, set down a tray with six decanters of various coloured homemade wines, soon a necklace of plates with all sorts of appetizing snacks was formed round the trays and decanters, the servants moved about smartly, bringing in covered plates through which one could hear the sizzling of butter. The loafer Yemelyan and the thief Antoshka were coping excellently with their job; these nicknames were given them only for the sake of encouragement. Petukh was not particularly fond of abuse, he was a kind-hearted man, but a Russian likes spicy words; he needs them as much as a glass of vodka for his digestion. What's to be done about it? Such is his nature. He doesn't like anything without flavour.

The savouries were followed by dinner. At dinner their good-natured host showed himself to be an absolute out-and-out bandit. As soon as he noticed that a guest had only one piece left on his plate he helped him to another, saying as he did so: 'Without a mate neither man nor bird can live in the world.' If the visitor had two pieces on his plate, he helped him to a third, saying, 'Two isn't much of a number is it? God loves a trinity.' If the guest ate all three, he would say: 'Have you ever seen a cart with only three wheels? And who builds a cottage with only three corners?' For four he had another saying, and for five, too.

Chichikov ate almost a dozen slices of something and thought to himself: 'I'm sure our host won't find anything more to say now.' But he was mistaken: without uttering a word Petukh put on his plate a piece of ribs of veal roasted on a spit with the kidneys, and what veal it was!

'I reared that calf on milk for two years. I looked after it as I would after my own son.'

'I'm sorry, but I can't manage any more,' said Chichikov.

'You try it and then say you can't.'

'It won't go in, there's no room.'

'Why, there was no room in the church, either, but as soon as the mayor arrived, they found room for him. And there was such a crush, there wasn't even enough room for an apple to drop. You just try. This piece of veal is the mayor.'

Chichikov tried and, to be sure, the piece of veal was like the mayor. Room was found for it, and yet it did seem there was no more room for anything more.

'Now, why should a man like that want to go to Petersburg or Moscow? Such hospitality will ruin him there completely in three years!' Chichikov, in fact, did not know that even this has now been improved upon: even without hospitality one can now run through a fortune in three months, let alone in three years.

Petukh kept filling their glasses. What his guests did not manage to drink, he gave to his two sons, Alexander and Nicholas, who simply tossed off one glass after another; it was quite obvious what branch of science they would take up on their arrival in the capital. It was not the same with the visitors: they could hardly drag themselves to the veranda and they were only just able to sink into their armchairs. Their host fell asleep as soon as he sank back into his own armchair, an armchair that could easily have held four. His corpulent body, transformed into a blacksmith's bellows, began to emit such sounds through his open mouth and nostrils as could not often be imagined even by a modern composer: there was a drum and a flute and some sort of abrupt, reverberating noise like the barking of dogs.

'Listen to him snoring,' said Platonov.

Chichikov laughed.

'Well, of course, after such a dinner you can hardly be bored, can you? You just fall asleep. Isn't that so?'

'Yes,' said Chichikov, 'I suppose so. But if you will forgive my saying so, I can't understand how one can be bored. There are so many remedies against boredom.'

'What sort of remedies?'

'Why, there are all sorts for a young man. You can dance, you can play some instrument, or else you can get married.'

'To whom?'

'Why, there must be lots of beautiful and rich young ladies in the district.'

'I'm afraid there aren't.'

'Well, look for them in other places. Why not do a little travelling?' And a happy thought flashed suddenly through Chichikov's head. 'Yes,' he said, looking Platonov straight in the face, 'that is an excellent remedy.'

'What remedy?'

'Travelling.'

'Travelling where?'

'Why, if you're free you can come with me,' said Chichikov, and he thought to himself, looking at Platonov: 'A good idea, we could go halves over the expenses and he could pay for any repairs to my carriage.'

'And where are you going?'

'At present I'm travelling not so much on my own business, as on the business of another person. General Betrishchev, a close friend of mine and, if I may say so, my benefactor, asked me to visit some of his relatives. Well, of course, relatives are all very well, but at the same time I admit I'm partly travelling also on my account. For seeing the whirligig of men – say what you like, it's like a living book, a second science.' And having said that, Chichikov thought to himself: 'It really would be an excellent idea. I could make him pay all my expenses, and even make use of his horses while mine could stay behind in his village and fatten up at his expense.'

'Why not do a little travelling?' Platonov was thinking to himself meanwhile. 'I've nothing to do at home. My brother looks after everything as it is, so there would be no disorganization. Why shouldn't I do a bit of travelling?'

'And would you agree,' he said aloud, 'to spend a day or two on our estate? Otherwise my brother wouldn't let me go.'

'With the greatest of pleasure. Three if you like.'

'Well, shake hands on it. We'll go,' Platonov said, growing more animated: 'We'll go.'

They shook hands: 'We'll go!'

'Where, where?' asked their host, waking up and staring at them with wide-open eyes. 'No, my dear sirs, I've ordered the wheels to be taken off your carriage, and your horse, my dear Platonov, is grazing ten miles from here. No, you're going to stay the night here and after an early lunch tomorrow you can go.'

What was there to be done with Petukh? They had to stay. They were however rewarded by a wonderful spring evening. Their host arranged a sail on the river for them. Twelve oarsmen, plying twenty-four oars and singing as they rowed, took them for a sail on the smooth surface of the mirror-like lake. From the lake they sailed into a vast river with sloping banks on each side, passing frequently under ropes stretched across the river for fishing. There was not a ripple on the water; one beautiful prospect after another opened up before them in silence, one copse followed another, beguiling the eye by the infinite variety of ways in which the trees grew; seizing their twenty-four oars all at once, the rowers raised them suddenly in the air and the boat skimmed the glassy surface of the river like a bird. The choir leader, a broad-shouldered fellow, the third one from the tiller, struck up a song in a pure, ringing voice, which seemed to issue from a nightingale's throat. As he began its refrain, five others caught it up, six others joined in and the song flowed on, boundless as Russia. With a start Petukh joined in noisily whenever the choir got tired, and Chichikov himself felt that he was a Russian. Platonov alone thought to himself: 'What's so good about this melancholy song? It only makes you feel more mournful than ever.'

It was dusk when they returned. In the dark the oars struck the water which no longer reflected the sky. In darkness they reached the shore along which camp fires were blazing; the fishermen were cooking a soup of fresh, still quivering ruffs on tripods. Everything was at home; the cattle and domestic fowl had been driven home long ago, and the dust they had raised was laid, and the herdsmen who had driven them were standing at the gates, waiting for their jugs of milk and an invitation to help themselves to some fish soup. In the twilight could be heard the quiet hum of human voices and the barking of dogs from other villages far away. The moon was rising and the darkened countryside began to light up and soon everything was brightly illuminated. Wonderful scenes! But there was no one to admire them. Instead of racing past them on two mettlesome horses, Nicholas and Alexander were dreaming of Moscow, of pastry-cooks' shops and theatres, about which they had been told such a lot by a visiting cadet from Petersburg. Their father was wondering how he might stuff his guests full of food. Platonov was yawning. Chichikov seemed livelier than any of them. 'Oh, dear,' he thought, 'I really must get an estate of my own one of these days!' And his future buxom wife and his brood of little Chichikovs rose up before his mind's eye.

At supper they gorged themselves again. When Chichikov had retired to his bedroom and, getting into bed, felt his stomach: 'A regular drum!' he said. 'No room for any mayor there!' Unfortunately, his host's study was on the other side of the wall. The wall was thin and he could hear every word Petukh uttered. Under the pretext of an early lunch, his host was giving orders to the cook for a real banquet. And the way he was giving his orders would have given an appetite to a dead man.

'Make a four-cornered fish pie,' he was saying, smacking his lips and sucking in his breath. 'In one corner put a sturgeon's cheeks and dried spinal cord, in another put buck-wheat porridge, little mushrooms, onions, soft roes, and brains and something else – well – you know, something nice. ... And see that the crust on one side is well browned and a little less done on the other. And make sure the under part is baked to a turn, so that it's all soaked in juice, so well done that the whole of it, you see, is – I mean, I don't want it to crumble but melt in the mouth like snow, so that one shouldn't even feel it – feel it melting.' As he said this Petukh smacked and sucked his lips.

'Damn him, damn him!' thought Chichikov. 'He won't let me sleep,' and he buried his head in the blanket, so as not to hear anything. But even through the blanket he could hear Petukh saying:

'And as a garnish for the sturgeon, cut a beetroot into little stars and put in some smelts and mushrooms and, you know, a turnip and carrots and kidney beans and something else – you understand, something nice, so that there will be a lot of garnishing. And don't forget to put some ice in the pig's stomach so that it will swell up properly.' Petukh was ordering many more dishes. Chichikov heard him saying repeatedly: 'And see that it's well roasted and baked, and see that it's well basted.' Chichikov fell asleep over some turkey.

Next day the guests gorged themselves so much that Platonov could not ride home. The horse was sent back by one of Petukh's stable boys. They got into the carriage. Platonov's dog with the

311

enormous head followed the carriage lazily; he too had gorged himself.

'This is too much,' said Chichikov as soon as they had driven out of the yard.

'What I can't forgive him is that he isn't bored with it all.'

'If I had an income of seventy thousand roubles a year as you have,' thought Chichikov to himself, 'I'm sure I wouldn't be bored. Now take the contractor Murazov – worth ten millions. Now, that is something!'

'Do you mind if we pay a call on the way? I'd like to say good-bye to my sister and brother-in-law.'

'With the greatest of pleasure,' Chichikov said.

'If you're keen on farming,' Platonov said, 'you'll be interested to know him. You won't find a better farmer. In ten years he has increased the income from his estate from thirty to two hundred thousand.'

'Oh, well, he certainly must be a remarkable man! I would, indeed, be very interested to make his acquaintance. Why, it's – it's – er – what did you say his name was?'

'Kostanjoglo.'

'And his Christian name and patronymic?'

'Konstantin Fyodorovich.'

'Konstantin Fyodorovich Kostanjoglo. Yes, it will be very interesting to meet him. One could learn a lot from such a man.'

Platonov took it upon himself to direct Selifan, which was just as well, for Selifan could hardly sit straight on his box. Petrushka, sitting stiffly on the box, had already twice fallen off it, so that it was finally found necessary to tie him to the box with a rope. 'What a brute!' Chichikov kept repeating to himself.

'Look,' said Platonov, 'that's where his land begins. It looks quite different, doesn't it?'

And, indeed, trees had been planted across a whole field and the trees were all of the same height and as straight as arrows; behind it there was another tree plantation, a little taller and also recently planted; behind them was an old wood, and each wood was taller than the last. Then there was another stretch of plain covered with thick woods, and once more the young woods alternated with the old ones. Three times they drove through these woods as though through the gates of a wall.

'It took him about eight or ten years to grow all that, whereas another landowner would have taken twenty or more.'

'How did he do it?'

'You'd better ask him. He's such an expert agriculturalist that he uses everything up. He knows not only the property of the soil, but also which crops to rotate with which and what trees to grow or plant next to what cereals. Everything with him has to serve three or four purposes. His woods, for instance, are grown not only for timber, but also for providing more moisture for the fields, for helping to manure the soil with leaf-mould, and for giving a certain amount of shade. When there's a drought in the district, his land suffers from no drought. When there are bad harvests all around, his crops are unaffected by them. It's a pity I know so little about these things, for I would have liked to tell you more. He is up to all sorts of tricks. They call him the sorcerer.'

'He really must be a most remarkable man,' thought Chichikov. 'What a shame the young man is so superficial and can't tell me more.'

At last they caught sight of the village. Like a city, it spread over three hills with a multitude of peasants' cottages and each of the hills was crowned by a church, and the whole village was fenced in on all sides by gigantic stacks of corn and hayricks. 'Yes,' thought Chichikov, 'you can see that the landowner who lives here is a real man of property.' The peasant cottages were all strongly built, the village streets were all smooth and well-made; if a cart happened to stand anywhere, it was new and strong. If they saw a peasant, he had an intelligent expression on his face; the cattle was first class; even the pig belonging to a peasant had the air of a nobleman. It was evident that the peasants living here were digging silver with their spades, as the song has it. There were no English parks or lawns with all sorts of fanciful ornaments, but everything was as in the old days: a long avenue stretched from the barns and workshops to the very house of the landowner, so that the landowner could see everything that was going on around him; and to crown all, over the roof of the house there was a glass watch-tower from which the whole countryside for ten miles around could be seen. At the front steps they were met by servants, efficient fellows every one of them, who were quite unlike the drunken Petrushka, though they did not wear frock-coats but Cossack coats of homespun cloth.

The lady of the house came running out on to the front steps herself. She was as fresh as a daisy and as beautiful as a bright sunny day; she was the spitting image of Platonov, with the only difference that she was not as listless as he, but talkative and gay.

'How are you, Platon? I'm so glad you've come. I'm sorry Konstantin is not at home, but he'll be back soon.'

'Where is he?'

'He has some business in the village with some dealers,' she said, showing the guests into a room.

Chichikov examined with interest the house of this extraordinary man who had an income of two hundred thousand roubles, hoping to find in it some indication of its owner's character, just as one can find out from a shell the nature of the oyster or snail which had once lived in it and has left its imprint on it. But he could come to no definite conclusion. The rooms were all very ordinary, almost empty: no frescoes, no pictures, no bronzes, no flowers, no whatnots with porcelain, no books even. In short, everything showed that the main part of the life of the man who lived here was not spent indoors but in the open fields, and that he did not think out his ideas, Sybarite fashion, in a comfortable armchair before a lighted fireplace, but that they occurred to him wherever he happened to be engaged in doing his work, and that as soon as they occurred to him, they were put into action. All that Chichikov noticed in the rooms were the traces of careful feminine housekeeping: clean lime-wood planks were placed on the tables and chairs and the petals of some flowers were piled on them for drying.

'What's all this rubbish on the tables and the chairs?' asked Platonov.

'Rubbish?' replied his sister. 'It's the best remedy against fever. We cured all the peasants with it last year. And those herbs over there are for all sorts of infusions, and those are for jam-making. You're always laughing at our jam-making and pickling of vegetables, but when you eat it you can't help praising it.'

Platon went up to the piano and began to turn over the sheets of music.

'Good Lord,' he said, 'what old stuff it is! Aren't you ashamed of it?'

'I'm sorry, my dear, but I have no time for music. I have an eight-year-old daughter and I have to teach her. To put her into the hands of some foreign governess so that I should have more time myself for music – I'm very sorry, Platon, but I'm not going to do that.'

'What a bore you've become!' said her brother, going up to the window. 'Ah, here he is! Here he comes!' said Platon.

Chichikov too rushed to the window. A man of about forty, active, with a swarthy complexion, in a camel-hair coat, was walking up to the house. He did not seem to be particular about what he wore. He had on a serge cap. On either side of him walked two men of the lower orders, their caps in their hands. They were discussing something with him. One of them was an ordinary peasant and the other a visiting *kulak*, an old fox in a blue Siberian coat. As they stopped near the front steps, their conversation could be heard in the house.

'Now, that's what you'd better do. Buy your freedom from your master. I may help you out with a loan, and you can repay me by working it off later.'

'No, sir, why buy our freedom? We'd rather you took us over. Working for you, we'd learn all sorts of things, for there's no man cleverer than you in the whole world. You see, sir, the trouble is that today it's impossible to be sure of oneself. One glass of the spirits the publicans are selling now is enough to give you such a stomach ache that you feel like drinking whole bucketfuls of water. Before you know where you are, you've spent every penny you had. There's too many temptations, sir. Looks like the devil is in charge of the world, it does. Everything's done to confuse the peasants: tobacco and all sorts of things. What are we to do, sir? We're only human. You can't fight it.'

'Now, look here,' Kostanjoglo said, 'don't you realize that if I took you over you'd still not be free. It's true that you'd get all you want at once – a cow and a horse, but, you see, I demand of my peasants more than anyone else does. Work comes first with me, whether you're working for me or for anyone else is of no importance. I don't allow anyone to lie about. I myself work like an ox and my peasants do the same, for, you see, my dear fellow, I know by experience that if you don't work, all sorts of nonsense comes into your head. So you'd better discuss it all with your villagers and then among yourselves.'

'But we've discussed it already, sir. The old men say the same. After all, sir, every one of your peasants is well off and there must be some good reason for it. Your priests, too, sir, are so kind-hearted.

Our priests, you see, have been taken away and we've no one to bury our dead.'

'All the same, you'd better go and talk it over.'

'Yes, sir.'

'Now, sir, I think you ought to knock your price down a little,' said the visiting *kulak* in the blue Siberian coat, who was walking on the other side of Kostanjoglo.

'I've told you already: I don't like bargaining. I'm not like the landowner you come to on the day he has to pay his mortgage. I know you. You keep lists of all the landowners whose mortgages fall due. There's nothing much to it, is there? I mean, if a landowner is in difficulties, he'll sell you his produce at half price. But what do I want with your money? I don't mind if my produce lies in store for three years: I don't have to pay interest on any mortgage.'

'That is so, sir. But, you see, I only – er – what I mean is that I only want to do business with you in future. It's not a question of being greedy. I could let you have three thousand roubles by way of an advance.'

The *kulak* took out a thick wad of greasy notes from his inside pocket. Kostanjoglo took it very coolly and, without counting, put it into the back pocket of his coat.

'H'm,' thought Chichikov, 'just as though it were a handkerchief.'

Kostanjoglo appeared in the doorway of the drawing-room. Chichikov was struck even more by the swarthiness of his face, the coarseness of his black hair, gone prematurely grey in places, the lively expression of his eyes, and a kind of choleric residue of his passionate southern origin. He was not a pure Russian. He himself did not know where his ancestors had come from. He was not interested in his family tree, being of the opinion that it was useless and certainly no help to farming. He was, indeed, quite convinced that he was a Russian and, besides, he did not know any language but Russian.

Platonov introduced Chichikov. They embraced.

'To shake off my spleen,' said Platonov, 'I've decided to take a trip across various provinces and Mr Chichikov here has been good enough to offer to accompany me.'

'Excellent,' said Kostanjoglo. 'What places,' he went on, addressing Chichikov amiably, 'do you propose to visit?'

'I confess,' said Chichikov inclining his head to one side agreeably, and, at the same time, stroking the arm of his chair, 'that for the moment I'm not travelling on my own business, but for a close friend of mine, General Betrishchev, my benefactor, if I may say so, who has asked me to visit some relatives of his. Now, relations, of course, are all very well, but I'm doing it, if I may say so, for myself, for you see, sir, quite apart from the benefit it may be in the haemor- rhoidal sense, I'd like to see the world, for the whirligig of men is, as it were, a living book and as good as any science.'

'Yes,' said Kostanjoglo, 'it's not a bad idea to have a look at all sorts of places.'

'A most excellent observation, sir. Yes, indeed, it isn't a bad idea at all. You see all sorts of things which you would never have seen and you meet people you would never have met otherwise. I mean, sir, sometimes talking to a man is like being given a gold coin. Take, for instance, the chance I have now of having a talk to you. ... I crave your assistance, sir. Please teach me, teach me, quench my thirst by showing me the truth. I wait for your precious words like manna.'

'But what can I teach you, sir? What?' said Kostanjoglo, looking a little embarrassed. 'I was too poor to get a decent education myself.'

'Wisdom, my dear sir, wisdom! The wisdom of being at the helm of such a difficult ship, if you will forgive the metaphor, as estate management. The wisdom of getting a steady income, of acquiring real and not imaginary property and in this way performing the duty of a citizen and earning the respect of your fellow countrymen.'

'Do you know what?' said Kostanjoglo, looking at him reflec- tively. 'Stay a day or two with me. I'll show you how I'm running my estate and tell you all about it. There's no particular wisdom about it, as you will see.'

'Of course you must stay,' said the lady of the house and turning to her brother added: 'Do stay too, Platon. Why be in such a hurry?'

'I don't mind, I'm sure. What about you, Mr Chichikov?'

'I don't mind, either. I'll stay with the greatest of pleasure. There is one thing, though. A relative of General Betrishchev, a certain Colonel Koshkaryov —'

'But he's mad!'

'Yes, I believe he is. You see, sir, I wouldn't have gone to see him, but General Betrishchev, a close friend of mine and, if I may say so, my benefactor —'

'In that case,' said Kostanjoglo, 'why not go and see him now? He lives not seven miles from here. The trap is all ready. Go and see him at once. You'll be back in time for tea.'

'An excellent idea,' cried Chichikov, picking up his cap.

The trap was brought round and in half an hour he arrived at the colonel's. The whole village was in a jumble: buildings finished and half-finished, heaps of mortar, bricks, and beams thrown about in all the streets. Some of the houses looked like government offices. One was inscribed in golden letters: Depot for Agricultural Implements. On another: Chief Counting House. Others: Committee of Rural Affairs, School of Normal Education for Villagers. In short, there was no knowing what was there.

He found the colonel standing behind the desk of a tall bureau with a pen between his teeth. The colonel received Chichikov with extreme cordiality. In appearance he was the kindest and most considerate of men, he began by telling Chichikov how much it had cost him to bring the estate to the present state of prosperity; he complained with feeling how difficult it was to make the peasants understand the nature of the higher motives which enlightened luxury and the fine arts inspire in man, that he had so far failed to induce the peasant women to wear corsets, while in Germany, where his regiment had been stationed in 1814, the miller's daughter could even play the piano, and that, in spite of the obstinate resistance on the part of ignorance, he was sure that he would not fail to achieve a state of affairs in which, while walking behind his plough, a peasant of his village would read a book about Franklin's lightning-conductors, Virgil's Georgics, or some work on the chemical analysis of soils.

'Would he indeed?' thought Chichikov to himself. 'I haven't yet had time to finish reading *The Duchess de la Vallière*.'

The colonel had a great deal more to say about how people were to achieve happiness and prosperity. He attached great importance to dress. He said he'd bet his life that if half of the Russian peasants were dressed in German trousers, the level of culture would rise, trade would improve, and the golden age would dawn in Russia.

Looking at him intently, Chichikov thought to himself: 'I don't think I need stand on ceremony with this fellow,' and he at once told him that he was interested in buying dead souls and explained how the deed of purchase was to be completed and the rest of the necessary formalities.

'As far as I can gather from your words,' said the colonel, without looking in the least put out, 'it's a request, isn't it?'

'Certainly.'

'In that case put it in writing. Your request will go to the Office of Reports and Petitions. Having entered it into a book, the Office will send it over to me. I will send it to the Committee of Rural Affairs and from there, after all the necessary inquiries have been made, it will be sent on to my estate agent. The estate agent together with the secretary ...'

'But, good Lord,' cried Chichikov, 'this could go on for ever. Besides, how am I to put it in writing? It's a sort of business – er – I mean to say, the souls are in a manner of speaking – er – dead ones.'

'Very well, put it down in writing that the souls are in a manner of speaking dead ones.'

'But how can I write – dead? You can't write like that, can you? They may be dead, but the whole point is, you see, that they must appear to be living.'

'Very well,' said the colonel. 'you just put it down like that: "but it is necessary, or it is desirable, or it is advisable that it should appear that they are living". Without paper work you can't do anything. If you want an example look at England, or even at Napoleon himself. I will detail a commissionaire who will conduct you to all the necessary offices.'

He banged on a bell. A man appeared.

'Secretary, will you please call the commissionaire.'

The commissionaire appeared, a sort of blend between a peasant and a civil servant. 'He'll take you to the offices you need most.'

Out of curiosity Chichikov decided to go with the commissionaire and have a look at all those most indispensable offices. The Office for Handing in Reports existed only on the sign-board and its door was closed. Khrulyov, who was in charge of it, had been transferred to the newly established Committee for Rural Buildings. His place had been taken by Berezovsky, the colonel's valet, but he too had been sent somewhere by the Commission of Building. They tried the Department of Rural Affairs, but that seemed to be in the process of alteration; they woke up some drunken peasant, but could get no sense out of him. 'We're all at sixes and sevens here,' said the commissionaire at last to Chichikov. 'Our master is being led by the nose. It is the Committee of Construction that is giving all the orders, taking people away from their work and sending them where they please. The only place you can get something done is the Committee of Construction.' He seemed to be dissatisfied with the Committee of Construction. Chichikov did not want to see anything more, but on returning he told the colonel that everything in his village was in a mess, that it was impossible to get any sense out of anyone and that the Office for Handing in Reports did not exist at all.

The colonel boiled over with righteous indignation and pressed Chichikov's hand warmly in sign of his gratitude. He immediately snatched up a pen and a sheet of paper and wrote down eight severe inquiries: on what grounds did the Committee of Construction without any authorization dispose of officials who did not belong to that department? How could the chief agent permit the representative to go off on an investigation without first giving up his post? And how can the Board of Rural Affairs regard with indifference the fact that the Office for the Handing in of Petitions and Reports did not exist at all?

'Oh, what a mess!' thought Chichikov, and was about to take his leave.

'No, I'm not going to let you go. It's now a question of my self-esteem. I'll prove to you the importance of an organic and correct management of an estate. I will entrust your affair to a man who is worth all the others put together: he has just finished his course at the university. That's the kind of serfs I have. Not to waste your valuable time, will you please wait in my library,' said the colonel, opening a side door. 'Here are books, paper, pens, pencils, everything. Make use of them, make use of everything, you are master here. Education should be available to everyone.'

So spoke Koshkaryov as he led him into the library. It was a vast room, lined with books from top to bottom; there were even stuffed animals there; there were books on every subject: cattle breeding, pig breeding, gardening; specialist journals on every subject which are only sent to subscribers, though no one ever reads them. Seeing that they were all books that were not meant for light reading, Chichikov turned to another bookcase. But it was from the frying pan into the fire: they were all books on philosophy. Six enormous volumes caught his eyes. They were entitled: *A Preliminary Introduction into the Field of Reasoning, The Theory of Generality, Totality, and Essentiality and its Application to the Interpretation of the Organic Principles of the*

Mutual Bifurcation of Social Productivity. Whatever page Chichikov happened to open, he found such words as 'manifestation', 'development', 'abstract', 'occlusion', 'conclusion', and the devil only knows what. 'That's not my cup of tea,' said Chichikov and turned to the third bookcase, where all the books dealt with the arts. Here he pulled out a huge volume with immodest mythological pictures and began examining them. Pictures of that sort give pleasure to middle-aged bachelors and sometimes also to decrepit old men excited by ballets and other spicy entertainments. When he had finished looking through this book, Chichikov was about to pull out another book of the same kind when Colonel Koshkaryov appeared with a paper in his hands.

'All's done and done most admirably. The man I mentioned to you is absolutely a genius. For this I'll promote him above all the others and put him in charge of a whole department. Just look what a clear head he has and how he found a solution to your problem in a couple of minutes.'

'Well, thank God for that!' thought Chichikov and settled down to listen. The colonel began to read:

'Having carefully considered the commission entrusted to me by you, sir, I have the honour to report as follows:

'1. The petition of the Collegiate Councillor and Cavalier, Pavel Ivanovich Chichikov, is based on a misunderstanding, for he has erroneously described the souls on the census as dead. It is to be assumed that he probably meant those who are on the point of death rather than those who are dead. And, indeed, this same description already shows that the gentleman has obtained an empirical education which must have gone no farther than the parish school, for the soul is immortal.'

'The rogue!' Koshkaryov said with a self-satisfied smile, as he interrupted his reading. 'Here he has a go at you a little. But you must admit he wields a clever pen!'

'2. There are no unmortgaged souls on the estate either on the point of death or any others, for all of them have without exception not only been already mortgaged, but have been mortgaged twice over for an additional hundred and fifty roubles a soul, with the exception of those to be found in the small village of Gurmaylovka, the ownership of which is being contested in the courts by the landowner Predishchev, who, as a result, has obtained an injunction from the courts, as stated in a notice published in No. 42 of the *Moscow News*.'

'Then why didn't you tell me about it before?' Chichikov said angrily. 'Why did you keep me here wasting my time on all sorts of trifles?'

'But, my dear sir, it was necessary that you should see it all put down in writing. Anyone could have told you that; even a fool is able to grasp something unconsciously, but one has to see it all consciously.'

Chichikov grabbed his hat and, without concealing his anger, rushed out of the house, regardless of all the rules of propriety. He was furious. The coachman had the trap ready for him, knowing that it was no use unharnessing the horses since one had first to send in an application for their oats and the decision would only be made the following day. Rude and uncivil as Chichikov was, the colonel was extraordinarily courteous and considerate. He shook his hand warmly and pressed it to his heart, and thanked him for having given him an opportunity for seeing the working of his system in practice. He added that he would have to give them a severe talking to otherwise they were all liable to fall asleep and the springs of his administrative system might rust and grow weak. As a result of Chichikov's visit, he concluded, a happy thought had just occurred to him, to wit, to establish a new commission which would be called the Commission for Supervision of the Committee of Construction, so that then no one would dare to steal.

Chichikov arrived angry and dissatisfied. It was late and the candles had been lit for some time.

'Why are you so late?' asked Kostanjoglo, when he appeared in the doorway.

'What have you been discussing with him for so long?' said Platonov.

'I've never met a fool like that in all my life,' said Chichikov.

'That's nothing,' said Kostanjoglo. 'Koshkaryov is a comforting phenomenon. He is necessary, because all the stupidities of all our clever fellows are caricatured and reflected in him and therefore become more apparent to us. I'm referring to all those clever fellows who, without first acquiring a thorough knowledge of the state of affairs in their own country, pick up all sorts of nonsense abroad. Look at the new type of landowner we've got nowadays. Starting up offices and factories, schools, committees, and goodness only knows what. That's the kind of clever fellow they are. They've only just recovered from the French invasion of 1812 and they're beginning to upset everything again. Why, they've done more damage to our country than the French, so that today even some Pyotr Petrovich Petukh is a good landowner.'

'But he too has mortgaged his estate.'

'Why, of course, he's mortgaged everything and everything he has will be mortgaged.'

As he said this, Kostanjoglo began to show signs of anger.

'They've started up factories for making hats and candles,' he went on, 'brought expert candle-makers from London, turned themselves into cheap tradesmen. A landowner's is an honourable calling and now they've become manufacturers and factory owners. Spinning machines – muslin dresses for town sluts, for prostitutes.'

'But you've got factories, too, haven't you?' Platonov observed.

'But who started them? They started themselves. The wool accumulated, I couldn't get rid of it, so I began weaving cloth. Thick, plain cloth. It is sold cheaply in the local markets. The peasants need them. My peasants. For six years the traders have been dumping fish refuse on my bank of the river. Well, what was I to do with it? I began making glue and I got thirty thousand for it. Everything is like that with me, you see.'

'What a devil,' thought Chichikov, staring open-eyed at him. 'What a paw for raking in money.'

'And why did I set up these factories? Because, if I had not, thousands of workmen would have died of hunger. It was a year of famine, all thanks to those factory owners who had neglected their crops. I've lots of such factories, my dear fellow. Every year a new factory, depending on the accumulation of all sorts of refuse and waste. If you look more closely at your estate you will find that every bit of rubbish can provide you with a good income. So much so that you try to get rid of it. You say to yourself, I don't want it. But then, you see, I don't build palaces with columns and pediments.'

'That's amazing, but what I find most amazing is that every bit of rubbish yields a profit!' said Chichikov.

'Why, of course, provided you take things as they are. But today everyone is a mechanic, everyone tries to open the casket with some kind of complicated instrument but, as in Krylov's fable, all you have to do is to lift its lid. He'd go off specially to England for that purpose, the idiot!' As he said this, Kostanjoglo spat. 'And the trouble is that on his return from abroad he'd be a hundred times more stupid.'

'Oh, dear,' his wife said uneasily, 'you're angry again, Konstantin. You know it's bad for you.'

'But how can I help being angry? It's not as if it were something that did not concern me. I have a personal interest in all this. You see, I can't help feeling annoyed that the Russian character is getting spoilt. You see, a quixotic element has now appeared in the Russian which he never had before. if education becomes his fad, he becomes a Don Quixote of education, he will found schools such as no fool would ever dream of founding. The man who goes through such a school will be good for nothing, he'll be fit neither for the city nor the village, he'll turn into a drunkard who is full of his own importance. If philanthropy becomes his fad, he will become a Don Quixote of philanthropy and he will spend a million roubles on building all sorts of ridiculous hospitals and other institutions, great edifices with columns, and then he'll go bankrupt and his patients will have to go begging: that's philanthropy for you!'

But Chichikov was not interested in education. All he wanted to find out was how every sort of rubbish could yield a profit. But Kostanjoglo did not give him a chance to put in a word. Bitter speeches poured out of his mouth and he could contain himself no longer.

'They're thinking of turning the peasant into an educated man. Why, first of all they should make him a good and prosperous farmer and then he'll learn all that is necessary for him to know. You can't imagine how stupid the whole world has grown nowadays. The things these scribblers write! Some greenhorn publishes a book and everyone is anxious to read it. This is the sort of thing they are saying now: "The peasant leads too simple a life. He must be introduced to articles of luxury and be made to realize the need to possess things he can't afford ..." They don't seem to realize that it is because of these luxuries that they themselves have become trash and not men, have contracted goodness knows what horrible diseases, and that there isn't an eighteen-year-old boy who has not experienced everything: his teeth have dropped out and he is already as bald as a billiard ball – and so they want the peasants too to be infected. Why, thank God, there's still at least one healthy class of society left which knows nothing of these sophisticated fads! We ought to thank God for that. Yes, the man who tills the land is more worthy of respect than any. Why then interfere with him? The Lord grant we may all be tillers of the soil.'

'So you think, sir, that agriculture is the most profitable occupation?' asked Chichikov.

'It's the most righteous, which of course is not the same thing as the most profitable. "In the sweat of thy face shalt thou eat bread", it is written. It's no use being too clever about it. The experience of ages has shown that a man who works on the land is purer, nobler, higher, and more moral. I don't say that people should not do anything else, but that agriculture should be at the basis of everything. That's my idea. The factories will come into being by themselves and those factories will be legitimate, for they will be supplying people with the necessities they need on the spot and not with all sorts of things that have led to the degeneration of modern man. Not the kind of factories that stimulate supply and demand by using all sorts of despicable means and deprave and corrupt the unfortunate peasants. You can say what you like in their favour, but I shall never set up any of those manufactures which are meant to stimulate their so-called higher needs, such as tobacco or sugar, even if it means a loss of a million to me. If the world is heading for corruption and depravity, it is not going to be with my assistance! Let me at least be blameless before God. ... I've been living for twenty years among the peasants and I know what the consequences of this would be.'

'But what amazes me most of all, sir,' Chichikov said, 'is how, with wise management, you get a profit from all sorts of remainders and left-overs and every kind of waste and rubbish.'

'H'm,' Kostanjoglo went on without listening to him, with an expression of bitter sarcasm on his face. 'Political economists, indeed! Fine political economists they are! One fool sits on top of another fool and uses a third fool as a whip. They don't see farther than their own stupid noses. An ass, a silly ass, and he climbs on to the rostrum in the lecture-room, puts on his spectacles. ... The idiots!' And he spat in his anger.

'You're quite right, dear,' said his wife. 'It's just as you say, only please don't be angry. Can't you talk about these things without losing your temper?'

'Listening to you, my dear Mr Kostanjoglo,' said Chichikov, 'one seems to delve, as it were, into the deeper meaning of life and feel the very core of the whole business. But leaving aside for the moment the universal aspect of things, let me draw your attention to a personal matter. Suppose I were to become a landowner and got the idea of growing rich in a short space of time so that I might, so to say, be able to fulfil my vitally important duty as a citizen, how should I set about it?'

'How set about getting rich?' Kostanjoglo repeated. 'Why, this is how ...'

'Let's go and have supper,' said the lady of the house, and getting up from the sofa, she stepped into the middle of the room, wrapping a shawl round her as if she felt cold.

Chichikov leapt up from his chair almost with the agility of an army officer, offered her his crooked arm, and led her ceremoniously across two rooms to the dining-room, where a soup tureen was already standing on the table and, its cover taken off, spread its pleasant aroma of soup full of fresh greens and the first carrots of spring. They all took their places at the table. The servants promptly set down all the dishes in covered plates and everything else that was required and went out at once. Kostanjoglo did not like his servants to overhear the conversation at the table and still less their standing about and gaping at his mouth while he was eating.

Having finished his soup and drunk a glass of excellent wine that reminded him of Tokay, Chichikov turned to his host and said:

'If you don't mind, sir, I should like to bring you back to the subject of our interrupted conversation. I was asking you to tell me what I have to do and how I should best set to work ...'

[*Two pages of the manuscript are missing here*]

'If he asked forty thousand for the estate I would pay him cash down on the spot.'

'H'm!' Chichikov thought it over. 'Then why,' he asked with some diffidence, 'don't you buy it yourself?'

'Well, sir, one must know how far one can afford to go. I have, as it is, plenty of worries with my own estates. Besides, the nobility here are already raising a clamour against me because they say I'm taking advantage of their difficulties and their ruined position to buy up their land for a song. I'm sick and tired of it, damn them.'

'It is amazing how prone people are to malicious gossip!' said Chichikov.

'In our province particularly. You can't imagine how fond they are of spreading all sorts of scandalous stories. They never call me anything but a skinflint and a miser of the worst kind. They find all sorts of excuses for themselves. "It's quite true," one of them will say, "that I've lost all my money, but that was because I did my best to satisfy the higher needs of life. I encouraged industrialists, that is to say, rogues, and if I hadn't done that, I might have lived like a pig or, in other words, like Kostanjoglo.'

'I'd like to be such a pig!' said Chichikov.

'It's all lies and nonsense, of course. What are these higher needs? Who do they think they are bluffing? One of them may buy a whole library of books, but he never reads them. It all ends in gambling and drunkenness. And it's all because I don't give dinners and I don't lend them money. I don't give dinners because I find them depressing. I'm not used to them. But if anyone cares to come and share my meals, he is welcome. It's nonsense to say that I won't lend money. Let anyone come to me who is really in want, tell me all his circumstances, and explain what he wants my money for, and if I see from his words that he is going to spend it wisely and that my money will really be of benefit to him, I will not refuse him and I will not even charge interest on it.'

'I must keep that in mind,' thought Chichikov.

'I should never refuse him,' Kostanjoglo went on, 'but I'm not going to throw my money down the drain. They will jolly well have to put up with it. Why, damn it all, if one of them wants to give a dinner for his mistress, or is crazy enough to spend a fortune on furnishing his house, or goes with some slut to a fancy-dress ball, or gives a banquet to celebrate the fact that he has led a life of idleness, he can't expect me to lend him money, can he?'

Here Kostanjoglo spat and almost uttered some unseemly swear-words in the presence of his wife. A shadow of gloomy, black melancholy darkened his face. The lines which furrowed his forehead vertically and horizontally showed how deeply moved and angry he was.

'Allow me, my dear sir,' said Chichikov, emptying a glass of raspberry liqueur which really was excellent, 'allow me to bring you back again to the subject of our conversation which we haven't by any means exhausted yet. Suppose I acquired the estate which you were good enough to mention, how long and how soon do you think would it take me to grow as rich as ...'

'If you want to get rich quickly,' Kostanjoglo broke in abruptly and sternly, for he was in a bad humour, 'you will never get rich. But if you want to get rich without thinking of how long it will take you, then you'll get rich quickly.'

'So that's how it is,' said Chichikov.

'Yes, sir,' said Kostanjoglo abruptly as though he was angry with Chichikov himself. 'One must love one's work. Without that you can do nothing. One must love farming – yes, sir! And believe me, it is not at all boring. They've taken it into their heads that life in the country is dull and depressing. Why, I'd die, I'd hang myself from depression, if I had to spend one day in town as they spend it in their stupid clubs, pubs, and theatres. The fools, the stupid idiots, the breed of jackasses! A farmer can't be bored. He has no time to be bored. There's not an inch of emptiness in his life. It is completely full. Think of the diversity of his work and what work! Work that truly exalts the spirit. Say what you like, but in the country man walks hand in hand with nature, with the seasons, he participates and communes with everything that goes on in creation. Have a good look at the annual cycle of works: how even before the coming of spring everything in nature is already on the alert and full of expectancy. The seeds must be got ready, the corn in the barns has to be carefully sorted out, measured, and dried, new rates of taxation have to be fixed. The income and expenditure for the whole year has to be carefully considered and calculated in advance. And as soon as the ice starts breaking up and the high-water level of the rivers has gone down and everything is dry again, the earth begins to be turned over – the spades get busy in the kitchen gardens and the orchards and the ploughs and harrows in the fields: planting and sowing ... Do you understand what it all means? A trifle! It's the next harvest that is being sown! It's the happiness of the entire earth that is being sown! It's the sustenance of millions that is being sown! Summer comes. ... The mowing and haymaking begins. ... Soon harvesting time is upon us; after the rye comes the wheat, then the barley and the oats. The work is in full swing; there is not a moment to be lost; if you had twenty eyes there'd be work for them all. And when all this has been happily accomplished and all the grain has been carted to the threshing floors and stacked, and the winter crops have been sown, and the barns, the threshing barns, and the cow-sheds have been repaired for the winter and the women have completed all their work, and the balance of all of that has been drawn up and you can see what has been done, why, it's ... And winter! there's threshing on all the threshing floors and the carting of the threshed grain from the threshing floors to the barns. You go round the flour-mill and the factories, you have a look at the workshops, you pay a visit to the peasants to see what they are doing. For my part, if a carpenter knows how to wield his axe, I'm ready to stand for a couple of hours watching him: his work gives me such pleasure. And when on top of it you realize that this work is being done with some purpose and that everything around you is multiplying and multiplying, bringing in both fruits and profits, why, I can't tell you what one feels at the time! And not because your money's growing – after all, money's not everything – but because it's all the work of your hands; because you see that you are the cause and the creator of it all, and that, like some magician, you are scattering riches and abundance everywhere. Where could you find any delight to equal it?' said Kostanjoglo, lifting his face from which the wrinkles had suddenly disappeared. Like an emperor on the day of his solemn coronation, he looked transfigured and it seemed as though rays of light were issuing from his face. 'Yes, nowhere in the world will you find anything to equal this delight. It is here, yes, here that man imitates God. God has left the work of creation to himself as one of the highest delights and he asks man also to be a like creator of prosperity all around him. And they call that dull work!'

Chichikov listened with delight to the sweet sound of his host's words like the singing of a bird of paradise. His mouth watered, his eyes grew moist and shone with sweetness, and he could have listened for ever.

'Konstantin, it's time to get up,' said the lady of the house, getting up from her chair.

They all got up. Crooking his arm, Chichikov led the lady of the house back to the drawing-room. But there was not the same adroitness in his movements, for his thoughts were occupied with more important things.

'You can talk as much as you like,' said Platonov, who was walking behind them, 'but it's boring, all the same.'

'Our visitor isn't a stupid man,' thought Kostanjoglo. 'He's measured in his words and he isn't a scribbler, either.' And as he thought this, he became even more cheerful, just as though his own words had warmed him up and he was celebrating the discovery of man who knew how to listen to wise counsel.

When afterwards they had settled down in a comfortable room, lighted by candles, facing the veranda and a glass door leading into the garden, and when they saw the stars twinkling in the sky over the tree-tops of the sleeping garden, Chichikov felt more cosy than he had felt for a long time. It was just as though after long wandering he had been welcomed under the roof of his old home and, to cap it all, had obtained all he had ever desired and, flinging away the pilgrim's staff, said: 'Enough!' Such was the entrancing mood the wise words of his hospitable host had induced in him. There are certain words which are nearer and dearer to a man than any others. And it often happens that in some remote, god-forsaken corner of the country, in some deserted spot, you unexpectedly meet a man whose warming words make you forget yourself and the impassability of the roads and the discomfort of the night's lodgings, the senselessness of the noisy contemporary world, and the deceitfulness of the illusions that lead mankind astray. And an evening spent in that way will be forever imprinted on your mind and your memory will retain everything: who was present and who sat in what place and what was in his hands – the walls, the corners, and every trifle in the room.

So Chichikov too noted everything that evening: the charming and unpretentiously furnished room, the good-natured expression on the face of his wise host, the pattern of the wallpaper, and the pipe with the amber mouthpiece handed to Platonov and the smoke he blew in Yarb's broad face and the way Yarb snorted, and the laugh of the pretty hostess, interrupted by her words: 'There, don't torment him', the gay candles, the cricket in the corner, the french window, and the spring night outside looking in at them from the garden, leaning on the tree-tops, studded with stars and loud with the songs of the nightingales warbling loudly from the depths of the thick green foliage.

'Your words are like sweet honey to me, my dear, dear Mr Kostanjoglo,' said Chichikov. 'I may say that in the whole of Russia I have not met a man equal to you in intelligence.'

Kostanjoglo smiled. He himself felt that Chichikov's words were not unjust.

'No, sir,' he said, 'if you want to know an intelligent man, we really have one who may be called truly intelligent, a man the latchet of whose shoes I am not worthy to unloose.'

'Who could that be?' Chichikov asked with surprise.

'It's Murazov, our government contractor.'

'This is the second time I've heard of him,' cried Chichikov.

'He's a man who could manage not only a landowner's estate, but administer a whole kingdom. If I were the ruler of a state, I'd immediately make him my minister of finance.'

'And I'm told he's a man of quite astonishing abilities. I'm told that he's made ten millions.'

'Ten millions? More than forty, I should think. Soon half of Russia will be in his hands.'

'Good Lord!' cried Chichikov, staring open-mouthed at him.

'Most certainly. It's quite clear. A man who has a few hundred thousand grows rich slowly, but a man who has millions has a greater radius of action: whatever he gets hold of increases two-fold or three-fold. His field of action is so wide. He has no longer any rivals. No one can compete with him. Whatever price he fixes, stands. There is no one who can sell at a higher price.'

'Dear Lord!' said Chichikov, crossing himself. He gazed into Kostanjoglo's face and his breath failed him. 'It's inconceivable! One's mind boggles at the very idea! People are astonished at the wisdom of Providence as they examine a beetle, but to my mind what is more astonishing is the fact that such vast sums can be concentrated in one mortal's hands. May I ask you one thing? Tell me, am I right in thinking that in the first place this was not obtained quite honestly?'

'In the most irreproachable way and by the most fair means.'

'Incredible! I mean, if it were just a case of thousands, but millions! ...'

'On the contrary, it is difficult to obtain thousands honestly, but millions are made easily. A millionaire has no need to resort to crooked ways: he can keep to the straight path and take everything that lies before him. Another man would not be able to pick it up. Not everyone has the strength to do so. But the millionaire has no competitors. His radius of action is vast, I tell you: whatever he gets hold of increases two-fold or three-fold. And what will a few thousands bring in? Ten or twenty percent if you're lucky.'

'What is most incredible is that the whole thing probably began with a few coppers.'

'It's always like that. It's the natural order of things,' said Kostanjoglo. 'He who was born with thousands and brought up on thousands will never make money, for he has formed all sorts of expensive habits and all sorts of other things. One has to start from the beginning and not from the middle, from a copeck and not from a rouble, at the bottom and not at the top. It's only then that one will acquire a thorough knowledge of life and men with whom one will have to deal afterwards. When you have experienced it all in your own person and learned that every copper has to be taken care of before you can treble it, and when you've been through all sorts of trials and tribulations, you will become so schooled in the ways of the world that you will never make a mistake and never come to grief in any enterprise. Believe me, that's the truth. One must start from the beginning and not from the middle. If a man says to me: "Give me a hundred thousand and I'll get rich in no time", I would not believe him: he is counting on chance and not on a certainty. One must begin with a copeck.'

'In that case,' said Chichikov, thinking involuntarily of his dead souls, 'I shall get rich, for I'm really beginning from nothing.'

'Konstantin,' said the lady of the house, 'it's time we gave Mr Chichikov a chance to rest and sleep, and you keep on chattering.'

'I'm quite sure you will get rich,' said Kostanjoglo, taking no notice of his wife. 'Rivers and rivers of gold will flow into your hands. You won't know what to do with your income.'

Chichikov sat spellbound; his thoughts whirling round in a golden world of daydreams and castles in the air. He gave full rein to his imagination which was embroidering golden patterns on the golden carpet of his future profits. And in his ears rang the words: 'Rivers and rivers of gold will flow. ...'

'Really, Konstantin, it's time for Mr Chichikov to go to bed.'

'Why are you so worried? Go to bed if you feel like it,' said their host and stopped short, for at that moment Platonov's loud snoring resounded through the room and after him Yarb snored still more loudly. Realizing that it really was bedtime, he shook Platonov, saying: 'Stop snoring!' and wished Chichikov good night. They all went to their rooms and were soon fast asleep in their beds.

Chichikov alone did not feel like sleeping. His thoughts kept him awake. He kept thinking how to become the owner not of an imaginary but of a real estate. After his conversation with his host everything had become so clear. The possibility of becoming rich seemed so self-evident. The difficult business of estate management now seemed so easy and intelligible and was apparently so well-suited to his own nature. All he had to do was to mortgage the dead souls he had acquired and buy himself an estate that was not imaginary. He already saw himself the real owner of such an estate which he managed just as Kostanjoglo had instructed him: efficiently, carefully, without introducing any new-fangled methods before having made a thorough study of the old ones, looking at everything with his own eyes, getting to know all his peasants, denying himself all superfluities, and devoting himself entirely to work and the management of his estate. He already experienced a foretaste of the pleasure he would feel when everything was running smoothly and all the springs of the household machine were working briskly, keeping everything in motion. The work would be in full-swing, and as in a mill the grain is swiftly ground into flour, so all waste and rubbish would be ground into ready cash. His wonderful host was constantly before his mind's eye. He was the first man in the whole of Russia for whom he felt a personal respect. Till then he had respected people either for their high rank or for their great wealth. He had never respected a man simply because of his intelligence. Kostanjoglo was the first. He realized that Kostanjoglo was not a man to try all sorts of tricks on. He was absorbed in another project – that of buying Khlobuyev's estate. He had ten thousand roubles of his own; and he thought of borrowing fifteen thousand from Kostanjoglo, for Kostanjoglo had declared that he was ready to help anyone wishing to get rich; the rest he would try to get hold of in some way or other, either by mortgaging his dead souls or simply by asking his creditor, that is to say, Khlobuyev, to wait. That, too, was quite feasible, for he would hardly go to court about it. He kept thinking about it for a long time. At last slumber which, as they say, had held all the household in its embrace for the last four hours, took Chichikov too in its embrace. He slept soundly.

Chapter 4

THE next day everything was arranged in the best possible way.
Kostanjoglo was glad to lend him ten thousand roubles without
interest or security, simply upon a signed receipt, so ready was he to
help anyone to acquire a fortune. He took Chichikov on a tour of his
own estate. Everything was so simple and so intelligently managed.
Everything was so organized that it seemed to go by itself. Not a
minute was wasted and not a single case of carelessness could be discovered in the work of any peasant. The landowner, like some
omniscient magician, made him bestir himself instantaneously. There
was no sign of a sluggard anywhere. Even Chichikov could not help
being struck by the fact of how much this man had achieved quietly
and without fuss, without drafting any grandiose projects and
treatises about conferring prosperity upon mankind. And how completely wasted was the life of any city dweller who kept scraping his
feet on parquet floors and paying compliments to women in drawing-
rooms, or of the man who kept dictating all sorts of grandiose projects in his hovel in some remote corner of the country. Chichikov
was terribly excited at the idea of becoming a landowner and he was
getting more and more convinced of its rightness. Moreover, Kostanjoglo not only showed him everything on his own estate, but undertook to accompany him to Khlobuyev's in order to look over his
estate with him. Chichikov was in high spirits. After a substantial
breakfast they set off, all three of them, in Chichikov's carriage;
Kostanjoglo's trap followed them empty. Yarb ran on ahead, chasing the birds off the road. The woods and the arable land belonging to Kostanjoglo stretched for about twelve miles on either side of
the road. They were constantly passing woods alternating with grass
land. Not a single blade of grass was wasted here. Everything looked
like a huge park. But as soon as Khlobuyev's land began, they fell
silent involuntarily: instead of woods, they saw bushes cropped by
cattle, and the rye, smothered with weeds, was barely visible. At last
they caught sight of dilapidated, unfenced peasants' cottages, and in
the midst of them an uninhabited stone house which had not been

completed. The owner, it seemed, had not had enough money for the roof. So it remained covered with thatch which had turned black. The owner of the estate lived in another house which was only of one story. He ran out to meet them in an old frock-coat, dishevelled and in boots that were all in holes. He looked sleepy and down at heel, but there was something good-natured in his face.

He was delighted to see his visitors just as though they were his long lost brothers.

'Konstantin Fyodorovich! Platon Mikhailovich! It is so good of you to come! Let me rub my eyes! I really thought that no one would ever come and see me again. Everyone avoids me like the plague. They all think I'm going to ask them for a loan. Oh, it's a hard life, a hard life, Konstantin Fyodorovich! I realize it's all my own fault, but what is there to be done? I live like a pig. I'm sorry, gentlemen, for receiving you in this attire. My boots, as you see, are all in holes. Will you have a drink?'

'Let's not stand on ceremony,' said Kostanjoglo. 'We've come on business. I've brought you a purchaser, Pavel Ivanovich Chichikov.'

'Very glad to meet you, sir. Let me shake hands with you.'

Chichikov gave him both hands.

'I'd be delighted, my dear Mr Chichikov, to show you over my estate, which is deserving of attention. But first, gentlemen, let me ask you: have you had dinner?'

'We have, we have,' said Kostanjoglo, who was anxious to get on with the business. 'Don't let's waste time. Let's go round the estate now.'

'Yes, let us by all means,' Khlobuyev said, picking up his cap.

The visitors put on their caps and they all set off through the village street. On either side of it were blind hovels with tiny windows stuffed with rags.

'Come and let us inspect my disorder and disgrace,' said Khlobuyev. 'Of course, you did well to have had your dinner. You see, Mr Kostanjoglo, I haven't a hen in the place – that's what I've come to.'

He heaved a sigh, and no doubt feeling that he wouldn't get any sympathy from Kostanjoglo, took Platonov by the arm and walked ahead with him, pressing his arm tightly to his chest. Kostanjoglo and Chichikov remained behind and followed them at some distance arm-in-arm.

'It's hard, Mr Platonov, it's hard,' said Khlobuyev to Platonov. 'You can't imagine how hard it is. No money, no bread, no boots. Why, it must be all Greek to you. I shouldn't have cared a hang if I were young and alone. But when all these misfortunes come upon you in your old age, when you have to provide for a wife and five children, you can't help feeling a little sad. Yes, indeed!'

'Well, if you sell your estate, that will set you right, won't it?' asked Platonov.

'Set me right?' said Khlobuyev with a despairing wave of the hand. 'It will all go to pay my debts and I don't believe I shall have a single thousand left for myself.'

'So what are you going to do then?'

'God knows.'

'But how is it you're not doing anything to extricate yourself from such a position?'

'What can I do?'

'You'll get some sort of post, won't you?'

'Well, you see, I am a provincial secretary. What sort of post would they give me? An insignificant one. And what salary would I get? Five hundred roubles? I've a wife and five children, you see.'

'Why not get a job as an estate agent?'

'But who will trust me with his estate? I've ruined my own.'

'But when faced with starvation and death, one has to do something. I'll ask whether my brother could not get you some job through someone in the town.'

'No, sir,' said Khlobuyev, heaving a deep sigh and pressing his hand warmly, 'I'm no good for anything now. I've grown decrepit before I'm old, my former misdeeds have left me with a pain in the back, and I've got rheumatism in my shoulders. What could I do? Why waste government money? As it is, there are hundreds of people who get themselves jobs in the Civil Service simply for the sake of drawing large salaries. God forbid that in order to get myself a salary I should be responsible for increasing the taxes of the poorer classes.'

'These are the fruits of a disorderly life,' thought Platonov. 'It's worse than my inactivity.'

While they were talking like this, Kostanjoglo, walking with Chichikov behind them, was beside himself with anger.

'Just look at it,' said Kostanjoglo, pointing with a finger. 'He has reduced the peasants to such poverty. There's not a calf or a horse to be seen. If there is a cattle plague, it's no use worrying about your own property. You have to sell everything and provide the peasants with cattle, so that they do not remain for a single day without the means of carrying on with their work. But now it will take years to put it right. And the peasants too have grown lazy and taken to drink. You see, if you let them go about without work for one year, you have spoilt them for ever: they will have acquired the habit of going about in rags and living the life of vagabonds. And look at the land! Look at the land!' he said, pointing to the water-meadows which soon appeared behind the cottages. 'It's all water-meadows. I'd sow flax, and make five thousand roubles from the flax alone; I'd sow turnips and make another four thousand roubles. And look there – the rye coming up on the hillside, it's all self-sown. He did not sow any corn. I know that. And look at those ravines over there – why, I'd plant such woods there that even a raven wouldn't be able to fly as high as the tree-tops. To neglect such a treasure of a land – why, if he had nothing with which to plough, he should have used the spade himself and made his wife, his children, and his house-serfs do the digging. It isn't a trifling matter. He should have gone on working even if it killed him. He would at least have carried out his duty instead of gorging himself like a pig at some dinner!'

Kostanjoglo spat as he said this and his face clouded over with bitterness.

When they came nearer and stood over the steep ravine, grown over with broom, they caught sight of the flashing bend of the river and the dark spurs of the hills in the distance and of a part of General Betrishchev's house hidden in the woods in the middle distance and behind it a wooded hill looking a dusty blue which Chichikov suddenly realized must be Tentetnikov's estate.

'If one were to plant woods here,' Chichikov said, 'the view would be more beautiful than –'

'Oh, so you're an admirer of fine views, are you?' said Kostanjoglo with a sudden stern look at him. 'Let me warn you, if you start chasing after views, you'll be left without bread and without views. Always think of what is useful and not of what is beautiful. Beauty will come of its own accord. Let the towns serve you as an example: so far the best and the most beautiful towns are those which have grown up naturally, where everyone built according to his needs and according to his taste. Those which have been constructed in straight lines look like barracks. ... Never mind beauty! Concentrate on the things that matter.'

'A pity one has to wait so long,' Chichikov said. 'One would like to see everything as one would wish.'

'Why, you're not a young man of twenty-five, are you? A restless, fidgety fellow? A Petersburg official? A strange business! Patience, that's what you want. Work hard for six years on end, plant, sow, dig the ground, without a moment's rest. It's hard, hard. But afterwards, when you've dug up the earth, it'll begin to help you and it'll bring you more than a million roubles in interest. Yes, sir, in addition to your seventy or so hands, seven hundred invisible ones will be working for you. Everything will increase ten-fold. I don't have to move a finger now: everything is done by itself. Yes, nature loves patience and that is a law given it by God himself, who favours those who are patient.'

'One feels an access of strength from just listening to you. One's spirits rise.'

'Look, how that land has been ploughed!' cried Kostanjoglo with a bitter feeling of grief, pointing to the hillside. 'I can't stay here any longer. It makes me sick to look at this waste and neglect. You can settle your business with him without me now. Take this treasure away from the fool as soon as you can. He only dishonours God's gifts.' As he said this, Kostanjoglo's face darkened with bitterness. He said good-bye to Chichikov and, overtaking Khlobuyev, began to take leave of him too.

'Good Lord, Mr Kostanjoglo,' said the astonished Khlobuyev, 'you've only just arrived and now you're off again!'

'I'm sorry, but I can't stay, I have to get home at once,' said Kostanjoglo, and taking his leave, he got into his trap and drove off.

Khlobuyev seemed to have understood the reason for his departure.

'Kostanjoglo couldn't stand it,' he said. 'A farmer like him can't enjoy seeing such disgraceful mismanagement. You see, Mr Chichikov, I haven't sown any wheat this year. I don't mind confessing, I had no seeds, not to mention ploughs. Your brother, Mr Platonov, is said to be an excellent estate manager, and as for Mr Kostanjoglo, we all know what he is. He's a Napoleon at his work. I often ask myself why one man should be given so much intelligence. Why not let me have a tiny drop of it in my silly brain. Be careful as you walk across

338

the bridge, gentlemen. Don't fall through it into the water. I gave orders for it to be repaired in the spring. It's the poor peasants I'm most of all sorry for. They need an example and what sort of an example can I be to them? But I'm afraid I can do nothing about it. You'd better take them over, Mr Chichikov. How can I teach them to be orderly when I am so disorderly myself? I'd have given them their freedom long ago, if that were of any use. I realize that they have to be taught how to live first. What they need is a stern and just man, someone who would live among them a long time and inspire them by the example of his own indefatigable activity. A Russian, to judge by myself, cannot carry on without a taskmaster: otherwise he will only drowse off and go to seed.'

'It's certainly strange,' said Platonov. 'Why is a Russian so prone to drowse off and go to seed? I mean, if you don't keep an eye on a peasant, he is sure to become a drunkard and a rogue.'

'From lack of education,' Chichikov remarked.

'Goodness only knows why. We are educated, we have attended lectures at a university, and yet what are we good for? Now, what did I learn? I did not learn to lead an orderly life. All I learnt was the art of wasting money on all sorts of new refinements and to become familiar with things that cost a lot of money. All I learnt was to spend a lot of money on all sorts of luxuries. Why is that? Is it because I did not study sensibly? No, my fellow-students were all the same. Two, or three of them, perhaps, did derive real benefit from their studies, and that was perhaps because they were intelligent by nature, but the rest did nothing but try to learn what undermines your health and eats up your money. Yes, indeed! Sometimes I can't help thinking that the Russian is a hopeless case. He wants to do everything but he does nothing. You keep thinking that from tomorrow you'll start a new life, that from tomorrow you will go on a diet, but nothing of the sort happens: on the evening of that very day you gorge yourself so much that all you can do is to blink and you can hardly utter a word. You sit there glaring like an owl at everyone, you do. And everyone is like that.'

'Yes,' said Chichikov with a chuckle, 'I suppose that does happen.'

'We were not born to be sensible. I don't believe that any of us has any sense. If I see any of us leading a decent life, making and saving money, I don't trust even him. When he grows older, the devil will be sure to lead him astray: he will squander it all later on. And everyone is like that, the educated and the uneducated. Yes, there's something lacking here, but what it is I don't know myself.'

Conversing like that, they went through all the cottages, then drove across the meadows in the carriage. These places would have been beautiful, if the trees hadn't all been cut down. Again views opened up. On one side, the hills in the distance showed blue, the same hills which Chichikov had seen only a short while before, but neither Tentetnikov's village nor General Betrishchev's estate could be seen. They were hidden by the hills. Descending to the meadows, where there were only small willow-trees and low poplars, the large trees having been cut down, they inspected a dilapidated water-mill and had a look at the river, on which timber could have been floated, if there had been any timber to float down. From time to time they saw some lean cows grazing. Having inspected it all without getting out of the carriage, they again returned to the village. They came across a peasant scratching the small of his back and yawning so loudly that he frightened the headman's turkeys. The roofs also yawned. Looking at them, Platonov too yawned. 'One patch on top of another patch,' thought Chichikov as he caught sight of a gate lying on top of a cottage instead of a roof. It was the system of Trishka's coat that reigned on this estate: the cuffs and the tails were cut to patch the elbows.

'That's how things are with me,' said Khlobuyev. 'Now let's have a look at the house.' And he led them into his house.

Chichikov wondered whether in the house, too, he would find rags and things that induce yawns, but to his surprise everything was tidy inside. As they entered the rooms, they were amazed by the mixture of poverty with glittering knicknacks of the latest fashion in luxury. A Shakespeare sat on the ink-stand, an elegant ivory hand for scratching one's back lay on the table. They were welcomed by Khlobuyev's wife, who was tastefully dressed in accordance with the latest fashion; their four children were also well-dressed and they even had a governess with them; they were all good-looking, but it would have been better if they had been dressed in coarse homespun skirts and ordinary shirts and had been running about the yard in no way different from peasant's children. Very soon a friend of the lady of the house arrived, an empty-headed chatterbox, and the ladies retired to their part of the house. The children ran after them. The gentlemen were left alone.

'And what is your price?' said Chichikov. 'I should like you, if you don't mind, to name your lowest price, for the property is in a much worse condition than I expected.'

'Oh, in a most lamentable condition, sir,' said Khlobuyev. 'And that is not all. I won't conceal from you the fact that out of every hundred souls on the last census only fifty are alive. Cholera is mostly responsible for that. The rest have run away without a passport so that you may count them as dead. If you try to get them back through the courts, you will have to sell the whole estate to cover your legal costs. That is why I'm only asking thirty-five thousand.'

Chichikov of course began to bargain.

'Thirty-five thousand for such a property! Thirty-five thousand! Take twenty-five.'

Platonov felt ashamed.

'Buy it,' he said. 'The estate is worth that price. If you won't give thirty-five thousand for it, my brother and I will club together and buy it.'

'Very well,' Chichikov said, alarmed, 'I agree, but only on condition that I pay you half the amount in a year's time.'

'No, sir, I cannot possible agree to that. You must pay me half of it now and the rest within fifteen days. You see, if I were to mortgage my estate I would get the same amount. Only I haven't got enough to feed the leeches, I mean, to pay the clerks.'

'Well, I don't know,' said Chichikov. 'I've only got ten thousand now.' He was lying. He had in all twenty thousand, including the money borrowed from Kostanjoglo. But he could not help feeling reluctant to part with so much money at once.

'No, sir, I tell you I simply must have fifteen thousand now.'

'I'll lend you five thousand,' Platonov said.

'Oh, well, in that case,' said Chichikov, and he thought to himself: 'It's a good thing he offered me the loan.'

Chichikov's box was brought from the carriage and he at once took out ten thousand roubles and gave it to Khlobuyev. He promised to bring the remaining five thousand the next day. He most certainly promised, but he intended to bring only three thousand and the rest in a day or two and, if possible, put it off for a couple of days more. Chichikov had a particular dislike for letting money out of his hands. If it were absolutely necessary to do so, it always seemed to him better to pay tomorrow rather than today. In fact, he behaved as we all do. We all like to keep a man waiting: let him cool his heels in the hall! And, indeed, why shouldn't he wait? What do we care whether or not every hour is precious to him and that his business may be suffering from the delay: 'Come along tomorrow, my dear fellow, I have no time for you today.'

'And where are you going to live?' Platonov asked Khlobuyev. 'Have you some other estate?'

'I'm afraid I'll have to move to the town. I have a house there. Besides, I have to do it for the sake of the children. They'll want teachers. I suppose I could get a scripture teacher here, but I should never find any music or dancing teachers here, however much I were to pay them.'

'Hasn't a crust of bread, but wants his children to be taught dancing,' thought Chichikov.

'Strange!' thought Platonov.

'However, we must have something to sprinkle our deal,' said Khlobuyev. 'Hey, there, Kiryushka, bring us a bottle of champagne!'

'Hasn't a crust of bread, but has champagne!' thought Chichikov. Platonov did not know what to think.

Khlobuyev could not help getting his champagne. He had to send for drinks to the town. What was he to do? He had to have something to drink. The shops wouldn't let him have even *kvass* on credit. But the Frenchman who had recently arrived with wines from Petersburg gave credit to everyone. So there was nothing to be done about it; he had to have champagne.

The champagne was brought in. They drank two or three glasses and felt much more cheerful. Khlobuyev was more at ease, he became clever and charming, and regaled them with witticisms and all sorts of anecdotes. It could be gathered from his words that he had a great knowledge of men and the world. He saw many things so well and so accurately. He knew how to sketch so neatly and cleverly in a few words the landowners who were his neighbours; he saw their mistakes and shortcomings so clearly; he knew the life history of the noblemen who had all come to grief so well, and why and how and for what reason they had become ruined men; he could reproduce all their idiosyncrasies in so original and humorous a manner that Platonov and Chichikov were completely enchanted with his talk and were quite prepared to admit that he was a most intelligent man.

'What I can't understand,' said Chichikov, 'is how it is that with all your intelligence you cannot find ways and means out of your difficulties?'

'I have the means,' Khlobuyev said, and at once unloaded a whole heap of projects on them. They were all so absurd, so odd, and showed so little knowledge of men and the world that all they could do was to shrug their shoulders and say: 'Good Lord, what an immense distance there is between knowledge of the world and the ability to make use of it!' All his plans were based on the necessity of obtaining at once a hundred or two hundred thousand roubles from somewhere. Then he imagined everything could be arranged in the best possible way: the estate would be properly run and all the tears would be patched up and his revenues would be quadrupled and he himself would be able to pay all his debts. And he ended his speech by saying: 'But what would you have me do? I simply cannot find the benefactor who would agree to lend me two hundred thousand or at least one hundred thousand roubles. It seems that it isn't God's will.'

'I should think so, too,' thought Chichikov. 'As if God would send two hundred thousand roubles to such a fool.'

'As a matter of fact,' said Khlobuyev, 'I've got an aunt who is worth three million roubles. She is a very pious old lady, she gives lots of money to churches and monasteries, but she is a little tight-fisted when it comes to giving to her relatives. I'm afraid my aunt belongs to a different age, but she is well worth seeing. She has four hundred canaries and pugs and women companions and servants such as you won't find anywhere nowadays. The youngest of her servants must be about sixty, though she still addresses him as: "Hey, boy!" If any of her guests does not behave himself properly, she'll tell her servants to leave him with a dish short at dinner. And they'll do it, too. That's the sort of woman she is.'

Platonov laughed.

'And what's her name and where does she live?' asked Chichikov.

'She lives in our town, Alexandra Ivanovna Khanasarov.'

'Why don't you appeal to her?' Platonov asked sympathetically. 'It seems to me that if she got to know the position of your family, she wouldn't be able to refuse you.'

'Oh, yes, she would. My aunt is a tough character. She's as hard as nails, the old woman is. And, besides, there are lots of others who are trying to ingratiate themselves with her and are constantly running in circles round her. One of them is aiming at becoming a governor:

343

he too claims to be a relative of hers. Do me a favour,' Khlobuyev said suddenly, turning to Platonov, 'I'm giving a dinner to all the dignitaries of our town next week. ...'

Platonov stared at him in astonishment. He did not know as yet that in the towns and capitals of Russia there are lots of clever people whose life is a complete and inexplicable enigma. A man seems to have squandered all he has ever possessed, he owes money all round, he has no means whatever, and yet he gives a dinner and all who dine with him say to themselves that it is the last dinner he'll ever give, because tomorrow he'll be dragged off to the debtors' jail. Ten more years pass and our clever fellow is still about, he is more deeply in debt than ever and he still gives a dinner which all his guests believe is the last dinner he'll ever give and that he'll be dragged off to the debtors' jail next day.

Khlobuyev's house in town was something quite extraordinary. One day a priest in his vestments would be holding a service in it, and next day some French actors would be having a rehearsal. One day there would not be a crust of bread in the house and the next a banquet would be given to all the actors and artists in the town, and each one of them would receive some generous gift. There were times so hard, that another man in his place would have hanged or shot himself. But he was saved by his religious turn of mind which was so strangely combined with his disorderly way of life. In these bitter moments he used to read the lives of the saints and martyrs who trained their minds to be superior to misfortunes of all kinds. At such times his soul completely melted, his spirit was deeply moved, and his eyes were filled with tears. He prayed and, strange to say, almost invariably some unexpected help would come to him from somewhere: either one of his old friends would remember him and send him money, or some wealthy woman he had never met, hearing about his straits when visiting the town, would send him a handsome present with the impulsive generosity of a woman's heart, or some lawsuit of which he had never even heard would be settled in his favour. At such moments he would reverently acknowledge the infinite mercy of Providence, hold a thanksgiving service in his house, and once again start the same disorderly life.

'I'm sorry for him, I really am,' Platonov said to Chichikov, after they had taken leave of him and had driven away from the house.

'A prodigal son,' said Chichikov. 'It's no use being sorry for people like that.'

And very soon both of them stopped thinking about him: Platonov because he regarded everyone's position apathetically and half-somnolently as indeed he did everything else in the world. His heart was full of compassion and ached at the sight of the sufferings of others, but somehow they did not leave a deep impression on his heart. He did not think of Khlobuyev because he did not think of himself, either. Chichikov did not think of Khlobuyev because all his thoughts were concentrated in all seriousness on his newly acquired purchase. He grew pensive and his ideas and thoughts became more sober, and his face assumed a grave expression. 'Patience! Work! That's not so difficult. I've been acquainted with them, if I may say so, ever since my swaddling days. It's nothing new to me. But will I have as much patience at my age now as I had when I was a young man?' Be that as it may, from whatever point of view he examined his purchase, he had to admit that it was a profitable one. He might mortgage the estate after having sold the best parts of the land. Or he might manage the estate himself and become a landowner after the model of Kostanjoglo, profiting by his advice as a neighbour and benefactor. He might even adopt the course of selling the estate (if he didn't care to manage it himself, of course), and keep the dead and the runaway peasants. Then another idea occurred to him: he could abscond altogether without repaying Kostanjoglo the money he had lent him. A strange idea! Not that Chichikov actually thought of it, but it occurred to him suddenly as though of itself, teasing and mocking him and winking at him. 'The slut! The temptress!' And who is the author of these suddenly occurring thoughts? He felt pleased with himself, pleased because he had now become a landowner, not an imaginary but a real landowner, one who owned lands, property, and serfs, serfs that were not imaginary, that did not exist only in his mind, but real ones. And little by little he started bobbing up and down and rubbing his hands and winking at himself, and putting his fist to his mouth he blew a march on it as on a trumpet, and he even addressed himself with a few encouraging words and nicknames, such as: 'Funny face! Fatty!' But remembering that he was not alone, he grew suddenly quiet and tried to suppress his too enthusiastic outbursts of delight, and when Platonov, mistaking some of these inarticulate sounds for words addressed to him, asked him 'What?' he replied 'Nothing.'

Only then, as he looked round him, he saw that they had for some time been driving through a very beautiful copse; a charming avenue of birch-trees stretched on their right and on their left. Gleaming like a snowy palisade, the white trunks of birch-trees and aspens rose slim and light in the young foliage of the newly opened leaves. The nightingales sang loudly, as they kept vying with each other from inside the copse. Wild tulips glowed yellow in the grass. Chichikov could not suppress his astonishment at having suddenly found himself in such a beautiful place when only recently they had been driving through open fields. Through the trees he caught sight of a white brick church and on the other side a trellis appeared out of the copse. At the end of the road a man appeared walking towards them, wearing a cap and carrying a gnarled stick in his hand. An English hound was running ahead of him on long, slender legs.

'Ah, that's my brother,' said Platonov. 'Driver, stop.' And he got out of the carriage. Chichikov followed him.

The dogs had already had time to greet each other. The quick, thin-legged Azor licked Yarb on the face with his quickly darting tongue. Then he licked Platonov's hand and then, jumping up on Chichikov, licked his ear. The brothers embraced.

'Good Lord, Platon, how can you treat me like this?' said Platonov's brother whose name was Vassily.

'What do you mean?' Platonov replied unconcernedly.

'Why, I haven't had any news from you for three days. Petukh's stable-boy brought your horse: "He has driven away with a gentleman," he said to me. Why didn't you let me know where you were going and why and for how long. Good heavens, my dear fellow, how can you behave like this? You can't imagine what I have been thinking all these days.'

'Well, I am sorry, I forgot,' said Platonov. 'We went to see Kostanjoglo. He sends you his regards and so does our sister. Mr Chichikov, let me introduce you to my brother Vassily. Vassily, this is Pavel Ivanovich Chichikov.'

The two gentlemen, who had been thus introduced, shook hands and, taking off their caps, kissed each other.

'Who is this Chichikov?' thought Vassily. 'Platon is not very discriminating in his acquaintances.' And he scrutinized Chichikov as much as was consistent with good manners and saw that he was a person who looked very respectable.

Chichikov for his part also scrutinized Vassily as much as was consistent with good manners and saw that the brother was shorter than Platon, that his hair was darker than his brother's, and that he was far less handsome, but there was a great deal more of life and animation in his face and he gave one the impression of being a much more generous person. One could see that he did not doze so much.

'I've decided, Vassily, to go on a trip across holy Russia with Mr Chichikov. It may help me to get rid of my spleen.'

'How could you have decided it so suddenly?' asked Vassily, looking bewildered, and he nearly added: 'And travel with a man you've only just met who may be a worthless person and goodness knows what!' Filled with mistrust, he looked sideways at Chichikov and saw a man of quite amazing respectability.

They turned right and went through the gates. The courtyard was old, and the house too was old, the sort of house that is no longer built nowadays, with eaves jutting out from under the high roof. Two enormous lime-trees, growing in the middle of the courtyard, cast their shade over almost half of it. There were a great number of wooden benches under them. Flowering lilac and bird-cherry bushes, which grew along the fence surrounding the yard like a necklace of beads, completely hid the fence under their blossom and leaves. The manor house was completely concealed and only the windows and doors peeped out charmingly through the branches. The kitchens, storerooms, and cellars could be seen through the trunks of the trees which were as straight as arrows. All this was inside the copse. The nightingales trilled loudly, filling the whole copse with their song. Involuntarily one's soul was filled with a kind of serene, pleasant feeling. Everything seemed to take one back to those carefree days when everyone lived happily and everything was simple and uncomplicated. Vassily asked Chichikov to sit down. They sat down on the benches under the lime-trees.

A lad of seventeen in a handsome pink cotton shirt brought and set down before them a few decanters of soft fruit drinks of all sorts and colours, some as thick as oil and others as fizzy as lemonade. Having set down the decanters, he picked up a spade which was leaning against a tree and went off into the garden. The brothers Platonov, like Kostanjoglo, had no servants: they were all gardeners or, rather, they had servants, but they all did some gardening in turn. Vassily maintained that servants were not a class by themselves, that anyone could serve at table and that it was not worth having special people for that purpose; that a Russian was good and efficient and no sluggard so long as he walked about in a Russian shirt and a peasant coat, but that as soon as he put on a European coat, he became ungainly and inefficient and lazy, never changed his shirt, stopped going to the bathhouse, and slept in his coat, and that bed-bugs and fleas in great numbers began to breed under his European coat. In this he was perhaps right. On their estate the peasants were dressed with particular smartness: the women's national head-dresses were all trimmed with gold braid and the sleeves of the men's blouses were like the borders of a Turkish shawl.

'Our house has long been famous for its fruit drinks,' Vassily said.

Chichikov poured himself out a glass from the first decanter. It was just like the mead he had once drunk in Poland. It was as effervescent as champagne, so that the gas mounted with a pleasant sensation from his mouth to his nose.

'Nectar!' he said. He tried a glass from another decanter and it was better still.

'It's the drink of drinks!' said Chichikov. 'I can now say that I've drunk a most excellent liqueur at the house of your brother-in-law and a most excellent fruit drink at your house.'

'Why, the liqueur is also ours,' said Vassily. 'It was my sister who introduced it. You see, my mother was a Ukrainian. She was born near Poltava. Nowadays people seem to have forgotten how to make their own food and drink. What parts of the country do you propose to visit?'

'You see, sir,' said Chichikov, swaying gently on the bench and stroking his knee with his hand, 'I'm travelling not so much on my own business as on another person's. General Betrishchev, a close friend of mine and, I may say, my benefactor, has asked me to visit some relatives of his. Now relatives of course are all very well, but to a certain extent, if I may say so, I'm travelling on my own business, for quite apart from the benefits in the haemorrhoidal respect, I'd like to see the world and the whirligig of men, which, if I may say so, is in itself a living book and a second science.'

Vassily pondered. 'The man speaks in rather a stilted way, but there's some truth in what he says.' After a short pause he said, turning to Platon:

'I can't help thinking, Platon, that a journey might quite well shake you up a little. Your trouble is simply a sort of lethargy of the spirit. You are simply asleep, and you're asleep not from any surfeit or exhaustion, but from lack of vivid impressions and sensations. Now, I am quite the opposite. I wish I did not feel so keenly and did not take everything that happens so much to heart.'

'What do you want to take things so much to heart for?' said Platon. 'You seem to be asking for trouble. Inventing worries for yourself.'

'Why invent them when there is always some unpleasantness at every turn,' said Vassily. 'Have you heard the trick Lenitsyn played on us while you were away? He has seized our waste land. Well, to begin with, I do not intend to part with that waste land for any money. On it my peasants celebrate the Red Hill festival every spring and all the traditions of our village are connected with it. I regard custom as something sacred and I'm ready to sacrifice everything for it.'

'He doesn't know about it and that's why he's seized it. He is a new man. He has only just arrived from Petersburg. You'll have to explain it to him. Talk it over with him.'

'He knows all about it all right. I sent to tell him, but he sent a rude answer.'

'You should have gone and explained it to him yourself. Talk it over with him.'

'Oh, no, he's too full of his own importance. I'm not going to see him. You'd better go yourself if you like.'

'I'd go, but you know I try not to interfere in your affairs. He may easily take me in and deceive me.'

'If you like, I'll go,' said Chichikov. 'Just tell me what it is all about.'

Vassily glanced at him and thought: 'What a keen traveller!'

'Just give me an idea what sort of man he is,' said Chichikov, 'and what it is all about.'

'I'm ashamed to impose such a disagreeable commission on you. In my opinion, he's just trash. He comes of a family of quite ordinary small landowners of our province. He's retired with a high rank after serving in Petersburg where he married somebody's natural

349

daughter, and now he's begun to give himself airs. Behaves as if he were a grand gentleman. But we aren't such fools here, either: fashion is not the law for us and Petersburg is not a holy of holies for us.'

'Of course not,' said Chichikov, 'but what is it all about?'

'You see, he needs land. In fact, if he had not behaved like that I would willingly have let him have some land in another place without charging him anything for it, much better land than the waste land, but now this quarrelsome fellow will think ...'

'In my opinion, it's better to talk it over with him. Perhaps we could settle the matter amicably. I've been entrusted with such affairs before and no one has regretted it. General Betrishchev, for instance ...'

'But I'm ashamed that you should have to talk to a man like that ...'

[*The continuation is lost in the manuscript*]

[*The beginning of the sentence is lost.*] '... and taking particular care that it all should be kept secret,' said Chichikov, 'for it is not so much the crime itself that is harmful as the temptation.'

'Ah, that is so, that is so,' said Lenitsyn, bending his head completely to one side.

'How nice it is to meet a man who thinks like you!' said Chichikov. 'I too have some business which is both legal and illegal. It looks illegal, but it's actually quite legal. Being in need of a mortgage, I do not want to involve anyone in the risk of paying two roubles for a living soul. I mean, anything might happen: I might go bankrupt, which God forbid. And it would be unpleasant for the owner. And that is why I decided to make use of runaway and dead serfs, who have not yet been removed from the census register, acting like a Christian and at the same time relieving the poor serf owner of the burden of paying taxes on them. We shall make out a deed of purchase in a formal way just as if they were living serfs.'

'It's rather a strange business,' thought Lenitsyn to himself, moving his chair back a little.

'The business is – er – is rather – er,' he began.

'And there will be no temptation since the whole thing will be transacted in private and by persons who are absolutely above suspicion.'

'All the same, it's the sort of business that – er –'

'No temptation whatsoever,' Chichikov replied quite frankly and straightforwardly. 'It's the sort of thing we've both been discussing: between trustworthy persons of reasonable age and, I believe, also of good rank, and, moreover, transacted in private.' And as he said this, he looked straight at his face, openly and honourably.

However resourceful Lenitsyn was, however experienced in all sorts of business affairs, he seemed to be utterly bewildered now, particularly as he appeared to have got himself entangled in a most strange way in his own net. He was entirely incapable of any unjust action, and he did not want to do anything unjust, even in secret. 'What an extraordinary business,' he thought to himself. 'How is one now to become close friends even with good people! There's a problem for you.'

But fate and circumstances seemed, as though on purpose, to favour Chichikov. Just as though to assist him in this difficult transaction, the young lady of the house, Lenitsyn's wife, a pale, short, thin woman, but dressed in Petersburg fashion and a great admirer of *comme il faut* people, came into the room. She was followed by a nurse carrying in her arms a first-born infant, the fruit of the tender love of the newly wedded couple. Skipping forward adroitly, his head leaning to one side, Chichikov completely charmed the Petersburg lady and her infant child. At first the baby began howling, but by uttering an 'Agoo, agoo, agoo, little darling!' and snapping his fingers as well as by the beauty of the cornelian seal on his watchchain, Chichikov succeeded in luring him into his arms. Then he began to swing him up almost to the ceiling and succeeded in evoking an entrancing smile on the baby's face, at which both parents were exceedingly delighted. But either from delight or from some other cause, the infant suddenly misbehaved himself.

'Oh, dear,' cried Lenitsyn's wife, 'he has ruined your coat!'

Chichikov looked and indeed the sleeve of his brand-new dress-coat was completely spoilt. 'Damn you, you little devil!' he thought angrily to himself.

Lenitsyn, his wife, and the nurse all ran for eau-de-Cologne. They began wiping him down on all sides.

'It's nothing, nothing, absolutely nothing,' Chichikov said, trying, as far as he could, to impart a gay expression to his face. 'How could a child spoil anything at this golden age?' he repeated, thinking to himself at the same time: 'The little beast has certainly done his work well! May the wolves devour him! The dirty little rascal, damn him!' This apparently insignificant circumstance completely won Lenitsyn over to Chichikov's side. How could he refuse anything to a visitor who had shown such affection for his baby and had paid so magnanimously for it with his own dress-coat. Not to set a bad example, they decided to settle the affair secretly, for it was not so much the affair itself as the temptation that was so harmful.

'Do let me repay you with a favour for the favour you've done me,' said Chichikov. 'Let me be an arbitrator between you and the brothers Platonov. You want land, don't you?'

[*Here ends the manuscript of the first four chapters of Part Two of* Dead Souls]

ONE OF THE LAST
CHAPTERS

EVERYONE in the world manages his affairs in the best way he can. 'You scratch where it itches', the proverb says. The tour of the trunks was carried through with success, so that something of that expedition was put away in Chichikov's private box; in short, everything was arranged most satisfactorily. Chichikov did not so much steal as take advantage of a favourable opportunity. Everyone, alas, takes advantage of something or other; one man profits by government timber, another by economizing government funds; one man steals from his children for the sake of some actress on tour, others fleece their peasants in order to be able to buy furniture made by Gambs of Petersburg, or the latest type of carriage. What is to be done if the world has become so full of tempting things? Expensive restaurants with crazy prices, fancy-dress balls, all sorts of promenades, and dances with gypsy girls. It is difficult to restrain oneself if everyone is doing the same thing and if fashion dictates it. Just try and restrain yourself! One can't always control oneself. Man is not a god. Chichikov, too, like the large number of people who love every kind of comfort, turned the affair to his advantage. He should have left the town long ago, but the roads were in a disgraceful condition. Meanwhile the town was getting ready for another fair. A noblemen's fair this time. The previous fair had been mainly a fair of horses, cattle, raw materials, and all sorts of peasant wares bought up by cattle dealers and *kulaks*. The new fair, however, was to sell all sorts of manufactured materials bought at the Nizhny-Novgorod fair by cloth merchants and then transported here. The destroyers of Russian purses were there in full force: Frenchmen with pomades and French women with hats, the destroyers of the money earned by sweat and blood, the Egyptian locusts, as Kostanjoglo called them, who would not only devour everything, but would leave their eggs behind them buried in the ground.

Only the bad harvest and, indeed, the bad year, kept many of the landowners on their estates. But the civil servants who care nothing for bad harvests were all there and, unfortunately, also their wives. Having read many books published recently with the sole purpose of stimulating all sorts of new needs, they were all obsessed by an extraordinary desire to experience all sorts of new delights. A Frenchman opened a new establishment unheard of till then in the province, a pleasure garden where suppers were served at extraordinarily low prices and half on credit. That was enough not only for the heads of departments, but also for the office clerks who showed up in force hoping to get the money back later by taking bribes from petitioners. A desire arose to show off carriages and drivers. What a clash between the various classes for the sake of enjoying themselves! In spite of the foul weather and the muddy roads, elegant carriages kept driving rapidly back and forth. Where they all came from goodness only knows, but they would not have disgraced their owners even in Petersburg. Merchants and shop assistants, smartly doffing their hats, asked exorbitant prices. Bearded men in shaggy fur caps were rarely to be seen. Everyone was dressed in European clothes, with their chins shaven, everyone looked degenerate and had rotten teeth.

'Come in, please, come into the shop, sir,' the shop boys were yelling in places.

But the shopkeepers, who were already well-versed in European ways, looked at them with contempt, uttering only from time to time with a feeling of dignity: 'Psst, psst!!' or 'Here we have materials *kiver*, *claire*, and black!'

'Have you any cloth of gleaming cranberry colour?' asked Chichikov.

'Excellent cloth,' said the merchant, raising his cap with one hand and pointing to his shop with the other.

Chichikov went into the shop. The shopkeeper lifted the flap of the counter and emerged on the other side of it with his back to his wares, piled up in rolls to the ceiling, and facing his customer. Leaning smartly with both hands on the counter and swaying slightly with his whole body, he said:

'What sort of cloth would you like to see, sir?'

'Olive or bottle-green and as near as possible to a cranberry ground, as it were,' said Chichikov.

'I may say, sir, that you will get a first-class article here. You won't find anything better in the most cultured capitals, sir. Boy, get down the cloth No. 34 from the top shelf. No, no, not that one. Why do you always aspire above your station, like some proletarian? Chuck it down here. Here's the material, sir.'

And unrolling it from the other end, the shopkeeper thrust it under Chichikov's very nose so that he could not only stroke its silky sheen with his hand, but smell it.

'It's excellent, but not quite what I want,' said Chichikov. 'You see, I used to be a customs officer, so I must have the very best quality material. I want one more of a reddish tint, more like cranberry than bottle-green.'

'I see, sir. You'd really like to have the sort of colour which is now coming into fashion in Petersburg. I have a cloth of the most excellent quality, sir, but I must warn you that it's not only of the highest quality, but rather expensive.'

The European shop assistant clambered up. The roll fell down. He unrolled it with the skill of a bygone age, having for a moment forgotten that he belonged to the most modern generation. Holding it up to the light, he went out of the shop into the open air in order to display it in the daylight and, screwing up his eyes in the light, said: 'A most excellent colour, sir. A cloth of the smoke and flame of Navarino.'

Chichikov liked the cloth, they agreed on the price, though, as the merchant asserted, it had a *prix fixe*. A deft tugging and pulling with both hands followed, and the piece of cloth was wrapped in paper, Russian fashion, with quite incredible rapidity. The parcel spun round under a light piece of string, which gripped it in a quivering knot. The string was then cut with scissors and the parcel was at once put into the carriage.

'Will you please show me some black cloth?' a voice said.

'Damn it, it's Khlobuyev!' Chichikov said to himself and turned away so as not to see him, thinking that it would be unwise on his part to enter into a discussion with him about the inheritance. But Khlobuyev had already spotted him.

'You're not trying to avoid me, Mr Chichikov?' Khlobuyev asked. 'I couldn't find you anywhere, and you realize, no doubt, that affairs of this kind must be discussed seriously.'

'My dear sir, my dear sir,' said Chichikov, pressing his hand warmly, 'believe me, I'd have loved to have a talk with you, but I was too busy.' And he thought to himself: 'The devil take you!'

Then he suddenly saw Murazov entering the shop. 'Good heavens,' he cried, 'is it you Mr Murazov? How are you?'

'How are you?' Murazov said, taking off his hat.

The merchant and Khlobuyev also took off their hats.

'I'm afraid the pain in my back is still worrying me and I'm not sleeping too well, either. I wonder whether it's lack of exercise that causes it?'

But instead of probing into the cause of Chichikov's illness, Murazov turned to Khlobuyev:

'I saw you go into the shop, Mr Khlobuyev, and followed you. There's something I'd like to discuss with you. Would you mind coming to my house?'

'Of course not, of course not,' Khlobuyev said hastily and went out with him.

'What could they have to talk about?' thought Chichikov.

'Mr Murazov is a very highly esteemed and intelligent man,' said the shopkeeper. 'He knows his business, but I'm sorry to say he has no culture. You see, sir, a merchant is not just a merchant, he is a big business man. He has all sorts of things to consider: his budget and reaction, for otherwise the result would be pauperism.'

Chichikov just dismissed it all with a wave of his hand.

'I've been looking for you everywhere, Mr Chichikov,' a voice said behind him. It was Lenitsyn.

The shopkeeper took off his hat respectfully.

'Ah, Mr Lenitsyn!'

'For God's sake, come along to my house. I have something to discuss with you,' he said.

Chichikov glanced at him: Lenitsyn looked terribly upset. Chichikov paid the shopkeeper and went out of the shop.

[Part of the manuscript is missing here]

'I've been waiting for you, Khlobuyev,' said Murazov, as Khlobuyev came in. 'Please come into my room.' And he led Khlobuyev into the room which is already familiar to the reader, a room which a civil servant, receiving a salary of seven hundred roubles a year, would have considered too modest for him.

'Tell me, I suppose your circumstances are much easier now, aren't they? You did get something after your aunt's death, didn't you?'

'Well, how can I put it, sir?' Khlobuyev said. 'I'm not sure whether my circumstances are easier or not. All I got was five hundred serfs and thirty thousand roubles, out of which I have to pay off part of my debts – and I'm afraid I shall have nothing left after that. The main thing is that there's something wrong with the will. You see, sir, there's some kind of fraud involved there. I'll tell you about it now and you'll be surprised at what's been happening. That Chichikov ...'

'If you don't mind, Mr Khlobuyev, I'd rather talk about yourself before discussing that *Chichikov*. Tell me, how much do you think you would want to put your affairs in order?'

'Well, sir,' said Khlobuyev, 'my affairs are certainly in a mess and to put them in order, to pay off all my debts, and to be able to live on a most moderate scale I should have to have at least a hundred thousand, if not more. In short, I can't possibly do it.'

'Well, but supposing you had that, what sort of life would you lead?'

'Well, sir, I'd rent a small flat and devote myself to my children's education. It's not good for me to think of myself any longer. My career is at an end, and I'm not fit for anything any more.'

'But then you would still be leading an idle life, and idleness is the cause of all sorts of temptations such as no man who has any work to do would dream of.'

'I'm sorry, but I can't do anything. I'm no good for anything. I've grown dull and listless, my back aches.'

'But how can you live without work? How can you exist without a post, without a job? Good heavens, man, just look at any of God's creatures: every one of them does some work, every one has its own part to play in life. Even a stone has its uses, and man who is the most intelligent of all creatures must be of some use, mustn't he?'

'But I won't be entirely without an occupation. I will be busy with my children's education.'

'No, sir, no! That is the most difficult thing of all. How can anyone hope to educate his children, if he has not educated himself. The only way to educate children is by personal example. And do you really think that your life can serve as an example for them? What will they learn from it? To spend their time in idleness and playing cards? No, sir, you'd better let me take your children. You will only spoil them. Think it over seriously. It was idleness that was your undoing. You must turn your back on it. How can one live without some attachment to something. Someone has to do his duty. A day-labourer too renders some service to the world. He may be eating dry bread, but then he earns it, and he takes an interest in his work.'

'I assure you, sir,' said Khlobuyev, 'I've tried to overcome my weakness. I've done my best to overcome it. But what's to be done now? I've grown old and incapable. What am I to do? I can't get a post in the service, can I? I mean, at forty-five I can't sit down at the same desk with young office clerks, can I? Besides, I'm not very good at taking bribes. I'd only be a hindrance to myself and a nuisance to others. You see, they've got their own caste system in the Civil Service. No, sir, I've thought about it, I've tried, I've examined all sorts of posts – I'd be no good anywhere. Except perhaps in the workhouse ...'

'A workhouse is for those who have worked. To those who have spent their youth enjoying themselves, one can only repeat the reply given by the ant to the grasshopper: "Go and dance!" Besides, even in the workhouse one has to do some work. One doesn't play whist there, my dear sir,' said Murazov, gazing at him intently. 'You're deceiving yourself and me too.'

Murazov gazed intently at him, but poor Khlobuyev could say nothing in reply. Murazov felt sorry for him.

'Listen, my dear fellow,' he said, 'you do go to church, don't you? You say your prayers? You don't miss morning or evening mass? You may not like getting up early, but you do and you go to mass at four o'clock in the morning when no one else is up.'

'That's a different matter, sir. You see, I know that I'm doing it not for man, but for the sake of Him who ordered us to live in the world. What's to be done? I believe that He is merciful to me, that however loathsome and abominable I may be, He would forgive me and accept me, while man would kick me aside and even my best friend would betray me and tell me later that he had betrayed me for a good cause.'

A pained expression appeared on Khlobuyev's face; the old man shed a few tears, but he did not gainsay him.

'Then serve Him who is so merciful to you. Work is as welcome to Him as prayer. Take any job you like, but do your work just as though you did it for Him and not for man. Pound water in a mortar, but you must think you're doing it for Him. At least you'll have no time left for evil, to lose money at cards, to gorge yourself with gormandizers, to waste your time in high society, and that's already something! Dear, oh dear, Khlobuyev! Do you know Ivan Pota-pych?'

'Yes, sir. I know him and I respect him greatly.'

'He was an excellent business man, worth half a million roubles, but as soon as he saw that everything was bringing in a profit he let himself go. Had his son taught French, married off his daughter to a general. He no longer spent his time in his shop or on the Exchange. All he was concerned about was to get hold of a friend and take him to a tavern for a cup of tea. He used to spend whole days drinking tea and in the end he went bankrupt. And then misfortune overtook him. His son died and, as you see, today he is one of my shop assistants. He's started from scratch again and his affairs have improved. He could do trade again to the amount of half a million, but he doesn't want to: "I've been a shop assistant and I'd like to die a shop assis-tant," he says. "Now that my health has improved, I'm feeling well again, whereas before I'd grown a paunch and was beginning to suffer from dropsy. No, sir," he says. And now he doesn't even have a drop of tea any more. All he has is cabbage soup and buckwheat porridge. Yes, sir. And he says his prayers better than any of us. And he helps the poor better than any of us, for, you see, many a man would be glad to help, but has squandered all his money.'

Poor Khlobuyev sank into thought.

The old man took both his hands in his.

'Look here, Khlobuyev, if only you knew how sorry I am for you. I've been thinking about you all the time. Now, listen. You know there's an anchorite in our monastery who sees no one. He is a man of great intellect, of so great an intellect that I know no one to equal him. I began telling him that I had a friend – I did not mention his name – who was suffering from such and such a complaint. He started listening to me, and then suddenly interrupted me with the following words: "God's business comes before yours. They are building a church, but there isn't enough money: funds must be collected for the church." And he slammed the door in my face. "What does it mean?" I thought to myself. "Apparently he doesn't want to give advice." So I went to see our archimandrite. As soon as I entered his room, he asked me whether I knew anyone who could be entrusted with collecting funds for the church, anyone of the nobility or of the merchant class who had better education than others and who would regard this work as a matter of personal salvation. "Why," I thought to myself at once, "that monk has appointed Khlobuyev for this job. The open road would be good for his illness. As he passes with his collection book from landowner to peasant and from peasant to artisan, he will find out how people live and what each of them is in need of, so that after he has been through several provinces, he will have learnt the locality and the countryside better than those who live in towns. And it is men like that that we need most now. You see, the prince was telling me the other day that he would have given a lot to have an official who had practical experience and did not obtain his knowledge of affairs from official documents, for, he said, you can find out nothing from documents: everything is in such an awful mess there.'

'I feel utterly confused and embarrassed, sir,' said Khlobuyev, looking at him in astonishment. 'I can't even believe that it's me you are telling this to. For this sort of work you want an energetic, indefatigable man. Besides, how can I abandon my wife and children who will have nothing to eat if I leave them.'

'Don't worry about your wife and children. I shall take care of them and I shall get tutors for the children. Rather than go about begging for yourself, it would be nobler and better if you begged for God. I will let you have an ordinary covered waggon. Don't be afraid of being jolted about: it's good for your health. I shall also give you money for the journey to distribute among those who are more in need than others. You could do a great deal of good there: you're not likely to make a mistake, and whoever receives from you will deserve it. Travelling all over the country like this, you will get to know everybody, his position and his circumstances. That's not the same as some official whom everyone is afraid of and from whom everyone is hiding; knowing that you are asking for a church, people will readily talk to you.'

'I can see that it's an excellent idea, and I'd very much like to fulfil even a part of it. But I'm afraid that's beyond my powers.'

'But what is not beyond our powers?' said Murazov. 'There's nothing that is within our powers. Everything is beyond our powers. Without help from above nothing is possible. But prayer concentrates our strength. Crossing himself, a man says, "Lord, have mercy on me," and he pulls at his oars and reaches the shore. This is not something one should spend a long time thinking about. It must be accepted simply as God's will. I'll have the covered waggon made

360

ready for you at once and you'd better run and see the Father Archimandrite and get the book and his blessing, and then you can start on your journey.'

'I shall do as you say and accept it as a sign from on high. Bless me, O Lord,' he said inwardly, and felt immediately strength and courage flooding his soul. Even his mind began to be roused with the hope of an escape from his melancholy and hopeless position. There was a glimmer of light in the distance.

But let us leave Khlobuyev, and return to Chichikov.

Meanwhile, petition after petition was reaching the courts. Relations turned up of whom no one had ever heard before. Like carrion birds swooping down on a carcass, so everybody swooped down on the immense property left by the old lady; information was laid against Chichikov, who was accused of having forged the old lady's last will, other information having already reached the authorities accusing him of having forged the first will too, and evidence was produced of theft and misappropriation of certain sums. Evidence also reached the authorities about Chichikov's purchase of dead souls and smuggling of contraband goods when he was serving in the Customs. Everything was dug up and all the past history of his life became known. God only knows how they got on the scent of it and how they managed to find it all out. Evidence was even produced about matters which Chichikov believed no one knew but himself. For the time being, however, all this was still known only to the legal authorities and had not reached his ears, though a trustworthy note he had received from his legal adviser a short while before made him realize that there was trouble brewing. The note was brief, and read as follows: 'I hasten to inform you that there's going to be some trouble in your case, but please remember that there is no need to worry. The main thing is to keep calm. We shall fix it all.' This note completely reassured him. 'That fellow is a real genius,' Chichikov said to himself. To cap the good news, the tailor brought him his new suit just at that moment. Chichikov was very anxious to have a look at himself in his new dress-coat of 'the flame and smoke of Navarino'. He pulled on the trousers which fitted him beautifully, so much so that he could have sat for his portrait in them. They fitted gloriously round the thighs and round the calves too; the cloth outlined every little detail, making the calves look even more resilient. When he tightened the buckle behind him, his stomach was like a drum. He banged it with a clothes brush, saying: 'What a fool and yet it completes the picture.' The dress-coat appeared to be even better made than the breeches: there was not a wrinkle anywhere, it fitted perfectly round the sides, curved at the waist disclosing all the lines of his figure. In reply to Chichikov's remark that it cut him a little under the left armpit, the tailor merely smiled; that, he explained, made it fit much better round the waist. 'Don't worry, don't worry about the cut,' he kept repeating with undisguised triumph. 'You won't get another such cut anywhere except in Petersburg.' The tailor himself came from Petersburg and he had put on his signboard: 'A foreigner from London and Paris.' He disliked being trifled with, and he was anxious to ram these two towns down the throats of all the other tailors, so that in future not one of them should come out with those names, but should merely put on his signboard: 'Karlseru' or 'Kopengara'.

Chichikov very magnanimously settled the tailor's bill and, left alone, began examining himself at his leisure in the looking-glass like a true artist – with aesthetic feeling and *con amore*. Everything seemed to be a great deal better than before: his plump cheeks looked more interesting, his chin more alluring, the white collar lent tone to the cheeks and his blue satin cravat lent tone to the collar, the new-fashioned pleats of the shirt-front lent tone to the cravat, the rich velvet waistcoat lent tone to the shirt-front, and the coat of 'the smoke and flame of Navarino', gleaming like silk, lent tone to everything. He turned to the right – it was perfect. He turned to the left – it was still more perfect. The curve of his waist was like that of a court chamberlain or of a gentleman who speaks French like a native and who does not know how to swear in Russian even when he is in a rage, but will swear in the French dialect: the refinement of it! Bending his head a little on one side, he attempted to assume a pose such as he might adopt when addressing a middle-aged lady of the most *avant-garde* views: it made a perfect picture. Artist, take up your brush and paint! Chichikov was so delighted that he leapt lightly in the air, executing a kind of *entrechat*. The chest of drawers shook and a bottle of eau-de-Cologne fell on the floor; but that did not worry him in the least. He called, as might have been expected, the stupid bottle 'a fool' and thought to himself: 'Whom shall I pay my first visit to? Best of all ...' When suddenly there was a clanking of boots with spurs in the entrance hall and a gendarme, fully armed, just as though he personified a whole platoon of soldiers, came into the room and said: 'You're commanded to appear at once before the governor-general.' Chichikov was dumbfounded. Before him stood a monster with a huge moustache, a horse's tail on his head, a crossbelt over one shoulder, a crossbelt over the other shoulder, and a huge sword at his side. He fancied there was a rifle hanging on the other side and goodness only knows what else: a whole army in one person! He tried to protest, but the monster retorted rudely: 'You're ordered to come at once!' Through the door leading into the hall, Chichikov saw another monster of the same kind; he glanced out of the window – a carriage! What was he to do? He had to get into the carriage just as he was in his coat of 'the smoke and flame of Navarino' and trembling all over he set off for the governor-general's with a gendarme beside him.

In the entrance hall he was not even given time to pull himself together. 'Go in, the prince is expecting you,' said the official on duty. As through a mist, he caught a glimpse of the anteroom with couriers receiving envelopes, then of a drawing-room through which he passed, thinking to himself: 'This is how men are seized without trial and sent straight to Siberia!' His heart was pounding more violently than the most passionate lover's. At last the fateful door was opened: before him was a study with portfolios, bookcases, and books, and the prince looking the very personification of anger.

'My destroyer! My destroyer!' said Chichikov to himself. 'He'll destroy me utterly! He'll slay me as a wolf does a lamb!'

'I spared you, sir, I allowed you to stay in the town when you should have gone to jail. You've disgraced yourself again by the most dishonest swindle a man has ever disgraced himself with.' The prince's lips trembled with anger.

'What most dishonest act and swindle, your Excellency?' asked Chichikov, trembling all over.

'The woman,' said the prince advancing more closely on Chichikov and looking him straight in the face, 'the woman who at your instigation signed the will has been arrested and you will be confronted with her.'

For a moment everything went black before Chichikov's eyes.

'Your Excellency,' he said, 'I will tell you the whole truth. I am guilty. Yes, I am guilty. But I'm not altogether guilty: my enemies have defamed me.'

'No one can possibly defame you because there are more abominations in you than the worst liar could think of. I don't think you have done anything in your life that was not dishonest. Every penny you have obtained has been obtained dishonestly, by theft and dishonesty for which a man deserves to be whipped and sent to Siberia. No, sir, we've had enough of you. You will be taken to prison at once and there, side by side with the lowest scoundrels and brigands, you will wait for your fate to be decided. And that is only just and merciful because you're a hundred times worse than they: they walk about in peasants' coats and sheepskins, while you ...' He looked at the dress-coat of 'the smoke and flame of Navarino' and, pulling the cord, rang the bell.

'Your Excellency,' cried Chichikov, 'have mercy on me! You're the father of a family. Spare my old mother, if not myself!'

'You're lying!' the prince cried angrily. 'Just as once before you implored me to take pity on your wife and children which you never had, so you now appeal to me to spare your mother.'

'Your Excellency, I'm a villain and the meanest rogue,' said Chichikov in a voice which ... [*The sentence is unfinished in the manuscript.*] 'I was indeed lying, I have no wife and no children, but, as God is my witness, I always wished to have a wife and do my duty as a man and a citizen so as to earn eventually the respect of my fellow-countrymen and the authorities. But what a disastrous concatenation of circumstances. One must earn one's daily bread, sir, with one's blood. Yes, sir, with one's blood. At every step snares and temptations, enemies, destroyers, thieves. My whole life has been like a whirlwind or like a ship tossed by the waves at the mercy of the winds. I am a man, your Excellency.'

Here tears suddenly gushed from his eyes. He fell at the prince's feet, just as he was, in his coat of 'the smoke and flame of Navarino', his velvet waistcoat, his satin cravat, and his hair beautifully waved and giving off a sweet scent of the most expensive eau-de-Cologne. He fell at the prince's feet and struck the floor with his forehead.

'Keep away from me!' said the prince. 'Call the guard to take him away!' he said to the man who entered the room.

'Your Excellency!' Chichikov shouted, clasping the prince's boot with both hands.

A shudder of revulsion ran through every vein of the prince.

'Keep away from me, I tell you!' he said, trying to pull his leg out of Chichikov's embrace.

'Your Excellency, I will not move from this spot until you have mercy on me,' said Chichikov without letting go of the prince's boot and being dragged along on the floor in his dress-coat of 'the smoke and flame of Navarino'.

'Go away, I tell you,' said the prince with that indescribable feeling of revulsion a man feels at the sight of a hideous insect which he hasn't the strength to crush underfoot. He gave such a violent shake with his leg that Chichikov felt his boot strike him on the nose, lips, and rounded chin, but he did not let go of the boot and held it still more tightly in his embrace. Two stalwart gendarmes dragged him away by force and, taking him under the arms, led him through all the rooms. He was pale, crushed, in the state of terrible numbness a man finds himself in when confronted with black and certain death, that monster that is so repugnant to our nature. ... In the doorway on the stairs he saw Murazov. With superhuman force he tore himself in one instant out of the hands of the two gendarmes and fell at the feet of the astonished old man.

'Good Lord, my dear Chichikov, what's the matter?'

'Save me! They're taking me to prison, to death!'

The gendarmes seized him and led him away without letting him even be heard.

A dank, damp cell reeking of soldiers' boots and puttees, a plain deal table, two rickety chairs, a barred window, a broken-down stove, which let smoke through cracks but gave no heat, such was the abode in which our hero, who had begun to taste the sweets of life and to attract the attention of his fellow countrymen, was placed in his thin new dress-coat of 'the smoke and flame of Navarino'.

He had not even been allowed to make the necessary arrangements, to take some of his most necessary things, his box in which he had his money which may have been sufficient to ... [*The sentence is unfinished in the manuscript.*] His papers, the deeds of purchase for the dead souls – all were now in the hands of the authorities. He flung himself on the floor and a feeling of hopeless grief wound itself round his heart like a carnivorous worm. It began gnawing at his heart which was utterly defenceless with ever increasing rapidity. Another such day of grief and there would have been no Chichikov left on earth. But over

Chichikov too, someone's unslumbering and all-saving hand was hovering. An hour later the doors of the jail were opened and old Murazov came in.

If a draught of spring water were poured down the parched throat of a worn-out, emaciated traveller, tormented by raging thirst and covered with the grime and dust of the road, he would not have been so refreshed by it as poor Chichikov was revived at the sight of Murazov.

'My saviour!' said Chichikov, leaping up from the floor upon which he had flung himself in his despairing fit of grief. He seized Murazov's hand, kissed it rapidly, and pressed it to his breast. 'May the Lord reward you for visiting an unhappy wretch like me.'

He burst into tears.

The old man looked at him with a pained and pitying expression and merely kept repeating:

'Oh, Chichikov, Chichikov, what have you done!'

'But what's to be done now, sir? The damned woman has ruined me! I did not know where or when to stop. Satan seduced me, made me lose my reason. Yes, I have transgressed, I have transgressed. But how can they treat me like that? A nobleman, sir, a nobleman! Fling him into prison without trial, without any preliminary investigation! A nobleman, sir! Not give me time to go home and make the necessary arrangements about my belongings? You see, sir, all my things have been left there now without anyone to look after them. My box, sir, my box! Why, all my property is there! Everything I've acquired by sweat and blood, by years of toil and privation. My box, sir! Why, they'll steal it all! They'll take it all away! O Lord!'

And unable to restrain the rush of sadness to his heart, Chichikov burst out sobbing in a loud voice that penetrated through the thick walls of the prison and echoed hollowly in the distance. He tore off his satin cravat and, grasping his collar with his hand, tore his coat of 'the smoke and flame of Navarino'.

'Oh, my dear fellow, how this property of yours has blinded you! It prevented you from realizing the terrible position into which you had got yourself.'

'My benefactor, save me, save me!' poor Chichikov cried in despair, flinging himself at his feet. 'The prince likes you. He would do everything for you!'

'No, my dear fellow, I can't do that, however much I'd like to.

You're now in the hands of implacable law and not in the power of any man.'

'Oh, that rascally Satan has seduced me, that enemy of man.'

He knocked his head against the wall and banged his hand on the table with such force that he made his fist bleed; but he felt neither the pain in his head nor the blow on his hand.

'Calm yourself, my dear fellow. Think how to make peace with God and not with man. Think of your poor soul.'

'But consider my fate, sir. Has any man been so treated by fate? Why, sir, I've earned my pennies with superhuman patience, by sweat and toil, sir, and not by robbing people or by defrauding the Treasury, as is usually done. And why did I save up my pennies? I did it in order to be able to spend the rest of my days in comfort, in order to leave something to my children whom I had intended to have for the good of my country. That is why I wished to have them! I've been a little dishonest, I don't deny it. I have been dishonest. But nothing can be done about it now, can it? But I was dishonest only when I saw that I could not get anywhere by following the straight path and that the crooked path led more directly to the goal. But, after all, I did work hard, I did do my best. If I did take anything, it was from the rich. What about these blackguards who take thousands from the Treasury in the courts, who rob people who are not rich, who take the last penny from those who have nothing! And think of my bad luck, sir! Every time I'm about to reach out for the fruit and, as it were, touch it with my hand, a storm suddenly blows up, my ship's flung against a submerged rock and breaks into splinters. I just had under three hundred thousand roubles of my own money. I had a three-storied house. Twice I've bought myself an estate. Oh, sir, how have I deserved such a fate? Why such blows? Was my life not already like a ship tossed about by the waves? Where is the justice of heaven? Where is the reward of patience, of my unexampled perseverance? Three times I had to start from scratch. Having lost everything I started again with a penny, while another man would have drunk himself to death from despair and rotted away in a pub. Think of the things I had to overcome, of the things I had to suffer! Why, every penny I earned was earned, if I may say so, with all the energies of my soul. Others, I dare say, got everything easily, but for me each penny was three times as hard to get, and God knows I got it by the exercise of iron will-power ...'

He could not finish and, bursting into loud sobs from the unbearable pain in his heart, collapsed into a chair, tore off the rent skirt of his dress-coat, and flung it away from him. He then grasped his hair, which he had been so careful before to keep tidy, and tore it mercilessly, taking pleasure in the pain with which he hoped to stifle the unquenchable anguish of his heart.

For a long time Murazov sat silently before him, looking at this spectacle of extraordinary suffering he had never seen before. And the unhappy, embittered man who had only recently been fluttering all over the place with the free and easy grace of a man of the world or a smart army officer, was now rushing about, looking dishevelled and disreputable, in a torn dress-coat and unbuttoned trousers, a bleeding. bruised fist, pouring out abuse on the hostile forces thwarting mankind.

'Oh, my dear fellow, my dear fellow, I can't help thinking what a man you would have made, if you had done some good work and if you had tried to accomplish something worthy with the same energy and patience. Dear Lord, how much good you would have done! If anyone of those men who love good, were to use as much effort to achieve it as you did for the acquisition of your pennies, and if any of them were willing without sparing themselves to sacrifice their own vanity and ambition for the sake of good, just as you did not spare yourself when acquiring your pennies – why, how our country would have prospered! My dear fellow, what I'm so sorry about is not that you're guilty in the eyes of others, but that you're guilty in your own eyes – before those rich gifts and powers bestowed on you. Your destiny was to have been a great man, but you seem to have lost your way and destroyed yourself.'

There are mysteries of the soul: however much a man may stray from the straight path, however much an inveterate criminal may become hardened and set in his life of crime, yet if you reproach him by drawing attention to himself, by pointing out his own good qualities which he has disgraced, he will be shaken in spite of himself and be deeply moved.

'Mr Murazov,' said poor Chichikov, grasping both his hands. 'Oh, if only I could regain my freedom and get back my property! I swear to you that I would then lead quite a different life. Save me, my benefactor, save me!'

'But what can I do? I'd have to fight the law. Supposing I made up my mind to do so, the prince is a just man, he would never go back on his decision.'

'Benefactor, you can do anything! It isn't the law I'm frightened of, I can find ways of getting round it, but the fact that I've been thrown into prison without cause, that I'm going to perish here like a dog, and that my property, my papers, and my box will – Save me!'

He threw his arms round the old man's legs and drenched them with tears.

'Oh, my dear Chichikov,' said Murazov, shaking his head, 'how this property of yours has blinded you! It's because of it that you don't think of your poor soul.'

'I'll think of my soul too, only save me!'

'My dear fellow,' said Murazov and paused for a moment. 'It is not in my power to save you. You see it yourself. But I'll do all I can to make it easier for you and to have you released. If in spite of everything I should succeed, I'm going to ask you to reward me for my trouble: give up all these attempts to make money. I tell you as an honourable man that if I were to lose all my possessions, and I have more of them than you, I should not cry over it. I assure you it isn't your possessions which can be confiscated that matter, but something no one can rob or deprive you of. You have lived long enough in the world. You yourself describe your life as a ship tossed by the waves. You have already enough to keep you in comfort for the rest of your life. Settle in some quiet corner near a church, and good simple people; or, if you are possessed by so passionate a desire to leave descendants, marry a good girl, a girl who is not rich but who is accustomed to moderation and simple housekeeping. Forget this noisy world and all its seductive luxuries. Let it forget you too. You won't find peace in it. You can see for yourself: everything in it is your enemy, your tempter, or your betrayer.'

'Yes, yes, I will! As a matter of fact, I was about to lead an honest life. I wanted to do so. I intended to devote myself to farming, to living modestly. But the demon, the temper led me astray. Satan, the devil, the fiend of hell!'

Some strange, unfamiliar feelings suddenly overwhelmed him, just as though something were trying to awaken in him, something remote, something that had been crushed in his childhood by the harsh and deadening precepts, the lovelessness and the dullness of his childhood years, the emptiness of his home, the solitude of his life, the poverty and the meanness of his first impressions; and it was as though everything that had been crushed by the stern glance of fate, which had looked dully at him through a kind of opaque window, covered with snow by a blizzard, was now trying to fight its way through into the open. A moan burst from his lips and, burying his face in his hands, he cried in a mournful voice:

'It's true, it's true!'

'Neither your knowledge of men nor your experience were of any assistance to you once you had embarked on this lawless path. If only there had been some lawful purpose for what you did! Oh, my dear fellow, why did you ruin yourself? Wake up! It's not too late. There is still time.'

'No, it's too late, too late,' he moaned in a voice that nearly broke Murazov's heart. 'I'm beginning to realize, to feel, to hear, that I've not been living as I should, that I've not been following the right path, and that I can't do anything about it. I'm afraid I haven't been brought up properly. My father always repeated all sorts of moral precepts to me, he beat me, he made me copy out all sorts of rules of upright behaviour, but he himself stole wood from his neighbours and even forced me to help him. He started an unfair lawsuit, while I still lived with him, and he seduced an orphan girl whose guardian he was. Example is stronger than a moral code. I can see, sir, I can feel that I'm not leading the right sort of life, but I'm afraid vice does not fill me with any great disgust: my nature has grown coarse, I've no love for good, I lack the fine aptitude for good deeds that are pleasing to God, an aptitude that becomes man's second nature, his habit. There's no willingness to do good that is in any way comparable to my desire for the acquisition of property. I'm telling you the truth. There's nothing I can do about it!'

The old man heaved a deep sigh.

'My dear fellow,' he said, 'you have so much will-power, you have so much patience. Medicine may be bitter but the patient takes it in the knowledge that it will help him to get well. You have no love for good, force yourself to do good without any love for it. That will be accounted to you even more than to him who does good out of love for it. Force yourself a few times and then you will also learn to love it. Believe me, everything is done ... [*The sentence is unfinished in the manuscript.*] A kingdom divided against itself, it is written. Only by

370

striving forcibly towards it – one must try to strive forcibly towards it, to take it by force. Oh, my dear fellow, you possess the strength to do it, which others do not possess, iron perseverance – so why should you not overcome it? Why, it seems to me you could have been a real legendary hero, for nowadays people are all lacking will-power, they're all weak!'

It could be seen that these words penetrated into Chichikov's very soul and stirred something that yearned for glory at its bottom. His eyes flashed if not with resolution, then with something firm, something resembling it. 'If,' he said firmly, 'you succeed in getting a pardon for me and the means of leaving this town with some money, I give you my word that I shall start a new life: I shall buy myself a small estate, become a farmer, and save up some money not for myself but to help others. I shall try to do good as much as I can. I shall forget about myself and all the gormandizing and feasts of the towns. I shall lead a simple and sober life.'

'May the Lord strengthen you in this resolve,' said the old man, looking very pleased. 'I shall do my best to get the prince to set you at liberty. Whether I shall succeed or not, God alone knows. In any case, your lot I'm sure will be made much easier. Oh dear, come embrace me and let me embrace you. How you have gladdened me! Well, wish me luck. I shall now go and see the prince.'

Chichikov was left alone.

He was deeply shaken and softened. Even platinum, the hardest of all metals, and the one most resistant to fire, can be melted: when the temperature in the crucible is raised, the bellows pumped, and the unbearable heat of the fire goes up into the chimney, the obstinate metal turns white and is transformed into a liquid; the strongest of men gives in in the crucible of misfortunes when, growing more intense, they burn petrified nature with their insupportable fire.

'I don't know how to do it and I don't feel like doing it, but I shall use all my energies to make others feel like doing it; I'm a bad man myself and I can't do anything, but I shall use all my energies to inspire others; I'm a bad Christian myself, but I shall use all my energies not to lead others into temptation. I shall labour, I shall work in the sweat of my brow on my land, and I shall do so honestly, so as to be able to exercise a good influence on others. I'm not quite worthless, am I? I have a natural bent for farming, I possess all the qualities of economy, efficiency, and prudence and even that of steadfastness. I've only to make up my mind.'

So thought Chichikov and it seemed that he did grasp something with the half-awakened forces of his soul. It seemed that by a kind of dark intuition his nature was becoming aware of the existence of a duty which man must perform on earth, a duty that can be performed everywhere, in any corner of the world, under any circumstances and in spite of the confusion and changes to which man is constantly subject. And a life of honest toil, far from the noise of the cities and the temptation which, forgetting work, man has invented out of idleness, began to present itself in so forceful a light to him that he almost forgot the unpleasantness of his situation and was perhaps even ready to thank Providence for this hard lesson, provided he was set free and given back at least a part of ...

But ... the door of his filthy cell was suddenly flung open and there walked in a certain official, a man by the name of Samosvistov, an epicure, a daredevil of a fellow, broad-shouldered, slim-legged, an excellent boon companion, a rake, and a crafty villain, as his own friends called him. In wartime this man would have worked miracles: sent to make his way through some impassable and dangerous places, to steal a cannon under the very nose of the enemy, he would have done it. But lacking a military career, which would perhaps have made an honest man of him, he turned his hands to any unsavoury job that came to hand. It's simply incredible what strange convictions and rules he had: with his bosom friends he was good, he did not betray any of them and, having given his word, he kept it; but those in authority over him he regarded as a sort of enemy battery through which he had to make his way, taking advantage of any weak spot, gap, or failure to take precautions.

'We know all about your position, we've heard all about it,' he said as soon as he saw that the door was closed behind him. 'Never mind, never mind! Don't lose courage. Everything will be put right. We shall all work for you, and we're all your servants. Thirty thousand roubles for everything and nothing more.'

'Do you mean it?' cried Chichikov. 'And shall I be completely cleared?'

'Completely. And you will get compensation too for damages.'

'And for your trouble?'

'Thirty thousand, all included, for our fellows and for the governor-general's and for his secretary.'

'But one moment, please. How can I do it? All my things, my box, it's all been sealed up and is under supervision.'

'You'll have it all within the hour. Shall we shake hands on it?'

Chichikov gave his hand. His heart was beating violently and he could not believe that it was possible.

'Good-bye for the time being. Our mutual friend has asked me to tell you that the main thing is calm and presence of mind.'

'H'm,' Chichikov thought to himself, 'I see. My legal adviser.'

Samosvistov disappeared. Chichikov, left alone, still could not believe what he had been told, but in less than an hour after their conversation, his box was brought to him: his papers, his money, everything was in perfect order. Samosvistov had appeared at Chichikov's lodgings as though authorized to do so: he swore at the sentries for their lack of vigilance, ordered an increase in the number of sentries for greater security, took not only the box but removed all the papers which could in any way incriminate Chichikov, tied it all up in a bundle, sealed it, and told one of the soldiers to take it immediately to Chichikov under cover of essential articles for going to bed, so that Chichikov together with his papers received all the warm things he needed to cover his frail body. This prompt delivery delighted him. He was again full of hope and again began to dream of all sorts of amusements: an evening at the theatre, the ballerina he was running after. The country and a life of peace and quiet grew dimmer and the city and the noise began to grow brighter and more vivid. Oh, life!

In the meantime the case was assuming vast proportions in the courts of justice and government offices. The clerks' pens were busily at work, and as they took pinches of snuff, the legal luminaries laboured with a will, admiring like artists their crooked briefs. Like a mysterious magician, Chichikov's lawyer was invisibly manipulating the whole mechanism; he got everyone in a hopeless tangle before they had time to realize what was happening. The confusion grew. Samosvistov excelled himself by his unexampled boldness and insolence. Having found out where the arrested woman was kept under guard, he went straight there and with such a swagger and an air of authority that the sentry saluted him and stood to attention.

'Have you been here on duty long?'

'Since the morning, sir.'

'Is it long before you're relieved?'

'Three hours, sir.'

'I shall want you. I'll tell the officer in charge to send another in your place.'

'Yes, sir.'

And on returning home, so as not to involve anyone in the affair and so that no one should be the wiser, he dressed up as a gendarme himself, disguised himself with a moustache and side-whiskers, so that the devil himself could not have recognized him. Arrived at the house where Chichikov was imprisoned, he got hold of the first woman he came across and handed her over to two young officials, daredevils like himself, who were initiated in the plot. He himself went off in his moustache and whiskers, and armed with a rifle, all as it should be, said to the sentry: 'You can go now. Your commanding officer has sent me to take your place.' They changed guard and Samosvistov took up his post. That was all that was needed. Meanwhile, the place of the woman prisoner was taken by the other woman who knew nothing and understood nothing. The first woman was hidden away somewhere, so that they never found out what had become of her. While Samosvistov was carrying out his plan in the guise of a warrior, Chichikov's lawyer was working miracles on the civilian side: he let the governor understand that the public prosecutor was writing a denunciation against him; he let the gendarme's clerk know that a secret government inspector, who was staying in the town, was laying information against him; and he reduced everyone to such a state that they all had to apply to him for his advice. The result was absolute chaos: one denunciation followed another and things were being discovered which had never seen the light of day and, indeed, such as had never existed at all. Everything was turned to good account: who was the illegitimate son of whom, his origin and profession, who had a mistress and whose wife was flirting with whom. Scandals, infidelities, everything got so mixed up and entangled together with Chichikov's case and with the dead souls that it was quite impossible to make out which of them was the more absurd. It all seemed equally nonsensical.

When at last the papers began to reach the governor-general, the poor prince could not make head or tail of them. A very clever and efficient official who was told to make a précis of the case nearly went out of his mind: it was quite impossible to get a clear idea of the affair. The prince was preoccupied at the time with a multitude of other official business, one thing more unpleasant than the other. There was a famine in one part of the province. The officials who had been sent to distribute bread had apparently not acted as they should have. In another part of the province the dissenters became restive. Someone seemed to have spread a rumour among them that the Antichrist had appeared who would not leave even the dead in peace and who was buying up some kind of dead souls. They did penance and sinned, and on the pretext of catching the Antichrist, murdered lots of people who were not Antichrists. In another place the peasants had revolted against the landowners and the rural police officers. Some tramps had spread rumours among them that the time had come when peasants were to become landowners and wear frock-coats, while the landowners were to put on peasants' coats and become peasants. And the whole district, without reflecting that there would be too many landowners and rural officers in that case, refused to pay their taxes. It was necessary to resort to force. The poor prince was in a most distraught state of mind. At that very moment the arrival of the government contractor was announced.

'Let him come in,' said the prince.

The old man came in.

'So this is your Chichikov! You stood up for him and defended him. Now he's mixed up in an affair which even the worst thief would not have attempted.'

'I'm afraid, sir, I don't quite understand the case.'

'The forgery of a will. And what a forgery! A public flogging is the punishment for such a crime.'

'Your Excellency,' said Murazov, 'I'm saying this not in order to defend Chichikov, but because the case against him has not been proved. The investigation is not yet at an end.'

'We have the evidence: the woman who had been dressed up to impersonate the dead woman has been arrested. I should like to question her in your presence.'

The prince rang and gave orders for the woman to be brought.

Murazov was silent.

'It's a most disgraceful affair and I'm sorry to say some of the leading officials of the town are mixed up in it, including the governor

375

himself. He should not be among thieves and good-for-nothing idlers,' said the prince warmly.

'But the governor is a relative of the dead woman. He has a claim on her inheritance. And as for the others who came flocking on every side, that, sir, is just what you can expect people to do. A rich woman has died without making any sensible and fair arrangements and quite naturally all sorts of people have come rushing in from all directions to get some of the pickings – it's only human nature.'

'But why commit such abominations? The blackguards!' said the prince with indignation. 'I haven't a single decent official. They're all scoundrels.'

'But, your Excellency, which of us is as good as he should be? All the officials of the town are men. They have their good qualities and many of them are very efficient at their work. Everyone is not immune from sinning.'

'Listen, Murazov, tell me, you're the only honest person I know: why are you so eager to defend every sort of scoundrel?'

'Your Excellency,' said Murazov, 'whoever the man may be whom you call a scoundrel, he is still a man. How is one not to defend a man, when you know that half of the wicked things he does are the result of his coarseness and ignorance. Why, we commit all sorts of injustices at every step without the slightest evil intention. Every minute we are the cause of someone's unhappiness. Why, your Excellency, you too have done a great injustice.'

'What?' the prince cried in astonishment, completely taken aback by such an unexpected turn in the conversation.

Murazov paused as though considering something, and at last said:

'Well, sir, take the case of Derpennikov.'

'Sir, a crime against the fundamental laws of the state is equivalent to a betrayal of his country.'

'I'm not justifying him. But is it just to condemn a young man who has been led astray and seduced by others through inexperience just as though he were one of the ringleaders? For Derpennikov got the same sentence as Voronov-Dryannoy, and yet the crimes are not the same.'

'For God's sake,' said the prince with undisguised agitation, 'do you know something about it? Tell me. You see, I only recently sent a request for the mitigation of his sentence.'

'No, your Excellency, I'm not saying this because I know something you don't know. Though there is indeed a circumstance which might have been in his favour, but he would not himself agree to make use of it because someone else might have suffered. What I'm driving at is that your Excellency may have been in too great a hurry at the time. I'm sorry, your Excellency, but I'm judging merely by my own weak understanding. You asked me several times to speak frankly to you. You see, sir, when I was in authority over other people, I had all sorts of workers, good and bad. One ought to take into account a man's past life, for if one does not examine everything coolly, but starts shouting from the very beginning, one only frightens the man and never gets a real confession from him. But if you question him sympathetically, as one might one's own brother, he will tell you everything and not even ask for mitigation of his sentence, and will feel no bitterness against anyone because he realizes clearly that it is not I who am punishing him but the law.'

The prince pondered. At that moment a young civil servant came in and stood waiting respectfully with his portfolio. His youthful and fresh face wore a look of anxiety and hard work. It was clear that he took his work of being sent on special missions very seriously. He was one of the few officials who did their work *con amore*; without being anxious to make a profit out of his job and without being impelled by ambition or by a desire to imitate others, he worked simply because he was convinced that his place was here and not anywhere else, and that this was the purpose of his life. To investigate, to take to pieces and, having unravelled all the threads of the most tangled case, to make it clear – that was his job. And his labours, his efforts, and his sleepless nights were amply rewarded if the case he was engaged on began to become clear and its hidden causes revealed, and he felt that he could put it all in a few words clearly and distinctly so that it would be comprehensible and obvious to everyone. It can be said that no student rejoices more when the meaning of a most difficult sentence is made clear and the real sense of the thought of a great writer becomes apparent than he did when he succeeded in disentangling a most complicated case. On the other hand ...

[*The sentence is unfinished and there is a gap here in the manuscript*]

'... With bread where there is a famine, I know that part of the country better than the officials; I will look into it personally and see who needs what. And with your permission, your Excellency, I shall have a talk with them peacefully. The officials will never be able to settle things with them peacefully. The officials will never be able to do that: a correspondence will be started and, besides, they have got so involved in their documents that they are unable to see the actual state of affairs for the sheets of paper. And as for money, I am not going to ask any of you, for when people are dying of starvation it is shameful to think of making profit for myself. I have a store of corn ready for distribution. I sent some to Siberia a short time ago and by next summer I shall be able to get more.'

'God alone can reward you for such a service, Murazov. I won't say anything to you because you realize yourself that words cannot express my gratitude. But let me say one thing about your request. Tell me yourself: have I the right to leave this place without further investigation and will it be just, will it be honest on my part to forgive these blackguards?'

'Your Excellency, I assure you on my word of honour that one ought not to call them that, particularly as many of them are very worthy men. A man's circumstances are very difficult, very difficult indeed, your Excellency. Sometimes it seems that a man is guilty beyond a shadow of doubt, but when you examine his case carefully he is not the guilty man at all.'

'But what will they say themselves if I drop it? You see, there are some among them who will turn up their noses more than ever and will even say that they have frightened me. They will be the first to lose respect ...'

'Allow me to tell you what I really think, your Excellency. Call them together, tell them all you know, and put your own position before them in exactly the same way as you were good enough to put it before me, and ask them what each of them would do if he were in your place.'

'Do you really think that they are capable of more honourable sentiments than carrying on intrigues and filling their pockets? I assure you, they will only laugh at me.'

'I don't think so, sir. A Russian, even one who is worse than any-one else, has a sense of justice. Perhaps some might do so, but not a Russian. No, your Excellency, you have nothing to hide. Tell them exactly as you told me. You see, sir, they abuse you as an ambitious and proud man who does not want to listen to anyone, who is sure of himself – so let them now see what you really are. What do you care? Your cause is just. Speak to them just as if you were not speaking to them, but opening up your heart to God himself.'

'I will think about it, Murazov,' said the prince thoughtfully, 'and meanwhile let me thank you for your advice.'

'And tell them to release Chichikov, sir.'

'Tell that Chichikov to get out of the place as quickly as possible, and the farther he goes the better. Him I would never pardon.'

Murazov bowed and went straight from the prince to Chichikov. He found Chichikov in good spirits, very calmly absorbed in doing justice to a decent dinner which had been brought to him on china dishes from a very respectable kitchen. From the very first sentences of their conversation the old man at once perceived that Chichikov had already managed to have a talk with some of the officials engaged in this complicated case. He even realized that the hidden hand of Chichikov's expert legal adviser had something to do with it.

'Now, listen, Chichikov,' he said. 'I've got you freedom on condition that you leave the town at once. Collect all your belongings and go without a moment's delay, for your affair is even worse than I thought. You see, my good sir, I know that there's a man here who is egging you on. So let me tell you in secret that something new is about to be discovered and that no power on earth will save that man. He, of course, is only too glad to drag others down with him for company, but the whole affair is now about to be exposed. I left you in a good frame of mind, in a better one than I find you now. I'm telling you this seriously. I assure you it has nothing to do with the inheritance over which men are at loggerheads and ready to murder each other, just as though it were possible to plan our life on earth without thinking of another life. Believe me, my dear fellow, that so long as people refuse to give up everything for the sake of which they attack and devour each other on earth, that so long as they refuse to think of putting their spiritual fortune in order, there will be no fair distribution of earthly fortunes, either. A time of famine and poverty will come and the people as a whole as well as every individual in it will suffer. ... That, my dear sir, is clear enough. Whatever you may say, the body depends on the soul. How then can you expect that things will arrange themselves as they should? Think not of dead souls, but of your own living soul and follow a different path with

God's help. I too am leaving the town tomorrow. Make haste, remember that when I'm gone there will be trouble.'

Having said this, the old man went out. Chichikov pondered. Again the meaning of life seemed to him to be a matter of the highest importance: 'Murazov is right,' he said to himself. 'It is time to take a different path!' Having said this, he walked out of prison. One sentry carried his box after him and another the mattress [?] and his linen.

Selifan and Petrushka were overjoyed to see their master a free man again.

'Well, my good fellows,' said Chichikov, addressing them graciously, 'we must pack our things and be off.'

'We'll roll along famously, sir,' said Selifan. 'I expect the road must have set by now. It's been snowing enough for that. It's time we got out of this town, sir. I'm sick and tired of it. Can't bear the sight of it.'

'Go to the coachmaker and let him put our carriage on runners,' said Chichikov, and himself went off to the town though he did not intend to pay any farewell visits. After what had happened, it would have been rather awkward, particularly as all sorts of most unfavourable stories were spread about him in the town. He avoided meeting anyone he knew and only went stealthily to the merchant from whom he had bought the cloth of 'the flame and smoke of Navarino'. He took four yards for a coat and trousers and went straight to the tailor. For double the price the tailor agreed to redouble his zeal and set the tailoring population to work all night by candlelight, working away with their needles, their irons, and their teeth, and the suit was ready next day, though a little late. The horses were harnessed; Chichikov, however, tried on the coat. It was excellent, exactly like the first but, alas, he noticed streaks of white showing in his hair and he murmured sadly: 'Why did I have to give myself up to such despair? I certainly ought not to have torn out my hair!' Having settled his bill with the tailor, he drove out of the town at last in a strange frame of mind. This was not the old Chichikov; this was a sort of ruin of the old Chichikov. The inner state of his mind could be compared to a building that has been pulled down in order to erect a new one in its place, and the new one has not yet been begun, because the final plan has not yet arrived from the architect and the workers are left in a state of bewilderment. An hour earlier old Murazov drove out of the town together with Potapych in a covered waggon, and an hour after Chichikov's departure an order was issued that the prince wished to see all the officials without exception in connexion with his departure for Petersburg.

All the officials of the town, beginning with the governor and ending with the titular councillors, assembled in the large ballroom of the governor-general's house: chiefs of departments, councillors, assessors, Kisloyedov, Krasnonosov, Samosvistov, those who took bribes and those who did not take bribes, those who acted against their consciences, those who only did so by half, and those who did not do so at all – all of them waited for the governor-general to appear, not entirely without agitation or apprehension. The prince came out looking neither gloomy nor cheerful: his glance as well as his step was firm. All the assembled officials bowed, many of them from the waist. Responding with a slight bow, the prince began:

'Before leaving for Petersburg I have thought it proper to meet you all and even to explain to you partly the reason for my departure. A very scandalous affair has come to light here. I think that many of those present know what affair I am speaking of. That affair led to the discovery of others no less dishonourable, in which persons whom I had hitherto regarded as honest have been involved. I am also aware of the fact that the secret aim of this affair has been to make everything so complicated that it would be impossible to disentangle it in a formal way. I know, too, who was the chief instigator of this affair and by whose secret ... [*The sentence is unfinished in the manuscript*] though he very cleverly concealed his share in it. But the point is that I do not intend to prosecute anyone in the formal judicial way and through documents, but by a summary court-martial, and I hope that the Emperor will empower me to do so when I put the matter before him. In a case like this when there is no possibility of invoking the authority of the civil courts, when cupboards full of papers have been burnt, and when, finally, efforts are made by a mass of false evidence and false reports to obscure a case which was sufficiently obscure already, I think that a court-martial is the only means left of dealing with the culprits and I should like to know your opinion.'

The prince stopped short, as though expecting an answer. All stood with their eyes fixed on the floor. Many of them turned pale.

'I know also of another affair, although those responsible for it are convinced that no one knows about it. This case will be investigated, not in accordance with the ordinary legal procedure, because I shall be the defendant and the petitioner myself and I hope to bring forward convincing evidence.'

Someone among the officials shuddered, and several of the more timid ones looked embarrassed.

'I need not tell you that the principal ringleaders must be punished by deprivation of rank and property and the rest by dismissal from their posts. Neither need I tell you that among those a number of innocent persons will suffer. But then what is to be done? The whole affair is far too dishonest and cries aloud for justice. Though I am perfectly well aware that it will not even be a lesson to others, for others will take the place of those dismissed and those who have hitherto been honest will become dishonest and those who have been deemed worthy of trust will deceive and betray – in spite of the fact that I'm perfectly well aware of it all, I must act harshly because justice is crying out aloud. I know that I shall be accused of being harsh and cruel but I also know that those will be even more ... [*The corner of the page of the manuscript has been torn off*] I must therefore become a callous instrument of justice, an axe which must fall on the heads of the guilty ones.'

A shudder involuntarily passed over all their faces.

The prince was calm. His face expressed neither anger nor deep indignation.

'Now the man in whose hands the fate of many lies and whom no supplications were able to move, this very man now flings himself at your feet and entreats you all. Everything will be forgotten, erased, forgiven; I will myself be the intercessor for you all if you do as I ask. This is what I ask: I know that it is impossible to eradicate injustice by any means, by any threats, by any punishments: it is too deeply rooted. The dishonest practice of taking bribes has become a necessity, something that even people who were not born to be dishonest cannot do without. I know that it is almost impossible for many people to swim against the stream. But I must now – as at a decisive and sacred moment when we all have to do our best to save our country, when every citizen bears everything and makes every sacrifice – I must now appeal to those at least who have still a Russian heart beating in their breasts and who still know the meaning of the word honour. What's the use of talking about which of us is more guilty among us? I am perhaps the most guilty of all; perhaps I received you too sternly at first; perhaps by excessive suspiciousness

I repelled those among you who sincerely wished to be useful to me, though for my part I too could [reproach them?]. If they really cared for justice and the good of their country, they should not have taken offence at the haughtiness of my manner, and they should have overcome their own personal vanity and sacrificed their personal dignity. It is not possible that I should not have noticed their self-denial and their great love for goodness and not have accepted their useful and sensible advice at last. It is, after all, more customary for a subordinate to adapt himself to the character of his superior. It is, at any rate, more lawful and easier to do so because subordinates have only one chief, while a chief has many subordinates. But let us leave aside the question of who is most to blame. The point is that the time has come for all of us to save our country, that our country is on the verge of ruin not because of the invasion of scores of foreign nations, but because of ourselves; that besides our lawful government, besides our lawful rulers, new rulers have appeared, far stronger than our lawful ones. These rulers have put up their own conditions, their own values, and even their prices have now become generally known. And no ruler, though he be wiser than all legislators and rulers, has it in his power to correct the evil however much he may curtail the activity of bad officials by putting them under the supervision of other officials. It will all be in vain until every one of us feels that as at the time of the general rising up of all the peoples, he armed himself against [his enemies?], so he must now rise up against injustice. As a Russian, as one tied to you by bonds of birth and blood, I now appeal to you. I appeal to those of you who have some idea of what is meant by nobility of thought. I invite you to remember the duty which every man, whatever post he may occupy, has to perform. I invite you to examine more closely your duty and the obligations of your earthly service because that is something which all of us are only dimly aware of, and we scarcely ...'

[Here the manuscript breaks off]